'I LOVED it. Whip-smart, original and so funny,
found it impossible to put down and lost count
of the number of times I laughed out loud'
**Beth O'Leary, *Sunday Times* bestselling
author of *The Switch***

'Hilarious and heartfelt. Had me laughing aloud
within its first five pages and kept me bouncing
between anxiety and delight until its very last. Utterly
clever, deeply funny, and altogether charming, this
book is sure to be one of the best of the year'
**Emily Henry, *New York Times* bestselling
author of *The Beach Read***

'Gloriously screwball crime caper (with a dusting of
romance) which will have you snort-laughing' *Red*

'Brilliant, wicked and dead, dead funny'
Andi Osho, *Asking For A Friend*

'A dazzling debut full of humour and love.
A comedy caper, doused in black humour,
comical references, mixed with romance – fans
of *Crazy Rich Asians* will love it' *My Weekly*

'*Dial A For Aunties* is one of the funniest, smartest,
most compelling books I've read in a long time and
I couldn't put it down' **Lucy Vine, *Hot Mess***

Praise for *Dial A For Aunties*

'Rejoice over *Dial A For Aunties*' *Elle*

'This smart, funny charming novel has all
the right ingredients to make you laugh out
loud . . . A heartfelt rom-com' *Platinum*

'A tightly-plotted, highly comic romp, *Dial
A For Aunties* keeps you guessing till the very
last twist' **Lauren Ho,** *Last Tang Standing*

'Has redefined what "page-turner" means with
laugh out loud humour and delightful twists
and turns at every corner' *Buzzfeed*

'A rip-roaring treat! Dark comedy at its finest
and a set of catastrophes that had me roaring'
Abigail Mann, *The Lonely Fajita*

'The comedy jackpot! Fresh, funny and
fabulous' **Kirsty Eyre,** *Cow Girl*

'A laugh-out-loud read' *Bella*

'Dark humour at its best. We had such a laugh
reading through' *Magic Radio Bookclub*

'This laugh-out-loud read is a real
breath of fresh air' *Fabulous*

Jesse Sutanto is the author of books for children and adults. She is the author of YA novel, *The Obsession*, and *Theo Tan and the Fox Spirit*, the first book in a middle grade series. *Dial A For Aunties* is her debut adult novel.

Jesse received her Masters from the University of Oxford. She grew up in Indonesia and Singapore and currently lives in Jakarta with her husband and two daughters.

You can find out more about Jesse on her website www.jesse-qsutanto.com and follow her on Twitter @thewritinghippo and on Facebook and Instagram @JesseQSutanto.

DIAL A FOR AUNTIES

Jesse Sutanto

ONE PLACE. MANY STORIES

HQ
An imprint of HarperCollins*Publishers* Ltd
1 London Bridge Street
London SE1 9GF

www.harpercollins.co.uk

HarperCollins*Publishers*
1st Floor, Watermarque Building, Ringsend Road
Dublin 4, Ireland

This edition 2021

1
First published in Great Britain by
HQ, an imprint of HarperCollins*Publishers* Ltd 2021

ISBN: 978-0-00-844588-1

MIX
Paper from
responsible sources
FSC™ C007454

This book is produced from independently certified FSC™ paper
to ensure responsible forest management.

For more information visit: www.harpercollins.co.uk/green

This book is set in 11.1/16 pt. Sabon

Printed and Bound in the UK using 100% Renewable Electricity at
CPI Group (UK) Ltd

For Mama and Papa,
who would definitely help me
move a dead body.

PROLOGUE

Eight Years Ago

There is a curse in my family. It's followed us all the way from China, where it took my great-grandfather (freak accident on the farm that involved a pregnant sow and an unfortunately placed rake), to Indonesia, where it claimed my grandfather (a stroke at the age of thirty, nothing quite so dramatic as great-grandfather's demise but still rather upsetting). My mom and aunts figured that a Chinese curse wouldn't follow them to the West, so after they all got married, they moved to San Gabriel, California. But not only did the curse find them, it mutated. Instead of killing the men in my family, it made them leave, which is so much worse. At least Yeye died loving my Nainai. The first one who left was Big Uncle. Then Second Uncle, and then—then it was my dad, who left without a word in the dead of night. Just up and disappeared, like a ghost. I woke up one morning, asked where he was, and Ma slapped down a bowl of congee and said, "Eat." That was when I knew the curse had claimed him. When my male cousins graduated, they left too, opting for schools like NYU and Penn State instead of any of the perfectly fine colleges in California.

"Ah, Nat, you sooo lucky," Big Aunt says, the day my mom announces that I've applied to eight schools, all of them in California. The farthest one is Berkeley, and we've had countless arguments over *that*. Ma thinks anything farther than UC Irvine is too far; she won't be able to drop by randomly and clean my dorm and nag at my roommate to go to sleep early and drink lots of water. Big Aunt's son, Hendra, is at Boston College and ignores 99.999 percent of her calls. The other 0.001 percent is when he runs out of money and has to ask her for more.

"Oh, so lucky," Second Aunt says, patting her chest and smiling sadly, probably thinking of my cousin Nikky in Philly, who never calls and only comes back once a year. Her other son, Axel, is in New York. I last saw him two years ago, when he moved out. *Finally*, he'd said. *When it's your turn, Meddy, fly far and don't look back.* "Daughters never leave you. Girl is such blessing," Second Aunt says. She reaches out and pinches my cheek.

Fourth Aunt grunts and continues shelling roasted, salted pumpkin seeds. Ma is her biggest nemesis, and she'd rather choke on a pumpkin seed than agree that Ma's the lucky one out of all of them. But when Ma isn't looking, she glances over at me and gives me a wink. *I'm proud of you, kid.*

I smile weakly. Because I sort of kind of totally lied to Ma. I did apply to eight schools in California, but I also applied to a ninth school. Columbia. I don't know why I did;

it's not like I'd ever get in, and plus, how would we even pay the exorbitant tuition?

Months later, I hold the acceptance letter in my hand and stare, and stare, and—

I crumple it. Throw it in the trash. I'm not like my boy cousins. I'm not like my father and my uncles. I can't just abandon my family. Especially not my mom. I'm not stupid enough to think that the curse will skip me. Years later, after my future husband leaves me, all I'll have left are Ma and my aunties. So I tell them I'm going to UCLA. Ma cries. My aunts (even Fourth Aunt) whoop and gather around, hugging me, patting my cheeks, and bemoaning the fact that they don't have daughters.

"You so lucky," Big Aunt says, for the millionth time, to Ma. "She stay with you forever. You always have companion."

Is it true? Am I doomed to stay with them forever, just because I'm the only one not heartless enough to leave? I force a smile and nod benignly as they fuss about me, and I try to look forward to the rest of my life, living here in the same house with my mom and aunts.

PART 1

GIRL MEETS BOY

*(There might be insta-love and also
someone might die. We'll see.)*

1

I take a deep breath before pushing open the swing doors. Noise spills out, a cacophony of Mandarin and Cantonese, and I step aside so Ma can walk inside before me. It's not that I'm being nice—I mean, I am, but I'm also being sensible. Ma grew up in Jakarta's Chinatown, a place heaving with people, and she knows how to make her way through a crowd. Any crowd. If I'm the one leading the way, I'd be squeaking, "Excuse me—oh, sorry, Ah Yi—um, could I just—I have a reservation—" My voice would never be heard above the din, and we'd be stuck outside the restaurant forever. Or at least until the dim sum rush died down, sometime around 2 p.m.

As it is, people surge behind Ma as she scythes a path through the throng of families waiting for their tables, and I would've lost her if I wasn't keeping a death grip on her arm as if I'm all of three years old. She doesn't bother stopping at the front desk. She strides in as if she owns the place, eagle eyes scanning the large dining hall.

7

How can I describe the chaos that is a dim sum restaurant in the heart of San Gabriel Valley at 11 a.m.? The place is filled with close to a hundred round tables, each one occupied by a different family, many of them with three to four generations of people present—there are gray-haired, prune-faced Ah Mas holding chubby babies on their laps. Steaming carts are pushed by the waitresses, though if you called them "Waitress" they'd never stop for you. You must call them Ah Yi—Auntie—and wave frantically as they walk by to get them to stop. And once they do, customers descend like vultures and fight over the bamboo steamers inside the cart. People shout, asking if they've got siu mai, or har gow, or lo mai gai, and the Ah Yis locate the right dishes somewhere in the depths of their carts.

My Mandarin is awful, and my Cantonese nonexistent. Ma and the aunts often try to help me improve by speaking to me in either Mandarin or Indonesian, but then give up and switch to English because I only get about 50 percent of what they're saying. Their grasp of the English language is a bit wobbly, but it's a heck of a lot better than my Mandarin or Indonesian. It's yet another reason why I find it extra hard to order food at dim sum. More often than not, everything good is gone by the time the Ah Yi notices me and understands my order. Then all that's left is the lame stuff, like the doughy vegetarian dumplings or the steamed bok choy.

But today, ah, today is a good day. I manage to get my hands on two lots of har gow, something that Big Aunt will certainly appreciate, and I even get hold of lop cheung bao—

Chinese sausage rolls. Almost makes the whole ordeal of coming to weekly dim sum worth my while.

Big Aunt nods her approval when the Ah Yi puts the bamboo steamers down in the center of our table, and I feel an almost overwhelming need to beat my chest and crow. I got those shrimp dumplings! Me!

"Eat more, Meddy. You should keep your strength up for tomorrow," Big Aunt says in Mandarin, plopping two pieces of braised pork ribs on my plate while I carefully place dumplings on everyone else's plates and pour them tea. Second Aunt cuts the char siu baos into two each and places one half on everyone's plate. The table being round means all the dishes are equally within reach of everyone, but Chinese family meals aren't complete without everyone serving food to everyone else, because doing so shows love and respect, which means we all need to do it in the most attention-seeking way possible. What's the point of giving Big Aunt the biggest siu mai if nobody else notices?

"Thank you, Big Aunt," I say dutifully, placing a fat har gow on her plate. I always reply in English no matter which language my family is speaking because Second Aunt says listening to me struggle through Indonesian or Mandarin makes her blood pressure rise. "You eat more too. We're all counting on you tomorrow. And you, Second Aunt." The second-biggest har gow goes on Second Aunt's plate. Third biggest goes to Fourth Aunt, and the last remaining one goes on Ma's plate. That shows that Ma has brought me up well, to look out for others before ourselves.

Big Aunt waves off my platitudes with a heavily jeweled

hand. "We are all counting on each other." Heads of big coiffed hair nod. Fourth Aunt has the biggest hair, something that Ma is always complaining to me about in private.

"Always such an attention hole," Ma said once, which was equal parts horrifying and hilarious. I asked her where she heard "attention hole," and she claimed that she heard it from our neighbor Auntie Liying, which is such a lie, but I've had twenty-six years of living with Ma and I know better than to argue with her. I simply told her it's "attention ho," not "hole," and she nodded and muttered "ho, like ho ho ho" before going back to chopping scallions.

"Okay," Big Aunt says, clapping once. Everyone sits up straighter. Big Aunt is older than Second Aunt by ten years, and she basically raised her sisters while Nainai went to work. "Hair and makeup?"

Second Aunt nods, bringing out her phone and putting on her glasses. She uses her index finger to tap on it, muttering, "Apa ya, the name of that app—Meddy make me use for hairstyle. Pin-something."

"Pinterest," I pipe up. "I can help you find it—"

Big Aunt shoots me a stern look, and I wilt. "No, Meddy. You mustn't help. If Second Aunt can't find the app tomorrow when she's with the bride, we will lose face for sure. We're supposed to be professionals," she says. Or at least I think that's what she says. She's speaking so fast I find it hard to follow, but I definitely caught the Mandarin words for "lose face"—a favorite phrase of hers.

Second Aunt's mouth purses, and her left cheek twitches a little. Just as Fourth Aunt irritates the crap out of

Ma, Second Aunt and Big Aunt have a lot of friction between them. Don't ask me why; maybe it has to do with being the two oldest. Maybe it's something in their complicated pasts. There's been a lot of drama with my mom's family, especially back in Jakarta. I've heard bits and pieces over the years, mostly from Ma.

"Ha!" Second Aunt crows, brandishing Pinterest on her phone as if it's a sword she's just managed to pull out of a stone. "I got it. This is the style that the bride chose. I practiced on Meddy's hair and it looked wonderful." She turns to me and switches to English. "Meddy, you got photo I take of your hair?"

"I do," I say, quickly taking out my phone. I call up the picture and Second Aunt holds it side by side with her phone, showing off the two pictures to everyone.

"Wah," Ma says. "It's so similar to the model's! Very good, Er Jie."

Second Aunt gives her a warm smile.

Fourth Aunt nods and replies in English, "Yes, they're nearly identical. How impressive." Her English is the best of all of theirs, yet another thing Ma will never forgive her for, even though Ma's English is better than her older sisters'. Ma insists that Fourth Aunt has a penchant for using big words (i.e., anything with more than two syllables) just to needle Ma. I think Ma might have a point there, but it's just one of the many truths we will never know.

"The curl not show up well with Asian hair," Big Aunt says. The fact that she's speaking English means she's half-directing the admonishment at me. My insides writhe with guilt, even though this is very definitely not my fault. "Why you choose blonde hairstyle?"

Second Aunt glowers. "I didn't choose. The bride choose. Customer always right, remember?" She stabs her har gow and bites it angrily.

"Hmm." Big Aunt sighs. "Should have tell her it look different on Asian hair than on blonde hair. But," she adds, when Second Aunt looks about ready to burst, "never mind. Too late now. Moving in—"

"On," Fourth Aunt says.

"Eh?" Big Aunt says.

"On. It's moving on, not moving in. Moving in is what you do when you move houses."

"Moving on. Okay." Big Aunt smiles at Fourth Aunt, and Fourth Aunt beams back so hard she might as well be a kid again. Ma says Fourth Aunt is Big Aunt's favorite because she's the baby of the family, and she was such a needy baby that she stole Big Aunt's heart right out of her chest.

"She snatch it right out," Ma has grumbled many times. I didn't bother asking if Ma, as the second-youngest sister, had been Big Aunt's favorite right up until Fourth Aunt was born.

"Flowers?" Big Aunt says in Mandarin once more. I relax a little.

Ma's back straightens. "All taken care of. Lilies, roses, peonies. Ah Guan will take everything to the island in the morning."

The island she's talking about is Santa Lucia, a large, privately owned island off the coast of Southern California that boasts pristine golden beaches, dramatic cliffs, and, as of a month ago, one of the most luxurious, exclusive resorts in the world—the Ayana Lucia. Tomorrow is the start of a two-day wedding weekend extravaganza for Jacqueline Wijaya, daughter of Indonesia's largest textiles company, and—I kid you not—Tom Cruise.

Sutopo, that is. Yeah, the groom's name really is Tom Cruise Sutopo. I checked. It's exactly the kind of thing Chinese-Indonesians love naming their kids after—famous people and/or brand names (I have a cousin named Gucci, who moved very far away as soon as he was legally able to), or some form of misspelling of a popular Western name. Also case in point: Meddelin. My parents were aiming for Madeleine. Growing up, my cousins called me Meddlin' Meddelin, which is why I never, ever meddle in anyone's business, ever. Well, that and also the fact that my mother and aunts meddle enough for the whole family.

Anyway, Tom Cruise Sutopo's parents own . . . something. Something large. Palm oil plantations, coal mines, that kind of thing. So it's a wedding between two billionaire families in a newly built resort, which is why Big Aunt and all the rest of us are understandably nervous. How we managed to land these people as clients, I have no idea. Well, I do. Fourth Aunt's husband is—let me get this straight—Jacqueline's cousin's father-in-law's brother. So we're practically relatives. Everything in Chinese-Indo culture is like that; everybody is somehow related to everybody else, and deals happen because somebody's in-law knows someone else's friend's cousin.

I thought that our cheesy-as-hell company motto, which Big Aunt is supremely proud of—*Don't leave your big day to chance, leave it to the Chans!*—would've scared away the bride and groom, but they actually found it funny. Said it made them even more certain that they wanted to hire us to cater their big day.

Ma rattles on about how she's managed to get the rarest flowers. "The arrangements are going to look—what do you say in English, Meddy? Exsqueezed?"

"You mean exquisite?" Fourth Aunt says, and Ma gives her the deadliest side-eye in the history of all side-eyes.

"Very good," Big Aunt says hurriedly, breaking the radioactive glares between Ma and Fourth Aunt. "And last one, songs, all okay?"

Fourth Aunt's face goes from icy glare to satisfied smirk. "Of course, the band and I have been practicing night and day. People keep coming by the studio to listen to me sing, you know." There are two versions of Fourth Aunt's life story. Version one has to do with her being a celebrated child prodigy with a voice that newspapers described as "angelic" and "a national treasure." She was well on her way to stardom, but chose to leave it all behind when all her sisters decided to move to California. Version two has her as a so-so singer who cunningly convinced her entire family to uproot themselves and move to California so she could pursue her pipe dreams of breaking out in Hollywood. One version is Fourth Aunt's; the other is Ma's.

"And the cake?" Second Aunt says, side-eyeing Big Aunt. "Our centerpiece needs to be perfect, unlike that unfortunate thing you made for Mochtar Halim's daughter's wedding." She gives a dramatic sigh. "Nobody has a face anymore." Hmm, that can't be right. I parse the words slowly in my head. I think she's saying Big Aunt has made all of us lose face. I really need to brush up on my Mandarin.

Anyway, the point is, Second Aunt has made a really low blow. Cheriss Halim's wedding is her favorite topic, because Cheriss had requested a fiendishly tricky cake—a five-layer upside-down tower, with the bottom layer as the smallest one and the top as the biggest. Big Aunt, with years and years under her belt as head pastry chef for Ritz-Carlton Jakarta, was confident she could do it. But something went wrong. I don't know what, maybe she didn't build enough structural support, or maybe it was just an impossible task for a beach wedding in the middle of a SoCal summer. Whatever it was, amid the guests' horrified gasps, the humongous tower had leaned over in slow motion before collapsing on one of the flower girls. It was the only time we'd ever gone viral, and Second Aunt hasn't let Big Aunt forget about the incident since.

Big Aunt's nostrils flare. "I'm just here to buy soy sauce."

Okay, that definitely can't be right. I lean toward Ma and whisper, "Why's Big Aunt talking about buying soy sauce?"

"Tch," Ma says. "This is why I always say to you: pay attention in Chinese class! Big Aunt is saying to Second Aunt to mind her own business."

"Thank you for being sooo caring, Meimei," Big Aunt is saying. Phew, she's really mad now. She only refers to the rest as meimei—little sister—when she wants to remind them who's the eldest. "Of course everything is ready. The cake will be perfectly fine; please don't worry about me." She gives Second Aunt a smile that I can only describe as "so sweet it's deadly" and then turns her attention to me.

I shift in my seat. Big Aunt, like her title, is larger than all her sisters. I guess twenty years as a pastry chef will do that to you. She wears her size well, and it makes her more majestic, more convincing. There's a reason she's the one who meets with potential clients. I hate the thought of disappointing Ma, but the thought of disappointing Big Aunt actually keeps me up some nights. Maybe it's the result of spending most of my life in the same house as my mom and her sisters. Ma and I only got to move into our own place a year ago, after the family business started turning a steady profit. We all still live in the same neighborhood, a mere ten-minute walk away from one another, and I feel the weight of their expectations, as if I have four mothers and all of their hopes and dreams have been placed on my shoulders. I'm basically driven by a mixture of caffeine and familial guilt.

Big Aunt turns to face me, and my spine straightens instinctively. Maybe she senses how nervous I am about tomorrow, because she gives me an encouraging smile and switches to English for my sake. "Meddy, everything okay with camera, ya? You ready for big day?"

I nod. I checked and rechecked my camera, my backup camera, and all five of my lenses yesterday. They'd all been sent for a maintenance and proper cleanup weeks ago, in preparation for this wedding. I hate that the documenting of my family's hard work—Big Aunt's towering cakes,

Second Aunt's complicated hairstyles and flawless makeup artistry, Ma's gorgeous flower arrangements, and Fourth Aunt's dynamic performances—all falls on my shoulders. Every wedding, I try to capture everything, and every wedding, I miss something. Last wedding, I forgot to take pictures of Fourth Aunt from her "good side, the one that makes me look twenty again," and the wedding before that, I failed to capture the centerpiece at table 17, which was apparently significantly different from all the other centerpieces.

"My gear's in perfect condition," I assure them, "and I've memorized the list of pictures I need to take for our social media."

"You good, filial girl, Meddy," Big Aunt says, and I force a smile. Ah, filial piety, the foundation of Asian parenting. From ever since I can remember, I've been taught to put my elders—that is, Ma and the aunties—above everything. It's the reason why I, out of seven kids in my generation, am the only one involved in the family business, even though I desperately want out. For their sake, I pretend to love all of it—the fuss and the huge production and everything—but it's slowly eroding what I love about photography. For months now, I've toyed with the idea of leaving the wedding business, of going back to what I love about photography—to be able to take my time, play around with different lenses and lighting and angles instead of rushing to take photo after photo of the same stuff. Not that I can ever reveal any of this to my family.

"Yes, you are a good, filial girl," Ma chirps in Indonesian.

Ma and the aunties are equally fluent in Mandarin and Indonesian and switch seamlessly from one language to the other. She's smiling really wide. Uh-oh. Why is she smiling? "That's why we have a surprise for you."

Now all of my aunts are grinning down at me. I shrink back in my seat, the siu mai in my mouth turning to stone. "What's going on?" I say, my voice coming out even smaller than usual with my family.

Ma says, "I found the perfect husband for you!" At the same time, all of my aunts say, "Surprise!"

I blink. "Sorry, you found what now?"

"Perfect husband!" Ma crows.

I look over my shoulder, half-expecting some guy Ma has probably ambushed at the Ranch 99 market to come up behind me.

"Aiya, he's not here, silly girl," Ma says.

"Is he tied up in the trunk of your car?"

"Don't joke, Meddy." Big Aunt tuts. "Your mama is doing all of this so that you can have a good life."

I nod, contrite. I'm an adult and yet all it takes is a single admonishment from Big Aunt to make me feel all of three years old again. "Sorry, Ma. But I don't—"

"Don't but this but that," Ma says. "Why is it so difficult to get you to date? I tried setting you up with Uncle Awai's son, but no, you didn't let me. I tried setting you up with my lily supplier, Ah Guan—Ah Guan is very handsome, you know—but you refused that too. Didn't even want to meet him."

"Meddy is probably cautious because last time when you

tried to set her up with Wang Zhixiang's son, he turned out to be, you know," Fourth Aunt says.

Ma waves an irritated hand. "Why do you keep bringing up Zhixiang's son? So he turned out to be some maniac. How was I supposed to know?"

"Kleptomaniac," I mumble. By the time our date was over, he'd stolen my makeup bag from my purse and, somehow, one of my shoes. I mean, the guy's an asshole, but you've gotta give it to him. Or let him steal it.

"Anyway, sayangku," Ma says, using the Indonesian term of endearment she saves for really special occasions, like the day I graduated from UCLA, "this guy is so good. I'm telling you, no one is better than him. He is so handsome, so kind, and so smart! Aaand . . ."

Oh god, here it comes. The final nail in the coffin. What is it going to be this time? With my luck, he'll turn out to be a second cousin or something.

"He's the hotel owner!" Fourth Aunt cries.

Ma glares at her. "I was just going to say that. You stole my thunder!"

"You were taking too long," Fourth Aunt says.

They all turn back to me, grinning expectantly.

"Uh." I put down my chopsticks. "I mean. Am I supposed to be happy about that? It sounds like a huge liability. Do I have to give you guys a refresher course on how bad I am at dating? What part of this is a good idea, exactly?"

"Ah," Ma says, smiling smugly. "I know you're not so good at dating—"

"It's because you're such good girl," Big Aunt says, loyally.

Second Aunt nods. "Yes, you're not a whore, that's why you're so bad at dating."

"Auntie! Can we not slut-shame women, please?"

She shrugs, not contrite in the least.

"Anyway," Ma says, "it doesn't matter. It's okay that you're terrible at dating, because this boy, oh, he is so in love with you, Meddy. He knows all your flaws and how awkward you are in person and everything, but he says it makes him like you even more!"

"Whoa, whoa!" I raise my hands. "Hold up. Okay." I take a deep breath. "There is so much here. Can we please switch back to English? Because I'm pretty sure I'm misinterpreting everything. First of all, he knows all my flaws? What the f—what gives, Ma? How does he know any of this stuff about me?"

"She met him online!" Fourth Aunt cries, triumphantly. I guess she's been bursting with the secret this whole time, because her entire face is shining with excitement. "Your mother went online, to a dating site, and has been chatting with him for weeks!"

"What?!" Oh my god, so it's not a loss in translation. She really did go and find me a random guy to go out on a date with. "Ma, is this for real?"

"Yes, very good idea, right? This way, you and him get to know each other before the date, which is tonight."

"Tonight?" I squawk. "But I *don't* know him! I know nothing about him, aside that he's been chatting with my mother for weeks. I mean, good grief, that is some messed-up shit, Ma."

"That why I tell you now," Ma says, completely unfazed. Meanwhile, my cheeks are so hot they're practically melting off my face. "Oh, he is such a good boy, so respectful of his elders."

"How would you know?" I realize how loud my voice is when heads at the next table swivel round. To be loud enough to attract attention in a dim sum restaurant during the lunch rush is damn near impossible, which just goes to show how fucking pissed I am.

"He buy his parents house! A mansion in San Marino, very good location."

My three aunties nod solemnly. San Marino is basically my family's Holy Grail—close enough to SGV for those late-night Taiwanese bubble teas, far enough to be surrounded by non-immigrants. Ma and her sisters have had their eye on San Marino ever since they immigrated here.

"And he loves cooking," Ma says, with a pointed glare at me. "Very good because no matter how many times I teach you, you still don't know how. How can you be good wife, you can't even cook rice?"

"Stay on the topic," Fourth Aunt says.

For once, Ma listens to her. "He has two dogs. You always want dog. Now you can have two! They are so well groom. Look!" She brandishes a photo of two glossy golden retrievers that are so golden and so perfectly shaped they look like they could be some pet magazine models.

"I tell him, I say, 'I'm wedding photographer,' and he say, 'Wow, so impressive!' and I say—"

"Wait." I have to take a second to let the words sink in. "Did you just—Ma. Did you—go on a dating site as *me*?" I sit there with my mouth open, not breathing or blinking or anything.

"Of course she did!" Second Aunt says. "How else can she meet the boy? If she say her real age, fifty-six—"

"Fifty-three," Ma interjects.

Fourth Aunt snorts.

"If she say her real age, then she will matching with men her age," Second Aunt explains very slowly, nodding and smiling at me encouragingly. "You see? Is why she has to pretend she is you."

I can't even think right now. What is my life? While my mind sputters to catch up with the situation, Ma regales me with more of the deep, soulful messages that Jake the hotel owner has sent me. He's seen my pictures and apparently finds me "breathtaking."

"Do you have any photos of him, at least?"

"I ask him, but I think maybe he a bit shy," Ma says.

"You realize that means he's a complete troll?" Fourth Aunt says.

Ma waves her off. "I think is because he so handsome, he don't want show off photo, he wants to make sure you falling in love with him, not his face."

"Also, he's Taiwanese, so his Mandarin very good," Second Aunt says. "Maybe you can improve your Mandarin with him. Whenever you speak Mandarin, aduh, give me headache."

"Sorry," I mumble. I'm so flustered by everything they're

throwing at me that I don't know how to react. "I need to—can I see these chat messages?"

"Aduh, no time for that," Ma says. "You trust me, okay, this one is very good boy. Very good. If you don't go, you miss out."

And, to my horror, despite the awfulness of everything, part of me is being won over, which clearly means I have lost my damn mind.

But the last time I went on a date was . . .

Last summer? Last fall? Christ on a cracker. Has it really been that long? And don't even get me started on the last time I got laid. As my best friend Selena likes to remind me, "Girl, you need to get some before that thing closes up shop for good." I look down at my lap, at that "thing." Why can't Selena just say "vagina"? *You're not gonna close up shop for good, are you?*

Okay, I have just started talking to my vagina. Maybe Ma's right. I desperately need to go out on a date. And so what if it's been set up in the weirdest, most awkward way ever?

"Must go, ya," Ma is saying, unaware that I've quietly talked myself—and my vagina—into agreeing.

"Must not cancel," Big Aunt says. "If you cancel last minute it so offensive, you know."

"*So* offensive," Second Aunt says. "But we know you not do that. You are nice girl."

"You'll jeopardize the wedding weekend," Fourth Aunt says. "You must go, be your lovely, sweet self. He'll fall in love for sure."

I stare at my mother and my aunts. They stare back at me, smiling and nodding in that way cats do when they've cornered a mouse.

"Fine." I sigh. "Tell me everything I'm supposed to know about my date tonight."

2

"You are NOT putting cut-up hot dog and kimchi in yours," I say, wrinkling my nose.

"Oh right, you can put that panda thing in yours, but I can't put hot dog and kimchi in mine?" Nathan says, stirring his bizarre mug cake batter.

"Pandan is a legit cake flavor, you caveperson. What kind of mug cake has hot dog and kimchi?"

"The best kind," Nathan says easily. "You know mine's gonna come out tasting way better than yours, and then you're just going to end up eating it all."

"Not. Possible."

Ten minutes later, I give a cry of frustration when my spoon hits the bottom of his mug. "Is that all there is?"

Nathan laughs. "Told you. Although I have to admit, panda is delicious."

"It's pan-DAN. We're not eating the animal. It's a plant."

"OH! This whole time I thought we were eating, like, a secretion from pandas' glands or something."

25

Now it's my turn to laugh. Seriously, this guy. "You are such a dork. Oh my god, I can't believe—which gland?"

"Obviously anal."

"Gross."

He gives that grin, the one that makes his eyes almost fully close. The one that makes me want to throw up. Just to be clear, it makes me want to throw up because it's so cute it does weird things to my stomach, not because it disgusts me. When I told Selena about the nauseating grin, she said, "Well, you either have stomach flu or you're in love. Either way, stay away from me. I can't afford to get sick."

In love. I watch as Nathan gets up and heads to the fridge to make another hot dog and kimchi mug cake for me, and I know, of course I know, that I'm stupidly, annoyingly check-my-phone-every-half-minute in love with him. Ever since we got to know each other during freshers week, Nathan and I have become fast friends. It feels meant to be. We've even got the same last name: Chan. What are the chances of that? Okay, so it's the most common surname in Hong Kong, which is where his dad's from, and one of the most popular surnames in China, which is where my grand-dad's from, but it feels like fate. We hang out almost every day and do lots of random stuff. We've located the best spots to nap in the library, we've found the best ice cream sandwich combo at Diddy Riese (white chocolate macadamia nut cookie with butter pecan), and today, he came over to my dorm's common room to make mug cakes. It's like my friend-ship with Selena, except with stomach-turning attraction on my part. On his part—

Well, I don't know. Sometimes I think he's attracted to me too. Sometimes I catch him watching me with his eyes all soft, which makes my stomach lurch (thank you, stomach). But then he'll do stuff like rest his elbow on the top of my head when we're waiting for the red light to change, and then I'm pretty sure he sees me as just a friend. Which I'm totally cool with. I'm down for platonic friendship, yeah. I'm chill. Totes chillax.

Nathan places a hand on my shoulder and I practically leap out of the chair. "Whoa, you okay?"

I snort. "Duh, of course, why wouldn't I be?" It's not as if I was interrupted mid-daydream about his abs, which I swear are visible through his UCLA hoodie.

"Did you hear what I said?"

"What?"

"About the party at Phi Kappa?"

A grimace takes over my face. "A frat party? What about it?"

"Um, do you wanna go? My friend's a member, and he says their parties are great. I don't know, could be fun."

"You do realize a frat party is where every bad thing happens? Alcohol poisoning, date rape, hazing . . ."

"Okay, okay." Nathan laughs. "I get it, you don't have to go."

Argh, why do I have to be such a killjoy? I do want to go. I just—I don't know, I guess I'm deathly afraid that Nathan might realize I'm into him, and that would be massively embarrassing.

Thankfully, the microwave dings then. Nathan busies

himself with taking out the mug cake. He moves so effortlessly around the shared kitchen, always with this liquid grace that reminds me of some feline creature. Like a lion, or a lynx. He sprinkles freshly cut chives over the mug cake and slides it over to me. I thank him even though I've lost my appetite.

"Anyway, I gotta go. I promised Matt I'd hit the gym with him."

"Thanks for the cake," I say in the world's most casual voice. "Have a good workout," I call out at the last minute, and then immediately regret it. That sounded like nagging.

He flashes me that grin again, and is gone. I slump back to my room. Selena barely looks up from her calculus textbook when I flop dramatically onto my bed. "Blue balls?" she says, scribbling in her notebook.

"The bluest balls," I groan into my pillow.

"Pretty sure the book's called *The Bluest Eye*."

I turn my head and glare at her. "You're not very empathetic."

"Did he ask you to go to the Phi Kappa party?"

"How did you know about that?"

Selena rolls her eyes. "Because I have a social life? And Nathan was very casually asking if you were going."

I groan. "I am the worst at parties. If he ever saw me at one, he'd realize I am the most unamazing person in the world."

"That's why you haven't gone to any parties here?" Selena gawks at me. "Boy, you have issues. Okay. It's settled. You're going to this one."

"No."

"Yes."

"No, you can't make me, I won't. I won't!"

Friday night, Selena and I stand outside Phi Kappa, a house that's quite literally vibrating with music. I mean, I can actually see the windows rattling with each deep bass beat.

"This is a bad idea," I moan. The only parties I like are the sit-around-playing-board-games kind.

"Focus," Selena says, grabbing me by the shoulders. "You look hot as shit, and we're gonna go in there and you're gonna find Nathan, and I'm gonna find some hot girl or guy, whichever comes first, and we're both gonna score tonight."

"Score?" I squeak.

"You know, smash?"

I narrow my eyes at her.

"Bone? Coitus? Do I really have to say 'sexual intercourse'?"

My voice comes out several octaves higher than most human voices usually go. "I wasn't going to—I'm not ready to—"

Selena cackles. "Oh god, your face. I'm just kidding. No fucking tonight, okay? You and Nathan are too adorable to fall for the drunk one-night-stand bullshit. We'll just find him, he'll take one look at you in this outfit, and that'll be that. He's going to DIE."

"Not literally, I hope," I mutter under my breath, just in case the curse is listening in. I take a deep breath and follow Selena as she struts confidently into the heaving frat house.

It's even worse inside than I thought it would be. The music is so loud my teeth rattle to the beat. Selena dives into the crowd, slithering between the hot, pulsing bodies, pulling me along with her. I have no idea where we're headed or how she even knows where to go. Someone spills an icy drink down the tight jeans Selena's lent me for the night and I squeal, letting go of Selena's hand, but any sound I make is immediately swallowed by the din. The bodies heave and close behind Selena. I cry out her name, but even I can't hear my own voice.

And now I'm alone. I take a deep breath, which is a mistake. Frat houses probably don't smell great at the best of times, and an hour into a roaring party, it smells radioactive. I gag, steel myself, and plunge back into the crowd, calling out for Selena. Some drunk guy stumbles and crashes into me, his sudden momentum making me stumble. I'm about to be trampled. This is not a good way to die—

"Whoa, hey," someone says, pulling me off the sticky floor.

"Nathan," I breathe.

He blinks. "Meddy?" Then he seems to actually see me for the first time, and his eyes widen. "Wow."

I gnaw on my lip. Selena would be so proud of his reaction, but I feel stupid, as if I'm wearing someone else's clothes. Which I am. Selena's stuffed me into a pair of jeans so tight I'm pretty sure they're going to have to be cut off my legs, and a shimmery, backless tank top that doesn't allow for a bra. She says it's fine since bras are really only for women with boobs. Harsh but true.

"Oh, hey," I say, as if I totally was not expecting to see him here, as if I didn't expressly come here half naked just to surprise him into loving me back.

"What?" he shouts.

"I said 'Hey!'" I shout back.

"Hey yourself," he shouts. At least, I think that's what he shouts.

"What?" I shout. We both shake our heads and laugh, and whatever awkwardness there was between us melts away like a little piece of marshmallow. He takes my hand and squeezes it before leading me across the room. My heart squeezes painfully—argh, he's going to notice how sweaty my palms are and then he'll let go and I'll lose him in the crowd the same way I lost Selena—but Nathan keeps a tight grip on my fingers and weaves through the crowd slowly, turning back every few steps to make sure I'm okay. And then suddenly, we're out in the backyard, chilly night wind stinging my face and my bare back, making me break out in goose bumps. Nathan closes the glass door behind us, and the thumping music is cut off, thank god.

"You made it," Nathan says, giving me a one-armed hug. "Where's Selena?"

"Somewhere inside." I check my phone and send her a quick message letting her know I'm in the backyard.

While I'm on my phone, Nathan greets the other people out here. There's a handful of them, all of them carrying red plastic cups or bottles of IPA. Okay, I can do this. It's way more relaxed out here. I shove my hands in my pockets, or try to, anyway. It turns out these stupid jeans are way too tight to fit even a pinky in. Nathan introduces me to his friends, whose names I immediately forget, but when I tell them mine, a couple of them light up and glance at Nathan, who narrows his eyes back at them. My heart clatters against my rib cage. *Does that mean he's told his friends about me? DOES THAT MEAN HE LOVES ME IN A MORE THAN JUST FRIENDS WAY?*

Okay, slow down, bunny boiler. It doesn't mean anything. A girl hands me a bottle of IPA and holds out a bottle opener to me. "Just hang it on that hook when you're done." She points at a hook that's been nailed onto a tree in the middle of the yard.

I do as she told me, and when I turn around from the tree, I walk right into Nathan's chest. "Oof."

"You okay? Sorry, I thought you knew I was right behind you."

I rub my nose. "Geez, are you wearing a breastplate under your shirt?"

He flexes his biceps dramatically. "What can I say? I'm just really cut."

"More like bony." He isn't, though. Not by a long shot. I tear my horny eyes away from his pecs. What is it about guys' pecs that I find so attractive? It's like I'm a boob man, but the reverse. A pec girl. Then my gaze lands on Nathan's hands, and I think, *Mmm, he has nice hands.* Maybe I'm a hand girl. Or maybe I'm just a Nathan everything girl.

I lean back against the tree trunk in an effort to look, well, effortless, but that turns out to be a massive mistake.

Pro tip: don't lean against a tree trunk when wearing a back-less top. "Shit," I hiss, rubbing at my back. "What's on this stupid tree, razor blades?"

"Um, that would be tree bark. Let me see your back." And before I know it, Nathan's fingers are on my bare skin. A warm, strong hand against my chilled back. My muscles melt into water. My stomach is basically a puddle. I swallow, remind-ing myself to breathe. "Just a scratch. You'll live." But his hand doesn't leave my back. Instead, his fingers splay across it, making my entire body tingle. "You cold?"

I can barely speak as he takes off his jacket and drapes it over my shoulders. This is it. This is when I tell him that I've been having sex dreams about him—no, that I have a mas-sive crush on him, that I think he's as perfect as humans come. His jacket's so big it hangs off my shoulders.

"Has anyone ever told you how ridiculously tiny you are?"

"Excuse you, I am five feet two—"

"On a good day, in heels," Nathan murmurs, giving me that dimpled smile. He pulls the jacket closed around me and gives a little tug, as if he doesn't want to let go. I don't want him to let go. "Hey," he says, his voice soft velvet.

I look up and fall into his gaze. "Hey." For once, there are no jokes, no smartass remarks, no thick layer of friend-ship between us. It's just him, and me, and the chilly desert night, and string lights glowing like stars around us.

"I'm glad you came," Nathan says.

And for once, I'm 100 percent honest with him. "I came to see you."

That smile again, and then he dips his head, stooping low as I raise mine, and our lips meet in a soft crush that obliterates whatever other thoughts I had.

Okay, okay. Okay. I've kissed boys before. Okay, two boys. Okay, one of them was the back of my hand. The kiss with the other boy wasn't great; I mean, my hand was better, honestly. I've never liked the look of those Hollywood open-mouthed kisses; I eat way too much fermented shrimp paste to have any qualms about me being a great kisser. When it comes to kissing, it's closed mouth all the way for me.

But this? Holy shit. Nathan is the perfect counter to my prudish mouth. His lips are soft, and his breath is a heady mix of rum and mint, and he doesn't just slip his tongue in like Christian Miller did in ninth grade. Nathan takes his time, touching his lips to mine so gently, so feathery soft, until I'm a boneless, watery mass. I wrap my arms around his broad, strong shoulders for support, and he half-lifts me off my feet. And then before I know it, my mouth parts, and I'm really kissing Nathan Chan, and it is hot as hell.

In this moment, I know this is it. There is no one like Nathan, not the way he's holding me, so firmly, the length of my body pressed up against his. And the moment I realize it, I know I'm pretty much screwed.

3

Meddy [7:03PM]: This is such a bad idea. How in the hell did I let them talk me into doing this?

Selena [7:04PM]: By being yourself?

Meddy [7:04PM]: 👍

Meddy [7:05]: It's all your fault! If you'd been at dim sum, you would've run interference and I wouldn't be sitting here waiting for some dude my mom's been catfishing!

Selena [7:06PM]: Right, like I would've dared stop your fam's plans of setting you up. Plus, this is fun!

Meddy [7:08PM]: You are the worst. Know what I'm gonna do? I'm gonna tell them this date went so well that they should do the same for you.

Selena [7:09PM]: If your mom can find me a rich hotel owner to date, I'm down. What's the problem?

I sigh and lower the phone to the table. If I told her the truth, that I'm still hung up on Nathan, she'd tell me to stop being so pathetic.

"Hello, Meddelin?" A warm, low voice says.

I startle, shaking all thoughts of Nathan out of my mind. *Do not start off this date being haunted by Nathan's ghost.* I look up, and—okay, Ma, you did well. Fourth Aunt was wrong. Jake is definitely not a troll. He's not as devastatingly gorgeous as Nathan—ugh, stop it, self—but he's definitely good-looking. He'd fit into a K-pop band for sure. Tall, lithe, flawless skin, and a slightly impish smile that I find impossible not to return. Fourth Aunt would be all over him. I stand to give the handsome man before me a—oh god, hug or handshake? He reaches out and pulls me into a hug, solving my minor crisis and hiding my social ineptitude, his hand lingering on my lower back. By the time we break apart, I'm blushing a little. That wasn't a normal "Nice to meet you" hug. Or was it? Have I been out of the game that long?

Jake must have sensed my slight unease, because he gives me a sheepish grin and says, "Sorry if that was too much. I'm just so excited to finally meet you in person."

Of course. For him, we are not complete strangers. We've been chatting for weeks. The poor sucker. I can't believe my mom catfished someone into dating me. Okay, focus. I manage a smile. "Um, me too."

"You are even more beautiful in person," he says, and reaches across the table to take my hands.

Uhhh.

My smile freezes into a Chrissy Teigen–esque grimace-smile, but he doesn't seem to notice. He flags down a waiter and says, "Bring us a bottle of your best champagne."

Is there a polite way of pulling my hands back? My mind is short-circuiting, trying to work its way through the mess. Okay, so obviously things have gotten deep for this guy. Deeper than Ma led me to believe. Damn it, why didn't I try harder to see the chat messages? If I pulled my hands away, would he feel hurt? Betrayed? Oh god, even worse, what if he realizes it wasn't me he's been talking to but my mother? He'll lose his shit for sure, and then would he try to get us fired? Bad-mouth us to the bride and groom at the very least? Jesus, what if he sues us? Is that even possible?

"You okay?" he says.

I blink and refocus on him. I take a deep breath. "Sorry, yeah, I'm fine."

"Something on your mind?"

You suing me and my family for fraud. "Um, nothing. Just. Work, I guess?"

He nods. "Like I've told you before, your work is amazing."

Heat rises up my neck. I almost blurt out, "You've seen my work?" But manage to stop myself in time. Of course he's seen my work. It would've been one of the first things Ma revealed to him. Our website, with thousands of pictures of happy couples, is pretty awesome, if I do say so myself.

37

"You capture all those emotions so well," he continues. "Honestly, sometimes I'm like, damn, Jake, how did you get this lucky?"

I laugh weakly. He is in deep, the poor guy. I'll be nice. I've got to give this a good go, if only for his sake. I almost stupidly say, "And what is it you do?" when I recall that I do actually know what he does. "You're too kind. So tell me, how did you get into the hotel business?"

Jake shrugs. "I was working in finance right out of college. Worked on Wall Street for a while, and then I thought, *Well, I've made a fortune—a couple of fortunes, really . . .*" He laughs. I don't really see what's funny, but I laugh along anyway, then feel like a complete idiot. "I toyed around with a few ideas and then decided I wanted to build a resort where my family and friends could visit and have fun. Why not, right? It's a perk of being filthy rich."

I'm spared having to answer when the waiter returns with our champagne. It's hard to imagine how this guy managed to charm my mom into—oh, who am I kidding? At twenty-six, I'm as good as a spinster. Ma would've dished me out to any guy as long as he has a pulse. I'm so nervous by now that I take a gulp of champagne before Jake says, "Cheers."

"Right, sorry. Cheers." I clink my glass against his and down it. If I'm going to get through tonight, I'm going to need a lot of champagne.

Maybe it's the champagne, or maybe it's the fact that the food at the restaurant is excellent; whatever it is, halfway through dinner I realize that I'm actually having an okay time. Jake has a way of dropping little obnoxious hints about how rich he is—"so rich that when I sweat, I drip diamonds"—but aside from that, he's actually got a good sense of humor, and he does seem to be genuinely interested in me, which is a pleasant surprise. What I do doesn't normally interest men; in fact, most men seem to think that just because I'm in the wedding industry, that must mean I'm in a rush to get married myself. The truth is, being in the wedding industry is a surefire way of making me not want to get married.

I tell Jake as much, and he laughs. "Maybe it's just that you haven't met the right guy," he says.

My heart gives a squeeze, and my smile wanes. It's not that I haven't met the right guy, I want to tell him. It's that I've met him, and I know that no one else compares. But I have just enough sense not to blurt that out. Plus, it's been four years since Nathan and I split up, and I seriously need to forget him. Pretty sure being hung up on an ex for four years counts as, if not pathetic, then at least bordering on creepy.

"You must meet so many bridezillas," Jake says.

"Actually, the brides have largely been okay, save for one or two exceptions. Surprisingly, it's been the grooms who have been trickier to handle."

"Really? I find that hard to believe. Don't you often get brides asking you to Photoshop them to look thinner, or whatever?"

I shrug, taking another swallow of champagne. "Sure, sometimes. But thinning down's easy. Know what's really tricky? When grooms ask me to make them taller. I can make them look more swole, but height is a real pain to edit."

Uh-oh, I'm straying too close to ranting about my favorite subject: groomzillas. There are just so many of them, but for some reason, brides get all the bad rep. "What about you? You must deal with difficult customers a lot of the time."

"Nah, I've got people to deal with them for me. That's why we've got a whole customer service team, you know?" He laughs again. It's starting to grate on me. I drink more champagne.

By the time we're done with the meal, I'm tipsy enough to know that I probably shouldn't drive home. "I'm gonna call a Lyft," I tell him, taking my phone out and noticing, with some dismay, that the battery is at 4 percent.

"What? No. Let me drive you. Give me your keys."

"That's okay, really. I'll take a Lyft and then come back for my car in the morning."

"The parking structure opens at eight a.m. Didn't you say you need to be at the harbor by eight-thirty tomorrow? You won't make it in time."

I curse under my breath. He's right. I need my car early tomorrow morning. Damn it, self! Why'd you have to go and get all tipsy? "But what about you? Don't you need your car in the morning? I don't want everything to come screeching to a halt because I've made you late."

"I have other cars I can drive, and the hotel should be running smoothly enough by now not to fall apart just because I'm a couple of hours late. In fact, you probably won't see much of me tomorrow. I'll be mostly working behind the scenes," he answers easily, holding out his hand. I can't see a way out of this. If I keep refusing his offer, he's bound to get offended, and then there goes our big wedding weekend. I mean, one would hope that he's professional enough not to let a bad date get in the way of business, but can I really risk my family's biggest wedding of the year? And anyway, it's just a drive home. It's really not a big deal. I live with Ma, so if he tries to weasel his way inside, I can always use her as an excuse.

As I fumble for my car keys, my hand brushes against the heavy Taser that I carry everywhere. I really should stop taking it everywhere I go; it's heavy, it's cumbersome, and it probably makes me seem like a paranoid idiot. Still, as I hand over the keys to my Subaru, I can't help feeling glad that I have that Taser. And then, of course, I feel silly for feeling relieved.

Jake puts his hand on my lower back as we walk across the parking lot, which seems awfully forward, but again, I don't feel comfortable enough to tell him to stop. When we get inside the car and close the doors, the silence is suddenly all I can think about. I can hear every noise we make—each inhale and exhale and even my own heartbeat. Then Jake turns on the engine and Maroon 5 spills out of the speakers. I relax a little. He gives me a reassuring smile as he adjusts the mirrors. I smile back. This is okay. I'll be home before I know it, and tomorrow when we see each other, we'll be friendly and pleasant and totally professional. Everything's fiine.

"So that was fun, huh?" he says, as he drives out of the parking lot into the darkened street. It's late, and though we're on the main road, there are hardly any cars about. He glances at me, and I nod.

"Yeah, super-fun." Super-fun? What am I, fifteen? "I had a good time," I add. That's stretching it a little, but I guess I didn't have a *bad* time, so.

"Me too. You're a great gal, Meddy." He gives me a wink, and then—oh dear god—he reaches over and rests his hand on my knee.

I shift, pulling away, but his hand remains there, its heat radiating up my thigh. Come on, dude, that's the universal sign for *Take your goddamn hand off my leg!* Okay, I can't. I cannot deal with this. Not even for the family business. Sorry, Ma and aunties. Heart racing, I gently push his hand off my leg, as if it's a hamster I need to handle with care. He glances at me and grins.

"So you wanna play it like that, huh?"

A sick feeling bubbles up in my stomach. "Um." Think fast, Meddy. "I think I'm feeling okay now. You can just stop right here and I'll drive the rest of the way back myself."

He pouts at me. "And leave me stranded in the middle of nowhere?"

"Um. I'll call you a Lyft, wait here with you until it arrives. I really don't want to trouble you, and tomorrow's going to be such a long day for the both of us—"

He laughs. "God, you're sweet." The way he says it doesn't sound at all like a compliment. It sounds dirty, as if he's talking about an overripe peach he can't wait to sink his teeth into. He turns down a side street, and it's as if we've left the city of L.A. behind. Everything is dark down here, even the trees look menacing, and there's not a single car or person in sight.

"Stop the car," I say, my voice coming out tight with fear. "Stop right now!"

Instead, he speeds up. I scramble for the door, but it's locked, and even in my panic, I know we're going way too fast for me to take the jump. At best, I'd break an arm. At worst, I'd die.

Oh god.

The sickening realization hits me. I might actually die tonight. Bile rushes up my esophagus. I can't tell how long I sit there, frozen, while we speed even farther away from civilization. I no longer recognize my surroundings. Outside, there are only what look like abandoned factories. There is no one to save me.

"Calm down, Meds. Hey, c'mon, we're just having fun, right?" He glances at me and actually smiles. "Don't be such a tease; I know you're not shy. Those texts you sent me, I know you're a dirty girl deep down inside. So I'll tell you how this goes. We're gonna find a nice spot, and get real cozy—"

The Taser darts shoot out and hit him right in the neck. Jake jerks like a doll. The car swerves to the side. I open my mouth to scream. Darkness.

4

"This is unreal," I breathe out as I gaze out the airplane window.

"Yeah."

I look down at my hand, nestled in Nathan's. It looks so tiny in his paw. He gives it a squeeze, and we smile at each other. Holy shit, I'm actually doing this. In about ten hours, we'll be landing at London Heathrow airport, where we'll be greeted by his parents. Oh my god. I cannot.

"Stop freaking out."

"I'm not."

"Okay, tell your face to stop freaking out."

I force a smile, which comes out as a grimace.

"That is officially the weirdest smile in the history of smiles," he says, leaning over to kiss me. "Mmm, I love it when I kiss your teeth."

That gets a laugh out of me, which makes me feel a tiny bit better. But not much. Because holy SHITBALLS, man! I'm on a plane with Nathan! On the way to meet his family! For Christmas! In England! What is this life?

"Hey, how come you don't have an English accent?" I never thought of it, but now that we're actually on our way to London, it strikes me that Nathan sounds about as American as it gets.

"It's because my parents moved around a lot when I was little, so I was always put into international schools. Even in England, they put me in an international school. Easier to transfer my grades that way. Do you want me to sound English? Oi can talk Brit-ish for you, luv."

"Oh god. Okay, you can't carry it off." I shudder, and he laughs.

"By the way, I got Selena those AirPods she's been lusting after for Christmas. Signed it from you and me."

I gape at him. "Really? That's so generous." I'd given her an assortment of moisturizers from Bath and Body Works.

"Well, yeah, none of this would've been possible without her help."

"True." Over the last two years, Selena has come home with me on many weekends. She's a hit with my family; my aunts tell her she's the daughter they wish they had (which—hello, what about me? But whatever), and Ma tells her she's the sister she wished I had, which I have to agree with. And when Nathan invited me to his home for Christmas, Selena gave me the best gift anyone could come up with. She'd told Ma she wanted me to come back with her to Northern California for Christmas, and Ma had agreed without hesitation, since my family doesn't celebrate Christmas anyway.

Nathan takes out his tablet from his backpack and sets

it up on our tray table. "I downloaded *Immortals* for the flight."

"Ooh, you are a godsend, Nathan Chan."

"I figured shots of a topless Henry Cavill would help take your mind off meeting my folks."

I roll my eyes. "There is way too much boobage in *Immortals* for you to act all selfless."

"True." He laughs, then leans in and lowers his voice. "But yours are my favorite."

I smack his arm, but honestly, I'm sort of grinning at that. He pulls me closer so I can rest my head on his shoulder and we settle down to watch the movie. At some point, we both fall asleep. When the air attendant wakes us up hours later, I find to my immense horror that my head is stuck at a weird angle.

"Oh, no. No, no." I try to turn it, but pain shoots down my spine, and I squeak.

Nathan stretches, yawning. "What's up, funsize?"

"I fell asleep badly, and now my neck's refusing to turn."

He stares at me for two beats before bursting out laughing. "Are you secretly a ninety-year-old woman?"

"Don't insult me, kid. I'm only eighty-seven. Ugh. I can't meet your parents like this!" I gesture wildly at my slanted head.

"Calm down. Come here." Nathan places a hand on the back of my neck and begins to massage it.

"Ow, ooh, ah." Is it painful or is it good as hell? I can't decide.

"Stop twitching."

"Please put on your seat belts and face forward," an air attendant reminds us with a pointed look.

We do as we're told. Despite Nathan's best efforts, my head's still stuck at an angle. Whenever this happens, I usually have to wait until I can sleep it off before I regain normal flexibility in my neck. So. I really am going to meet his parents with a slanted head. Okay, that's totally fine. I am not at all freaking out about that.

Once we get off the plane, Nathan tries again to massage some movement back into my neck and shoulders, then he says, "Well, this'll be fun." He laughs when I hit him, catching my fist and kissing it. "It's so cute when you hit me with your teeny-weeny hand. It'll be okay. They are going to love you so much they won't let you go back to the States."

And, despite the crooked neck, he's right.

As soon as we get our bags and go into the arrivals hall, there's a shout and suddenly his parents are right there. His mom, a beautiful tall blonde, gives me a quick hug, and his dad, an Asian man who looks like what I imagine Nathan will look like thirty years down the road, gives me one of those awkward hugs that my mom and aunts often do.

"Oh, it's lovely to have you two here," his mom says.

"Hi, Mrs. Chan."

She pooh-poohs at me. "Call me Annie, none of that Mrs. Chan business. And that's Chris." She points at Nathan's dad, who smiles at me.

"Alright then, son?" Chris says.

"Alright, Dad."

Huh. Nathan does speak British after all.

When we walk outside, I gasp at the sharp, unforgiving cold, which slices right through my hoodie. Nathan takes out a jacket he's brought for me, which is about three sizes too big but is delightfully warm and smells of him.

The drive from Heathrow to Oxford takes almost two hours, and by the time we get off the freeway—or motorway, as it's called here—I'm exhausted. Though Chris and Annie are perfectly pleasant, they're so different from Ma and my aunts that I'm constantly on edge, desperate to make the best impression possible. Conversation with them is somewhat stilted, and I wonder if this is what all English families are like, if they all use words like "lovely" and "delightful" instead of shouting and flapping like my family does.

It only cements the decision I've made about keeping Nathan from my family for as long as humanly possible. Which is getting tougher and tougher to pull off. Nathan wants to meet Ma. And all my aunties. It's a bit of a sore spot in our otherwise perfect relationship. I'm so worried that he thinks I haven't introduced him to my family because I'm ashamed of him. Why don't I take him home with me one weekend? he'd ask. They'd be delighted, they would. And they would, if they knew about him.

But.

It's not even just the stark differences in our families that's holding me back from taking him home. My whole life, I've followed all of Ma's rules. I even chose to stay in L.A. for her. I love Ma, but I also want to be separate from her. Even thinking it makes me wince; it feels so much like a betrayal. But I do. I'm a horrible, selfish person, and I know I need to keep that part of me buried. I know that after college, I'll have to go back home, be with Ma. And for now, I just want Nathan all to myself. I want to keep him as separate as I can from Ma and my aunts. If that's selfish, then let me be selfish, just for now, just until we graduate. I don't want him to be swallowed up by my loud, overbearing family. I don't want him to see me the way I am with them—quiet and benign. I want him to see the real me—the one on campus, where I can really be myself, free and sarcastic and sharp. A challenge instead of a shadow. Then, of course, there's the curse. What if taking him home means it finds me even sooner than it had found my mom and aunts? I've tried explaining my reasoning for keeping him away from my family, but each time I just end up verbally flailing, and then the conversation ends with him hurt and disappointed.

His parents' house is worthy of an interior design magazine. In fact, it has been featured in *Home & Garden* magazine, Nathan tells me when my mouth drops open once we walk inside.

Nathan takes me up to his bedroom, and I gape at how tidy and tasteful everything is. It has a navy blue color scheme, and I can imagine what a neat kid he must've been because everything is in its place. I think back to my own room back in San Gabriel and how, just last weekend, I'd found a forgotten coffee mug that had actual mushrooms growing in it. Not even mold but like full-grown mushrooms, with stalks and heads and everything.

"So this is my childhood home, and that's my family,"

Nathan says, dropping our bags on the carpeted floor. "You okay? I'm sorry, I know they can be a bit much."

"Are you kidding? They're amazing. And your house is amazing." Not at all like mine, I want to say, but I don't, because honestly, I'm embarrassed. Ma and my aunts are practically hoarders. They say it has to do with growing up poor. The bathroom, for example, has no fewer than twenty-seven bottles of face cream. I know, I counted them when I was fifteen, and the pile hasn't moved in the last five years. They're all almost empty. When I asked Ma why she doesn't throw them away, she says, "Maybe one day I need, then how?" I guess a grower of mushrooms in coffee cups is not one to judge.

Nathan wraps his hands around my waist, his fingers brushing underneath my shirt. I shiver when he touches my skin. "Hey, none of that, not right now. Your parents are right below us," I scold, smacking his arm.

He grins and kisses me. "I'm not doing anything," he says, in between kisses. "I just love touching you here." His hands splay across my back, and I melt against him.

"You've got your horny face on," I say.

"What does my horny face look like?"

I lean back and try to imitate it, and Nathan bursts out laughing.

"Seriously? If my horny face looks like that, why did you ever start sleeping with me?"

"Out of pity." Then I squeal as he catches me and flings me over one shoulder as though I'm a sack of potatoes. "Don't make me fart while my butt's right next to your face!"

"I dare you to." Nathan laughs, but then he lowers me gently onto his bed and kisses me again, this time slow and deep. By the time he stops, I'm out of breath and aching for him. He presses his forehead against mine. "I'm so glad you're here."

"Me too."

I bite my lip against my smile, then gasp as he starts sucking lightly at my neck. Maybe it's because we were friends before we started seeing each other. Whatever it is, Nathan seems to know exactly what I want and how I want it. Every touch is addicting, the smell of him intoxicating. It's weird, finding out that we're not just compatible as friends. Shirts are flung off, jeans tugged down, and soon we're in our underwear, and the touch of his skin against mine is so good my entire body is blushing. We've done this probably close to a hundred times by now, but still, when Nathan takes off my bra, he does so with reverence, his breath coming out slow and sweet as my breasts are laid bare before him.

As always, I have to fight the instinct to cover them, but Nathan is so gentle, bending down to kiss my jawline, my neck, my chest, before his mouth finds my nipple and I am lost. I forget everything—the curse, my ma and aunts, even my own name. I bury my fingers in his hair, and there's just me and Nathan. Everything Nathan. Nathan's mouth, Nathan's fingers, Nathan's body. The first time was a bit awkward and lasted all of four minutes. But by now we've found a rhythm that drives all thought from my head and turns me into a being of need. And when our eyes meet, neither of us looks away until the very last gasp.

Later, lying in bed next to him, I realize something. We've been together for almost two years now, and he's the first one I tell everything to—when I get my papers back, when we're assigned terrible coursework, when the leader of the photography club says anything dumb, which is all the time. And he does the same, telling me every interesting detail about his econ classes, sharing his wildest dreams of owning a fancy hotel in the future, even telling me how much weight he's doing at the gym. I guess the last one's him showing off, but I don't mind. I like that Nathan wants to impress me, because I want to impress him too. And he does impress me. Even after two years, which involves a lot of farting and embarrassing bedroom stuff (queefs, anyone?), I still find Nathan impressive as hell. I love him. I want a life with him.

To hell with the family curse. It doesn't matter. I'm in Oxford, England. This is where curses go to die. I almost laugh out loud at the thought. I haven't really stopped to think about how much half-believing in the curse has weighed me down, but now I realize that I've always felt it lurking behind my back, felt it giving me an expiration date. But it's stupid. Why damn the relationship when there's nothing wrong with it? I make a choice.

When I get home, I'm going to tell Ma about Nathan. I'll tell her everything. I'll even tell my aunts. I'll tell them all over Sunday dim sum, since they're always happy when they're eating dim sum. That'll go over well.

5

"Fuuuck."

Pain. So much of it, it lurches from deep in my bones, squeezing my chest with a red fist, and then it erupts out of me in a moan, and the sound of my voice, so hoarse with pain it's alien, brings me back. I blink. Blink again.

Right. I'm in my car. Not in England with Nathan. My car.

Light flashes at the edge of my vision. It's my turn signal, which is making an infernal clicking noise. I reach out to turn it off, and the movement makes pain burst through my chest.

"Jesus—"

With one last heroic try, I manage to hit the turn signal switch. Sweet, blessed silence. I glance down, not daring to turn my head too much. My seat belt's digging into my chest. With a swallow, I push myself back slightly, still unsure what's broken and what isn't. Moving back makes the crushing sensation around my chest ease a little. I take a small

53

breath, then another, a bigger one. It hurts, but not too much. Ribs bruised, not broken. I release a shuddering laugh. Unbelievable. I'm okay. I'm—

I turn and barely stifle the shriek clawing its way up my throat.

Jake!

"Oh god," I moan. "Jake—" My voice catches. Every question that pops into my head seems so stupid, so unnecessary. *Are you okay?* It's obvious he's not, not when he's lying against the dashboard like that. *Are you . . . dead?* I moan again. Oh my god. I think he is. There's blood trickling out of his goddamn ear, down his neck, staining the collar of his shirt. Somehow, it's that small detail, the growing stain of blood on his white polo, that really hits home. He's dead. I killed him.

My panicked, gulping breaths fill the silent car. I look around wildly. "Help," I whisper. But there's no one in sight. The street is deserted. I don't even know where we are. I hit my seat belt lock, wrench the door open, and lurch out of the car, barely making it out onto the pavement before my dinner comes back out.

There's a dead man in my car.

A man. Dead. In the driver's seat of my Subaru. This is not at all on-brand for Subaru. Subarus aren't killers' cars. Jeep Wranglers are. Or, um, whoever makes those window- less white vans. Who makes those, anyway? I mean, those are creepy AF—

Focus!

A sob warbles out. No. I can't afford to freak out right now. If I start crying, I'm never going to stop. What do I do?

Cops.

Yeah. 911. Right.

I open the back seat and reach inside, shielding my gaze from Jake's body, focus on finding my purse—there it is. Cell phone. Nothing happens when I hit the power button. I moan. No, please. Out of power. I inhale shakily and reach for Jake's pocket. Maybe his phone's in there. My teeth grit so hard when the tips of my fingers brush against his pants that I almost crack my molars.

Empty.

The thought of groping about his pants for his phone is nauseating.

Okay. This is fine. This is totally and utterly okay. I'll just . . . I'll wait here until a car drives by.

Except. Except god knows how long we've been here, and no one's driven past. There are no houses or convenience stores or anything that might contain human life around me. The factories look like they haven't been used in years; many of the windows are broken and they're completely silent. I can't wait here much longer. I can't stand it. I glance back at the car. Incredibly, despite having crashed into a tree, it looks largely okay. The hood's dented, obviously, and there's a large crack running up one side of the windshield, but aside from that, it looks . . . drivable.

"No," I mutter to myself. I can't possibly drive it. Not least because there is a dead guy in the driver's seat.

Then move him.

My whole body recoils at the thought of touching him again. But my mind is like a caged wild animal, throwing itself against the bars and hissing. I *need* to get out of here. I can't stay here another minute, hoping for someone to drive by, hoping they'd be nice enough to stop.

Gulping in shallow gasps of air, I open the door to the driver's side, yelping when Jake's body slumps onto the pavement. Oh god, I was definitely not expecting that to happen. Hang on. I should check for a pulse. Or should I? He's so clearly dead. Yes, yes, I should. Whimpering slightly, I press a trembling finger against his wrist. I manage to keep it there for all of two seconds before I yank my hand back and wipe it furiously on my shirt. Dead. Very dead. I take another deep breath, fanning at my face, trying to put out the flames in my cheeks, then I reach out and grab Jake's arms.

They're still warm. Argh. Somehow, that makes it so much worse. Bile rushes up, but I grit my teeth and pull hard. Thanks to my job, I've had to work out religiously—carrying my two heavy cameras plus all those lenses for ten hours straight is hell on my back and shoulders, so I do everything possible to increase my strength and endurance. I even splurge on a weekly session with Dinah, the best personal trainer that my gym has to offer. Which means when I pull, Jake's body actually moves, surprisingly easily. Dinah would be proud.

Okay, Dinah would definitely not be proud of the fact that I can move a 180-pound man whom I've killed. And why am I even thinking of Dinah right now? Because—my mind argues as I yank Jake across the pavement, to the back of the car—because you need to think of anything and everything else that isn't, "Holy shit, I'm moving a dead body!"

Holy shit, I'm moving a dead body.

Where? Where do I move him to? I can't leave him here. That's way too cruel. But I can't stomach the thought of having it—him—in the back seat of the car while I'm driving. I eye the trunk. Okay. Trunk it is.

As an afterthought, I take a hoodie that I keep in the back seat and drape it over his face. Jake was an asshole when he was alive, but now that he's dead, I feel an inexplicable need to treat him with respect. I'm going to need so much therapy to unpack all of this.

Once I slam the trunk shut and Jake's out of sight, I feel somewhat better. More in control. In control? Who am I kidding? I have a literal corpse in my car. I shake my head. Let's not dwell on that. Shuddering to myself, I slide back into the car. Please, start, please—

The engine rumbles to life as soon as I turn the key. My breath releases in a whoosh, and I take a moment to calm down. Or try to, anyway. I'll just drive until I find a pay phone, and then I'll call 911. Right.

I back out slowly, wincing at the scraping sound my bumper makes along the road. Maybe I should get out and try to fix that, but no. I really can't stomach another second at this cursed spot. My breath is still coming out in shallow, panicked gasps as I drive along the road, and the brighter the streets become, the more panicky I feel. This is nuts. What have I done? I've put a body in the trunk of my car. What would the cops say when I called them? What would I even say? Why the hell did I do that? What kind of sane person would do that?

Question after question assaults my mind until a scream rips out of me, and in that instant, I realize: I can't go to the cops. They'll think I'm guilty of murder, that I'm some crazed killer, and they'll arrest me.

There's a gas station in the distance. This is my chance. I can stop there, rush inside, and beg for help. But my foot presses down on the gas pedal, refusing to let up, and I zoom right past it. It's as though my subconscious has gotten hold of my body and is forcing it to keep driving, not looking back, until I hit the entrance to the 405. I take it, heart drumming painfully at the familiar road sign, head throbbing as I join the traffic zooming down the freeway. I'm driving down the 405 with a dead body in my trunk. A hysterical laugh bubbles out. It sounds cracked, slightly mad. Tears spring into my eyes when I see the sign for the 10. So close to home. To safety. A lump catches in my throat. For the first time in years, I can't wait to get home to Ma.

6

The stage is set. By stage, I mean our table is groaning under the weight of all the dim sum dishes stacked in the middle and I've poured the tea for everyone, and now, all I need to do is . . . tell them. Just blurt it out, Meddy. Just do it. Do the thing!

"Um, so—"

"We have a big announcement!" Ma says in Mandarin. Her eyes are all twinkly. Seriously, they're like Christmas lights. She claps like an excited child.

"Oh?" I sit back, heart hammering from almost word vomiting about Nathan. Calm down, heart. I'll try again after their big announcement.

Ma nods at Big Aunt, who straightens up regally. She clears her throat. "We have decided to make a family business."

"Um. Okay . . . wow. That's huge." My mind swims. What business could they possibly put together?

"All of us," Big Aunt says, and for once, Second Aunt doesn't contradict her. They're all smiling and looking at me.

"Okay . . ." Why are they looking at me like that? Dread creeps up my stomach. Oh my god, this is where they tell me they've used the house as collateral against the loans they've taken out for this mystery business. Or maybe the business is dealing coke. Or human trafficking. Wow, I have a low opinion of my family. "What's the business?" I say, when I can't take the anticipation any longer.

"Weddings!" Fourth Aunt shouts, throwing her hands up with a flourish. Big Aunt frowns at her.

"I was about to tell Meddy that," Big Aunt scolds.

"Sorry," Fourth Aunt says, not looking sorry in the least.

"Weddings?" I frown.

"Yes," Big Aunt says. "I'll do the wedding cakes. I already do big birthday cakes, very good ones."

I nod slowly, thinking of Big Aunt's towering birthday cakes. She does do good cakes, there's no denying that. But the others . . .

"I'll do makeup and hair for bride," Second Aunt says. "I have so many loyal customers at the salon. If I quit, they'll all follow me."

"I'll do the flower bouquets and flower arranging," Ma says.

"And I'll do the entertainment!" Fourth Aunt finishes. "I have so many fans in the Asian community, you know. No doubt they'll all want to hire me as a wedding singer."

Ma rolls her eyes and says in a loud whisper, "She's just tagging along. She's family, so we have to give her a job."

"Says the minimum wage supermarket worker," Fourth Aunt mutters.

The two of them glare at each other until Big Aunt snaps her fingers between them and says, "And, Meddy, sweet Meddy." All eyes turn to me. I shrink back in my chair.

"Yeah?" I squeak.

"You'll be the photographer."

The breath is knocked out of me. I guess I should've seen it coming. Of course they'd want me to be their photographer. It makes sense; I am studying photography, after all. But still.

"Um. I need a minute." I leap out of my chair and weave through the crowd until I'm outside the restaurant. I gulp in a few deep breaths and try to make the swirling thoughts in my head less swirly. I'm upset, but I don't really know why. I guess there's that part of me that's fighting back and yelling, "Don't I get to choose what to do with my degree?" But then when I actually stop and think about it, I like the idea of doing wedding photography. I guess I'm mostly railing against the fact that they've all made this decision without me. Which is stupid, right? I shouldn't feel angry that they've made a good decision. And it *is* a good decision; they're right, they can do all those things. Ma's flower arrangements are gorgeous. Big Aunt is wasted on birthdays, and Second Aunt does have a loyal following at the salon. As for Fourth Aunt, well, she thinks she's a celebrity, and she does have a decent voice. We could make it work.

And as soon as I think that, tendrils of excitement unfurl inside me. We could do this. This could be my family's way out of the crappy little house we're all cramped in.

The door to the restaurant opens, noise spilling out. Ma brightens when she spots me.

"Aiya, why did you come outside? I was looking for you in the bathroom, but you weren't there." She peers at me and frowns. She must've sensed that I'm having A Moment, because she switches from Indonesian to English. "You okay? Why so sad?" The fact that she switches to English, despite her not being fluent in it, makes my stomach clench with guilt. She's already sacrificed so much for my sake, and I can't even communicate with her in her mother tongue.

I force a smile. "I'm not sad. I'm just trying to digest this whole family business thing."

"Ah, yes. Very big deal. But if you not interested, it's okay. We don't need photographer."

I stare at her. "But inside, you guys were like, 'Meddy, you should be our photographer.'"

"Yes, of course we want you to be our photographer. You are the best photographer."

I laugh bitterly. "Ma, you don't know that. I'm a total newbie. I'd probably make a mess of everything."

"It's okay, we are all new babies. We start slow. You do that thing, what is it called? Spirit another photographer?"

"Shadow."

"Ah, yes. You become a shadow to wedding photographer, you learn first, then when you graduate, you can do this. But if you think, no, I don't like this wedding photography, then no need to join family business, it is okay."

I take her hands in mine. It's hard for her to tell me it's okay, that I don't have to join them, because I can see plainly how excited she is about the idea of us all working together. "I'll do it, Ma."

"Really?" She looks so happy it breaks my heart.

"Yeah, of course. I'll look into wedding photography. I want to do this with you."

"Aduh, sayangku." Ma pulls me into a hug. It's not as tight as the ones Nathan's family gives, but it's sweet in its own way. "You make your mama so happy."

I hug her back and close my eyes. I guess I'll tell them about Nathan some other time.

7

Present Day

I sit in the garage for what seems like hours, wondering just how the hell my life has spun so out of control. And what in the world am I even doing here? Why am I home, instead of at the police station? It might not be too late. I could probably still go to the cops, explain everything. They'd be sympathetic, maybe. But when I think about turning the engine back on and driving out of the garage again, every drop of energy leaks out of me. I slump against the wheel, boneless. I just need to stay here for a bit. Gather enough courage. Decide what I would say to the police.

There's a sharp knock on the window. I jump so hard I bump my head on the roof of the car. Now I know what the saying "jumped out of their skin" means.

"What are you doing in there? You drunk? Aduh, were you drunk driving?" Ma calls out in Indonesian, her voice muffled through the window.

I open the car door, heart thundering. "Ma, you scared me!"

She frowns at me. "What is it, Meddy? What's wrong?"

I wasn't planning on telling her anything. Of course I wasn't—the last person I want to tell is Ma. She wouldn't know what to do, or say, or—

"Ma, I killed him." Tears spring into my eyes when I hear myself say those words out loud. I killed him. How many more times would I have to say that?

"Kill him? Kill what? Aduh, Meddy, how many times must I tell you, don't drink so much. You see, now you're not making any sense."

"I killed him, Ma. Jake. The guy you set me up with!" And now, finally, I let the tears flow, because saying his name is awful. It's not just some body in my trunk; it's a body who used to be a someone.

Ma stops her nattering mid-sentence. Her mouth claps shut, and she stares at me for a while. When she next speaks, it's in halting English. "This is like what you and Selena like to say? You kids always saying, 'Wah, you killing it!' Like that, ya?"

"No!" I cry. "I mean I literally killed him, Ma!" Not knowing what else to do, I take out my car key and hit a button. The trunk pops open with a click that might as well be a gunshot inside our small garage. All noise is suddenly amplified; I can hear my own heartbeat, and Ma's sharp intake of breath.

"Meddy," she whispers, "this is joke, right? You just joking with me?"

"No, Ma, this isn't a joke."

A strangled laugh from Ma; then she shakes her head.

"You kids, ya, you always think you are so funny." She wags a finger at me and strides to the back of the car, still shaking her head. "My daughter, such a joker, so—AIYA wo de tian ah!" She stumbles back, hands covering her mouth.

I wince.

"Meddy," she hisses. "Meddy! This is not funny." She looks back and forth between me and the trunk. "Are those fake legs? What you call it—man-ee-kween?"

I shake my head, fresh tears springing to my eyes. "No, Ma, it's not a mannequin. It's really Jake, I swear."

She utters a noise that's somewhere between a howl and a whimper, then takes a moment to steel herself before peering closer into the trunk. She whimpers again when she sees the rest of the body. I imagine what she's seeing from her vantage point. First the shoes—brown loafers, no socks— then the legs, the torso, and then the hoodie covering his face.

"Why you cover the face?" she says. "Something horrible happen to it, is it?" She shudders. "Is there something sticking out of the eye? Aiya, don't tell me, I don't want to know." She flaps, grimacing. "Is it broken glass in his eye?"

"No, Ma. There's nothing sticking out of his eye. I just thought it would be, I don't know, more respectful."

"Oh." She nods. "Yes, you right, more respectful." She pats me on the cheek. "I raise you so well."

Hysteria rises from deep in my stomach and I have to swallow it. Trust Ma to take pride in my etiquette when I've just shown her my date, whom I've killed, in the trunk of my car.

"I did just kill a person, so I don't know that you can say you've raised me well."

"Oh, he must deserve it."

I bite my lip to keep from bursting into tears again. I'm so grateful that I don't have to explain myself to her.

"Okay!" Ma says, straightening up, all of a sudden in control. She's not even breathing hard anymore. There's a glint in her eye that she gets the week before Chinese New Year, when she goes absolutely berserk and cleans the house like Marie Kondo on crack. "You. Inside. Now." She slams the trunk shut and herds me through the back door into the house.

Inside, she tells me to sit at the kitchen counter. I follow her instructions, too exhausted and defeated to argue. And, as much as I hate to admit it, I'm glad she's taking over, because I don't know what the hell to do in this situation. So I slump onto a chair, rest my elbows on the kitchen counter, and bury my face in my hands. Please let me wake up and find out that all this was a nightmare. Any moment now.

A steaming cup of tea is placed in front of me.

"TCM," Ma says. "You drink now. You got too much 'yang,' your insides very hot. Your breath smell so bad." She shuffles out of the kitchen.

I stare at her retreating back. Traditional Chinese medicine, seriously? Who would think about bad breath at this particular moment? Still, I take a sip, and the herbal tea is like an elixir, spreading its sweet warmth through my entire body, down to my freezing hands. I take another sip, then another, and before long, I've finished the entire cup and actually feel a little better.

Ma strides back into the kitchen. "Okay, I call Big Aunt already. She will be here in few minutes."

"WHAT?" I jump out of my chair. "Ma, oh my god, I can't believe you did that."

She looks genuinely confused for a second, but then her face clears and she laughs, waving me off. "Oh, no worry, no worry, she say she will call everyone else for me, okay? Won't just be Big Aunt coming here, you don't worry, all your aunties will come too."

"WHAT??" I cry. I throw my head back and stare up at the ceiling. This can't be happening. "Ma, that's not—we shouldn't be telling everyone about this!"

Ma frowns. "Not everyone. Just your aunties."

"That's everyone!"

"Meddy!" She tuts, disapproving. "They are family. It's different."

"It's murder!" I cry. "Or, well, not murder, it's more like self-defense, but still. Ma, there's a dead guy in my car. This is not the kind of thing you share with everyone, even if they're family."

"It's exactly kind of thing you share with family," Ma says.

"What do you mean, it's exactly the kind of thing you share with family? What other things have you guys shared that are in any way like this?"

Ma waves me off and says, "Come, help me cut mango for aunties. If we don't offer any food very ngga enak."

"Seriously, Ma? You care about saving face right now? I think we're kinda beyond that, aren't we?"

She gives me a look as she bends down to open up the fruit drawer in the fridge. "Meddy, how can you say that? Your aunties coming over, so late at night, coming to help us get rid of body, and we don't even offer them any food? How can? Oh, we have dragon fruit, good, good. Big Aunt's favorite. Wah, got pear too. Very good. Help me peel, don't be so rude to your aunties, you will bring shame."

"Oh, right, it's the lack of fruit that'll bring shame, not the dead body in the car."

But less than a minute later, I'm standing at the kitchen island with a peeler in one hand and a Korean pear in the other. My mind keeps going, *Bwaaa, this is so surreal. There is a dead body in my car and I'm standing here peeling fruit!* For some reason, I continue peeling and cutting. I suppose I might as well, since I don't have any better ideas.

Just as I finish cutting up the giant pear, the doorbell chimes.

"Go get door," Ma says. She's still slicing up the last dragon fruit.

I head for the front door, still in that weird I-must-be-dreaming state of mind. I don't even know what to say to my aunts. Thank you for coming to help figure out what to do with this guy I killed?

But I'm spared having to say that, because the moment I open the door, Big Aunt pats my cheek and says in Indonesian, "My dear Meddy, it's okay, don't worry. Go sit down," and then strides past me. Second and Fourth Aunts follow, each one clucking, "Don't worry, we're here now, stop crying."

"I'm not crying—"

Second Aunt tuts, as though my lack of tears were a personal affront to her, before joining the others in the kitchen. Noise explodes from the kitchen, though not of the "Oh my god, Meddy did what?" variety. More of the "Wah, dragon fruit! Aduh, you shouldn't have bothered!" variety. I can hear Ma pulling out chairs and shouting merrily at them to sit down and have some mangoes. "Ah Guan gave me a whole crate when he came back from Indo. A whole crate!"

Taking a deep breath, I steel myself and go into the kitchen.

"Meddy!" Big Aunt shouts.

Oh god, here it comes. Now they'll start freaking out about the body.

"Have you eaten?" Big Aunt says. "Come! Come here and sit down, oh, you look so pale." She gets up from her seat.

It's as though a switch clicks on inside me. I automatically hurry over, pushing her back down onto the chair, saying, "Please, Big Aunt, don't bother yourself. I'll grab a chair. You sit and enjoy the fruit, okay? Can I get you anything else?"

From the corner of my eye, I sense Ma's approval, and it makes me want to laugh out loud *and* sob. I mean, seriously, I've just killed a man, and she still cares about me being respectful to my elders.

Big Aunt spears a sliced mango and takes a dainty bite. "Wah, so good." She takes another bite and sighs. "Nothing beats Indonesian mangoes."

"Yes, Indonesian mangoes are the sweetest," Ma says. "Does anyone want herbal tea? I boiled a pot for Meddy and I have some left over."

"Tch, no thanks, I don't believe in that old-fashioned TCM stuff," Fourth Aunt says.

Ma glowers at her. "Traditional Chinese medicine is real medicine!" She launches into one of her usual tirades about how TCM has been medically proven to work and is much better than Western medicine and so on and so forth.

I'm stuck in a nightmare. I know it. Maybe I got a concussion from the accident. Maybe I'm actually in a coma, and my coma-brain is coming up with this weird-ass scenario, because there is no way that I'm actually sitting here, in the kitchen, watching my oldest aunties eat a mango and Ma and Fourth Aunt argue while Jake lies cooling in the trunk of my car. Just when I'm about to scream, Big Aunt puts down her fork with a meaningful clatter.

Everyone sits to attention.

"So," she says, turning to me and switching to English. Behind the kindly wrinkles that I know so well I could sketch them in my sleep, her gaze is eagle sharp. "Tell Big Aunt what happen. Start from beginning."

I don't hesitate. There's just something about Big Aunt, a mix of firm authority and motherly warmth that nobody can say no to. I'm feeling so guilty about having them rush here in the middle of the night—to help me with a dead body, no less—that I try relaying the story in Indonesian. But not even one sentence in, Second Aunt tells me my atrocious Indonesian is giving her a headache and I should just stick to English. With some relief, I tell them about my date with Jake, about how he insisted on driving me home, and the things he said.

My aunts and mother cover their mouths with horror and shake their heads.

"How could you set Meddy up with such a douchebag?" Fourth Aunt snaps at Ma.

Ma's face is as red as a Louboutin sole. "He was so nice online! Perfect gentleman, even offer to cook terong for me—er, for Meddy."

"What's terong? Is that fermented shrimp paste?" I say.

"Tch, no," Ma says, switching to English. "Shrimp paste is terasi. Terong is eggplant."

Something clicks inside me. "He offered to cook me eggplant? That's weirdly specific."

Ma nods furiously. "It's why I think, wah, this boy is meant for you. He even know what is your favorite food."

"I need to see these chat messages."

Ma takes her phone from her pocket, and my aunts all take out their glasses. As Ma hands the phone to me, Fourth Aunt swipes it from her hand.

"Hey!" Ma says.

Fourth Aunt ignores her and starts scrolling. Her eyebrows shoot up, almost disappearing in her hairline, and she bursts into hysterical laughter.

"Why you laugh? What is so funny?" Ma snaps.

Still laughing so hard she can't catch her breath, Fourth Aunt pushes the phone to me. I skim through the messages, and . . . Oh. My. God. It is so much worse than I thought.

Jake1010Hotelier: Hey

Meddelin Chan: Hello!

I look up at Ma, aghast. "You used my real name on this site? And is that—" I tap on the little icon next to my name, and it enlarges to show an actual picture of me.

"I don't know you are supposed to use fake name! How am I supposed to know that?"

"Maybe by not pretending to be me and making a fake dating account? I mean, for god's sake, look, Jake didn't upload any pictures of himself!" Ma looks so hurt that I immediately regret saying that. "I'm sorry, Ma, I know you just wanted to help."

She gives a tiny nod, and I resume reading.

Jake1010Hotelier: Love your pic

Meddelin Chan: Thank you!! You so sweet!!

I grit my teeth in an effort to not snap at Ma again. How many exclamation marks can the woman use in a single reply?

Jake1010Hotelier: So, wedding photography, huh? That must be interesting.

Meddelin Chan: Oh yes! Very interesting!! What do you do?

73

Jake1010Hotelier: As you might have guessed from my screenname, I'm a hotelier. I own hotels. Many of them, actually.

Meddelin Chan: Wahhh! So impressed!

It goes on like that for a while, Jake bragging, describing in great detail each and every one of the hotels he owns, and Ma replying in the most bimbotic way that's humanly possible. Anyone reading this would think I'm desperate for Jake's approval, but I know that this is Ma being polite. This is how she's raised me, to encourage others to talk about themselves, and then find the good things in what they say and show appreciation. I can't tell whether it's a Chinese thing or an Indonesian thing, but whatever it is, it worked on Jake. After only a few days of messaging back and forth, he sends this message:

Jake1010Hotelier: I feel so comfortable chatting with you, Meddy.

Meddelin Chan: Me also!

Jake1010Hotelier: It's so hard finding someone I really click with, you know? I feel as though I've known you for a long time.

Meddelin Chan: I agree!

Jake1010Hotelier: Sooo wanna meet up?

Meddelin Chan: Yes! So happy you ask now! Yesterday my body not taste so delicious, but today is better.

Oh. My. God. Noooo. In Indonesian, the phrase "tidak enak badan" means "not feeling well," but its literal translation is "body not delicious." Behind me, Fourth Aunt resumes cackling, while the others go, "What? What's so funny?"

I read on.

Jake1010Hotelier: Oh. Wow, okay. Damn, girl, you're even thirstier than I thought. 💦

Meddelin Chan: Haha! No, no, not thirsty! I have a lot to drink. Quite wet now.

Jake1010Hotelier: Wow. Damn. If I'd known, I would've asked you out sooner. 🍆

Meddelin Chan: Wah! How you know eggplant my favorite??

Jake1010Hotelier: It is, huh? Well, I've got a real big one for you.

Meddelin Chan: Oh! I can't wait! LOVE eggplant!!

I slam the phone down and stare at Ma. Fourth Aunt is literally lying on the floor, laughing.

"What? What is it?" Big Aunt says. "He sound like very nice boy, offer to cook eggplant for you."

"Right?" Ma cries, gesturing wildly. "I read that and I think, wah, this boy is so lovely, so caring for my daughter, even ask her, is she thirsty?"

I bury my face in my hands. "Nooo! Ma, those emojis—the water droplets and the eggplant—they're sexual innuendos!"

Three pairs of eyes stare at me in utter confusion while Fourth Aunt howls with laughter.

"Sexual . . . what? In-you-when-what?" Second Aunt says.

I can't believe I'm having this conversation with my aunts and mom right now. "Sexual innuendos. You know, like, sexual wordplay. The eggplant symbolizes the—um—the male uh, the um." This is ridiculous. I'm twenty-six, for god's sake, and yet I can't say the word "penis" out loud in front of my mom and aunts because part of me is sure they'd scold me for saying it. Instead, I use my index finger to air-draw the universal symbol for penis.

"Eggplant," Big Aunt says. "Yes, he say eggplant, we know that."

"No—"

"She means PENIS!" Fourth Aunt howls, and then doubles over again, laughing.

"What?" Ma gasps. "No. But—"

"That sound not right. I think you wrong," Big Aunt says stridently. She snatches the phone from me and frowns at it again. "See, he say, 'If I'd known, I would've asked you out sooner . . . I've got a real big one—' Oh." She drops the phone on the counter as if it's turned into a cockroach.

Ma's standing there, frozen, a look of horror on her face.

"Ma, you okay?"

She turns to look at me slowly, then says, in a voice full of horrified wonder, "Eggplant is penis?"

"Yeah." I sigh, feeling so ashamed of my generation.

"I thought he mean, you know, fried eggplant. I thought—" She looks so lost and small that I can't help but feel sorry for her. I put an arm around her shoulders and squeeze.

"It's okay, Ma. I know."

"Yes, it's okay, everyone has to learn how to sext at some point," Fourth Aunt says.

I shoot her a dirty look.

"Sext?" Ma says.

"Don't worry about it," I say, patting her shoulder. "So, um. Okay, so this clarifies some things. Not that it excuses Jake's behavior in any way, but I see now why he was so . . . uh—"

"Horny?" Fourth Aunt says. She grins when I shoot her another dirty look.

Ma's hand flies to her mouth again. "Meddy, is it . . . did I get boy killed because I say I want to eat his eggplant?"

I open my mouth to answer, but my aunts beat me to it, shouting, "NO!" in unison.

"So what if you say you want eat eggplant?" Second Aunt says. "Maybe one day you want eat eggplant, but then another day you don't want, is okay you change mind."

"Yes, he is very bad boy, very bad," Big Aunt says.

"But if I don't say, 'Wah, yes, I want to eat your eggplant,' then maybe he not so—you know—"

"Meddy, when he said those things to you in the car, what did you say to him?" Fourth Aunt says.

"I told him no, I wasn't interested in that. I moved his hand off my knee. I was pretty clear about what I wanted and didn't want."

"See?" Fourth Aunt says, triumphantly. "The eggplant doesn't matter. That was just flirting. Everybody does it. But he chose to take it further after Meddy said no. It's not your fault."

I nod emphatically. "It really isn't your fault, Ma." A tiny voice in my mind says: *Well, it kind of is, in that if she hadn't impersonated me in the first place . . .*

I squash the voice down. No use pointing fingers now.

"Okay, back to what happen," Big Aunt says. "So this baggy douche try touch you—"

"Douchebag," Fourth Aunt says.

Big Aunt waves her off. "Douchebaggy try touch you—"

"Um, and then I kind of freaked out—panicked—and uh. I may have Tased him a little."

Four pairs of eyes stare at me, horrified.

"Meddy," Second Aunt breathes. "You have Taser?"

I can't help cringing as I nod. Here it comes. They're going to—

"Can we see?" Second Aunt says.

Huh?

"Wah, wonder what model you got," Big Aunt says. "Is

it like my one?" She picks up her handbag from the kitchen counter and rummages in it, looking over her reading glasses.

Fourth Aunt sighs. "They got distracted again. Hey!" She claps at them, like they're raucous puppies. "Focus! It's very late and we have an early morning."

Big Aunt straightens up, clearing her throat. "Ah, sorry. You show me Taser later. Okay, so you Tase him. You get him where? Neck? Cheek?"

I gape at her. "Um, the neck."

They all nod. "Always go for neck," Ma says. "I hear neck is best place to Tase. Very sensitive. Good, Meddy." She pats my cheek with approval.

It takes a second for me to gather my thoughts from the mess of WTF-ness. "And then, uh, then he crashed the car, and when I came to, he was—uh. Well, you know."

"He die already," Ma says, flatly.

None of my aunts seem surprised by this, which means Ma must have told them over the phone before they came, or maybe it means that MY FAMILY IS A BUNCH OF PSYCHOPATHS. I choose to go with the former.

"Then how?" Second Aunt says.

She can say that again. We sit there for a bit, silent, each of us deep in thought. For the record, my thoughts are still stuck in WHY ARE THEY SO CALM WHAT IS GOING ON ALSO OMG I KILLED A MAN.

Big Aunt takes off her reading glasses with a sigh. "Okay. Where is Jake now?"

"In the trunk of my car," I say, wincing again at how insane it sounds.

She nods. "Nobody see you, right?"

"I mean, I don't think so? There was no one around. It was a quiet street, I think he chose to go down that street because, uh, you know, he wanted to—you know."

My aunts and mother all mutter curses in various languages—lots of F-words being tossed around in Hokkien, Mandarin, Cantonese, and Indonesian.

"I tell you, ah," Ma hisses, "it is good thing he already dead, otherwise I kill him."

Even Fourth Aunt nods in solemn agreement to this. Hearing this makes tears spring to my eyes again. The fact that there's no question among them that I did the right thing in defending myself is as soothing as a tight hug, and I just want to melt in their arms and sob and let them take care of everything.

"Okay, so we getting rid of body," Big Aunt says, with her usual authority.

"Hang on," Fourth Aunt says, "why should we do that? Why not just go to the police? I mean, it sounds like a pretty clear-cut case of self-defense."

Ma scowls at her. "Yes, we know it is self-defense, but police don't know. They see we got dead body in trunk, they will for sure say, 'Oh my god, you murder him!'"

Fourth Aunt glares back at her, opens her mouth to say something, stops, turns to me, and says, "Why did you put the body in the trunk?"

Despite being the youngest of the lot, Fourth Aunt is still formidable. All the women in my family are. Except for me, I guess. I quail under her gaze, my voice coming out flimsy. "Um. I freaked out. I didn't want to wait another second longer for someone to come by, my phone was dead, and I didn't want to drive back with it next to me. In hindsight, I guess I made the absolute worst choice I could've made."

"No, worst choice is you leave him there, on side of the road," Second Aunt says.

"Ohhh, yes, that one even worse," Ma says, nodding gratefully at her before shooting Fourth Aunt another dirty look. Fourth Aunt ignores her.

"Surely if we go to the cops and explain everything, they'll see that Meddy is no killer. Look at her!"

I'm suddenly the subject of four pairs of shrewd eyes once more. I try my best to not cringe away from the attention. Big Aunt exchanges a look with Ma. Though the question is unspoken, I know what she's asking Ma: It's your daughter, what do you want to do?

Ma straightens up. "We are not going to police. No, I don't trust them. We don't know what they say. They might say she temperating the body—"

"Tampered with the body, you mean," Fourth Aunt says.

Ma shoots her a look of pure venom. "They might say she block justice—"

"Obstructed justice," Fourth Aunt says.

"It's very clear what I mean!" Ma snaps. "Yes, we know your English is very good, no need to show off, okay?"

Fourth Aunt throws her arms up. "I'm just helping!"

Big Aunt catches her eye and gives a small shake of the head, and immediately Fourth Aunt deflates, her breath

81

coming out in an angry sigh. She mumbles, "Do whatever you want."

It's as though there's a fire under my skin. My cheeks are red-hot. My mom and aunt are fighting because of me. I mean, okay, Ma has never gotten along with Fourth Aunt, and they fight every chance they get, but still, it sucks to be the reason they're fighting now.

Big Aunt nods. "Okay, no police. Come, we go see body."

8

"—and they say want twelve lily tower!" Ma practically shouts at me over the phone.

"Wow, that's amazing, Ma," I say, lowering the volume on my phone to the minimum. I can't see her face. As usual, she's got the camera pointing too high, so it's only showing her forehead and her permed bangs.

"Yes, it all go so well, Meddy. When you finish school and come home, it will go even better, especially then we have photos of everything we done."

I don't even have to force my smile. The family business, sans me, has been surprisingly successful. I have to admit that my mom and aunts have exceeded my expectations, even though I was somewhat dubious about the idea to begin with. I've been helping out here and there whenever I'm home, taking as many photos as I can of Ma's flower arrangements and Big Aunt's cakes. I even set up a website for them. It doesn't look half bad, but I can't wait to be able to spend a lot more time streamlining everything and making

83

it look all shiny and impressive. Weirdly, I'm actually really looking forward to graduating and plunging headfirst into the business. Who woulda thunk it?

There's a knock at my door. A second later, Nathan pops his head in. I quickly tell Ma I have to go and cut the call short. Still haven't told her about Nathan. I figured we're so close to graduating, and once we do, I'll definitely tell them about Nathan because he'll be coming round to our house all the time. With them constantly fussing over him, I'd lose him to them. So for now, I choose to be selfish again. Keep him all to myself. Just for the time being. There's plenty of time to serve him up to the sharks. At least with graduation looming, Nathan's stopped asking when I'll introduce him to my family. He knows it won't be long now, so he can afford to be patient.

"I've got news," Nathan says, dimples on full assault as he walks in.

"Oh?" Three years together and the sight of him still makes my breath catch. Maybe I have asthma. I shouldn't still be so breathless around such a long-term boyfriend. But seriously, those stupid dimples. They should be outlawed.

"No horny face," he scolds, grinning. "Not yet, anyway." He takes both of my hands in his. "Okay, so. You know how I was interning at JLL last summer?"

I gasp. "Did they offer you a position? That's awesome! I knew they would!"

"They did."

I squeal and leap into his arms, and he lifts me right off the floor, laughing. "Wait, I'm not done telling you the offer yet."

I'm peppering his entire face with kisses, so I miss the next thing he says. Or rather, I hear it, but my brain says, *Does not compute*. I pause mid-kiss. "Come again?"

"It's in New York. That's where their headquarters are."

"I—oh. Can you put me down?"

He does so, gently, and the second my toes touch the floor, I start pacing about the small room. Thoughts race through my head at Nathan's news. What does it mean? It means, dumbass, that he's going to move to New York. Wait, does it mean that? He hasn't said he accepted. But how can he not accept? It's the biggest business consulting company in the country, if not the world. And it's New York! But what about his dream of staying here in California and opening a hotel? *What about it? It was obviously just that, a dream.*

"You okay?" Nathan says, rubbing his hands up and down my arms. "I wasn't actually done telling you stuff."

"Oh?" My head pops up like a meerkat. Maybe he's going to tell me he got an even better offer, from an even bigger consulting firm that I have never heard of. Which would be totally plausible.

Nathan's eyes grow soft, and he takes my hands again. "I'd love it if you'd come with me, Meddy."

My mouth drops open. No sound comes out of it. My mind, whatever's left of it, has short-circuited.

"Meddy? Hmm. Did I break you?" He waves a hand right in front of my face. "Hey."

"Sorry. What? Come with you? To New York?"

"Yeah," he laughs. "Come with me. We'll explore the Big Apple together. We can get an apartment together; we'll wake

85

up next to each other every morning. I'll make you a latte and get you fresh bagels every day. It's a great city for photographers. You'd have your work in galleries, Meddy, I know it. You're brilliant."

My knees grow weak. God, I want all those things so badly. I want me and Nathan in a tiny New York City apartment with exposed brick walls and wood floors and those old school radiators.

But.

New York. That's so far away, it might as well be another country. What would Ma do without me? I'd be no better than my male cousins, leaving home as soon as they could. No, I'd be even worse, because I gave Ma and my aunties false hope, led them to believe that I'd stay before ripping their hearts right out. Ma would be devastated. Big Aunt would shake her head with disappointment and say, "Wah, turn out girl not blessing. Same as boy, leave us behind." And Second Aunt and Fourth Aunt would give me disapproving looks as they comfort Ma.

No, I'm better than my cousins. Better than my uncles— and I sure as hell am better than my father. I won't abandon my family. Not for love, not for anything.

"I—" I pause. I can't just tell Nathan that I won't go with him to New York. What if he decides to stay in California because of me? I can't do that to him. I won't. I won't make him give up his dreams for me, not when I'm not prepared to give up mine for him. And let's not forget about the curse. I've always known our relationship is doomed, that there will come a time when Nathan will leave me. I should take

86

matters into my own hands and make sure this will work out okay for Nathan. As it should. It's too good of an opportunity for him. The thought makes me want to vomit, but it's clear what needs to happen.

This, then, will be my gift to Nathan.

I turn away from him. I can't do this while looking at his beautiful, beloved face. I make myself laugh a little. "Well, that's good. I, uh, I wasn't sure how to tell you this before, but um. I think it's best if we, um, if we break up. Yeah."

"What?"

My gaze darts toward him, just long enough to register the plain shock on his face.

"Yeah, we've been together like basically all of our adult lives. I kind of want to see what else is out there. Don't you?"

Nathan looks like he could put his fist through the wall. "No, I don't. What the hell, Meddy?"

My chest squeezes like a fist, threatening to crush my heart, my lungs. I struggle to breathe. "I'm sorry, I was planning to tell you after graduation, but this feels like a good time. Now that you're going to New York, and I'll be staying in L.A. . . . it's all for the best, you know?"

His face is a picture of pain and betrayal. "No, I don't know. What the—how long have you been feeling this way?"

It's a struggle to keep from falling apart. I swallow the lump in my throat. Don't cry. Don't fucking cry. "Um, a while."

"A while?" He gapes at me for a bit, then barks a mirthless laugh. "Jesus." He shakes his head and rakes a hand through his hair. Takes a long, shuddering breath. "I was gonna . . ." He shakes his head again. "Never mind. I—I'm gonna go. I'll, uh, come by for my stuff later. Or something."

I manage a small "Okay" and stay unmoving as he leaves my room. Dear god, what have I just done? I feel as though everything inside me has just been scooped out, leaving me an empty husk of a person. I can't watch. I can't stay here and look as the boy I love walks out of my life. But I do. As the tears finally fall, I make myself stare, because I know it'll be the last time I see Nathan, and I don't want to miss a single second of him, even when he's leaving me.

9

Present Day

Fourth Aunt perks up a little as we walk out of the kitchen. "I've never seen a dead guy before," she says.

"You are too young," Big Aunt says. "Wait until you are fifty, then all your friend parents here die there die, then you see dead people all the time."

"Well, obviously I've been to funerals before. I've seen bodies in coffins. This is different. I mean I've never seen a dead guy who isn't, you know, at a funeral."

A couple of steps away from the garage, Second Aunt suddenly gasps and says, "Wait! Cannot go out there!"

We all jump, and in the ensuing silence, I swear I can hear all of our hearts beating a mad rhythm.

"What is it?" Ma says.

Second Aunt's face is stricken. "We cannot see the body! Cannot go near it!"

"Why not?" Fourth Aunt demands, obviously irritated. She glances with anticipation at the garage.

"Tomorrow is big wedding weekend. So unlucky if we

are near dead body now, and then we bring the bad luck to the wedding, how can? We will curse bride and groom and their whole family!"

Fourth Aunt groans. "Not this superstitious BS again."

I don't usually agree with Fourth Aunt, but I very nearly groan out loud with her, because as soon as Second Aunt says it, both Ma and Big Aunt actually pause to consider what she's saying. My pulse goes so fast I feel as though I might faint. I can't believe I might end up going to prison because of a superstition.

"But isn't the belief that you shouldn't go to a wedding after you've been to a funeral?" I point out.

My aunts' eyebrows rise.

"I mean, this isn't a funeral, technically. We're not doing any burial rites or anything."

Eyes shining, Ma snaps her fingers and points at me. "Meddy is correct. We just don't bury body now. We—maybe we put him in freezer? Then on Monday, after wedding, we can bury body."

Fourth Aunt blanches. "Uh, hang on, I didn't mean—"

Big Aunt nods. "Okay, it sound good."

Second Aunt chews her lip, hesitating, and Big Aunt glares at her. "And anyway," Big Aunt says, "since hotel owner die, wedding probably cancel tomorrow, when he not show up. So we be back early, then we bury body."

With that, they resume walking toward the garage, Fourth Aunt leading the charge, Second Aunt being pushed along by Ma, me trailing at the back.

"Ah, you leave light on," Big Aunt says, walking through the back door into the garage.

"Yes, dead body cannot be in the dark," Ma says.

Big Aunt nods. "Yes, good thinking."

"More superstitious BS," Fourth Aunt mutters.

"Just wait until you see what Meddy do to the body. She was very respectful," Ma says.

I can't believe she's taking this moment to boast about me being respectful. This is peak Asian parenting.

We all crowd around the trunk of the car. My breath catches, my chest painfully tight, not enough room for my lungs to expand and take in air. I think I might faint. As though sensing my near-panic, Ma pats my arm before opening the trunk.

And there he is, just as I left him, lying in there with his long legs bent, knees at his waist, the hoodie covering his face. There is a mix of noises from my aunts—Big Aunt is tch-tching and shaking her head, muttering, "This what happen when parents don't raise the son well," Fourth Aunt is staring openmouthed with what I can only describe as horrified glee, and Second Aunt is . . .

"What are you doing, Second Aunt?"

She hardly glances at me as she goes into a deep lunge. "Snake Creeps Through the Grass," she mutters.

"What?"

"She doing Tai Chi," Ma says. "Doctor tell her do it for high blood pressure."

"Uh. Okay." I suppose we all have our ways of dealing with stress.

Fourth Aunt reaches toward the hoodie, and Ma smacks her hand.

"Ow! What?"

"What do you think you're doing?" Ma demands.

"Isn't it obvious? I want to see his face!"

"Aiya! You so disrespectful. People already dead, you want to see his face for what?"

"She's right, Mimi," Big Aunt says, gently. "We try not to disturb him too much."

I have to turn away from the body. The sight of it brings back the trauma of the accident, and I can't stop seeing flashes of Jake, again and again. Of him smiling, his hand on my knee. Now his hands are lying limply against his hips.

"Now what?" Second Aunt says, going through her Tai Chi moves a lot faster than they call for. "This boy so tall. How we get rid of him?" She shudders before going into a different pose with arms outstretched. "Maybe we can chop him up, cook some curry, then throw away bit by bit?"

"That's a lot of curry," Fourth Aunt says.

My stomach lurches. Calm. Down. They're not being serious. They're not. They're just being their usual selves. Their usual *murdery* selves. What is going on right now?! Maybe one of the Chinese dramas they're always watching is a crime show. Or maybe this is a mom thing: once you have a kid, you lose the ability to be truly shocked by anything. I mean, this is not normal, right? *Right?*

"No curry," Big Aunt scolds. Second Aunt glares at her.

"You got better idea is it?" Second Aunt says.

Big Aunt sighs. "I think first."

"Um," I squeak, and they all look at me. I charge ahead

before I lose whatever tiny bit of courage I have. "Maybe we should take him to the desert and bury him there?"

They mull this over. We've been on family trips to Vegas a couple of times; we all know the route well, the empty desolation between California and Nevada that people pass through and never stop at.

"Good idea," Ma says, smiling with obvious pride at me.

Second Aunt nods. "Yes, very good."

"Better than your curry idea," Big Aunt chides. "Okay, we do that when we come back from wedding island. Definitely got no time to do tonight, we need to be at pier tomorrow by eight-thirty."

Oh my god. In all the panic and confusion, I haven't forgotten that we still need to work a wedding tomorrow, but I have forgotten the details of it—the fact that it's at Santa Lucia and that we have to congregate tomorrow morning at the pier to catch one of the private yachts that will be taking us to the island. The thought of it exhausts me. Driving to the desert, digging a hole, filling it, and then driving back is out of the question for tonight. As it is, I can barely stay on my feet.

"We cannot leave him in trunk for whole weekend," Ma says. "Later he will stink up my house, then will be very hard to get rid of smell."

Big Aunt nods again. "We need to put him in fridge."

Lord help me, we are literally talking about fridging the dude.

"My fridgerator not big enough," Ma says.

"Only you got fridge big enough," Second Aunt says to Big Aunt.

The only sign that betrays Big Aunt's dismay at the realization that it would have to be her fridge is a flicker of displeasure, but then she nods and says, "Okay. Anyway, I will feel better with body in my fridge than if body in someone else fridge; who knows, maybe that person is not so responsible." She gives Second Aunt the side-eye. Second Aunt's nostrils flare and she opens her mouth to speak, but Big Aunt says, "We go now."

"Um, could we move him into your trunk?" I say. "It's pretty obvious my car's been in an accident, and I don't want us to get pulled over."

"Okay. My car already in your driveway. Come, we move him."

We all crowd around Jake's body.

"We can't carry him out like this," I say. "What if someone sees?"

"Yes, cover him with something," Second Aunt says. "Nat, you got big bag or not? You know, when Hendra go ski, he take his ski in this very big bag. I always think, wah, can fit me inside that bag."

"Why you think that? Such unlucky way of thinking," Big Aunt scolds.

Before Second Aunt can snark back at Big Aunt, Ma quickly cuts in. "No, Meddy don't ski. Maybe garbage bag? Can it fit or not?"

We regard the body. "I think he's a bit tall to fit in a trash bag, Ma," I say.

"We'd have to cut him up first," Fourth Aunt says, her eyes shining with what I can only describe as horrified glee.

Has she always been this murderous? Have they always been this blasé about chopping bodies up?

"Such silly idea," Ma scoffs. "So messy, and the garbage bags always leak. You will make big mess in my garage."

"That's because you always buy the cheap ones," Fourth Aunt shoots back. "I told you to buy Glad brand. Haven't you seen their ads? Glad bags will hold his cut-up body just fine, no leaks!"

I look at the ceiling. Pretty sure that when Glad was planning their marketing campaign, they didn't think their target market would be a bunch of middle-aged Chinese women arguing about how to best dispose of a body. "What about a blanket?" I say. "We just need something to cover him while we move him to Big Aunt's car. All it has to do is make him look less . . . like a dead body."

"Good idea," Big Aunt says.

Ma flushes with pride. The woman really needs to get her priorities straight. I run back inside the house, grab a couple of old blankets from our storeroom, and rush back into the garage, where they've moved on from the trash bag issue to arguing over some other thing. "Here it is!" I say loudly.

I pass one blanket to Big Aunt and shake out the other. We approach the body, blankets raised, and pause.

Fourth Aunt growls, "Come on, do it!"

Teeth gritted, I put my blanket over the top half of his body.

"Tuck the sides under him," Fourth Aunt says. "Wrap him up like a burrito."

"Oh god," I whimper, but I do as she says, tucking the

blanket underneath his body, cringing at how warm it feels. "He's still warm," I hiss, face scrunched in revulsion. I hesitate. "Should we—uh. I think we should check his pulse."

"No, no, that very bad luck, touching corpse," Ma says, shaking her head firmly.

I stare at her. "What are you talking about? I literally just touched it. Can I also point out you guys were talking about cutting him up moments ago? Would that not involve touching him?"

"Is different," Ma says. Everyone else save for Fourth Aunt nods.

"How is it different?" I cry.

"Touching dead body to cut it up, get rid of it, is okay. But touching dead body to try and find life inside, ohhh, very bad luck."

"WHAT?" I swear my head has exploded. "How is cutting up a dead body better than just a small touch to make sure it's actually dead?"

"Aiya, if you don't understand, no use trying to explain," Second Aunt says.

"When someone doesn't understand, that's exactly the time you should explain." I shake my head. Why am I wasting precious time arguing with them? Without giving myself time to chicken out, I grab Jake's wrist, cringing, and feel for a pulse. Ugh, god, this is so gross. I feel about, pressing here and there, but my hand is trembling too hard and my palm is all sweaty and—

"Sudah!" Ma snaps, yanking my hand back. While still holding on to me, she reaches over and knocks on the door,

96

saying, "Aduh, knock on wood. Why my daughter insist on bringing bad luck on us? Knock on wood deh."

"Aiya, come here, give that to me. He's clearly dead." Fourth Aunt pushes me aside and grunts as she lifts Jake's upper body. "Ooh, he *is* still warm. Interesting! Would've thought he'd have gone all stiff. Must be because it's such a warm night. Meddy, pull the blanket round from underneath him—yes, okay, good. Top wrapped. Let's do the legs."

We're all staring at her, dumbfounded. Fourth Aunt is a D-list singer, a total diva with big hair and tight, sequined clothes. Being efficient with wrapping up dead bodies is not a quality I would've guessed her to have. But her tone is so authoritative that even Big Aunt obeys without question. We lift Jake's legs until Fourth Aunt finishes wrapping the second blanket around them. When we're done, we all step back with a visible shudder.

"Right, to Da Jie's car!" Fourth Aunt says.

I stop Ma in time from opening the garage door, telling her I'm going to turn off all the lights first.

"Oh, yes, good thinking," she says, clearly rattled by the whole experience. My heart twists at the sight of her lined face. I've done this to her. I've made her worry. The least I can do is try to fix it, try to stay on top of things.

Once the lights are off, we open the garage door, wincing at the whirring noise. We should've just carried the body through the house and gone out through the front door. God, I hope the garage door's crazy loud whir doesn't wake any neighbors.

"Let's go," I whisper. I brace myself and, before I can chicken out, grab the top half of Jake's body. He seems so much heavier than I remember. How the hell did I even manage to carry him out of the driver's seat and into the trunk in the first place?

Adrenaline. Right. My blood might as well have been Red Bull at the time. I could've moved boulders if I'd had to. But now, hours after the accident, I'm exhausted, my arms noodly, my legs stiff and slow. I manage to lift Jake's torso a few inches up, my muscles trembling hard. "I can't do this on my own," I gasp, and am about to drop him when Ma catches his head.

"Er Jie, you take his hips," she barks. "Da Jie, you take his legs."

Big Aunt rushes to take Jake's legs, as she's told, but Second Aunt is frozen, her eyes wide. "I can't—I don't—" Big Aunt snorts, and Second Aunt glares at her. "What? I don't want touch dead body, is that wrong?"

"Your family in need and you don't even want to help," Big Aunt says. "You tell me, is wrong or no?"

"It's okay, I'll take the hips," Fourth Aunt says, running forward. She waves Second Aunt away. "You open Da Jie's trunk." She lifts, and together we heave Jake out of the trunk.

It's hard to describe the walk to Big Aunt's car, which, as promised, is waiting for us just a few feet away. Jake is heavy, warm, and limp, and even under the layers of blankets, I'm acutely aware that we're carrying a dead human. We're moving as fast as we can, but we have to adjust to one another's speeds, which slows us down. Any moment now,

Mr. Kim next door is going to wake up, get a glass of water from his kitchen, glance out the window, and see us. Or maybe, from across the street, Mabel's chihuahua will wake up and ask to go outside.

Somehow, we manage to make it to Big Aunt's trunk without any neighbor shouting "Hey, what are you doing?" Through unspoken agreement, we lower him gently instead of dropping him unceremoniously. I guess we have hearts after all, even though we've just moved a dead body.

10

The drive to Big Aunt's bakery, which is only a ten-minute walk away from ours, is tense and interminable. Ma, Fourth Aunt, and I are all squished up in the back seat, and nobody says anything. Big Aunt's bakery is on Valley, a few blocks away from the huge Ranch 99 supermarket. It sits in between a beauty salon, which conveniently belongs to Second Aunt, and a florist, which conveniently belongs to Ma. She parks at the back of the bakery, and we spill out of the car. I take big gulps of air, grateful to be out of the suffocating, thick silence of the car.

This time of night, there are no cars around, nobody in sight. It's as though the entire world is asleep and this moment belongs to us, this awful, dark moment that will forever be tucked into my memories as the worst night of my life. I'm so grateful that I have my family with me. It's a strange thought to have as we heave Jake out of Big Aunt's trunk and move him, with much difficulty, across the parking lot and through the bakery's back door.

Big Aunt locks the door behind us and turns on the lights. Brilliant white light fills the kitchen, blinding us.

"Aiya! Turn off lights! Someone will see!" Ma cries.

"Nobody will see, got no windows back here," Big Aunt says. "Put him down there—no, not there, too close to my flour. Yes, there, okay. Make sure he not touch anything." With that, she hurries over to the giant industrial-sized refrigerator. She pulls the handle and opens the heavy door with some effort. We crowd around behind her and—

"Wah," Ma says. "Very beautiful."

I can only nod, speechless at the towering piece of art that stands in refrigerated glory before me. It's stunning—eight tiers of perfectly round cake covered with flawless buttercream, each layer made to look like poured marble in different shades of dusky pink and gray. Flowers adorn it in a gently weaving cascade—peonies and hydrangeas and roses, all made with loving hands out of sugar paste, their petals as thin as tissue paper. It's incredible. I've seen Big Aunt's wedding cakes plenty of times before, of course, but she's outdone herself. She's always been good at her job, but this isn't just a cake, it's pure artwork.

"It's amazing, Big Aunt," I breathe. "It's perfect."

"This is your best yet," Fourth Aunt says.

Big Aunt is way too traditional to show pleasure at compliments. She waves our compliments off, muttering, "Ah masa? Is nothing." But there's just the tiniest quirk to the corners of her lips that makes it obvious that she's fighting off a huge smile.

"Is not bad," Second Aunt grunts, and the quirk leaves Big Aunt's mouth.

Big Aunt's expression hardens. "Anyway, no room in fridge for body. Then how?"

"Just move cake out," Second Aunt says. "Is covered in fondant, it can last forever outside refrigerator."

"Is not fondant," Big Aunt says, smirking triumphantly. "I know maybe you think is fondant because the surface so smooth, right? But is buttercream. Bride say no fondant, I say no problem, I can do buttercream. Customer always first—"

"I can't believe it's not fondant," I cut in. There's no telling how long Big Aunt's speech would go on for, left unchecked. "Big Aunt's right, we can't risk the cake spoiling. Maybe we could put the body in one of the coolers until morning, and then once the cake's out, we can transfer the body into the fridge."

Big Aunt turns the idea over, chewing on her bottom lip. "Can. Tomorrow Xiaoling and mover man come over at seven-thirty, move cake into van, then you all can come and help move body into fridge." I cringe at the thought of Xiaoling, a spry young pastry chef that Big Aunt hired to be her assistant, being in the same room as the dead body. We'll have to make sure she and the mover don't go anywhere near the wrong cooler. Big Aunt sighs. "Dead body in my fridge, so unhygiene."

A crushing wave of guilt nearly knocks me off my feet at the trouble I'm causing everyone. "I'm so sorry, Big Aunt. I'll buy you a new fridge, or pay for this one to be professionally cleaned afterward."

"Aduh, don't so silly, is okay." She goes to the shelves, where there are three giant coolers and numerous boxes stacked in neat rows. She points to the biggest cooler and waves us over to help slide it out.

It's a monstrous thing, easily big enough for Jake, provided we're able to fold his legs up, which is a hell of a thing to think of, but here we are. We look at one another and nod. This is it. We unwrap Jake from the blankets and carry him to the cooler. It takes a few tries, a lot more arguing from my aunts and mom, and quite a few curse words, but finally, Jake's in. Fortunately, because it's such a warm night, we're able to fold all of Jake's limbs easily enough, though we did have to take off his shoes. We fold the blankets up neatly and put them on top of him, covering him from sight, and then Big Aunt gets us to pile all sorts of baking supplies on top of the blankets, covering them. By the time we're done, we're all sweaty and the cooler looks like it's filled with bags of flour and confectioners' sugar.

She writes out: CAN NOT OPEN on a Post-it and sticks it to the top of the cooler.

"If you write 'Can Not Open,' people will surely open," Second Aunt says.

Big Aunt glowers at her. "Maybe you one of those people opening things not theirs, but most people more better than that."

Second Aunt tuts and grabs the pen. She writes down on a new Post-it note: BAKING SUPPLYS, NO OPEN, HAVE TO BE COLD and slaps it down on top of Big Aunt's original note.

"That's probably fine," I say, quickly. "Thank you, Big Aunt. Thank you, Second Aunt," I say in Indonesian. They've helped me move some guy I killed; the least I can do is thank them in their preferred language. I turn to Fourth Aunt and Ma and thank them too.

"Aiya, thank us for what, we did nothing," Big Aunt says, waving me off.

"You literally just helped me move a dead body." I don't know how to put into words what I'm feeling, so I give her a big hug, tears shimmering in my eyes. We're not usually big touchers in my family, but Big Aunt accepts the hug fully, her strong arms encircling me tightly. "Thank you," I whisper.

"Ya, sayang," she says, patting the back of my head.

We let go and push the cooler back next to the other coolers, and then pile sacks of flour on top of it. By the time we're done, it looks like the world's most innocent cooler, definitely not like one that contains a dead human inside it.

"Tomorrow we come back here seven forty-five. Xiaoling will be finish up with move, and then we move body into fridge and I lock it," Big Aunt says. She mutters to herself, "Must bring lock."

Even Second Aunt nods in agreement without snarking at Big Aunt. We're all so tired by this time that we're swaying a little on our feet. Bed has never seemed so good to me. It's a good thing that we all live on the same street. Big Aunt drives us back, dropping us off at our respective homes, and Ma and I shuffle, zombie-like, into the house. I just about manage to peel off my sweaty clothes and take a scalding hot shower before trudging into my bedroom. I'll have to deal with the clothes tomorrow. Burn them or something. Same with my car. Clean it, burn it, whatever it is, I don't have the energy to deal with it now. At the sight of my beautiful, cozy bed, my muscles turn to water and I fall, face-first, into the pile of pillows. Only then does it hit me that we've forgotten to search for Jake's cell phone. Shit. I make a mental note to retrieve it first thing in the morning. We have time. When we move the body from the cooler into the fridge, there will be plenty of time to find his phone, if it's on him. The last thought I have right before exhaustion knocks me out is: I got through it. Nothing could be worse than tonight. The worst is over.

11

"—dy! Meddy!" Ma's voice slices through the room, shattering my sleep.

"Wha—?" I mumble, blinking and grimacing at the bright sunlight. Is it morning already? I feel like I could easily sleep for a whole week. "What time is it?"

"Time to go. You get up now. We need move body and then go to pier."

The events of last night come back in a dizzying, sickening rush. Jake, the car crash, the—oh god—the body. I bury my face in my hands. It wasn't a dream. It really did happen. I really did kill a man, and my family helped me move the body.

Ma bustles in and puts a glass of juice in my hands. "I make herbal tea for you. Wake you up. Cepat, drink."

I do as she says, too tired and dazed to argue, and I hate to admit it, but she's right. The TCM drink, whatever she's put in it, does perk me up a little, sliding hot and bitter down my throat. I finish it and have a shower, and by the time I'm dressed in my usual all-black photographer outfit, I feel more or less human and ready to face the gruesome task that awaits us. I send a quick text to Seb, my second photographer, to make sure he's ready for the day. He's supposed to get to the resort an hour after I do, to take pictures of the groomsmen while I handle the bridal party. Seb replies with a thumbs-up emoji. I pack my gear in the car before driving to Big Aunt's bakery with Ma.

As soon as we walk in through the back door, it becomes obvious something's wrong. Big Aunt and Second Aunt are already there, and they're snapping at each other in Indonesian, so deep into their argument that they don't even look up when we walk inside.

"Oi!" Ma has to yell above their voices. "Sudah! Done, stop! Stop arguing, what is it?"

Second Aunt scoffs and releases a laugh that sounds more like a cough-sob. "You tell them," she says, glaring at Big Aunt. "You tell them what happened."

Dread is like a stone deep in my belly, hard and jagged. I try to swallow, but my mouth is a desert. Whatever Big Aunt's about to say, I don't want to hear it.

Big Aunt's voice comes out hushed, trembly. "Xiaoling and the mover came early. And—"

I've never in my life heard Big Aunt's voice falter, but now it does.

"And they took the cooler!" Second Aunt crows. "You should've come earlier so you could supervise, but you didn't." Her eyes are bright with triumph as she turns to us and says, "She overslept."

Big Aunt doesn't meet our eyes as she mumbles, "I was so exhausted after last night that I slept through my alarm."

Ma and I stare in dismay at the spot where we'd pushed the cooler to last night, and sure enough, it's empty, all three coolers gone. It strikes me that this is bad news for all of us, including Second Aunt, but not even such catastrophic news is enough to distract her from the rare opportunity of rubbing Big Aunt's nose in it.

"So irresponsible," Second Aunt says. Big Aunt bristles visibly.

"I'm irresponsible?" she hisses.

Ma jumps in between her and Second Aunt. "Okay, sudah, cukup." She flaps her hands for a bit. "You better call Xiaoling now, quickly!"

"I already did. She said the coolers have all been loaded up to the yacht." Big Aunt sighs. "She sounded so happy and proud to have done everything without my help. Aduuuh, gimana ya?"

"We'll go to the pier now! Maybe the yacht hasn't left yet!" Ma cries.

It's left. We're told this after we arrive at the pier, sweaty and out of breath from running from the parking lot.

"But hey, no worries," the hotel—what's the correct title here, yacht organizer?—says. "There's another one coming in about five minutes. You ladies are early. The one that left fifteen minutes ago was just cargo, right? You're not scheduled to travel for another half-hour," he says, checking his tablet.

"We like to play it safe, get places early," I wheeze. "So, um, what happens to the cargo once it gets to the island?"

"What cargo you got?"

I exchange a glance with Big Aunt. "Um, cakes, mostly. There's the giant wedding cake and, um, a bunch of other desserts."

"Okay, that stuff will go straight to the kitchen. We've got orders to put them in the walk-in fridge. Sound good to you?"

I nod weakly. "Perfect."

"How everything go?" Big Aunt says. "Go okay?"

The yacht organizer smiles brightly. "Yeah, everything's going great."

"Great."

"Great."

We trudge a few paces away from the guy and go into a huddle. "They not know Jake is, you know—" Big Aunt mimes a cutting motion across her neck.

"Big Aunt!" I hiss. "Be more subtle, please." Just to play it safe, I switch to Indonesian. "Okay," I say. "Kami perlu uh . . . mikir . . . a plan." Wow, my Indonesian sucks. I try switching to Mandarin. "Wo men xu yao um . . . xiang . . . a plan."

Ma sighs. "I spend so much money on Chinese class for you, all wasted."

I give her a sheepish smile. "Um, so, a plan?"

"Aiya, so simple," Second Aunt says in Mandarin. "As soon as we get there, we'll find the cooler and one of us can take it back here. See? Easy."

"Easy?" Big Aunt sniffs, shaking her head. "I don't think it'll be that easy."

"Why not?" Second Aunt says, raising her chin.

Big Aunt shrugs. "Because it's never easy. Otherwise people would get away with murder all the time."

I wince at the word "murder," even though she said it in Mandarin. And even though I want to have faith in Second Aunt's simple plan of "get there, find cooler, bring cooler back," I have a feeling that Big Aunt is right. When it comes to hiding a dead body, it's never simple—a lesson I'm quickly learning from the previous night.

We gather our stuff from the back of the car and wait for the yacht to arrive. When it does, we sit in silence as the boat roars back to life and heads off from the mainland. Fourth Aunt, being the entertainment, won't be due at the island until this evening, so Big Aunt tells me to update her through our family WhatsApp. Of course, I can't say anything incriminating over WhatsApp, so I type out a cryptic:

Hi, Fourth Aunt, there's been a bit of a hiccup. We're headed to the island early. Call me when you get this.

Ma, reading over my shoulder, gives a loud sigh. "She won't see until she wake up after noon, that lazy bum." Fourth Aunt is the one who gets to sleep in during wedding season and the one who gets the most recognition for her work, and Ma won't ever forgive her for it, even though it's technically not Fourth Aunt's fault. Fourth Aunt loooves rubbing that in Ma's face. I guess their beef is like Big Aunt versus Second Aunt, going back decades, far older than me and my cousins.

It's a typical SoCal spring day, sunny and sweltering, wisps of white clouds in the deep blue sky. I stare out at the vast ocean, at the distant strip of land that I can hardly believe is the mainland. From this distance, it looks so small. For a moment, I almost feel better, escaping from everything that's happened back home, but when the island of Santa Lucia comes within sight, reality crashes back in. I'm not leaving my troubles behind. They're right here, awaiting me. And for all I know, maybe Xiaoling, well-trained helper that she is, would unpack everything. The thought of her doing that is so vivid. I can practically see her doing it, humming as she opens up the cooler. She'll bend down, remove all the packets of sugar and bric-a-brac we piled on top of the blankets, until she reaches the blankets. Maybe she'll stop with a confused frown—why would there be a blanket here—and then she'll pull the blanket up, and—

A loud horn bellows, and I jump up as though I've been electrocuted. "Ladies and gentlemen, welcome to Santa Lucia. We hope you enjoy your stay with us at the Ayana Lucia."

Gathering my heavy camera bag, I help Ma and the aunties to their feet. They're all a bit wobbly on the yacht, and cling to my arms as we make our way off the boat. We stagger across the bridge. At the pier, we're greeted by another hotel manager holding a tablet.

"The Chans, I gather?" he says, eyeing my camera bag.

"Yes."

He gives my family a once-over, then points to Big Aunt. "Cake and pastries?" he says.

My heart bursts into a gallop. Oh god. This is it. He's going to tell us that they've found the body, and then cops will jump out from behind those columns lining the pier, and then—

Big Aunt must be on the same train of thought as I am, because she's frozen, a look of horrified uncertainty on her face.

"Hello, cake and pastries?" he repeats. He turns to me, wearing an expression that says *Help me out here?*

"Um, is there a problem with the cake and pastries?" I say.

He frowns. "No. Why would there be?" he says snidely.

We all visibly sag with relief. "Yeah, she's the baker," I say.

"Good. That wasn't so hard, was it?" he snorts, then hands Big Aunt an ID with her name and the word BAKER on it. "Wear this at all times." He turns to Ma. "And who are you?"

"Flowers," she says.

"Florist," I add.

"Okay, here's your ID, and you would be the hair and makeup?" he says, turning to Second Aunt, who nods quickly. He hands her an ID and then gives me the last one. I turn it over in my hand, marveling at how meticulously planned this wedding is. I don't think I've ever done a wedding where we've had to wear ID cards on a lanyard before.

"I have question," Second Aunt says.

The guy visibly sighs. "Yes?"

"Erm, your boss—he okay? He very fierce? He in bad mood today?"

He stares at her with the world's bitchiest expression. "I mean, I don't know, it's not like we're besties or anything."

She leans closer. "So you not see him today?"

"Ugh, I don't know. I'm a busy guy. I don't keep track of everyone who comes on and off the yachts."

"Isn't that literally your job? Keeping track of who comes on and off the yacht?" I say.

He shoots me a glowering look and says, "Anyway, here's your buggy. You guys should go now. Toodles!"

We clamber up into the buggy, exchanging meaningful looks with one another. Still no luck finding out whether or not the hotel knows that Jake's not turning up today. It hits me that I don't even know if they're expecting him here. Last night, he'd told me that this is his seventh resort, so it's not like he's expected to turn up at every function that's being held at one of his hotels. But then this is his most ambitious project so far—an entire island owned by him, and this is the first wedding the resort is hosting, and the bride's parents are personal friends, so surely he'd be expected to show up and make sure that everything runs smoothly. Which means that at some point, someone will go, "Where's Jake? Why isn't he here yet?" and then someone else will be asked to ring his cell, and—

Holy. Shit.

His cell!

In the confusion and panic this morning, I've totally forgotten about it. I jump up and almost get flung off the moving buggy. Ma and Second Aunt yelp and catch hold of me, and the buggy halts suddenly, throwing us back in our seats.

"What happened?" the driver says. "You okay? Did you drop something?"

I can only shake my head and wave a weak hand at him, indicating that he should continue. Once I catch my breath, I say, "Kita lupa handphone nya dia."

"Handphone siapa—oh," Ma gasps, her hand flying to cover her mouth. "Ada dimana handphone nya?"

I don't know where it is. I shake my head.

"Pasti didalam kantung celana," Second Aunt says.

His pants pocket. Yeah, that's a fair assumption to make, and I only checked one. How loud is its ringtone? Would people be able to hear it ringing inside the cooler? They will probably start calling him soon, if they haven't already been calling.

"Here we are," the driver says, as the buggy stops at the entrance to the resort. We clamber out and then stop and stare at the grand entrance.

The lobby of the hotel is built atop a hill. The words "majestic" and "hallowed" come to mind. The resort has been designed with ancient Southeast Asian architecture in mind, with richly carved ornaments decorating the giant columns. The lobby is open on two sides, offering a stunning view of the resort and the ocean below. The ceiling is so high I have to tilt my head all the way back to see the top, and surrounding the lobby is a peaceful pond with brilliant orange koi and floating candles.

Despite the gorgeous setting, my chest is tight, my stomach knotted painfully. Ma, Big Aunt, and Second Aunt all wear the same strained expression. We're greeted by a receptionist, who tries to tell us where each of us needs to go, but Big Aunt interrupts her.

"No, they must come with me first," Big Aunt says.

The receptionist falters. "Um, but the rooms are in the opposite direction of the kitchen. It's a big resort. Hair and makeup is expected at the bridal suite soon. If you go to the kitchen first, you might be late—"

"Is okay, we be very fast," Big Aunt says, rising to full authoritative mode.

"But—" The harried receptionist spots someone and her whole demeanor changes, angling her face in a sweet way and smiling and fluttering her lashes. "There's the owner. He'll be able to help with your request."

The owner? For a second, my family and I freeze, making panicky looks at each other.

"Hi, Jeanine, everything going okay?" a smooth, rich voice that can only be described as molten chocolate says.

"Morning, sir," Jeanine says. "I was just telling the wedding vendors where to go." She bats her lashes at him again.

My family turns around and introduces themselves to him, but I'm frozen to the spot. Because even without turning around, I know who it is. I hear his voice in my dreams. I can still feel his touch on me, his strong, gentle hands on my skin.

"And you must be the photographer?" he asks.

Taking a deep breath to try to steady myself, I turn around to face him. The one that got away. The one who took a huge chunk of my heart, my soul, with him.

His smile freezes on his face, and I see years of history fly through his mind as I say in a hoarse voice, "I am. Hi, Nathan. It's been a while."

PART 2

GIRL FINDS BOY

(under very awkward circumstances)

12

The years have been kind to Nathan. He's obviously started working out; even in his button-down shirt with the sleeves rolled up to his elbows, I can see his biceps straining against the fabric. His face has lost its teenage softness, giving way to a defined jawline that makes my teeth clench because fuck, he's hot. So much hotter than I remember, and I remember him as the most gorgeous boy I'd ever laid eyes on in real life. My gaze skitters to his hands. No wedding band. Part of me—a very small part—squeals inwardly.

His expression is a mystery—surprised, obviously, but also a whole host of other emotions that I can't quite read. Is he happy to see me? Horrified? Maybe both?

"Meddy—" he says, and his voice is deeper, but still achingly familiar.

I'm momentarily distracted by my family's half-whispered discussion.

"Setan!" Second Aunt is saying. Ghost!

"Ssh," Big Aunt scolds her.

"Itu setan! It ownernya, kan?" Second Aunt hisses.

"Is everything okay, ladies?" Nathan says.

"You the owner of this hotel?" Ma says. "Mr. Jake, is it?"

"No, Ma, this is—"

"I'm Nathan. It's so nice to finally meet all of you."

Shit, my family's going to be like, "Finally? What you mean, finally?"

"We just need to go to the kitchen real quick," I say. "Just gotta—check on the cake. It's the centerpiece, you know. Gotta make sure it's perfect, okay, see you, bye!"

"I'll take you." He touches me lightly on the back, and just that small touch is enough to send an electric current racing down all the way to my feet.

"You must have a thousand things to take care of—"

"I can spare the time."

With my mom and aunts following behind and whispering among themselves, Nathan leads me through a side door marked "Staff," and we walk along what seems to be an endless maze of hallways.

"How have you been?" he says, glancing at me from the corner of his eye.

"Good! You?"

"It looks like your family business has really taken off. I bet you take the most amazing pictures." He gives me an inscrutable smile.

"It sure has. Don't leave your big day to chance, leave it to the Chans!" I laugh weakly. My stomach is not doing great.

He bites back a grin. "Did you come up with that slogan?"

"Obviously. And you've done well yourself. My god, Nathan. You're the owner of this place?"

"Well, part owner," he says, with a dimpled smile. "There are many investors involved."

"But you're running it?"

"Yeah."

Pride surges through me. This has always been a dream of his, for as long as I've known him. He's always wanted to work in the hospitality industry, run his own hotel, and he's definitely achieved that with the Ayana Lucia. "Nathan, wow—"

"Excuse, excuse," Ma says, coming in between us. "How you two know each other? Hi, I'm Meddy's mother. You call me Auntie Natasya, okay."

Nathan stops walking to give Ma a firm handshake, looking her in the eye as he says, "Hi, Mrs. Chan—I mean, Auntie. I'm Nathan. I was Meddy's—"

"Friend from college," I blurt out.

Everyone stares at me. It's clear that neither of my aunts nor my mother is buying the lie.

"College friend," Nathan says, and then gives me a forced smile I can actually read. One that spells disappointment.

It's not you, I want to shout at him. It's me, and my mother, and my aunts, and the fact that we're on our way to go look for the corpse of some dude I killed last night who was supposed to be YOU, apparently. But I can't tell him any of it, so we walk the rest of the way in painful silence.

I nearly breathe an audible sigh of relief when we finally go through a set of double doors and find ourselves in a bustling kitchen. Nearly there. The cooler must be around here somewhere. Nathan leads us past the busy chefs and chef underlings, all of them chopping and searing and stirring. They each glance up and greet Nathan as we walk by, and he greets them with an easy smile here, a pat on the back there. He was always effortlessly charming when I knew him back in college, but now he's even more so. It's obvious that everyone in here, from the head chef Miguel down to the dishwasher Ming, knows and adores him.

"This is your workstation," he says to Big Aunt, as we approach a work station. Xiaoling is already there, dozens of fondant flowers spread out in front of her. She jumps to attention, grinning widely at Big Aunt.

"Morning, chef," she chirps, and then her eyes widen when she sees the rest of us. "Oh, hi, Aunties. Hey, Meddy. Wasn't expecting to see you down here."

"Xiaoling," Big Aunt says, her voice terse. "Where are coolers?"

"Oh! Well, I thought I'd get an early start, do a bit extra, you know. I wanted to surprise you—"

"Coolers!" Big Aunt snaps, and we all jump, even Nathan. Big Aunt just has that kind of effect on everyone.

"Fridge!" Xiaoling cries, hurrying toward a big steel door. "Is something wrong? Did I do something? I just wanted to help—"

"No, you very good helper," Big Aunt says, forcing a smile. "You stay there and finish the flowers, okay, good job."

I'm about to go into the walk-in fridge with my family when Nathan takes my arm.

"Can we talk?" he says.

"Not right now. I need to help out with the—um, the cakes."

His thick eyebrows come together in confusion, and he gazes down at me from under his thick lashes. I swear, this man and his lashes. "You're the photographer, right? Why would you need to help out with the cakes?"

"For . . . the . . . photos, obviously." Yeah, that's it. "I'm taking photos of the wedding prep. You know how it is nowadays. People want to know everything there is to know about weddings, down to the prep work."

"Do they? Okay . . ." He sighs. "Maybe later? I don't know what your schedule's like. I'm guessing it's pretty hectic, but if we could—"

I struggle to keep the smile on my face when Ma pops into view from the square window in the steel door, mouthing at me to hurry up and get inside.

"Yeah! Totally, yeah, we'll talk later."

"Okay."

"Okay." I turn to leave, but Nathan catches my hand, giving it a squeeze.

"It's good seeing you again, Meddy," he says, quietly, and the sincerity in his voice almost makes me burst into tears. When he turns and walks away, I'm whisked right back to when we broke up all those years ago, when I'd forced myself to stay in my room and do nothing as he left, heartbroken. All sorts of emotions well up inside me, and I have to fight back the sob that's threatening to rise out of me. I watch him leave, struggling to get my breath under control, and then walk into the fridge.

"Lock the door!" Big Aunt commands in Indonesian as soon as I get inside.

I do as she says, wondering what we're going to say when someone needs to fetch some ingredient from here. The fridge is large and well stocked with crates of vegetables and fruit and other assorted ingredients, including crate upon crate of wine bottles. There is a separate section for meats behind a plastic curtain. My aunts and mom have located the right cooler and pulled it out from the shelves and into the meat section so it's not visible from outside the fridge.

"Okay," Big Aunt says. "Buka."

"You open it. It's your cooler," Second Aunt says.

Normally, I'd stand back and let them fight it out, because you don't ever get in between a tiff between Big Aunt and Second Aunt. But running into Nathan has rattled me. I feel untethered, wild. Without a word, I reach for the cooler and lift the lid up. I see what's inside the cooler, and I scream.

13

It's chaos. Big Aunt sees the contents of the cooler and immediately understands. Second Aunt and Ma, blocked from
view by me and Big Aunt, flap around us, yelling in such
rapid Indonesian that I beg them to stop and switch to English before my head explodes trying to make sense of anything. Meanwhile, Big Aunt is just standing there, eyes wide,
rattled for the first time I can remember seeing in my life.

Everything we've piled on top of Jake last night—the blankets, the baking supplies—are still inside, but instead of a neat
pile hiding his body, they're now a mess, packs of flour open,
white powder and colorful sprinkles all over. And Jake—

I have to look away before I lose my shit. Because Jake—
oh god, Jake—

"He not dead last night," Big Aunt says, her voice coming
out all dazed. "When we put him inside cooler, he still alive."

"What?" Ma and Second Aunt yelp.

Ma pushes me aside and takes a look at Jake, his face
now uncovered in what must have been his struggle to try
and get out of the cooler, and she shouts too. But what she
actually says is: "EH! THAT MY LILY GUY!"

All noise ceases, sucking the entire walk-in fridge into silence. As one, we all stare at Ma, who's staring at Jake. Jake, who's in a very different position than what we left him in last night. Jake, whose mouth is frozen open in what must have been a cry for help. Jake, who—

—is being prodded in the head by a carrot-wielding Ma.

"Ma! What are you doing?"

"I just check to see maybe he sleeping, maybe we can wake him up. Eh, Ah Guan, qi lai ah," she says. "Shi wo, Chan Ah Yi." She pokes his cheek again with the pointy end of the carrot but gets no response. "Aduh, he really dead this time. Wah, this so bad. So bad!"

My eyes fill with tears. It's too much, all of it. He was awful, but even he didn't deserve such a horrible death. "Ma, I'm so sorr—"

"Who am I going to get my lilies from now?"

I stop mid-sentence and stare at her. We all do.

"Why you all just stand like statues? This is big problem! Lily very expensive, you know! Ah Guan, he give me best price, and—" She freezes, a look of horror on her face. Maybe she's just realized how ridiculous she's being right now. "Aduuuuh! He suppose to bring in one last batch of lily for wedding!" I guess not. "Now my arrangements all will be lopsided! Aduh, gimana ya? How? How?" She flaps around at us.

Breathe, I tell myself. Fortunately, Ma's little meltdown seems to have had a calming effect on Big Aunt, who straightens up and brushes her hands down her front like she's cleaning invisible crumbs off herself.

"Okay, San Mei," she says. "Hey!" She clicks her fingers sharply, and Ma stops flapping. "Stop that," she scolds gently. "Is okay. You no need lily, your arrangements still be very pretty."

Ma smiles and gives an "Aw, shucks!" face. I mean, really now, the woman and her priorities.

"So this boy not Jake?" Big Aunt says.

Ma shakes her head. "This is Ah Guan, my lily supplier. Remember he brought mangoes from Indo for me! I think his English name is . . . Timothy? Tommy? Something like that."

"But Ma, how—I don't understand," I say. "You said you met him online. How come—I don't even know where to begin. Did you tell Jake—I mean, Ah Guan—about going online to find me a date?"

"Of course I tell him! I tell all my suppliers! Ah Guan, Lin Mei Auntie, Yi Mei Auntie, Rong Na Uncle, they all know. I always tell them my daughter, she so pretty and kind, but she still single, aduh, how she refuse to give me grandchildren. Every time I got good boy to ask her out, she say she don't want to. You not remember? I try to set you up with Ah Guan but you keep saying no, give me this reason, that reason. Ah Guan ask why. I say I don't know, but my daughter is torturing me, she never want to go out with boy—"

"Okay, so you've been telling everyone about my dating life," I say, through gritted teeth.

"Lack of dating life," Second Aunt says, helpfully, from the far corner of the room where she's—yet again—doing

Tai Chi. "Draw Big Watermelon," she says under her breath, swinging her arms out and up, "and then cut in half . . ."

I ignore her. "And what did Ah Guan say to you?"

"Wah, he so helpful deh," Ma says, smiling and nodding. "He tell me is okay if you don't want to get set up with him. He say I should make you go on Internet find boyfriend. I say, aduh, Meddy will not want to do that. He say it's okay, got very good website for young people. He show me dating website and say, why not create a profile for you, then easier to persuade you to use it."

My mind spins. "So he knew you were using it and pretending to be me?"

"Of course not, you so silly! I keep asking you to use dating website, but you don't want to, so finally I use it for you. I don't tell Ah Guan. I just use it, and then wah! Hotel owner message me, and so kind, make such good match—oh."

There it is, finally. Realization dawns on her face. Even Second Aunt pauses her Tai Chi movement to watch as Mama mentally digests what she's just told us. Her face scrunches up like a ball of tissue, and her mouth drops open in an enraged wail.

"He trick me? Use me get to my daughter!?"

Big Aunt nods solemnly. "I hear about this kind of Internet scam before. Is called goldfish."

"Catfish," I say.

"No, I'm sure is call goldfish. Because pretend got gold, but actually just a fish."

I know better than to argue with her. Second Aunt snorts from where she's wobbling on one leg.

"What is it?" Big Aunt snaps.

"Nothing," Second Aunt says, raising her other leg slowly.

Big Aunt turns back to face us. "Anyway—"

"Is just so typical," Second Aunt says. "Because you always know best, right, Da Jie? Da Jie always correct. Who decide to put this Ah Guan boy in cooler? Is you. We just follow blind, don't ask questions. Now turn out Ah Guan not dead, but we kill him by putting him inside cooler." She pushes her palms out in front of her slowly, moving her feet in a gentle circle.

Big Aunt takes a deep breath. "Anyway—"

"Now you going to tell us again what to do, even though so obvious you don't know also."

Big Aunt rounds on her. "And you do, is it? If you know what to do, then you say lah! Don't stand in corner doing Tai Chi; come tell us solution."

Second Aunt pointedly ignores her and continues moving her palms round. I'm sure Big Aunt is about to explode when her cell phone rings. She picks it up, still glaring at Second Aunt, and speaks in rapid Mandarin. "Si Mei, you're here already? Okay, good. Yes, I know it's very early, but we have a problem. Come meet us at the kitchen. Just ask them take you down here. Now, yes." She hangs up.

Fourth Aunt is here. I don't know why, but it makes me feel better to know that the whole family is here, even though realistically I know it doesn't make much of a difference.

"We need to decide what we're going to do," I say quickly, before Big Aunt and Second Aunt can get into it again. "Now that we know Jake isn't Jake, and the real Jake—Nathan—

is still alive, that means the wedding is definitely going to go on as planned. Which means, like it or not, we've got to show up and do our jobs and pretend that everything's okay."

They're all looking at me funny, and it takes a second to realize that I've just taken on a leadership role with MY AUNTS. Whoa. I quail under their gazes. "Um, sorry, that was just a suggestion, I didn't mean to—"

"No, you are right, Meddy," Ma says, smiling fondly.

Big Aunt nods. "You right. The wedding continue on. We must get rid of body before guests come. If we leave body here, only matter of time before someone find. Okay, we think of plan. Sekarang jam berapa?"

I glance at my phone. "Quarter to nine."

"I have to do hair and makeup for bride and mother and bridesmaids," Second Aunt says.

"Aiya! My other flower suppliers all coming soon also," Ma says.

"And I need to finish up welcome cakes," Big Aunt says. "Meddy, what time you start photos?"

"I just need to be there to take photos when the bride's makeup is nearly done, so I have time right now. I can take the cooler out and, um—get it onto a yacht and take it back to the mainland. I'll drive it back to your bakery."

"Okay, good, very good." Big Aunt takes out the key to her bakery and hands it to me. "He quite heavy you know. You take Si Mei with you."

I nod. Normally, I would hate to be such a bother to others, but I have enough self-realization to know I would struggle to carry Jake's—damn it, Ah Guan's—body out of the cooler and into Big Aunt's fridge. I'll need all the help I can get.

As though thinking of Fourth Aunt has summoned her, there's a knock on the fridge door, and I look through the plastic curtains to see Fourth Aunt's face peeping through the window. She waves at me, and I go to unlock the door and usher her through the plastic curtains.

"Why is everyone gathered inside the fridge?" she says, then she sees the open cooler with Ah Guan's body in it. "Why's that thing here? Wasn't he supposed to be at the bakery?" She looks closely at him, interest piqued. "Huh. He's not bad looking."

Sometimes I think that Ma and Fourth Aunt are always at odds with each other because they're just too similar. Priorities—neither one has them.

Big Aunt quickly fills Fourth Aunt in on what's happened and our plan, and Fourth Aunt groans when she's told she and I need to go back to the mainland to stash the body in the fridge. "I just got my nails done," she moans, showing us her nails, which have been blinged out with crystals and, on her pinkies, even feathers. Ma cringes.

"Who do nails like that? How do you wash your bum when you have feather on your nails?" Ma says.

"Very carefully, not that it's any of your business how I wash myself."

Ma wrinkles her nose and flaps a hand over it. "So unhygienic. So not practical. You won't be able to cook, bathe, clean—"

"I can do all of those things! I'm about to help your kid clean up her mess, aren't I?"

Ma turns red, and I wince. The lowest, most painful blows my mother and her sisters strike with is me and my cousins. That's how you know that Ma and her sisters are truly fighting—they talk shit about each other's kids. I hate that I've become a liability for Ma, that from now on, this will forever be dredged up as a trump card against her. *My nails may be impractical, but at least I didn't kill someone like your daughter did!*

"We are happy helping," Big Aunt says, giving Fourth Aunt a look. "Is what family do. Now go, quick. We lose so much time already."

Nodding, I replace the blanket on top of Ah Guan and close the cooler before grabbing the handle and pulling. It's heavy, but it rolls easily enough on all four wheels. The handle feels a bit shaky, and I wonder if it's built to carry the weight of a full-grown human male. I'll have to be very careful with it.

Big Aunt walks out of the fridge first, and then Second Aunt and Ma hold open the swing doors for me as I pull the cooler along behind me, followed by Fourth Aunt, who frowns at her nails as she walks. Big Aunt looks as imperious as ever, not a hint of guilt anywhere about her.

Xiaoling, who's busy putting gold luster dust on the decorative flowers, looks up at the procession. "The flowers are almost done, chef." She spots the cooler and comes toward me, saying, "Let me help you with that. The back wheel catches sometimes—"

"No," Big Aunt barks, and Xiaoling shrinks back, her eyes wide. I feel awful for her. All she's done is try to be helpful. "You doing more important things," Big Aunt says. "Must finish the flowers before guest arrive. Kuai yi dian!" She claps and Xiaoling positively jumps to attention, scrambling to finish painting the flowers.

I mouth a thank-you to Big Aunt and continue walking through the kitchen, trying my best to look like I'm not pulling a cooler full of dead dude behind me. Second Aunt, Ma, and Fourth Aunt walk ahead, which is good, as any and all attention is immediately attracted to them instead of me. With Fourth Aunt's flamboyant clothes—she's wearing a flamingo-pink sequined top and bright turquoise pants—it's impossible to take your eyes off her. In contrast, I'm in my "Don't look at me, I'm the help" all-black photographer's outfit. With any luck, everyone will assume I'm hotel staff all the way back to the yacht.

Fortunately, the kitchen staff is just as busy as before. No one gives us a second glance; everyone is too occupied with chopping and frying. We make it out of the kitchen without getting asked any questions and breathe a sigh of relief.

Out in the quiet hallway, our footsteps and the clack-clack of the cooler's wheels seem deafening. Mama glances back at me and says, "Meddy, you don't pull like that, you pull like this." She stops, adjusting my posture so I'm standing straight up. "No slouch, that is bad posture; later you will hurt your back."

"Actually," Second Aunt says, "I learn from Tai Chi Quan this is best posture." She comes close to me and readjusts my posture, muttering, "Knees bend a bit, yes." Between her and Ma's adjustments, I'm now standing awkwardly, slightly leaning forward, knees bent, arms all weird and stiff.

"Aiya, no," Ma says. "I been taking ballroom dance. I know good posture. Chin up, Meddy."

"No offense, but I don't think that right now is the best time to give Meddy posture adjustments," Fourth Aunt says.

I nod gratefully. "Fourth Aunt is right." Ma's expression looks like I might as well have punched her right in the heart. "But thank you for your help, Ma and Second Aunt. You're both right, my back was starting to hurt."

Ma and Second Aunt smile smugly and—thank god—resume walking. We walk the rest of the way to the lobby in relative silence, save for Ma muttering to herself, "Aiya, no more cheap lily."

The lobby is a lot busier than when we first arrived. Ma's underlings have arrived, wearing their trademark bright red and gold shirts, the colors of good fortune in Chinese culture. With an excited squeal, Ma rushes over to survey the arrangements. She's been working on these for weeks, designing each centerpiece and flower stand, overseeing the workmanship meticulously. Now, she beams with naked pride as the crates are opened and her workers take out the most elaborate flower sculptures and arrangements I have ever seen. She barks out orders—this tower to the ballroom, that vase to the bridal room—and is about to scurry off, giving out more orders, when she stops and turns back to me.

"Meddy, oh—I forget about the you know what—" she says, but I wave her away.

"It's fine, Ma. I've got everything under control."

"Okay. Okay, you be careful, ya." She squeezes my arm and then is off, shouting to a worker to be careful with the peonies.

My phone beeps with a text message.

Seb [09:51AM]: I'm here! Super early, but that's what you get from the world's best second photog!

Meddy [09:52AM]: Great! Go to the groom's suite and start taking photos.

Seb [09:53AM]: Aye, aye boss.

A hotel receptionist hurries toward us. "Excuse me, sorry, are you the hair and makeup artist?"

Second Aunt nods.

"Oh good, I've got instructions to take you to the bridal suite. Please follow me."

Second Aunt glances at me, her eyes questioning. "You going to be okay or not?"

I smile at her. "Go. I'll be fine."

"Okay, Auntie go first then. You be careful." With that, she leaves, and I'm alone with Fourth Aunt. And the body. "You doing okay, Fourth Aunt?" I can't even begin to describe how bad I feel about dragging her into this. I'm the least close to Fourth Aunt out of all my aunts. Maybe it's because of her ongoing feud with Ma, or maybe it's because she's the opposite of me in every way. Whatever it is, I've always felt a little awkward around her, and now we're supposed to go all the way back to San Gabriel Valley with a dead body. This is fiiine. I am totally okay with this plan.

"It's way too early for me to be awake." Fourth Aunt sighs. "I'm going to look so haggard at tonight's performance."

"You? Haggard? Never." I pull the cooler up again and resume walking. "You're looking great, Auntie. Very glamor—oh." Outside the lobby, the long, winding path leading back to the pier is made of loose pebbles. My stomach drops. How the hell am I going to wheel the cooler down this path? Why would anyone make a path out of pebbles?! This is a serious design flaw! What about people in wheelchairs, or parents with strollers, or people carrying dead bodies in giant coolers?

"Would you like me to call you a buggy, miss?" a hotel receptionist asks.

I startle, and the receptionist tilts his head at the cooler. "Let me call you a buggy—"

"Nope! No need!"

He frowns, confused. "But—"

"I get buggy sickness," Fourth Aunt says. "We'll be fine. This old thing is empty anyway."

We smile widely at the receptionist until he goes away, looking bemused.

"Now what?" I whisper to Fourth Aunt.

"Put those biceps to good use," she replies, pushing the end of the cooler. It rolls off the smooth marble and onto the pebble path. We wince at the horrible crunching noise it makes as I pull, and Fourth Aunt pushes it along the path.

"This is not working," I grunt, after only a few seconds. "People are going to wonder why we're not putting it on a buggy." Sure enough, when I glance back, people are taking notice, throwing strange looks our way. But that might also just be the effect that Fourth Aunt often has, being the equivalent of a human peacock.

"Pull harder," she gasps, shoving at the cooler.

It makes more of a crunching noise and barely moves an inch. "We're gonna have to carry it."

Fourth Aunt doesn't look happy, but as we've got no choice, I take the front of the cooler and lift, and she does the same with the back. Together, we heave the cooler up and stagger slowly down the pebble path. It's a long journey, but with every painful step, the resort is getting farther from view.

Until Fourth Aunt suddenly stops, her eyes going wide.

"What's going—" My words die in my mouth when I turn around, because there's a buggy headed toward us, and incidentally, it's occupied by Nathan and an elderly couple I quickly recognize as Tom Cruise Sutopo's parents, that is, the parents of the groom, a.k.a. the billionaires who are footing the staggering bill for this wedding.

Nathan's entire face lights up when he notices me, which does funny things to my stomach. My poor stomach—it can't decide whether to knot out of sheer terror due to body in cooler, etc., or flutter with pleasure because Nathan, etc. It compromises by giving a nauseated gurgle.

Nathan hops out of his buggy and says to Mr. and Mrs. Sutopo, "Here's someone I'd love you to meet."

I swallow, my mouth dry.

The old couple smile politely, obviously as confused as I am because I'm a nobody. But when they see Fourth Aunt, they actually gasp out loud and grab each other's hands.

"This is—"

"MIMI CHAN!" Mr. Sutopo positively squeals.

Mrs. Sutopo shakes her head in wonder, mouth agape. "Is it really her?"

Fourth Aunt takes this in her stride. She lowers her end of the cooler gracefully before sashaying to them. Nathan helps the older couple down from the buggy. They still can't take their eyes off Fourth Aunt, even as they clamber down.

"We're such big fans," Mrs. Sutopo says. Her English is flawless, her accent slightly British. Belatedly, I recall Googling her and reading that she met her husband while they were both studying at Oxford. "We've followed your career ever since you were a little girl."

"Oh, that's so sweet to hear! I love meeting my fans." Fourth Aunt gives them a big hug, and they practically melt into her, their faces beaming hard.

"You know, our son Tom booked your family's services for today because he knows we're your number one fans," Mr. Sutopo says.

Fourth Aunt's grin is as wide as a Cheshire cat's. We'll definitely be hearing more about this later, when Ma's around to listen to Fourth Aunt boast about how she's brought in good business for us. And I will have to nod and tell them that it's true. Ma's not going to like that.

"But where are you two off to?" Mrs. Sutopo says. "You're going the wrong way. The hotel's that way."

"Oh, we just need to . . ." My brain short-circuits. We just need to what? I almost tell them that we've brought the wrong cooler, but quickly realize that I would be admitting a mistake to our clients. Big Aunt would have my head for it. No, I can't tell them that. "We didn't want to take up too much room inside the walk-in fridge, so we're just taking this cooler back real quick."

"Back? You mean back to the mainland?" Mr. Sutopo says.

"That's a whole lot of hassle just to stow a cooler!" his wife says. "Nathan, dear, there must be a place for them to store it here. You can't possibly have these lovely ladies traipsing all across your island and across the water on such a big day."

"Of course," Nathan says. "I'm as surprised as you are." He turns to me and says, "You can store it in the walk-in fridge. It's plenty big enough."

"I really don't want to trouble you."

"It's no trouble, really."

"Nathan, dear, why don't you help the lovely girl take the cooler back to the fridge? We'll be alright here with Mimi. You take the buggy. We'll walk," Mrs. Sutopo says. She turns to Fourth Aunt and winds her arm through hers before saying, "Come, we must take so many pictures together. Oh my goodness, you are even prettier in real life!"

I watch in dismay as the Sutopos and Fourth Aunt walk away. "Um, I don't think it's a good idea to let them walk to the hotel. It's pretty far, and it's uphill—"

"I agree," Nathan says, easily. "We'll leave the buggy here for them, and I'll help move this cooler back to the kitchen."

"No, it's okay, don't bother, you must be so busy . . ."

He pauses, giving me that smile of his. Even after all these years, it still looks so disarmingly boyish on his rugged features, instantly taking years off and making him look all of five years old. "It's going to be a crazy weekend, isn't it?"

You have no idea, I want to say.

"Tell you a secret?" He lowers his voice and moves closer to me. My heart thumps painfully. "I may be pissing my pants a little at the thought of everything that needs to go well this weekend. Just a little. It's a huge deal for us, and I just—opening this hotel was my dream. My investors are pretty nervous at the expense. I really need this wedding to go perfectly."

I gnaw on my lip. Perfectly. Right. Which probably means no corpses being found on the premises.

Nathan rakes a hand through his hair and grimaces. "Sorry, I didn't mean to spill everything. It's just—" He smiles at me. "Seeing you . . . it's amazing, Meddy, and so unexpected. I mean, seriously, what are the odds? I'm so glad you're here. You've always got your feet firmly on the ground, and it's great to see you."

"It has been amazing," I say, meaning every word. "And I'm so glad to see how well you're doing. I mean, you opened your own hotel at twenty-six, Nathan. That's incredible."

He shrugs, blushing. "I had a lot of help. Met the right people at JLL, got seed money from my folks, got to know lots of investors . . . I didn't do all this by myself. I just got really, really lucky."

"Well, I'm sure you also worked your ass off."

"A bit," he laughs, and it's exactly like the old times, as though we've picked up right where we left off. We meet each other's eyes, and all of our beautiful history unravels in my mind's eye. I remember every single detail—every kiss, the exact way his eyelashes feel against my face, the solid warmth of his hands—with aching clarity. "So, um, are you seeing anyone?"

My heart stutters, and I shake my head furiously. "You?"

"My family has been setting me up with various blind dates, but nothing has stuck."

Oh god. I can feel my cheeks burning, because speaking of blind dates, mine's in the cooler right next to him. As though reading my mind, he picks up the cooler handle and pulls, frowning when it doesn't budge.

"It's impossible to move it on this pebble path," I babble. "Look, don't worry about me, you're slammed with work, and like you said, you've got investors up your ass. Just go, I'll call for a bellboy or something."

His frown deepens. "Let me do this for you," he says in a gruff voice, giving the cooler a hard yank. The top of the cooler pops up a couple of inches for one heart-stopping moment before I push it back down. Jesus. I could pass out right now, I really could.

Nathan looks down at the cooler and cocks his head to one side. "Is that—"

Oh god. It is. It's a corner of Big Aunt's blanket sticking

out like a fucking woolen tongue. I watch as Nathan moves in slow motion and reaches down to open the cooler. And I do the only thing I can, the thing I've been dreaming of doing for the last four years.

I grab his broad shoulders, feeling his muscles under my fingers, and pull him back to face me.

"Meddy—"

I don't wait for him to finish speaking. I reach up, still pulling him down, and let our mouths meet in a fervent kiss.

14

The kiss sears through my skin, singeing my flesh, reaching deep into my memories, reminding me of the heat of our romance. In the space of a few seconds, I taste those college days once more—the Diddy Riese cookies we used to share with Selena at 11 p.m. on a Tuesday, the scent of hookah smoke as we walked down Broxton Ave holding hands, the feel of his hand cupped firmly round my waist, sending hot waves running through my entire body. The way he made me laugh, a full-on, no-holds-barred belly laugh, and then how he'd climb on top of me and kiss me fully, with his entire being, his skin against mine—

By the time we break apart we're both breathless. I look at his face, and I know he's thinking of our UCLA days as well.

"Meddy," he whispers, leaning in again, catching my mouth with his. So soft, and warm. New and yet achingly familiar. "God, how I've missed you."

"I've missed you too." My voice catches with emotion. I have. So much.

He takes both of my hands in his, gazing down at me

with his beautiful eyes. "I've been wanting to kiss you since I saw you this morning." He sighs. "Ever since UCLA, I've wondered what happened with us. I've always wanted to reach out to you, but I wasn't sure if you wanted to talk to me—I mean, what happened back then?"

My stomach twists. "It's hard to explain."

"I know. I got the feeling, especially when I found out you never told your mom about us."

I cringe. It must've been quite a blow to discover that your girlfriend of three years never told her family about you. And for him to find out today, of all days . . . I am such a shit. "I'm sorry, I—it's complicated."

The dimples appear again. "I get it. Families often are. Honestly, I thought I'd be more upset about it, but seeing you after all these years . . ."

Relief surges through my chest. He's not upset about it! God, how is he this amazing? "I know."

"I—"

"Hey!" someone shouts from afar.

We break apart as if we're guilty teenagers. A middle-aged man with the world's bushiest mustache is climbing up the hill toward the resort. Halfway up, he pauses for breath, fanning himself with a piece of paper. When he finally gets to us, his face is tomato red.

"You—" he gasps.

"Hi, Sheriff," Nathan says. "Can I help you with something?"

Sheriff? I freeze. My insides have turned to stone.

"You can't—can't do this here!" the sheriff says.

"Do what?"

The sheriff straightens up, still catching his breath. "This large brouhaha the hotel is holding. Do you have the right permit for it? I doubt you do, because I sure as hell didn't sign one. And there's a storm coming, supposed to hit us later today. I don't think you should let this party go on."

Despite the weirdness of the situation, Nathan seems completely at ease. "Come on, Sheriff McConnell. It's a wedding, and I've got permits from the mainland to hold large functions here. It's all legit. I'll have someone come by and show you the papers. And yes, we're prepared for the storm if it does hit us. We'll get everyone inside. It'll all be okay."

"Mainland," the sheriff spits. "You mainland people think you're better than the rest of us. I'll be back, just you wait. You and your mainland permits." He strides away, muttering angrily to himself. I release my breath.

Nathan must have noticed how pale I look because he says, "Are you okay?"

I'm about to reply when Fourth Aunt calls out, "Oh, you kids are still here!"

"Done with the pictures?" Nathan says, cheerily.

"Yep." Fourth Aunt whispers to Nathan when she reaches us, "I think Mr. Sutopo is pretty tired. Might wanna get him to his room now."

Nathan nods and hurries back to where Mr. and Mrs. Sutopo are standing. Halfway there, he pauses and says, "I'll call a buggy down for you. That cooler's heavy."

"Don't worry about us," I babble, "we'll be fine. You go."

Nathan nods at me and gives me one last smile before

going. We stand there, waving at them as they drive away. I turn to see Fourth Aunt smiling slyly at me.

"Um. Everything okay?"

"I don't know, you tell me," she says.

"I have no idea what you're talking about."

She nudges me playfully with her elbow. "I saw that kiss."

My breath comes out in a heavy whoosh. Damn it. The last thing I need is one of my aunts finding out about my love life. "Please don't tell the others."

Fourth Aunt grins. "You have my word. Oho, I do so love knowing something your mother doesn't! She doesn't know about this, right?"

I shake my head. "Anyway, we need to focus on this." I nod at the cooler. "What do we do with it?"

"I give up trying to carry that thing all the way down to the pier," Fourth Aunt says. She wiggles her fingers at me. "I'll ruin my nails."

"Yeah, I don't think we can carry it that far either. Let's take it back to the fridge, and we can all carry it down together when the others are free. That'll be more manageable."

"Okay."

We struggle to push the cooler off the path, but once it's back on the smooth marble floor, it's pretty easy to wheel it all the way back to the kitchen.

Big Aunt's face lights up when she sees us, then falls when she spots the cooler behind us. "What happen? Why that thing back here again?"

I tell her about the pebble path and the impossibility of

wheeling the cooler on it, and she sighs, leading the way to the walk-in fridge.

"Push it there," she says, pointing to a corner. I do as I'm told and then we put containers of pastries on top of the cooler. "Maybe is okay there for now."

We survey the cooler. It looks so exposed here, in a place where people are constantly coming in and out. Just as I think that, one of the hotel chefs comes in, pausing when he sees us.

"Essential personnel only," he says.

"They with me," Big Aunt says coolly, and he frowns but doesn't say anything else. He grabs a crate of vegetables and leaves the fridge.

"We should get out of here," I say. "It's obvious we don't belong here." Not me in my photographer's outfit and Fourth Aunt in her sequined-flamingo outfit.

"You no worry, I keep eyes on cooler," Big Aunt says, as we walk out of the fridge.

"I really need to go do the bridal photos now, but once we have free time, we should meet here and move the cooler out."

The three of us nod, Big Aunt says she'll let Ma know of the plan, and I rush off to the bridal suite to update Second Aunt. And do my job.

The bride, Jacqueline, is radiant even before Second Aunt finishes doing her makeup. Her skin has the kind of glow that only years of meticulous, expensive skin care can achieve, and her nose has the perfect arch and slight upturn that only the best surgeon can give. She catches me staring at it and says with a wink, "Souvenir from Seoul." I like her immediately.

After the round of introductions—I've obviously met the bride beforehand, but there are many new faces here, including her mom and what seems like twelve hundred bridesmaids who are all wearing bathrobes and walking in and out, sipping flutes of champagne. The bridal suite is huge, easily bigger than my and Ma's house, with two bedrooms, a gorgeously decorated living room, and a dining room with a large chandelier. It's also a mess; every available surface has been covered by a carelessly flung dress, or heels, or handbags, or mascara, or champagne glasses. A waiter swans around with trays of champagne and chocolate-covered strawberries.

Second Aunt has set up a makeup station near the window for the best possible lighting. Next to her, her two assistants have their own work stations and are busily dabbing at bridesmaids' faces.

I take out my trusty Canon and fit my favorite lens on it—a fixed 50mm f/1.2. I bought it for myself as a Christmas present last year, and it's worth every goddamn cent. The pictures come out lush, the focus crisp and the background melting into a delicious blur. I usually have to settle for the 35mm when shooting inside hotel rooms because I need the wider angle to take everything in, but this suite is so huge that I can easily fit everything in with the 50mm. Heaven!

"Can I take photos of the wedding gown, please?" I say to Jacqueline.

"Of course! Miss Halim here will help you. She's the best maid of honor." Jacqueline grins up at a tall, slender bridesmaid, who rolls her eyes.

"She only says that to butter me up. I'm Maureen. Nice to meet you," Maureen says, with a wry smile.

"Yes, but it works so well." Jacqueline laughs.

"Only because I love you, you brat." Maureen turns to me. "Come, I'll help you with the dress. It's a two-person job."

She's not kidding. The dress is huge, and it takes the two of us to pull it off the mannequin and hang it up against the floor-to-ceiling window. The sunlight at its back makes it almost translucent, and every lace detail shines through. I was expecting a Vera Wang or an Alexander McQueen, but the silk label says Biyan, which is a nice surprise. An Indonesian designer. It makes me like Jacqueline even more. It strikes me, as I take pictures of the dress from various angles, that this is the first time I'm photographing a wedding dress by an Indonesian designer, and it feels special somehow. It rekindles the love I have for photography and why I decided to join my family's venture in the first place. If only wedding photography could be all about the intimate details—just me, my camera, pretty dresses, and happy couples, instead of the family obligation and drama that come with it. But now is so not the time to think about leaving the family business.

I take photos of all the other details: the bride's red-soled Louboutins, which will no doubt kill her feet, the luscious bridal bouquet Ma has created, the invitations.

"Tante Yohana," I say to the bride's mother. Tante means Auntie in Indonesian—I can never bring myself to call my elders just by their first name. "Can I take photos of the jewelry, please?" In Chinese weddings, the bride's jewelry is the last to go on, and is usually a gift from her parents. I've taken dozens of pictures of parents putting diamond necklaces on their daughters, and without fail, it's always a bittersweet moment, full of tearful smiles.

Tante Yohana smiles and ushers me into the bedroom. She takes out a velvet box from the safe and opens it. "What do you think?"

It's a gorgeous set—earrings, necklace, and a bracelet, all of them dripping with diamonds, arranged in a floral design. The smallest diamond in the set looks about one carat, the biggest easily over three. I'm looking at a set that must have cost them over a million dollars. "It's beautiful," I tell her, and she beams.

"It was designed by an Indonesian jeweler, you know," she says, with obvious pride.

I have her stay right there in the room as I take pictures of the jewelry. I never let myself be left alone with anything expensive, just in case that thing goes missing and I get blamed for it. When I'm done with the jewelry, I slide the box back to Tante Yohana open, so she can see that everything is still intact, and she smiles and returns it to the safe. I'm about to go back out to the living room when my phone boops with a text.

Seb [10:18AM]: SOS

Meddy [10:18AM]: What's wrong?

Seb [10:19AM]: Men.

A picture appears on my screen.

I stare at the phone in disbelief. Seb is in the groom's suite, which is down the corridor from the bridal suite and looks identical. Except instead of bridesmaids swanning around, chatting and laughing, the groomsmen are lying dead drunk on every available surface.

Seb sends another picture, and I groan out loud. The groom, Tom Cruise Sutopo, is lying half naked in the large, claw-foot bathtub.

Meddy [10:21AM]: Why are men??

Seb [10:21AM]: Tell me about it. I've been trying to wake them for the last fifteen minutes.

Meddy [10:22AM]: Where's the WP?

Seb [10:23AM]: I don't know, I don't keep track of the wedding planner. They're supposed to be keeping track of things like this!

I swear under my breath.

Meddy [10:24AM]: I'll be right there.

I slip out of the bridal suite and run all the way to the groom's suite. Seb opens the door and sweeps inside the room, saying, "Ta-da! Presenting the male *Homo sapiens*."

"Goddamnit." I survey the carnage. The room stinks of alcohol and vomit, and the groomsmen are so wasted that they don't even budge at the sounds of our voices. They're all in various states of undress; more than once I have to turn away quickly, my cheeks burning. "Um, 'scuse me, guys, you need to wake up now."

Seb laughs. "Right, you're gonna wake them up with your little teeny voice. Yo! Guys! Wake the hell up!"

I jump at Seb's shout, but none of the groomsmen even stir. "Are they alive?"

Seb nods, nudging one of the groomsmen on the leg with his shoe. The groomsman mumbles something before falling back asleep. Inside the marbled bathroom, Tom Cruise Sutopo is in a similar state. It's a bathroom fit for Pinterest—smooth marble everywhere, the bathtub a luxurious affair set behind a large picture window overlooking the hotel's gardens. I pat Tom's cheek gently. He grunts, but doesn't stir.

"You need to channel your inner Asian Auntie and do a shout that'll make your mom proud."

"Ha, ha. I can probably count on one hand the number of times I've raised my voice." It's probably the result of being raised by such loud women. I have a natural aversion to raised voices now. "You do it, Seb. Pleeease."

Seb sighs, clears his throat, and shouts loud enough to make my ears ring. Tom stirs, blinks a few times, and falls back asleep. I'm about to ask Seb to do it again when movement outside the window catches my eye.

Ho. Ly. Shit.

It's Big Aunt, Ma, and Fourth Aunt, and they're moving the cooler, staggering across the expansive lawn with it, and—oh god—the cooler must've popped open at some point without them realizing it, because there is a fucking *hand* sticking out of it.

"OH MY GOD!" I scream.

Tom startles awake. "Wh-wha?" he rasps, blinking around him and wincing. "My head."

"Nice job! I knew you had Asian Auntie within you," Seb says, lifting his palm for a high five, but I rush past him and head for the door. "Where are you going? You still need to wake the groomsmen."

"Just pour water over them. I gotta go." I run all the way down the hallway, holding down my precious camera and camera bag so they don't bounce too hard. My heartbeat is a constant roar in my ears. By the time I catch up to my mom and aunts, I'm breathing so hard I feel like I'm about to vomit out my lungs.

"Meddy, oh good," Ma says, cheerily. "You take that corner and lift."

"What are you doing?" I whisper-shout. "His hand's out!" I lift the cooler's top up slightly and shove Ah Guan's hand back inside. It's only when it's in that I realize I've just touched his corpse. A shudder runs through my body.

Ma, Big Aunt, and Fourth Aunt's eyes widen.

"Oops," Ma says after a second.

"Must be when we go over that bump," Big Aunt says.

"Why are you moving him now?" I cry.

"The fridge getting so crowded, people coming in and out, in and out. I think not safe there," Big Aunt says.

"And since got three of us, we think we can carry all the way down to pier, no problem," Ma says.

I blink. No problem? Their version of "no problem" is to struggle with the cooler all the way to the pier with his goddamn hand sticking out of it? The thought of what would've happened if I hadn't spotted them through the window makes my knees buckle. And who knows how many people have seen them?

"Yes, got three of us, no need your Second Aunt," Big Aunt says.

Inside me, a star implodes. This. This right here is the real reason why Big Aunt got Ma and Fourth Aunt to move the cooler now, of all times. Because Big Aunt wants to prove that Second Aunt isn't needed. I can just imagine the smug look on Big Aunt's face when Second Aunt finds out that we've resolved everything without her help. Big Aunt will be all, "You see? I can handling the thing just fine, you no need worry," and Second Aunt will be all inwardly going, "Fuck you," but then outwardly she'll have to smile and congratulate Big Aunt on a job well done. I can't believe my aunts' rivalry with each other is jeopardizing us getting away with murder.

"Anyway, now you here, we can definitely move body down to pier," Ma says. "Ayo, cepat."

I check the time. Still about twenty minutes left before

Second Aunt is done with the bride's hair and makeup. Jacqueline is nice, but she's not going to be pleased if I completely miss the shots of her getting ready. But then again, a disappointed bride is much better than, you know, getting arrested because you're found in possession of a dead body. And now that we're here, getting back to the kitchen will be just as troublesome. We may as well see this through right here, right now.

With a frustrated groan, I take one corner of the cooler. Together, we heave, and the cooler lifts off the ground. We walk as quickly as we can, and with each step, my shoulder muscles burn, and my thighs shriek and beg for me to stop.

It feels like an eternity before the pier comes into view, and I nearly whoop with joy at the sight of all those yachts tethered there.

"Ladies," the yacht organizer calls out as we approach. "Can I help you with something?"

We lower the cooler gently, and I turn to him. "We need (gasp) to get on (gasp) a yacht (gasp) back to L.A."

"Sure, hop right on."

"Oh, thank you, thank you." My family and I make excited faces at one another and lift the cooler back up.

"Whoa, whoa, what's this?" the yacht organizer says. What a douche. He would've seen that we were carrying the cooler down the pier, but he's waited for us to pick it back up before asking about it. Prick.

"Oh, it's baking supplies. My aunt's the baker, and we need to get this stuff back to the bakery. There's not much space left in the kitchen."

The yacht organizer's eyes narrow. "Ah. Caterers." He says it like a dirty word. "Sorry, this yacht's for guests only?"

We stare at him. "Is that a question?" Fourth Aunt says.

"No? I mean like, it's for guests only. Period."

"Technically, I'm not a caterer," Fourth Aunt says, flipping her hair back. "I'm the star of the show, so."

"Oh? I don't know who you are . . ." He narrows his eyes like he's trying to figure out who she is.

"Why don't you ask your boss who I am—"

"No, wait, it's okay, please don't bother!" I say quickly. If Nathan catches wind that—yet again—my family and I are struggling with the cooler, he's definitely going to get suspicious. "We'll just store this in the kitchen. Thank you!"

The yacht organizer gives us the fakest smile of the year and goes back to tapping on his iPad.

"Kenapa?" Big Aunt says, and I shoot her a look that says "Later." We struggle back up the pier with the cooler, and when we stop for a breather, I tell them about how Nathan had seen me and Fourth Aunt moving the cooler, and how he would definitely think it's weird that we're trying to move the same cooler again.

"Oh yes, that sweet boy," Fourth Aunt says, grinning widely. "Very true, Meddy. I forgot about him." She wiggles her eyebrows.

Ma looks back and forth between the two of us. "What? What is it?"

"Nothing!" I say hurriedly.

Fourth Aunt wiggles her eyebrows again.

"Obviously not nothing. What is it? Why you cannot tell

156

your own mama?" Ma frowns, apparently hurt that I'm keeping something from her.

"Aiyo, San Jie, if your daughter doesn't feel comfortable sharing secrets with you, you shouldn't force her. Maybe that's why Meddy doesn't want to tell you these things," Fourth Aunt says.

Aw, come ON! These sisterly rivalries are going to be the death of me. Plus, I tell Ma a lot of things. Okay, yes, I did keep my three-year relationship from her, but that's different. I tell her everything else. I'm as close to her as any daughter can be. I'm the good, filial one, remember? I want to shout. I stayed behind while everyone else left. So maybe I don't tell them everything, but what more do they want from me?!

"It's nothing! He's just someone I used to know. Anyway, we've got bigger problems right now." I gesture to the cooler. "Maybe we should focus on this?"

"Yes, Meddy is right, you two can talk about where you failed as a mother later," Fourth Aunt says.

For the love of god.

"Ma, I don't keep any secrets from you, you know that." Aside from Nathan. Literally the ONE secret I kept from her. I mean, I even told her about me killing Ah Guan. That's got to count for something.

Ma doesn't meet my eye. "I do everything for you, and this how you repay me? Begitu ya? What did I do to deserve such unfilial child?"

Heeere we go. "This is so not the time."

"Then when is the time?"

"After we get rid of the guy I killed!" Oh god. I didn't mean to say it quite so loud. But really, nobody drives me quite as nuts as Ma and my aunts. We all look around to see if anyone's heard, but luckily, the place is relatively deserted. "Please, Ma, can we shelve this for now? I will tell you everything later, I swear. I desperately want to tell you, Ma, I really do, but now, let's focus on cleaning this up, okay?"

With a sigh, Ma's shoulders sag. "Okay," she says in a small voice. "Where we take cooler now? Back to fridge?"

Big Aunt shakes her head. "Cannot, too many people. The head chef driving everyone crazy, people rushing in and out of fridge, looking here and there for truffle lah, for rosemary lah, for this for that, just matter of time before somebody open cooler."

My phone boops with a text.

Seb [10:43AM]: There is waaay too much vomiting going on right now. Can we switch, please?

Me [10:44AM]: I'll switch with you later. I'm in the middle of something.

Seb [10:45AM]: You're not in the bridal suite?? Where r u?? She's not going to be happy if you miss shots of her putting her veil on!

Me [10:46AM]: It's an emergency. On second thought, can you cover for me? Go take pics of the bride. Sounds

like you're not getting any good ones of the groom anyway.

Seb [10:47AM]: Excuse you, I am getting fantastic shots of the groom and his idiots.

He sends a photo of some guy with his head in the toilet. Behind him, another guy is taking a shower, fully clothed.

Me [10:48AM]: Go to the bridal suite. I'll see you in a few.

I stuff my phone back into my pocket and take a deep breath. We're running out of time. Time. Time! "It's time!" I cry.

The others look confused.

"Check-in time! Remember? They told us our rooms won't be ready until ten? It's past ten!" I could cry with relief. We'll be able to store the cooler without worrying about someone stumbling across it. Maybe we'll be able to get out of this unscathed.

15

The lobby is packed with aunties wearing Gucci pantsuits and huge visors, and uncles wearing Patek Philippe. All the handbags hanging off the aunties' arms are Birkin or Kelly. No Louis Vuitton or Prada; this crowd is strictly Hermès. What is with the Chinese-Indo community and their hard-on for Hermès? It seems like all of the guests have arrived, even though logically I know this is untrue; most of them are due to arrive at 2 p.m., in time to check in and freshen up before cocktail hour. But the extended family members have arrived—the aunties and uncles and cousins who are due early for the tea ceremony— and in typical Chinese-Indonesian fashion, this means close to a hundred relatives, all of them arriving at the same time.

"Wah, look at that one, crocodile skin Kelly," Ma whispers to Big Aunt. Fourth Aunt twists her head around so far to catch sight of the coveted bag that her grip on the cooler slips. It slams onto the floor, and one of the wheels snaps right off.

"Aiya!" All four of us say it.

Heads turn. Curious gazes follow us. A few conversations have stilled as the aunties and uncles watch us.

"Tch, why you so kaypoh?" Ma scolds.

"You distracted me!"

"It's fine, just pick it up," I whisper, which seems ridiculous, whispering in such a huge space packed with people. But I feel the weight of those stares, crawling over my skin, and I need to get out of here. Fourth Aunt picks up her corner of the cooler once more and we hurry to the reception desk, where to my dismay there is a large line of guests waiting to check in.

"No worry, I go talk to them," Big Aunt says. We set down the cooler and she goes round to the side of the reception desk. She says a few words to the harried receptionist, who glances at her and then turns back to the computer screen, apparently ignoring Big Aunt. Her face turns red, and she says something else to the receptionist. From where we're watching, I can tell from Big Aunt's pinched expression the exact tone of voice she's using. It's the one she brings out when she's displeased with us, a quiet voice filled with iron, impossible to ignore. The reason Big Aunt is the matriarch of our entire family isn't merely that she's the oldest. If that were the only reason, she'd have been dethroned ages ago. No, the reason is that she has The Voice.

I watch as she uses her superpower on the receptionist right now. Whatever it is she says to her, the receptionist's head whips up, and she stares at Big Aunt with a worried frown. Big Aunt raises her eyebrows and gives a nod. With a sigh, the receptionist starts typing with a vengeance, and within minutes, Big Aunt is handed a key card with a tight smile. She walks back to us with a triumphant smile, waving the key card.

"Wah, Da Jie, good job!" Ma says.

"Yeah, that was nothing short of amazing," Fourth Aunt says.

Their respect and admiration show clearly on their faces, and for one guilty moment, I'm glad that Second Aunt isn't here to sour Big Aunt's moment. It's nice, seeing the sisters get along.

"Aiya, is nothing, lah," Big Aunt says, though she's smiling widely and it's obviously not nothing to her. "I just say to her—"

"Hi, Meddy."

My entire body reacts to Nathan's voice before my brain catches up, whirling round and angling my head up to meet his gaze. I'm already biting my lip—stop it!—but the expression on his face makes it clear there's nothing romantic about this moment. He's wearing a puzzled frown.

"Hey. Hi."

"Everything okay here?" he says.

"Yeah, just checking into our rooms," I say quickly, hyperaware of the curious stares from my mom and aunts.

"I hope you're finding everything okay," he says.

Ma comes up and squeezes in between us. "Such a good boy," she says, and to my horror, reaches up to pat his cheek. "So handsome also." I shrivel up and die.

"Can I get someone to help you to your room, Auntie?" Nathan says. His glance darts to the cooler, and his smile wanes. "I see you're still struggling with that same cooler?" He looks at me with a world of questions in his eyes.

"Yeah, we didn't want to take too much space in the

fridge, and this is all non-essential stuff, so we thought we'd take it out of your way," I babble.

Ma is still touching Nathan all over appraisingly, as though he's a watermelon she's thinking of buying. "Very tall," she murmurs, "good height. You have braces when you were small?"

"I—what?"

"Ma!"

"Braces, you know, on teeth."

Big Aunt and Fourth Aunt smile up at Nathan expectantly.

"Um, no?" Nathan's face has that glassy expression I often see on people when Ma is talking at them.

"Wah, so your teeth naturally straight? So good! Meddy, he is very good specimen, will give good offspring. No need to spend money on braces for your kids."

My jaw crashes to the marble floor. Nathan's face is so red I'm sure we could boil a kettle on it.

"MA!" I give a pleading look to my aunties, and they finally stop grinning long enough to take Ma's arms and lead her away. Even so, I still hear Ma going, "Very good teeth on him kan?" I turn to Nathan. "I am so, so sorry about that. Please ignore her."

"Don't be sorry. I've always wanted people to notice how straight my teeth are." He grins.

I laugh. "Okay, they are freakishly straight."

"I've also been waiting all my life to be told what a good specimen I am."

"Uh-huh. You're a pretty damn good specimen." It's only after the words are out that I realize how heavy they sound.

Does he know that no other guy even comes close to him? That after him, I couldn't help comparing every other man I meet to him, and that none of them could compare? And also, that none of this matters because I have a literal dead body sitting in the cooler next to us?

Luckily, Nathan's distracted by an uncle wearing a giant gold Rolex, who strides to him with a booming, "NATHAN! My boy, what a place, eh? Your old man will be so proud!"

"Hi, Uncle Timmy, it's so good to see you here."

"Listen, Nathan, Auntie Sofie is tired after the boat ride here. Could you possibly get us checked in now?" The man nods at the long line of people at the reception desk.

"I'm in the middle of something, but I'll get someone to take care of that for you—"

"No, it's okay," I say quickly, "why don't you help him? I have to rush off anyway."

Nathan gives me an apologetic smile. "Okay. I'll catch you later, Meddy. Come, Uncle, I'll take care of this for you."

Once Nathan and the older man are gone, I hurry to my aunts and mom. "Okay, let's go."

"Meddy, wah, you must go for that boy, your mother correct, he is best specimen," Big Aunt says.

Fourth Aunt snickers.

"Can we please talk about my love life later? When we don't have you-know-what to take care of?"

My mom and aunts grumble but then bend over to pick up a corner of the cooler. A bellboy swoops in. "Please let me get that for you," he says.

"No—" I say.

"No worries, ma'am, I'll get this to your room. Room 202, is it?"

"Don't—"

He gives us a polite smile and grabs one end of the cooler. My mind short-circuits, but before I can say anything, Ma says, "Aiya! You bellboys always looking for tip. I got no tip for you, you go away."

Looking shocked, the bellboy says, "I wasn't—"

"You go, shoo." Ma literally shoos him away like he's a naughty puppy, and he walks off, shaking his head, muttering, "Asians."

I wince, feeling torn between anger at his muttered remark and embarrassment because of our awful behavior. Still, I don't have the time to worry about that right now. "Let's go before yet another bellboy accosts us."

We pick up the cooler and scurry off to the elevators, eyes following us as we go. I don't blame them. We make a weird-looking team—me in all black, Big Aunt and Ma both wearing big white aprons, and Fourth Aunt, glittered and sequined and feathered. It's only after the elevator doors close behind us that I release my breath, but still I can't shake off the horrible feeling that too many people have seen us with the cooler. Too many curious glances have been thrown our way. We need to get rid of the cooler, and fast.

16

Being in the hotel room offers huge relief. Once we get inside, I close the door, lock the deadbolt, and then—bliss. For just one moment, I allow myself a chance to relax. I lean my head against the door, closing my eyes and breathing deeply. *We'll get through this*, I tell myself. *We will.*

"Wah, look this room. Bagus banget!" Ma says.

Reluctantly, I open my eyes and turn around. She's right. Despite this being the cheapest room at the resort, it's beautiful—two queen beds piled high with fluffy pillows and even fluffier duvets, a floor-to-ceiling window that opens out to an expansive balcony, modern furnishings all around. And it's nicely air-conditioned, giving us respite from the unforgiving heat.

I take off my shoes and put them next to my mom's and aunts' shoes in the entryway. Already, Big Aunt and Fourth Aunt have grabbed the thick terry cloth robes in the closet and put them on over their clothes. Ma glares at Fourth Aunt. "Excuse you, your own room will have robe also, don't use mine."

Fourth Aunt shrugs, tying a knot around her robe. "I'll bring my robe by once I check into my room."

I hurry between them, breaking up the glaring contest between the two. Ma would never think to ask Big Aunt to remove her robe, so if she wants to wear one, she's going to have to fight it off Fourth Aunt. "I'll call and ask for an extra robe, Ma. But before that, we need to resolve the issue with the cooler."

"What issue?" Big Aunt says. She's already made herself at home on the chaise longue, leaning back like a fifteenth-century lady.

"Well, unfortunately, way too many people have seen us lugging the cooler around. I'm pretty sure it looks hella suspicious, so I think we need to get rid of it. Also, it's clear that if we keep the body inside the cooler, we're never going to be able to move it off the island before tomorrow evening, and I'm pretty sure he's going to start smelling by then."

"Aduh, amit amit deh," Ma says.

Big Aunt looks up at the ceiling, quiet for a while. "No use 'amit amit,'" she says, finally. "Meddy is right, by tomorrow body will smell. We cannot wait until then. We need new plan."

"Fortunately for us," Fourth Aunt says, jumping into one of the beds, "we're surrounded by the ocean. Just dump him in the sea and be done with it!"

My instinctive reaction is to refute her, because most of Fourth Aunt's ideas are flighty and not at all well thought out, and as Ma always grumbles, Fourth Aunt isn't the most responsible person around. But then I realize that she has a point. Aside from burying the body in the desert, the ocean isn't a bad option. We could put him in a duffel bag, fill it with rocks, and then dump him in the water. With any luck, by the time he's found, he'll be so bloated they won't be able to identify him.

Wow, my thoughts went to a dark place there. It's shocking how quickly I've adjusted to the thought of, you know, killing a guy, to getting rid of his body. I never thought I had it in me to think like this. Once, I found a wallet with $200 in it on the dance floor of a nightclub, and I actually turned it in. That's the kind of rule follower I am. But the thought of going to prison, and not just me but my family, because they've inadvertently helped to kill Ah Guan, is unthinkable.

"That's actually a really good idea, Auntie," I say. "All we have to do is—"

There's a knock at the door, and we all freeze.

"Room service. I've got your bags here."

Perfect timing! I rush to open the door, then step aside as the bellboy deposits all of our luggage inside the room. I've brought only a small overnight bag, but my mom and her sisters are chronic overpackers, and within minutes our room is filled with giant suitcases. I tip the bellboy, and he leaves.

Then I turn, grinning, and say, "Okay, all we have to do is put the body in one of these bad boys and weigh it down with rocks and then tonight, we . . ." I falter. We what? Climb up with a heavy-ass suitcase to the top of the cliff and throw him down to the jagged rocks below? Steal a yacht and drive it out to the middle of the Pacific Ocean and dump him overboard? All these things are easy in theory, but as I'm about to say them out loud, it sounds ridiculous. How would we manage to carry it up to the top of the cliff in complete darkness? That's an accident waiting to happen. And stealing a yacht? I don't know how to even begin to do that, and if we somehow managed to get our hands on the keys, none of us knows how to drive a yacht. Is that even what it's called? Driving? Or do you boat a yacht? This is hopeless.

"We what?" Ma says, her eyes wide with expectation. I can't bring myself to admit that I have no fucking clue what we do from there.

My phone boops with a text, and I groan, remembering that I'm way overdue at the bridal suite.

Seb [11:35AM]: Uh oh, someone told the bride about the groom and buddies being dead drunk and she's sent the MoH over to the groom's suite.

Seb [11:36AM]: Oooh, MoH is really laying into them. These idiots, I swear.

Seb [11:40AM]: Omg, turns out they only got done drinking at like, 9AM. No wonder these assholes are still passed out!!!

Meddy [11:41AM]: Does this mean I have more time before I need to rush over to the bridal suite?

Seb [11:41AM]: Yeah. I don't think she's gonna be done anytime soon. But you're missing out on a good show.

Meddy [11:42AM]: I'll be over in a bit.

I stuff the phone back into my pocket, my mind whirring, and with a click that's practically audible, everything falls into place. The passed-out groomsmen. The crates of alcohol in the kitchen. Things starting off with cocktail hour as soon as the rest of the guests arrive.

"This is it!" I cry.

All three women look at me quizzically.

"I've got it! Forget about the luggage and whatnot. We'll hide him in plain sight. We'll pretend he's one of the drunk guests and then at night, while everyone's busy at the reception, we can take him to the pier. No one's going to think twice about yet another drunk guy. When the coast is clear, we throw him in the water. Even if he washes up to shore, they'll just think he got drunk, fell off the pier, and drowned."

"Won't they be able to tell how long he's been dead for?" Fourth Aunt says. "In CSI, they can tell, you know."

"Well, technically, he's only been dead for—I don't know, less than ten hours? Because of the whole, you know, him not being dead when we put him in the cooler . . ." My voice trails off because honestly, when I put it that way, the full horror of the situation is rather staggering. The poor guy. He was a shit, but he didn't deserve to die like that.

"Oh! Yes, yes, good point, Meddy. Yes, it is like one of those fish in restaurant, you know, they alive in tank and then they kill right before eating . . ." Ma's voice trails off as she notices our blank stares. "Never mind, it is not like that at all," she says.

I love her for trying, though. "Anyway, I'm pretty sure that being in the water for a while is going to mess up the

170

forensics investigation, especially since the weather's been so hot lately. Yay, global warming," I cheer weakly. Bad for the environment, good for killers.

"This not bad idea," Big Aunt says. "Is not good idea, but we trapped here, cannot get off island without calling attention, so no choice. Okay, Meddy, good job, we go with your idea."

I have to bite back my proud smile. It's next to impossible to get approval from Big Aunt, and for a fleeting moment, I get the urge to crow about it to Selena. Then I realize I can never crow about it to anyone. It's not like I can WhatsApp Selena and go, "Big Aunt approves of my corpse disposal idea!!!"

I can't believe I'm sitting here mentally bragging about this moment. I must be dehydrated. "We should probably get rid of the cooler in the meantime. Maybe like, set up a red herring, you know?"

"What red hearing?" Big Aunt says.

"Red herring. It means a decoy, something to mislead people. So, for example, I'm thinking we fill the cooler with actual food, so if anyone was suspicious about it— which I think the entire lobby full of people were—then we can always be like, 'Nope, there's just food in here, see?'"

Big Aunt nods. "Okay, yes, good idea, this red hearing. I will go kitchen and bring back leftover ingredients."

"Let's take his body out first, and then I have to go to the bridal suite to take photos."

We all stand up, the mood in the room turning somber, and gather round the cooler.

"Open it," Fourth Aunt says.

"Why I open? You open!" Ma says.

"I'll do it," I say. It has to be me. It's my mess. The least I can do is open the damn thing. I inch toward it, and when I reach out with my right hand, I swear the skin on my hand crawls up my arm. Oh god, here it goes . . .

I flip it open and scamper back, shuddering.

My mom and aunts crane their heads forward.

"How bad is it?" I ask, from behind them. "Is he—ugh, is he oozing?"

"Huh," Fourth Aunt says.

"Hmm," Big Aunt says.

"My lily flowers," Ma sighs.

This is impossible. I push past them and look. And huh. I mean, as far as corpses go, it could be worse. The first thing I notice about him is how pale he is. Which should be expected, and in theory I knew he'd hardly be rosy-cheeked, but seeing it in person is still a bit of a shock.

"Okay. Let's do this," I chirp. No one moves.

Big Aunt orders, "San Mei, you take left arm; Si Mei, you take right one; Meddy, you take left leg. I take right leg." We all nod. Thank god for Big Aunt. Still none of us moves, not even Big Aunt. Nobody wants to touch a corpse. Big Aunt claps hard and barks, "Cepat!" And we all snap forward. This is it. I don't let myself think twice before grabbing one of the legs, right below the knee.

Oh god, oh god, I'm touching it. Argh. Whatever I thought about corpses and how they felt, touching an actual one is a million times worse. Rigor mortis must be setting in, because he's super-stiff. It feels as though he's flexing all of his muscles. Which is just so wrong, thinking of him flexing anything at all.

"Okay, now lift," Big Aunt says, and as one, we do so.

And Ah Guan burps. We all shriek and drop him and clamber over one another to get away from him. We crowd around the other end of the room, gasping and staring at the open cooler.

"Is he alive?" Fourth Aunt cries.

"Ah Guan, ah, is me, Auntie Natasya. Hello, Ah Guan? You awake or not?" Ma says, smiling manically, as though he could see her from here.

I'm the first to realize what must have happened. "I think it was just trapped air from inside him coming out. It's part of the dying process."

They all look at me with a mixture of horror and awe.

"Meddy, how do you know such things?" Ma says.

I shrug. "The Internet? I don't know, there is lots of random information you come across just by surfing the web." Or, more accurately, by spending your evenings stuffing potato chips in your gob and going through Reddit.

Big Aunt nods, still looking shocked. "Very good, Meddy, you study so hard."

And again, part of me wants to crow, "Big Aunt thinks I study hard!" A small part, though. Tiny.

Ma practically preens when Big Aunt says that, and Fourth Aunt rolls her eyes.

"Okay, let's do it again," I say, emboldened by my knowledge. "And don't be shocked if he burps again. Or farts."

Grimacing, we all tiptoe back to the cooler. I guess we're

all tiptoeing because even though logically we know I'm right about gas merely escaping a dead body, we're still half-expecting him to leap out of the cooler and, I don't know, attack us for killing him. Which I realize makes zero sense, but it's hard to be logical when it comes to moving a guy you killed the night before.

"Okay, so. Everyone take a limb." And this time, they actually do what I tell them. I don't think I've ever ordered Big Aunt to do anything before, and it's an incredible feeling when she takes Ah Guan's right leg. We lift him up once more, and this time, no noises come out of him, thank god. We stagger toward the nearest bed and drop him on top of it, then step back and survey our handiwork.

"If we want to disguise him as a drunk guest, we'll have to clean him up a little." Luckily, there's not so much blood on him. There's just a bit of dried blood on the side of his neck from his ear. Once we get that off and put sunglasses and a suit on him, he'll look the part.

A suit. Sunglasses. Where the hell are we going to get those?

"Need to dress him nicer," Ma says, as if reading my mind.

"Dress him nicer? You mean put him in a suit?" Fourth Aunt says. "Where are we going to get a suit from?"

"Is not bad idea," Big Aunt says. She's taken out a toothpick from somewhere—Big Aunt always has toothpicks on her—and is cleaning her nails with it. She always has sugar and fondant and stuff stuck under her nails, which makes sense. Usually, seeing her clean her nails grosses me out a little, but right now, it's surprisingly calming. Like, the sky could be falling and there's a dead body on my bed, but by god, Big Aunt will have clean nails. "I can get suit."

We all stare at her. She's not even looking at us; she's all focused on her nails. "Where, Big Aunt?"

She frowns as she maneuvers the toothpick through a tricky bit. "I notice laundry room next to kitchen. Guest send their dress and suit to laundry room to dry clean or iron. I go inside, take suit, done!" She looks up, smiling.

Could it really be that easy? But then again, it's not like we have any other choice. "Thank you, Auntie. That—yeah, that would be amazing. I have to run now, I need to get back to the bridal suite, but I'll get back here as soon as I can."

"Okay, you go, I check on flowers," Ma says, waving me off.

"I guess that leaves me to look after the corpse, then," Fourth Aunt mutters.

I grimace. "I'm so sorry, Fourth Aunt."

"Meh. Could be worse." She settles on the other bed, making herself comfortable, and grabs the TV remote. "Don't be too long."

We all promise we'll be back soon, and off we go to handle the next crisis. One thing I can say about the weddings we do: they are certainly never dull.

17

The bridal suite is a mess. I find Second Aunt in her work corner, trying to put the finishing touches on Jacqueline's hair while Jacqueline visibly tries not to cry. Maureen holds Jacqueline's hands tight, speaking to her in a low, comforting tone of voice.

"I can't believe he's drunk," Jacqueline says. "On our wedding day!"

"I know," Maureen says, rubbing Jacqueline's arms. "But I think he's sobering up right now. He'll probably be okay."

Second Aunt brightens up when she spots me. "Ah, photographer is here, you no cry anymore, okay? Later ruin picture."

"Who cares about pictures anymore? My groom is a dumbass!" Jacqueline cries.

"Oh, sweetie." Maureen pulls her into a hug.

I bite my lip and give the two of them a bit of space. The truth is, people often judge brides for being high-strung and call them "bridezillas," but honestly, without a groom like Tom, Jacqueline would've been a perfectly calm bride.

After a few minutes, I gently say, "Seb's over in the groom's suite, helping the groom and groomsmen get ready. It'll all work out okay."

Jacqueline's chin trembles, and her eyes shine with tears. "It's just—we've been planning this for over a year, and everybody's here, and—"

"I know." I crouch down so I can look her in the eye. "And everybody is going to enjoy themselves and remember this as one of the most beautiful weddings they've ever attended, with the most gorgeous bride they've ever seen."

A sad smile touches her lips. "But even if Tom and his groomsmen do wake up in time, they'll look awful, and Tom won't even be able to enjoy his own wedding day."

"If you want to call the wedding off or postpone it or whatever, you can," Maureen says.

My heart does some complicated gymnastics move. Yesss, call off the wedding! We'd be able to leave early with the body—

Jacqueline shakes her head. "People have flown all the way from Indo to get here. If I canceled it there would be hell to pay." She takes a deep breath. "I'll be fine. Tom's the right guy for me. I've just got to get through today, and then we'll be fine. He makes a shitty groom, but he'll be the perfect husband."

I have to consciously stop myself from sighing out loud in disappointment at the missed opportunity for us.

Second Aunt resumes putting on the finishing touches while I aim my camera at Jacqueline and take pictures. This is usually one of my favorite parts of the day—taking photos of the bride. There is no doubt that the bride is the highlight of every wedding. There's just something about taking pictures of a woman wearing a gauzy, frothy wedding dress that makes me love my job. Usually. Today, I just want to get everything over and done with. And knowing that the bride is secretly unhappy doesn't help matters.

Once we're done, Second Aunt and I leave, giving Jacqueline and Maureen some privacy to bitch some more about the idiot groom and his idiot friends. As we walk out of the room, I turn and catch a glimpse of Maureen giving Jacqueline a quick hug while speaking in a reassuring tone to her, and I'm glad that Jacqueline has such a good friend to lean on. Outside the bridal suite, I quickly fill Second Aunt in on what's happened.

"So now we just waiting for Big Aunt to steal suit from laundry room?" she says, incredulously.

Put that way, it does sound pretty crazy. It sounds like the kind of plan that has about a gazillion ways to go wrong. "Well, we couldn't think of anything else, and that cooler's been seen by just about everybody."

"Is all Big Aunt's fault," Second Aunt says, triumphantly.

"Well, I wouldn't say that. The fridge was just too busy, people coming in and out."

"Nobody notice cooler, especially if we stack at bottom. You see, this is what Big Aunt do. She think she knows better, so she just do something without asking everyone. In the end, she create bigger mess."

"I mean—it's a difficult situation. I don't think there are any right answers, you know?"

Second Aunt harrumphs. "I been telling everyone for so long, cannot just rely on Big Aunt, but everyone always ask, 'Big Aunt, is this okay? Is that okay?' How would Big Aunt know? No, cannot rely on her. I will think of something, better idea."

"Uh." This feels bad in a too-many-cooks-spoil-the-soup kind of way. "I really don't think—"

"You go back inside, tea ceremony going to start soon. You get ready." With that, she walks off, wearing a firm expression of someone who knows absolutely what she's about to do.

I stand there for a while, hesitating. I should stop her. Or should I? I don't know. I've been raised never to go against my elders. Like I said, it's a difficult situation with no right answer, and left to my own devices, I would . . . well, I honestly don't know what I'd do. Killing a dude and covering up said dude are all a bit out of my normal comfort zone.

It's barely noon. Unbelievable. I feel as though it's the end of a very long day, but now it turns out there's still some time before the penjemputan ceremony. In Chinese-Indo weddings, the groom and groomsmen go to the bride's house (or in cases where the bride's already at the hotel, to the bride's suite). The bridesmaids are supposed to greet them at the door and make them do a series of embarrassing stunts before they're allowed to walk through the door and jemput—pick up—the bride. I wonder what torturous stunts Jacqueline's friends have concocted, especially to get back at the guys for getting so shit-faced. Despite myself, I smile at the thought. They deserve a bit of ass-whooping, honestly.

"Well, at least somebody's having a good time."

I look up to see Nathan coming down the corridor. "Oh, hey." I can't stop the smile from spreading across my face. The sight of him. I can't describe it. I mean, objectively he's gorgeous, obviously, but there's also something about him that makes me feel that I've come home after a long day.

"Just came out from the groom's suite," he says with a sigh.

"Oof. How're they doing?"

"Well, they're awake, so there's that, but a couple of them are trying to shift the blame by saying that their drinks must've been spiked in order for them to get that drunk."

I stare at him in horror. "Seriously?" How fucking entitled can you get?

Nathan sighs again. "Yep, seriously. Unfortunately, this kind of thing isn't unique. You won't believe the number of times guests have blamed us for some random thing just to cover their asses or get a freebie."

"That sucks. I empathize. I deal with people on the most stressful day of their lives, so . . . yeah. I don't usually see the best side of them."

His mouth quirks into a crooked smile that doubles my heart rate. "Did you mean 'the happiest day of their lives'?"

"I meant what I meant, dude. Sure, it's a happy occasion with some truly beautiful moments, but it's also stressful as hell, especially when you're Chinese-Indo and need to invite two thousand people to your wedding."

"True." He continues smiling at me as if I'm very interesting instead of a wildly ranting weirdo. "So, um, I have a confession to make."

I have to swallow before speaking. "Yeah?"

"I've been thinking a lot."

"Uh-oh. Don't overdo it."

His smile widens, and I'm treated to a full view of its gorgeousness. It's a full-on assault. His face should be illegal, the way his dark chocolate eyes crinkle at the edges and the way those dimples appear. He looks like a combination of Daniel Henney and Lewis Tan, a combination that is waaay too hot for his own good.

"I've mainly been thinking about feet."

"Uh." Okay, this is not where I thought the conversation was going to go. "Well, I'm glad that you've picked up a fetish since college . . . ?" I smile in what I hope is a very open-minded way. I think the smile ends up looking slightly demented.

Nathan laughs. "Sorry, I wasn't being clear. Though it's interesting that that's where your mind went."

"Oh, like there's a different way to take 'I've been thinking about feet'?"

"Good point. Anyway, more specifically, I've been thinking about *your* feet." He winces and quickly adds, "Okay, wait, that came out a lot creepier than it should have."

"Yeah, that did come out pretty creepy." I laugh, though the thought of Nathan thinking about anything that has to do with me makes things inside me flutter.

"I've been thinking about how, when you go to sleep at night, your feet wag back and forth."

I bite my lip as memories come rushing back. Of us, tumbling about under the sheets, not leaving my bed for days. Of the conversations we had in between devouring each other, my head on his chest, listening to his heartbeat. We'd talk about everything, from physics to games to mutual friends, and we'd watch from bed as the sky went from inky black to smoky purple and wonder about how we'd just spent the entire night awake and didn't feel tired at all.

That first night we spent together, as I was dozing off, he said, "Do you always do that with your feet?"

My feet stopped still. "Do what?"

"No, don't stop. They were like, wagging back and forth under the covers." He turned his head to look at me, smiling. "That's so cute."

"Sorry," I moaned. "My mom said my future husband would complain about my restless feet."

He laughed. "Your future husband?"

"Well, according to her, I can only share a bed with one dude in life, and that's my husband." I wince inwardly at the magnitude of this statement. "Not that I'm saying you're my future husband, I mean, you're not the first guy I've shared a bed with. I've been with plenty others before. Not plenty, but like, you know. I don't want to marry you, is what I'm saying. I mean, not like—"

His mouth covered mine in a sweet kiss that ended with us giggling at each other, our lips still touching.

"I know what you mean," he said gently. "Don't worry. The feet don't bother me at all."

And then we had fallen asleep like that, in each other's arms, and I'd woken up with him hard against me, and—

I snap back to the present, with Nathan—my Nathan—

smiling down at me. I grin weakly, my stomach fluttering at the vivid memory of our first night together. Did he bring up the feet thing on purpose, to remind me of that night?

"This is probably the most important weekend of my career," Nathan says. "The success of this wedding will basically make or break the hotel."

I nod weakly. "I understand."

"I really should be focused on work and making sure everything goes well, but, Meddy—god, I haven't been able to stop thinking about that kiss." He leans close to me, and everything about him fills my senses. His scent floods me, that good, clean, fresh smell he has that has nothing to do with cologne. He's always smelled of fresh, warm laundry. "I should be focusing on making sure everything goes well, but I keep coming back to you."

Of course, now that he's talking about it, it's all I can think of too. He's so deliciously close to me, I can see his ridiculously long, thick eyelashes, and the way the muscles in his jaw move as his lips part ever so slightly. He dips his head toward mine. His lips are only an inch away when my phone goes off. We jump apart, and I scramble to pick it up. It turns out to be my alarm, set to go off five minutes before the penjemputan.

"Alarm. It's time for me to go in," I say, waving the phone vaguely. My heart is screaming. Can hearts scream? Mine's doing some weird shit, anyway.

Nathan gives a rueful smile. "Maybe later, when there's a lull, we can talk about us?"

"Yeah. Yeah, of course." More than anything, I long for

the chance to talk things out with Nathan, to close the years' worth of gap between us, to know everything that's gone on with him. But the dark worry of Ah Guan's body in my hotel room resurfaces from the depths of my consciousness like a swamp monster, and I step away from Nathan. "We'll talk," I say, and it comes out more curt than I wanted. Nathan's smile loses a wattage or two, but he nods before walking away, leaving me feeling like I've lost him for the second time in my life.

18

Chinese-Indonesian weddings are filled with small ceremonies. Before the penjemputan, there is a short veiling ceremony, where the parents of the bride kiss her on the cheek and then put the veil over her face, thus completing her transformation from woman to bride. It's usually a tearful occasion; in most Chinese-Indo families, no matter how old you get, kids usually live with their parents until they get married and move out. So for most families, this is goodbye, and the veiling ceremony is a visual reminder of it.

Jacqueline and her parents are no exception. I move swiftly and quietly, capturing as many pictures as I can of the intense emotions on their faces without detracting from the moment. When Tante Yohana and Om Hendrik pull the veil over Jacqueline's head, tears sting my eyes at the bittersweet smiles on their faces. These are my favorite moments of wedding photography. Capturing the in-betweens. The moments in between the big ones, when raw emotion is painted vividly and it feels as though I'm catching the tunes of their hearts with my camera.

Once that's finished, we wait for the groom and groomsmen to arrive for the penjemputan.

And wait.

And wait.

I send a text to Seb to see what the hell is the holdup. I mean, really now, I've got a dead body in my room and somehow I'm *not* the biggest mess at this wedding.

Meddy [12:17PM]: Yooo, where's everyone? They're late for the penjemputan.

Seb [12:18PM]: You won't believe these idiots. They're all rushing around, getting dressed, messing with their hair. Some of them can't find their shirts or pants or whatever shit.

I sigh and open up the chat group with my mom and aunts.

Meddy [12:19PM]: Everything okay?

Big Aunt sends a string of emojis that seem completely unrelated to each other instead of an actual response.

Whoever introduced my mom and aunts to emojis needs to be thrown off a tall building. Ever since they found out about emojis, my mom and her sisters think they're a perfectly acceptable way of communicating. Except everyone has a slightly different interpretation of emojis, and it takes me about three times as long to figure out exactly what they're trying to say. Like now, for example, the thumbs-up emoji means everything is okay, which is good, but then why is there an angry face emoji right next to it? And then the shirt emoji . . . does she mean to say that she managed to grab a shirt, but people are angry at her? But then why the thumbs-up emoji? *Why?*

Meddy [12:22PM]: I don't know what that means.

Ma [12:23PM]: Aiya, how can not figure out? So obvious.

Big Aunt [12:24PM]: [Another string of emojis]

Meddy [12:25PM]: Everything is okay, right??

Second Aunt [12:26PM]: [String of emojis]

I give up. Whoever said "It's as hard as herding cats" has obviously never tried to herd a group of Asian aunties. I'll just have to trust that since they haven't used the police car or police station or whatever other dire emoji, things are okay. Or at least they're not catastrophic.

Just as I shove my phone back into my pocket, there's a commotion outside the door. I perk up. Finally! The groom and his posse are here. I hold up my camera—I'm using the 35mm now, which gives me a wider angle so I can make sure to capture everyone—and snap the moments as the bridesmaids, who have been gathered at the suite door, call out, "Who's there?"

"The groom!" comes the answer, and the bridesmaids giggle.

They open the double doors and a cheer goes up, albeit a weak and straggled one as the groom and his friends are obviously suffering from a bitching hangover.

"You're late!" Maureen shouts.

Tom Cruise Sutopo—I really need to stop referring to him mentally by his full name every time, but then again, I can't stop thinking of him as a knock-off Tom Cruise—and the groomsmen in the front wince at her shout. Tom smiles weakly and says, "Let us in?"

"Only if you do a few things for us!" At this, all of the bridesmaids cheer, and the groomsmen groan theatrically.

I'm smiling as I take pictures of them all. I love the acara penjemputan. I've seen bridesmaids come up with the most creative trials for groomsmen to do: having them shave each other's chest hair, getting them to wear diapers over their pants, asking them the randomest questions about the bride and making them eat raw chilies when they get a question wrong.

Now, a Victoria's Secret box is passed from bridesmaid to bridesmaid until it reaches the maid of honor. "Don't come back until you've put these on." She laughs, passing it to Tom.

The guys all groan loudly again, but they're also laughing, some covering their faces as they fish out lacy lingerie from the box. Gamely, they put on the lingerie over their suits, and that's when everyone realizes there's a set of lingerie left in the box.

"Why's there a set left?" Maureen says, holding up the lace underwear. "All of y'alls need to wear these! Come on out, stop hiding! Who's missing?"

The groomsmen glance around, looking confused and . . . guilty. Huh. Why would they look guilty?

"Uh, Ryan isn't here," Tom says, finally.

"Why not?"

"He um—" He lowers his voice, leaning in a little, and says, "Please don't tell Jac, but he can't find his clothes."

"What?" Maureen cries. "For fuck's sake, Tom. Come ON. You guys had ONE job. One! Just show up. And you can't even—" She stops herself, takes a deep breath, and forces a smile. "Okay, whatever. Moving on. Time for the next trial." She nods to one of the bridesmaids, who taps something on her phone. Music blasts out. Kelis's "Milkshake." "Shake it, boys!" she shouts, and then hurries back inside the room, whispering something to a bridesmaid as she goes. The bridesmaid nods and takes her place at the front.

Maureen hurries through the living room and into the bedroom, where Jacqueline is waiting. Moments later, even through the din of the music, I hear Jacqueline go, "Seriously?"

I can't help but sigh. Honestly, can these groomsmen be more of a mess? I walk over to the bedroom and knock softly. Jacqueline looks up and says, "Oh god, Meddy, we're down a groomsman!"

"Yeah, I heard. Look, I know it seems like a huge deal, but it really isn't. You've got enough bridesmaids and groomsmen for people not to notice a missing one, and I promise the pictures will turn out just as good."

"But what about when they're walking down the aisle

after the ceremony? I can't send Becca down the aisle on her own; that's just too sad."

I think fast. "She can walk down with another pair. Have the groomsman stand in between two bridesmaids as they go down the aisle."

Jacqueline and Maureen look at each other, mulling over what I said, then Maureen shrugs. "She's right. That's the best option."

Jacqueline sighs. "Okay. Could you?"

"I'll let her know," Maureen says. "Don't you worry." She gives Jacqueline's hand a squeeze and leaves the room.

Jacqueline leans her head back against the wall and breathes out. "This day's a mess."

She doesn't know the half of it. "Weddings always are. But yours is going great, trust me. And you look amazing."

She crooks a half-smile. I tell her I'm going back to take pictures, and she nods. With that little snag resolved, the rest of the penjemputan ceremony passes by quickly. The guys pass all of their trials and tribulations and are allowed into the suite. I capture the moment when Tom sees his bride for the first time in her wedding gown, the expression on his face making everyone go, "Awww." He lifts her veil and gives her—as per Chinese-Indo tradition—a chaste kiss on the cheek. Her parents smile in approval. I snap the tearful moments when Jacqueline hugs her parents before leaving the bridal suite, and the acara penjemputan is over. The wedding festivities have begun.

19

Up next is the tea ceremony, a favorite for many couples. The bride and groom serve tea to their elders, and their elders bestow gifts upon them. Traditionally, the gifts come in the form of gold or red packets filled with money. With the more lavish Chinese-Indo weddings, the aunties and uncles often try to outdo one another; I've shot a wedding where an uncle gave his favorite nephew a car. Rare, but it has been known to happen. With Tom and Jacqueline's ostentatiously wealthy families, who's to say what the ceiling is when it comes to their tea ceremony?

The atmosphere inside the function room is electric. Seb and I take our respective positions, me behind the chairs for the elders so I can capture photos of the bride and groom, and Seb across the room. All the aunties and uncles and grandparents are side-eyeing one another as they await their turn to be served tea. The wedding organizer is perched next to the bride and groom, and she calls out the names of relatives, who go up two by two.

The first couple to go up is Tom's parents. My shutter snaps dozens of pictures as Maureen passes a tray with two steaming cups of wulong tea to Jacqueline and Tom. They each pick up a cup and present them, heads bowed, to Tom's parents. Tom's parents accept with gracious smiles, take a sip, and then place the cups back on the tray. Tom and Jacqueline bow to them, and then Tom's dad takes something out of his jacket and presents a piece of paper with a flourish.

The wedding planner announces, "A title deed to your new house!" and the guests ooh and aah and clap. Tom and Jacqueline hug Mr. and Mrs. Sutopo, and I take pictures of them holding up the title deed before Maureen places it in a prepared box.

The next ones to come up are Jacqueline's parents, who give Jacqueline the brilliant set of jewelry I'd taken photos of earlier that morning and a Chopard watch for Tom—"Limited edition, worth more than a BMW," announces the WP. The audience claps appreciatively, and the gifts are whisked away to join the title deed in the large velvet box. The rest follow, going from oldest relatives to youngest.

There are more watches—Cartier and Patek—and there are receipts for larger items, like a La Cornue stove from one of Jacqueline's aunties, and a Hastens bed from an uncle. Then there is jewelry—again, more Cartier, a couple of Bulgari, and a smattering of Tiffany. And of course, as usual, there are the red packets. These ones are bulging, stuffed with stacks of hundred-dollar bills. I catch sight of an auntie stuffing her red packet with more wads of cash; evidently she's feeling outmatched by all the insane gifts. I feel bad for her. No doubt about it, the tea ceremony is the most stressful one for the extended family.

By the time they're done, Maureen has had to ask for another box to hold all the gifts. Everyone claps and proceeds to a different hall to have lunch.

"Do you still need me around?" Seb says, glancing up from his camera screen. "Or can I head for lunch?"

"Go, I'll be fine. Thanks for dealing with the groomsmen and everything."

"Anytime. I'll see you later."

I see Maureen struggling to pick up both boxes and hurry toward her, slinging my camera strap over my shoulder.

"Let me help you with that."

She glances up, startled. "Oh, that's totally fine, I can manage."

I watch, hesitating, as she piles one box on top of the other and grunts, lifting. The top box wobbles precariously, and I leap forward, catching it just in time before it topples over and rains expensive jewelry everywhere.

"Oof, thanks. I guess I can't manage after all."

"How come no one else is helping out with this? The stuff's heavy."

Maureen smirks. "I'm the only one they trust with this."

"Ah, makes sense. You're a great maid of honor. She's lucky to have you."

Her smile wanes a little at that, and I wonder if I've said the wrong thing. We brisk-walk the rest of the way to the bridal suite in silence. When we get inside, Maureen says, "Just put the box down on the coffee table." I do as she says and hesitate again. Should I leave, or should I wait for her?

As though reading my mind, she says, "You can go now," dismissing me with a flick of her hand.

Outside, I check the schedule and breathe a sigh of relief. It's lunchtime, and after that there are a couple hours of break while everyone rests through the hottest part of the day. I won't be needed for a few hours until portrait time in the afternoon, after which will be the wedding ceremony, followed by the reception. I'm about to go to the restaurant, where lunch is provided for all the wedding vendors, when my phone rings. Second Aunt's face pops up onto the screen.

"Meddy, got problem."

My heart thumps to the floor. "What is it?"

"Ah Guan phone. It keep ringing, someone want to talk to him bad. Maybe I pick up and say—"

"Do NOT pick up! I'll be right there."

I run all the way back to my room. Even before I open the door, I can hear the faint sound of music. I tap the key card at the door sensor frantically and burst into the room. Fourth Aunt jumps up, then sighs when she sees me.

"You'll give me a heart attack!"

"What's that music?" I say, rushing inside.

"Shoes!" Fourth Aunt scolds.

Seriously? I kick my shoes off and rush toward the bed. Someone has put the duvet on top of Ah Guan, covering all of him save for his socked feet, which are poking out the bottom. His phone is on top of the desk, lying facedown, and the music is coming from it, because Second Aunt was right, someone keeps calling him.

"Why didn't you turn it to Silent mode?" I reach for the

phone and pause. What do I do? Now that I'm actually here, I don't know what I'm supposed to do. Answer it? Shit, no. I can't do that. I'm still standing there, frozen, when it stops mid-ring. Silence falls, thick and heavy.

"It's going to ring again," Fourth Aunt says. "Been ringing for the past ten minutes. Er Jie couldn't stand it; that's why she's out there."

"Out there?" I glance up and finally catch sight of Second Aunt out on the balcony, doing Tai Chi.

"That position's called White Crane Spreads Its Legs," Fourth Aunt says. I give her a look, and she goes, "What? I'm serious. You think I'm making these names up?"

"Yeah, actually." I shake my head. Why the hell am I arguing about Tai Chi position names right now? "Where are Big Aunt and Ma?"

"Went for lunch. You know how they get all angry when they're hungry. They get . . . hang-angry. Ooh, I just coined a new term!"

"The term's 'hangry,' and you didn't coin it." I focus on the phone. *Okay, Meddy. Think. Okay, first things first: we need to know who's been calling. Yeah. Okay.*

Taking a deep breath, I reach out while at the same time the rest of my body cringes away from the phone. Even my lips peel back, like my entire skin is trying to crawl off. I pick it up, grimacing, and tap the home key. The screen lights up, asking for an unlock code or a fingerprint.

I swear out loud.

"What is it?"

"I need his thumbprint."

"Oof. Mm, yeah, not going to help you with that." Fourth Aunt resumes plucking her eyebrows.

"Yep, don't worry about it," I mutter, walking to the side of the bed. "Okay. I can do this. No biggie. This is totally fine." I dart to the bathroom, retrieve a hand towel, and wrap it around my hand. Deep breath. I lift the duvet, gritting my teeth as I see his hand. His pale hand. Mannequin pale. Shit, shit, shit. Gingerly, I maneuver it so I can press his thumb up against the home key. Nothing happens. Argh. Okay, other thumb. Still nothing. With increasing desperation, I try his index finger and finally hit jackpot. The screen lights up, and the phone unlocks. Thank you, sweet baby Jesus. I drop his hand and do a full body shiver. Yech.

Then I look at my prize. Ah Guan's phone, unlocked. First things first: I go into Settings and turn off the phone lock, so I won't need his fingerprint again to access the phone. Then I click on the calls history list and—

"Shit."

"What is it?" Fourth Aunt says.

I look up at her, my mouth open, aghast. "It's Maureen Halim."

20

"Who Maureen Halim?" Second Aunt says, walking back in the room.

"The maid of honor." My voice comes out all dazed. I don't get it. Why would Maureen be calling Ah Guan? Just as I think that, a text comes in.

Maureen [1:32PM]: Where the fuck r u???

Maureen [1:32PM]: The things r ready!!

Maureen [1:33PM]: This was ur idea, don't tell me ur backing out now!!

Backing out of what? My fingers move faster than my mind does, and before I know it, I've typed out a reply.

Ah Guan [1:33PM]: Not backing out, but can't talk rn.

Maureen [1:34PM]: Can't talk?! R u fuckin kidding me rn?

She rings again, and this time, I pick up. I don't even need to say anything before she launches into a tirade. I don't even need to put her on speaker; in the small, silent room, her voice comes out painfully clear.

"You fucking shithead, you better get here right now and pick shit up, or else I'm gonna report your ass. Door's unlocked. I'm going into the dining hall before they realize I'm missing. Move. Your. Ass." With that, she disconnects the call, leaving me staring at the phone.

"Wah, this Maureen very angry girl," Second Aunt says from behind my back. "She need to do Tai Chi."

"I guess I need to pick up whatever Ah Guan was supposed to pick up so she doesn't realize he's dead," I say, weakly.

"I go with you," Second Aunt says. "I done my Tai Chi now, so I very calm. You need someone calm."

She is not wrong. I thank her, and we both leave the room.

"Where we going?"

"Well, when I left, Maureen was in the bridal suite, so I guess I'll start there." There's a dark suspicion unfolding in my mind as we walk, and I hope against all hope that it's not what I think it is, but when I get to the bridal suite, the deadbolt on the door has been left in the locked position, with the door slightly open, so that the door doesn't swing shut and automatically lock. My stomach is twisting, but I make myself knock and call out, "Maureen? You there?"

No answer. I push open the door slightly and peer in. "Maureen?"

Still silence. Second Aunt pushes the door wide open. Or tries to, anyway. There's something blocking it. We exchange a look and push harder, until the gap is big enough for us to get through. The object that's behind the door turns out to be a heavy duffel bag. I bend down and unzip it and—

"Ahhh, shit." I sigh.

"What is it? What inside—oh."

I suck in a breath through gritted teeth. "The tea ceremony gifts."

"Waaah, this one's gorgeous," Fourth Aunt cries, opening a velvet box and finding a diamond necklace inside. She strokes it with as much adoration as a mother stroking her newborn. "Can't I just keep one?"

"No!" I snap, snatching the box away from her. I slam it shut and put it back in the duffel bag. When I look back, Second Aunt looks up guiltily. She's doing Tai Chi in the middle of my hotel room, and on one outstretched arm she has on a thick gold Cartier bracelet and on the other she has a Patek Philippe watch on. "Second Aunt!"

"Not keeping them," she mutters. "Just want see what they look like when I do Tai Chi." She moves into a different pose and says, "Grasp the Bird's Tail pose. Oooh, look nice, ah?"

Fourth Aunt nods appreciatively.

I march over to her and hold out my palm. "Give them back."

"So spoilsport." She takes them off and drops them in my hand with a pout.

"I—or we—need to figure out what the hell's happening." I pace the room. "Okay, so it looks like Maureen and Ah Guan know each other somehow, and they plotted to steal the tea ceremony gifts. Maureen's moved the gifts from the boxes into the bag, and Ah Guan's supposed to pick them up, which we've done for him, and now . . . now what?"

"Have some tea, Meddy, you're too anxious," Fourth Aunt says, passing me a steaming cup of my favorite tea, Tie Guan Yin.

"Tea got caffeine, will stress her out even more. Better you just do Tai Chi, Meddy. Come, you do with me." Second Aunt plucks the teacup out of my hand and places it on the desk before launching into a Tai Chi pose. "Parting the Wild Horse's Mane," she says, stretching out both hands.

This is impossible. "I'm going to the balcony to think." I stride outside and close the sliding door behind me. Leaning against the balcony railing, I breathe out a huge sigh. Before me is the mountain view, which is a nice way of saying "not ocean view," but the sight of all the trees and greenery is soothing to me. Okay, so. Ah Guan was an even bigger shit than I thought. I close my eyes. Let's pretend to be him for a second. I've got a duffel bag filled with expensive gifts. What do I do?

I get off the island as fast as I can.

They'd sent us an e-mail with travel details. I take out my phone and open the e-mail, scrolling down to "Vendors boat timetable." Sure enough, there's a yacht for vendors who aren't staying overnight scheduled to leave in fifteen minutes. The next one leaves in six hours' time. Ah Guan would've wanted to leave ASAP. How would he have smuggled the duffel bag out, though?

The lilies. He would've arrived here with crates of them. I guess he could just stuff the duffel bag into one of those crates and nobody would be the wiser. Right. So. That was most likely his plan. Now that I've figured it out, what do I do? I took the duffel bag because I didn't want Maureen to find out that he's not here. I thought maybe it would be best to keep up the appearance of having him still be alive. But if I go along with their plan, it means I would be stealing from Jacqueline and Tom. And they don't deserve that. I'm already a killer; I really don't need to add "thief" to the growing list of crimes.

I'll return the gifts to them. Just gotta figure out how. Can't exactly march up to Jacqueline and tell her that her maid of honor is a lying, thieving jerk, because then I'd have to explain how I found out. Maybe I could just leave the duffel bag outside the bridal suite? But then Maureen would know that something went wrong on Ah Guan's end. Argh. Okay. I'll figure it out somehow. In the meantime, I'll just have a freaking dead body and a bag full of stolen goods in my room, because of course I do.

There's a knock on the glass door. I open it and Fourth Aunt says, "You're going to be here awhile, right? Er Jie and I are going to lunch. We're starving."

"Oh. Yeah, of course. Go. Thanks for watching the—you know—while I was gone."

"Of course, that what family do," Second Aunt says. They slip on their shoes, call out their goodbyes to me, and leave the room. I go back inside, closing the balcony door behind me, and sip the tea that Fourth Aunt had made for me. With a sigh, I plop down on the other bed, staring at Ah Guan. Or rather, the lump that's covered by the duvet. Oh lord, it's just hit me that one of us will have to sleep in this bed that housed a dead body for hours. Inconceivable. I'll just—I'll sleep in the bathtub. Or with Ma. Or on the floor. Anywhere but the bed Ah Guan's corpse is cooling down in. I look at the stocking feet sticking out. How surreal that there's an actual human body underneath that. A human body I killed. And there, on the desk, the duffel bag. I pick it up and put it inside the closet. Seems wrong to just leave a bag full of stolen jewelry and money out in the open like that.

Just as I'm sliding the closet door shut, there's another knock. Without thinking, I swing it open, saying, "Did you forget something, Fourth—" The last word chokes halfway up my throat. Because there, standing in front of me, isn't Fourth Aunt or Second Aunt.

It's Nathan.

21

"Nathan!" I cry, hoping that came out more "pleasantly surprised" than "shocked and horrified." Not that I would be shocked or horrified to see him under normal circumstances, that is, when I do not have a dead body AND a bag full of stolen things in my room. I slide out of the room and pull the door shut behind me, and only then do I breathe easier.

And there he is. My Nathan. "Hi."

"Hi," he says, smiling at me as though I'm the only person he wants to see in the entire world. He's had this effect on people since our college days. He'd smile at the cashier at Safeway, and the kid would just melt. "I had some free time—okay, I don't, actually, I made some free time—Meddy, I can't stop thinking about you."

"Me too." Technically a lie—I haven't been able to stop thinking about the corpse—but also not technically a lie, given that I've been obsessing over him for the past four years. I guess that's what he wanted to hear, because next thing I know, his arms are around my waist, pulling me close. He pauses, his lips only a single, lonely inch from mine, and the yearning inside me takes over and I close the distance.

Every kiss we have steals my breath, stops the spinning of the world, and this one is no different. Time stops, air molecules freeze, and in this moment, there's no me, or him, or everything else. Just us. I kiss him hungrily, and he kisses back with equal fervor. My lips part slightly, and he slides his tongue into my mouth. Molten lava fills my belly. I can't have enough of him. The taste of him is intoxicating, the gentle caress of his tongue on mine sending me spinning into mindlessness. His hands hold me tight, possessively, and when one of them moves to cup my breast, I arch my back like a cat, filling his palm, feeling my skin burst into flames at the touch. God, I want him so badly.

"Can we go inside?" he murmurs, his lips tracing the words against my neck, making me whimper with need. I wrap my arms around him even tighter, words tumbling out of my mouth without much meaning.

Inside. Where we could rip off each other's clothes, skin kissing skin, his warmth against mine, inside me—

Inside. Where Ah Guan's corpse lies, cooling. My eyes fly open. I might as well have gotten an electric shock. All of my muscles tense, and I turn into a salt pillar. "Inside?" I squeak.

Nathan pulls back a little. He searches my eyes. "Yeah, I thought—" He blushes. "Sorry if I'm moving too fast—"

"No! No, you're not. I really, really want to go inside with you. You won't believe how much I've been fantasizing about that. It's just—shit, actually, I just locked myself out." I pat my pockets for my key card. I'm not even lying. In my panic to close the door when I found Nathan here, I forgot to grab the key card from the desk.

"Oh. That's okay, I've got a master key." He takes a card out of his pocket and smiles. "Look, I know this is moving really fast, but um—I'd actually love to just be able to sit down with you and talk. We have so much to catch up on and if I'm being totally honest, you know, I still don't understand where we went wrong back in college. I drove myself crazy trying to figure out what I did, and I don't want to make that same mistake now."

"You didn't. It was nothing you did."

Confusion crosses his face.

"I was too scared to go east with you and I just freaked. I wanted to stay and help the family business, but I didn't want to risk you giving up on your job offer, so. Yeah. Biggest mistake of my life. Believe me, I kick myself every day for letting you go."

Nathan smiles, and god, it's beautiful. It's like years are shaved off his face. "So. I didn't fuck it up?"

"God, no! You were the love of my life. I want to talk too, properly—"

He waves the key card at the door before I can say "but," and the light above the knob turns from red to green. The lock slides with a click, and Nathan opens the door for me. My heart stops. My entire being has frozen.

But instead of walking in as I thought he would, Nathan remains outside.

He sees my startled, dazed gaze, and smiles ruefully. "It's clear that you're unsure about this, Meddy. And I'm not going to make you do anything you don't want to. We've got all the time in the world after this weekend to talk about us." He takes my hand, enveloping it with his warmth, and lifts it to his lips. My knees turn to water as he kisses my hand with exquisite reverence. "You're worth the wait." He tucks an errant strand of hair behind my ear and trails his fingers down the side of my cheek, to my neck, making me shiver with pleasure.

"After this weekend," I promise, "I'll be all yours, and I promise I'll explain everything about my family and why I was such an idiot and broke things off with you."

His smile lights up his face, same old Nathan, the boy I fell so wildly in love with all those years ago, and it's like watching the sun rise. I kiss him again, wanting so badly to memorize every delicious curve of his mouth, the addictive taste of him. When we break off, we're both breathless again. I slide back through the door, almost home free. His gaze flicks up somewhere behind my shoulder, and his smile freezes.

"Is that—?" A frown etches into his forehead as he cranes his neck to look through the gap at the door. When he speaks again, his voice has lost all of its warmth, and he's looking down at me like I'm a stranger. "Is there a guy in your bed?"

A supernova goes off in my head. Oh god, he's seen the body. HE'S SEEN THE BODY.

Instead of a look of horror, though, what settles on Nathan's face is disappointment.

He laughs a little awkwardly. "I thought you weren't seeing anyone, but—" He laughs again, an utterly humorless sound, and the look on his face is unbearable to see. Betrayal. My heart crumples at the sight of it. A small part of me insists this is worse, much worse than shock-horror. A small part of me wants to shout: "No! It's not a boyfriend! Just some blind date I killed last night; he means nothing to me, I swear! I didn't even know his real name before I killed the guy!"

But I stay there, blinking idiotically, letting the love of my life think I'm some cheating asshole who would go around making out with him while I'm still attached to some guy who's apparently napping in my room.

"Anyway." Nathan gives me a tight-lipped smile, the kind you give to the overly friendly cashier at Trader Joe's to get them to stop talking. "I'll see you around, Meddy." And with that, he leaves. I melt back inside my room, close the door and lean against it, tears already pooling in my eyes. My chest hurts, like someone's just reached in with an iron fist, shattering my ribs, grabbed my heart, and wrenched it out, but there's nothing I can do to stop Nathan from leaving.

22

Ma finds me curled up on the other bed, crying as if I've just been watching one of her K-dramas.

"Meddy?" She hurries to my side and gives my shoulder a little shake. "Kenapa? What happened? Why you cry?"

I look up and the sight of her round, lined face is too much to bear. A fresh wave of tears bursts out of me and I babble, "I'm sorry, Ma. I'm so sorry." It's all too much, all of it. Ah Guan. Ma and her sisters helping me with Ah Guan without a single word of complaint. And how in truth, I've been plotting to get out of the family business for months.

And, of course, Nathan. How I'd met my soulmate in college, fallen irrevocably in love, and never told Ma about it. It's stupid, but it feels like the biggest betrayal somehow. And now I've lost him again.

"It's just—" I take a breath. "Things have gotten so complicated. And I'm so sorry that I got you into all of this."

She breathes out. "Aiya. Of course I get into all of this." She gestures vaguely in Ah Guan's direction. "I'm your mother. I must protect you."

"But that's just it, Ma. I don't want you to protect me.

You've been doing it this whole time and I'm grateful, but I wish I weren't such a mess, you know? I wish you didn't need to protect me."

Ma gives me a small, sad smile and puts a hand on my cheek, the way she's done ever since I was big enough to remember. "You're not a mess. You just kill by accident only. Bad luck. Can happen to anyone."

That makes me laugh despite everything. "I don't think accidentally killing your date is something that can happen to anyone, Ma." I sigh. "I haven't been honest with you, and with everything that's been happening, I don't know if I'll get the chance to tell you the truth about Nathan, so . . . I want to tell you, Ma. I don't want to keep things from you anymore."

A light dawns on Mama's face, shaving off years and making her look so young and vibrant, I catch a glimpse of her as a twenty-something, full of fire and laughter. "Yes," she says. "Tell me."

Minutes later, we sit on the balcony, cupping hot mugs of tea in our hands.

"I met Nathan the first week of college. It was love at first sight, which I realize is cheesy as hell, but . . . Yeah."

She laughs. "You know, I meet your dad at wedding. He keep smiling, smiling at me, aduh, I was so irritated at him. I said, 'Eh, you look at me for what, ah? Can you stop looking?' and he said, 'I like staring at beauty.' And that's it, BAM, fell in love."

The thought of Papa and Mama being young and in love is a bittersweet one. "How come you can still talk about him so fondly, after everything that's happened?"

"Oh, Meddy. Because I got you. And your papa was very kind in the beginning. Always listen to me, very good man. We try hard to be good to each other. And it didn't work out, but it is okay, we got you, that is good enough."

I reach out and squeeze her hand. It's smooth, smoother than mine, and I remember the feel of it when I was young, stroking my hair as I cried in her lap after getting bullied or failing a test. My mother's always had such smooth hands, but now I see wrinkles and age spots on them too, and the sight is so jarring. When did she get old on me?

"So what happen with this boy?"

I sigh. "Everything. He was my everything, and I guess that's what scared me the most. I was eighteen. I wasn't ready to find my everything yet, you know? And of course there's the family curse."

"What family curse?"

I stare at her. "You know, the one that's taken all the men in our family! You and all the aunties used to mention it when I was a kid. You guys would be like, 'Ah, we are so unlucky, we are cursed to have our husbands leave us.'"

Ma laughs. "You mean family blessing?"

"What?"

"Aiya, we call it curse at first because yes, of course we are sad that our husbands all leave us. But after few years we realize actually, is not a curse. It is family blessing. Because your papa leave me, I become even more close to your aunties. And they become more close to each other too, because they have no husband, no son. And you, they see you as their daughter. It's like you grow up with four mothers. That is blessing, Meddy. We are very blessed, we have close family."

My eyes fill with tears. All these years, I have never seen it that way, but Ma's right. I did grow up with four mothers, and it really has been amazing. There's been so much love in my life that I took for granted.

"You're right, Ma."

"And anyway, it is not curse that take your papa away. We just not work out, it is okay, we move on. And your aunties are the same with your uncles. Maybe at first heart-break, but after a while it is okay. Don't miss out on love because you think we got curse, so silly, you. I thought you are more educated than that."

A laugh bubbles out. My superstitious mother is chastising me for believing in curses. Life could not get weirder.

"That is why you never tell me about this Nathan?"

"Yes and no." I take a deep breath. "The truth is, I was a different person in school than I was at home. I don't really know how to explain it. It's nothing against you or the aunties, it's just—I don't know—"

"You feel more free to figure out who are you."

I stare at her in wonderment. "Yeah. Exactly. How did you—"

"Aiya, you think you are the only one who go to school, is it? I go to college also, I know what you are talking about. At home, I am just Third Sister, no one special, not the oldest, not the youngest. Not the prettiest, not the smartest. But in school, I can be my own person. Not just Third Sister, but me. Natasya."

"Yeah, that's exactly it." All along, she's understood. Of course she has. Like me, she grew up in a huge, close-knit family filled with overbearing relatives. "So I didn't want to take him home at first because of that, and then as we became even closer and he became an even bigger part of my life, I didn't know how to take him home and tell you that we'd been together for more than a year. It felt like such a betrayal to you, and I didn't know how you'd take it. I'm sorry, Ma. I should've had more faith in you."

"Yes, you should have," she says, simply. I steel myself for a tirade of guilt-tripping, but for once, Ma is quiet.

"Anyway, then we graduated, and he got a job offer in New York, and I didn't want to move across the country just to be with him. I don't know. Or maybe I did, and it scared me to hell that I wanted to. That I would give everything up just for him. So I made myself choose something else. Something that would keep us far apart from each other. But I never could move on from him, because I knew he was the one, Ma." And the tears come again, as I admit it out loud for the first time. "He was my one, and it killed me, losing him that first time, and I can't believe I just lost him again."

"Why lose him again?" She frowns in confusion.

A shaky laugh rattles out of me. "He saw Ah Guan's feet and he thought it's my boyfriend, napping in my bed. I couldn't tell him the truth, obviously, so I let him think that."

Ma purses her lips. "Ooh. Bad luck, very bad luck."

"You can say that again."

"So how? Are you going to chase that boy?"

I shake my head. "I don't know that there's anything I can

say to change his mind without telling him the truth. And honestly, I don't want to lie to him. I don't want to make up some crazy story about how it was just my aunt or whatever who was napping—" Of course, once I say that, I get a glimmer of hope, like huh, maybe I *could* tell him that it was one of my many aunties underneath the duvet. But as soon as I imagine myself lying to him, everything inside me shrivels up. I have no desire to do so. I can't stand the thought of having to look him in the eye and feed him false words. "And anyway, I probably shouldn't be getting distracted by—whatever this is."

"Love is a good distraction. Maybe I get my grandbabies soon," Ma says with a grin.

I roll my eyes, but I can't stop the smile from tugging at the corners of my mouth. How does my mom do it, every time? She'll find me in pieces, and somehow, some way, she manages to put me back together. I reach out and squeeze her hand. "Thanks, Ma."

"Aiya, thanks for what?" She waves me off and takes in a sharp little breath. "Ah! I forget to tell you I find this outside. Aduh, you are so careless, how can you forget your own key card?" She digs in her pants pocket and brandishes a plain white card.

I frown as I take it from her. "That's not my key card. I put mine on the table over there." We both look at the table, and sure enough, my key card's lying there. I turn the card Ma found over in my hands. On the other side, in plain letters, are the words MASTER KEY. My breath comes out in a small "Oof."

"It's Nathan's card. He must've dropped it after he opened the door for me. Ugh, I'm gonna have to return this to him somehow." An idea pops into my head. "Right after I use it to return the tea ceremony gifts." I pace the room, working out how and when I should do it. It'll have to be tonight, right after the reception, while everyone is outside watching the fireworks. I'll steal back here, grab the duffel bag, use the key card to open the bridal suite, and put it—somewhere. Maybe under the bride's bed or something, where it wouldn't be found right away, so it gives us more time before Maureen realizes something's gone wrong with her plan.

I go over my plan again, poking and prodding at the details to look for flaws, and yeah, obviously there are flaws, but overall, it's the best plan anyone could come up with given the situation. For the first time since this entire fiasco started, I actually feel kind of good. Yes, there is still a dead body in my bed and a stolen stash of jewelry in my closet, but hey, at least I now have a viable plan to take care of the latter. In no time I will come up with another plan to get rid of the former. Hopefully.

"You think of something?" Ma says.

I turn to her, grinning wide, and am about to tell her my plan to return the stolen jewelry when Ah Guan's phone vibrates. The sound slices through the air, silencing both of us. I don't think either of us even dares to breathe. Our gazes shoot to the phone, buzzing on the table like some great big beetle. Reluctantly, I step closer, still holding my breath, and see Maureen's face on the screen. Argh, great. What now? God, I hope their plan didn't involve them meeting up once he got the duffel bag. I let the call go to voicemail.

Ma gnaws on her lip. "Maybe you can just ignore—"
The phone buzzes with a text.

Maureen [2:02PM]: SOS. Srsly, where tf r u?

SOS. Dread fills my stomach, leaden and hot. This isn't going to be anything good. With a deep breath, I pick up the phone and type out:

Ah Guan [2:04PM]: What is it?

The reply is practically instantaneous.

Maureen [2:04PM]: PICK UP THE PHONE U FUCKER.

Oh god, she's going to call again, isn't she. I quickly type:

Ah Guan [2:04PM]: Can't, w/ ppl right now

Maureen [2:05PM]: Get rid of them! This is an emergency!

Ah Guan [2:05PM]: Just tell me what happened.

Maureen [2:06PM]: Over text? R u high rn?

Right. She can't tell me over text because then it could be used as evidence if things go sideways. Okay. *Think, Meddy.*

Ah Guan [2:08PM]: I'll call in a sec but I won't be able to say much 'cuz ppl around me.

Maureen [2:08PM]: FINE.

"I'm going to call her back. Don't say a word while I'm on the phone with her."

Ma nods, and I take a second to gather myself. Deep breath. Okay. I tap on Maureen's name and call her. She picks up on the first ring.

"Dude, oh my god, things are so bad. I can't even—everything's going wrong!" Her voice is shaky, hoarse with tears.

Instinct kicks me to say something. It feels so wrong just standing here being silent. I opt for a Hugh Jackman as Wolverine grunt. "Hmm."

"They—shit—they found out the stuff's missing!" she hisses.

Oh! Hope soars. Maybe that's good. They'll catch Maureen and—oh. And they'll interrogate her, try to dig for the truth, and what if she spills then? What if she says Ah Guan came and got the stuff, and then they—I don't know, what would they do? Maybe search the entire resort? Would they do that? Who am I kidding? There's easily a couple million dollars' worth of jewelry and fine watches in that duffel bag; of course they would. They'd do anything to get it back. Shut off the island from the mainland. Tell every guest to stay in their room while they methodically go through everybody's room. Oh my god. This is bad. This is really, really bad.

216

"And the heat's on me," Maureen continues. "'Cause I was the last one with the stuff. I can't let them suspect—not her, oh god, I can't—change of plans, you hear me?"

I give my Wolverine grunt again.

"We'll have to pin it on the photographer."

"What?!"

"She was the one who helped carry the boxes back to the room—you sound weird, do you have a cold?"

It takes everything inside me to come up with another grunt.

"Anyway, she helped me carry the boxes back. I can tell them that I was careless, that she was still in the room when I opened the safe. Maybe she saw the safe code or whatever, and then came back later to take the stuff. That's believable, right? It'll buy us enough time. You need to—shit, what are we gonna do with the stuff? You need to put them in the photographer's room and—"

I hang up on her. My heart is racing, my mind shattered. I can barely string together a coherent thought.

"What did she say?" Ma asks, rubbing her elbows, her face lined with worry. She's so concerned she forgets to speak English and switches to Indonesian. "Meddy, you look so scared, what is it?"

I stare at the phone. I stare at Ma. Nothing comes out.

"Meddy!" Ma snaps her fingers. At the same time, the phone vibrates again. I jump, and reality comes rushing back in, like a flood.

I hit Reject, and then send off another text:

Ah Guan [2:11PM]: Can't talk now, but will take care of the stuff. Don't worry.

When I look up again, Ma raises her eyebrows. "Well?"

"They found out that the tea ceremony gifts are missing, and Maureen wants to blame it on me."

When I was five, there was a boy at my kindergarten who was always pulling my hair and pinching me. When Ma complained to the school about it, they laughed and said, "Awww, that's so sweet! Little Bobby has a crush on your daughter. Isn't that the cutest?" Ma rose to her full five feet two inches—even her breasts rose—and she got this look on her face, as if the soul of a warrior had just taken over her features. Mrs. Mallone, my teacher, was still stupidly grinning at her. She didn't even know what was coming. But by the time Ma was done with her tirade, Mrs. Mallone was in tears and had promised to have a talk with Bobby's parents about boundaries.

The expression on Ma's face reminds me of that moment. Everything about her is standing tall and proud and furious.

"That no-good thief wants to frame my daughter?"

It's right at this moment that the door unlocks, and in come all my aunties. They pile in, rubbing their bellies and chatting amicably in Mandarin, but then Big Aunt notices the look on Ma's face.

"What happened?" she says. "Is there trouble?"

"The thief wants to frame Meddy!" Ma cries.

My aunties gasp, shock and anger rippling through them. Big Aunt cries the F-word in Mandarin, Second Aunt immediately launches into some Tai Chi pose that no doubt has some ridiculous name, and Fourth Aunt slides her over-the-top nails across her neck, hissing. I want to hug them all to pieces. They're all so enraged on my behalf.

"We'll fix this," Big Aunt says, and for once, Second Aunt doesn't even come up with a snarky retort. She nods along while crouching into a pose that looks like it should be called something along the lines of Carrying an Extra Large Gourd and says, "Don't worry, Meddy. We'll fix this."

"No."

They all look at me. Ma steps toward me. "Meddy—"

"No, you've all helped me so much. I can handle this one by myself. I know exactly what I have to do. I'm going to get rid of this—" I heave the bag out of the closet. "And then I'll be back for the body."

23

A perk that comes with being one of the core wedding vendors: the wedding planner has shared a Google spreadsheet with me that includes the day's timetable, the phone numbers of everyone important, and a very handy list of everybody's room number.

I do a quick search for Maureen's name, and there she is.

Name: Maureen Halim
Role: Maid of Honor

And thief, the voice in my head snarks snarkily.

Phone number: (626) 526-1755
Room Number: 317

My mouth sets into a grim line and I sling the duffel bag over one shoulder and walk briskly toward the staircase. Level 3. I pop my head out before walking out to the hallway, careful to make sure that there's no one about. Luck's on my side, and I hurry toward room 317. I can't believe I'm doing this. I move fast, too fast to second-guess myself. There's no time for second-guessing anyway, and if I freeze now, if I chicken out, then I'll be caught with a bag full of stolen goods, and what good will that do anyone? So I walk, ignoring all of the panicky voices crowding my head, and before I know it, I'm here. Room 317.

Okay. Shit. Okay. I'm doing this. I really am. A day ago, the worst thing I've ever done was—well, it was probably breaking up with Nathan. And now, I've (1) accidentally killed someone, (2) hidden the dead body, and (3) carried around over two million dollars' worth of stolen goods.

Maureen must be with Jacqueline, so the room should be empty, but just in case, I knock on the door. "Hello?" I call out. "Room service." Wait two seconds. Knock again. Check the hallway once more. No one about. I slide the master key card out of my pocket and tap it against the door lock. A little green light blinks, and the lock opens with a whirr. Here goes nothing. I grab the door handle and go inside Maureen's room.

Maureen's room is a junior suite, with a living room and a separate bedroom. Okay, if I were a dirty, traitorous thief of a maid of honor, where would I hide a bag full of stolen goods that my dirty, traitorous, thieving hands grabbed from my best friend?

Bedroom for sure.

I hurry inside the bedroom and look around. Under the very tall four poster bed? Too obvious. Inside the closet? I open the closet and study it. The shelves go all the way up to the ceiling, which is stupid because no one could reach all the way up there. I can't even see what's on the top shelf—

Which makes it the perfect hiding spot. I grab a chair from the writing desk, drag it across the room, and climb up on top of it. As I straighten up, I wobble and for a terrifying second, almost fall off the chair with the heavy duffel bag, but I manage to grab one of the shelves for balance. I hoist the duffel bag over my head and push it as deep as I can, then hop off the chair. I look up, and with satisfaction, confirm that I can't see the duffel bag from my vantage point. Not even when I go on my tiptoes. The top shelf is way too high.

Just as I finish putting the chair back at the desk, I hear the worst sound in the world. The front-door lock whirring open. A split second later, the door clicks open, and someone bustles in. My mind short-circuits, and for a precious moment, I just stand there, frozen, like a hamster who knows it's about to get spotted by the hawk. Then my instincts kick in and I hurry—but where to? I look around me frantically. The closet I just hid the bag in? No, it's filled with shimmery dresses and it's likely that Maureen might need something from it. The bathroom? The—

The bed!

I leap onto the floor on the far side of the room just as the bedroom door is flung open. I lie down on the carpeted floor and as the person walks in, I roll under the bed. Luckily, Maureen is apparently too distraught to hear any small noises I make as I slither under the bed. She's sniffling loudly, her breath coming in shallow gasps. The bed creaks and sags slightly as she sits down and sobs. What the hell is going on? If I didn't know Maureen was a dirty thieving liar, I would be feeling really bad for her right now. In fact, I *am* feeling bad for her. I don't think it's humanly possible to listen to those sobs and not feel the tiniest bit bad.

As silently as I can, I pull Ah Guan's phone out of my pocket and switch it to Silent mode. Just in case she—

And just as I think that, she does call him. Thank god for prescience. I clasp the phone to my chest, unable to bear watching her face coming up on the screen. When it goes to voicemail, Maureen utters a little cry and flings her phone across the room, where it hits the wall and thunks onto the floor. Uh-oh.

This is where she goes to pick it up and notices a whole other human in the room with her.

But she doesn't. She just stays there, crying for what feels like an entire hour but is in fact only two minutes. I know, because I stare at Ah Guan's phone the whole time. Then she goes to the bathroom, probably to wash her face. Should I take this chance to leave? But even as I think that, Maureen comes out of the bathroom and swipes her phone from the floor. I freeze, but she doesn't spot me. Her feet remain there for a while, unmoving, and I'm wondering what the heck she's doing when I realize she's either making a call or typing a text message. Sure enough, when I check Ah Guan's phone, there's a new text.

Maureen [2:15PM]: Don't know y ur not picking up the phone, but everything better be ready. I'm gonna ask them to check the photographer's room.

Check the photographer's room. The photographer's

room. THE PHOTOGRAPHER'S ROOM WHERE AH GUAN'S CORPSE IS. Every single cell in my body shatters into panicky shrieks, and it takes all of my will to stop myself from leaping out from under the bed and choking her. Somehow, I manage to stay still until she leaves the bedroom. Moments later, I hear the front door slam shut. I slide out from under the bed immediately and call Ma. One ring. Two rings. Come on, Ma.

"Hallo?"

Thank. God. I have never been so grateful to hear her voice in my life. "Ma, are you still in my room?"

"Iya, of course. I cut mangoes and make more tea, your aunties all eating—"

Mangoes? Where did she get—never mind. I shake my head. "Ma, listen, you guys need to get rid of the body now. Maureen's going to tell them to search my room for the tea ceremony gifts. I'll come back—" My phone beeps with an incoming call. It's Jacqueline. Shit. Maureen's even faster than I thought. "I can't come back. I'm being called by the bride, probably to go to her room."

"Okay, no worry, we will get rid of body, no problem. You go to bride's room, you settle everything, we settle body, no worry."

"Okay . . ." She's sounding very confident for someone who's just been told at the last minute to hide a whole human corpse. "Um, where are you going to take him?"

"Aiya, you don't worry, we got plan. Okay bye-bye, we going to hide Ah Guan now, okay, bye, love you, bye."

The call cuts off and I accept Jacqueline's incoming call.

"Hello? Meddelin?" Her voice is frantic, the edges all shrill and brittle, ready to break. "Could you—um, could you come to my room now? Please?"

"Hey, yeah, sure." I swallow and say, "Everything okay?"

"Uh-huh!" she says, even shriller than before. "Just come to my room now, okay?"

I close my eyes, my stomach plummeting. So Maureen's really gone through with it. Jacqueline is probably being falsely cheerful to make sure I don't get scared away. "I'll be right there."

"Great!"

Deep breath. Even though I've gotten rid of the stolen goods, as I sneak out of Maureen's room and walk down the hallway toward the bridal suite, I can't help feeling like I'm walking straight into a trap. Outside the bridal suite, I pause to gather myself. My breath keeps catching, and then I have to focus to keep inhaling and exhaling. *Remember, you don't actually know that there's anything wrong.* Right. For all I know, I'm here to do the family portrait or whatever. Cool. I grasp my camera protectively and nearly drop it, my palms are so sweaty. I wipe them on my pants and knock at the door.

The bridal suite is filled with people, except this time the people aren't wispy bridesmaids dressed in pastels but stern-looking men in security uniforms. One of these stern-looking men opens the door, and glares down at me as I walk in, making me feel once again like a hamster, this time crawling into a hawk's nest.

I smile up at him and say, "Hi, I'm here for the family portraits." I wave my camera up at him.

His upper lip curls up in contempt, and he takes my arm. I look at his meaty hand on my upper arm. I look back at him.

"Could you not do that?" I try to pull my arm away, but he only tightens his grip.

"Don't think you can sneak away, thief—"

"Rob!" Nathan strides out of the bedroom and hurries toward us. "Stop that. Let her go."

"But, sir, she's the—"

"We don't know anything yet," Nathan says. His voice turns low and dangerous, his eyes narrowing at the security guard. "Let go of her arm."

With one last scowl at me, Rob releases my arm. I rub at it gingerly. I swear my entire head is on fire. I've never been manhandled like that before. It happened so fast.

"Meddy, glad you're here," Nathan says. "I'm sorry about Rob."

"What's going on?" I follow him to one side, away from the crowd of security guards stomping all over the beautiful living room. "Where are all the bridesmaids?"

"They've been asked to go back to their rooms. The bride didn't want them finding out."

"Finding out about what?"

Nathan exhales. "The tea ceremony gifts—all those watches and jewelry and cash—have gone missing."

I manage a small gasp. Let my mouth drop open, my eyes widen, my brows rise. Do I look genuinely surprised?

Nathan takes my hand, seems to remember where we are, and drops it. With another sigh, he says, "And the maid of honor claims you were the one who took them."

"What?" Am I hitting the right mix of shock and anger? Should I even be angry? Or just shocked? God, I am so bad at this. I need to stop second-guessing myself. Yes, I should definitely be mad. "Why would she think that?"

He shakes his head. "She says you were the one helping her carry the box back to the room and you saw the safe code." He lowers his voice. "Look, Meddy, obviously I don't believe a word of it, I mean, Christ. But she's pushing for them to search your room, and I need to follow protocol—"

"I understand," I say, quickly. It pains me to see his face so tortured. It's obvious he hates himself for having to tell me these things. "It's totally fine. I'm okay with my room being checked." As long as my mom and aunts manage to get the body out beforehand. I should probably give them more time.

"Are you sure?" Nathan's eyes search mine, and his are filled with so many unspoken things. Worry, anger, but most of all, need. Seeing it sparks the need churning deep inside me, and god, I can't believe we're here in this moment and I can't even touch him because of all these damn security guards. Well, and the thieving accusation against me. Keep it in your pants, Meddy. Now is so not the time. I tear my gaze away.

"Yeah, I'm sure."

"Right. Let's go inside."

I steel myself as Nathan leads me into the master bedroom. Inside, it's worse than I imagined. Or rather, it's just as I imagined, but worse because now it's real. I'm actually standing here, witnessing the fallout of Maureen's crime.

Jacqueline is sitting at the foot of the bed in a fluffy haze of white silk and ruffles, and she's crying. Maureen sits next to her, a protective arm around Jacqueline's pale shoulders, handing her more tissues. Tom's furiously tapping on his phone at the bay window, and both sets of parents are there. Mr. Sutopo is snapping at someone on the phone, and Mrs. Sutopo is snapping at someone else on her phone, and Jacqueline's parents are arguing with each other—"You should've come in here to make sure everything's fine after the tea ceremony." "Me? YOU should've done that! What were you doing?"

It's complete and utter chaos, and everything inside me squeaks to run the hell out. But Nathan's hand is on my back, and as if he can read my thoughts, he gives me a reassuring pat.

At that moment, Jacqueline glances up. "Meddy!" she cries, standing up in a rush. She trips over her dress and would have fallen if Maureen hadn't caught her. Maureen shoots me a glare as Jacqueline hurries over and clasps my hands. Her hands are cold and trembly.

"Meddy," she says, her gaze boring into mine. "Meddy, Meddy, please tell me the truth—" Her voice breaks in a sob.

Mr. Sutopo strides toward us and shouts, "There's the thief!"

"No!" Nathan says. "Calm down please, everybody. Let's hear what Meddy—Meddelin has to say."

The room goes silent, all eyes on me. Jacqueline takes in a shaky breath and says in a broken whisper, "Did you take the tea ceremony gifts?"

"No." The word slides out easily.

The room collapses in a collective sigh, then everyone reacts at the same time.

Maureen: "She's lying!"

Mr. Sutopo: "Of course she'd say that."

Tom: "Come on, let's just call the cops."

Jacqueline stares at me through her tears. "Really? They've gone missing, Meddy, and I don't know—"

"I didn't take them." My voice comes out solid. I squeeze her hands, hoping to give myself strength, and then let my gaze travel to Maureen. "She was the last one with them. I only helped to bring them here, but I left them with her." It's a strange thing, accusing someone else of a crime. Even though I know for a fact that Maureen was the culprit, even though she wants to frame me for it, it still doesn't feel great. I don't feel vindicated or anything; I just feel shitty. My insides squirm as if they're trying to crawl out of my skin, especially when Jacqueline utters a choked sob and glances at Maureen. The look on Maureen's face is equal parts fear, anger, and something else I can't quite put my finger on, but it's painful to see.

"It wasn't me," Maureen cries. "C'mon, Jackie O, you know me, I would never! Search her room; she's probably stashed them there."

Jacqueline turns back toward me, her expression apologetic but desperate. "I—is that okay, Meddy? I hate to do it, but . . ."

I lift my chin and meet her gaze. "That's fine. I've got nothing to hide." Aside from the dead body, that is, but I'm counting on my family to take care of that part.

24

The whole entourage marches out of the bridal suite, making the spacious corridor seem cramped. Leading the charge are Tom and his dad, followed by the security team, followed by Jacqueline and Maureen, the latter's arm still wrapped tightly around the former's shoulders. Nathan and I follow behind everybody. I don't even know how to process this mess of emotions raging inside me. Anxiety, stress, and anger, and of course there's that familiar thread of whatever it is I still feel for Nathan. I ache to reach for his hand, feel the warmth of his fingers around mine. I want to fall into his arms and have him crush me in a strong embrace. But I don't do either of these things. I keep my gaze straight and my chin up, and I follow the crowd of people who seem intent on having my head on a spike.

As we pass by the groom's suite, the door slides open ever so slightly, and I almost do a double take when I see Fourth Aunt's face behind the door, peeping out. She spots me and retreats into the room. I resume walking, my mind whirring madly. What's going on? Why's she in the groom's suite?

What does it mean? Are we about to find Ah Guan's body still cooling in my bed? Oh my god!

I take my phone out, but there are no messages. Nothing. I'm about to send a text to Ma when I realize it'll make me seem more suspicious. Plus, what if they check my phone and see that I've sent a message asking if "the thing has been moved"? Then they'd assume I'm talking about the stolen goods.

"I'm so sorry about this," Nathan murmurs.

I stuff the phone back into my pocket and mutter, "Don't worry about it." My voice comes out as though from afar. I barely recognize the sound. When we get to my room, one of the security guards glances back at Nathan, who nods with a sigh. The guard takes out a master key card and swipes it across the door lock. There's the familiar whirr of the lock, and he opens the door with what seems like an unnecessary flourish.

This is it. The moment of truth. I step forward, but my legs have turned to water and they buckle. I've never lost control of my body like this before. Nathan's arm shoots out, and I grab it.

"You okay?"

I nod. "Just tripped over the carpet." Come on, insides. I imagine them turning to iron. To steel. But then I see all these people barging into my tiny room, my little room with the dead body inside, and my muscles go all papery again. I can't go inside. I can't. "I'll just wait out here. Seems pretty crowded in there." At least my voice comes out somewhat normal-ish.

Nathan nods and I hold on to his arm, so reassuringly solid and strong, the muscles underneath his shirt tight under my palm. He leads me to the wall and I lean against it, hoping I look relaxed instead of floppy. He reaches forward, as though about to brush a stray strand of hair away from my face, but stops at the last second.

"Nathan, I—"

A fire burns bright in his eyes, and he takes another step toward me. "Yeah?"

I what? My voice trails off. I love you? I haven't stopped thinking about you since college? I have a corpse inside my room that you thought was my boyfriend but actually is just some dude I killed last night? I shake my head. "Nothing."

The light dies away, leaving his face slack with disappointment. Guilt scratches away at me. But any moment now, those people inside my room are going to wonder why the strange man in my bed isn't waking up with all the noise around him, and then—

"I'll go in and hurry them along." He strides into my room before I can answer.

I stay put, squeezing my eyes tight, hoping that my aunts and mother came through. Footsteps rush out, and my eyelids fly open. Maureen's right in front of me, her face flushed, chest heaving.

"You've hidden them somewhere. You must've stashed them—" I can't help but flinch away from the incandescent rage. "Where did you hide them?" she says.

In a flash, Nathan's behind her, taking her by the shoulder and arm and pulling her away from me. "That's enough," he says, and his voice, though low, has a dangerous tone to it that silences everyone, even Maureen. "We've encroached on Meddelin's privacy without any concrete cause and we've found nothing."

Nothing. I swallow the huge lump in my throat, concentrating on not crying uncontrollably. They found nothing. Ma and the aunties have managed to get rid of the body in time after all.

"But she must've hidden them somewhere else!" Maureen cries. "Aren't the rest of the vendors her family members? Maybe we should search their rooms too!"

Tom frowns. "True—"

"No." The expression on Nathan's face makes me think of a tumultuous sea. "We've done enough. And you should be apologizing to Meddelin."

"Apologize to her?" Maureen cries, shrilly. She looks so shocked that something inside me breaks then.

And I'm suddenly filled with rage. Overflowing, really. She's taken the gifts meant for her best friend and tried to have them planted in my room when she thought she was about to be found out. She is not in a position to judge me.

When I speak, the words come out as firm as a fist. "I think we should check *your* room now, Maureen."

Everybody falls quiet, all eyes crawling over to Maureen.

"But—" Whatever else Maureen was about to say trails away. She's staring at me, and I don't know what it is, but she must've spotted something in my expression, something that gives it away. Her eyes go wide with shock, and her mouth closes quietly. For the first time, I see it plain as day, written across her face. Fear.

She knows I've done something to thwart her plans.

And with her shock, her mask slips, just a little, and Jacqueline knows her best friend well enough to understand what's just happened. Her pale shoulders stop trembling, and she stares at Maureen. Then, quiet as a feather landing in the snow, Jacqueline says, "You were the last one with the gifts." So quiet, but impossible to ignore.

"No, Jackie, I swear—"

Jacqueline turns to Nathan and says, still in that painfully quiet voice, "I'd like to see her room, please."

Nathan gives a somber nod.

"No!" Maureen cries, but it's too late. The entourage turns like the tide, unstoppable, and before I even register it, we're marching down the hallway again, with Maureen stumbling after us, pleading with us to stop.

This doesn't feel good. It's definitely not something I want to celebrate, but I guess it's necessary. And when we get to room 317, I almost want to shout at them to stop, to turn around. But I stand back and let them open the door while Maureen goes back and forth between saying, "You know you won't find anything, god, what a waste of time" to "She must've done something, she must've arranged for something—" And I feel sick to my stomach.

I want to wait outside like before, but I don't want to be left alone with Maureen, so I follow everyone. Back in her room once again. I stay just inside the doorway, next to the bathroom door, as the security guards go through the room.

They're being respectful, probably because their boss is here, but still it feels like such a breach of privacy. An invasion. I understand the word now. All these burly men going through the beautiful hotel room, turning over every cushion, opening every cupboard. I imagine them riffling through Maureen's luggage, their hands sorting through her underwear, and it makes me feel ill.

"Make them stop," Maureen begs Jacqueline.

Jacqueline turns away from her, eyes downcast, and Maureen goes to Nathan. "You can't do this. I don't give my consent!"

"I'm sorry," he says, and I can see he's struggling too. He's not enjoying this, not one bit.

Tom's striding everywhere, peering over the guards' shoulders and snapping orders at them to look harder and faster. He actually says, "Look harder and faster," as if it makes one bit of goddamn sense. His eyes are alight. He looks more alive than I've seen him so far. He's not liking this; he's loving it. I decide then that I despise him. Jacqueline shouldn't be with someone so abrasive and entitled. She has a sweet disposition, whereas Tom is everything but sweet. Over time, he'll wear her down, strip her of her gentleness until only resentment remains, hard and sharp-edged.

Someone inside the bedroom shouts, "Found it!" I close my eyes, everything inside me sinking. That's it.

It's as though a gun's been fired. Everybody shoots up to attention, and the atmosphere is electric. The guard rushes out of the bedroom carrying the duffel bag, and Tom and his father rush over, grabbing it from him. Or trying to, at least. The guard barks, "Get back, please, sir," until Nathan holds out his hand and tells the overzealous guard it's okay. The bag is handed over to Mr. Sutopo, who rips it open.

Jewelry spills out like glittering intestines. It looks obscene somehow. I turn away as everyone gasps. Jacqueline utters a half-sob, half-sigh.

"No," Maureen moans. "No, this can't be. I need to—I—" She fumbles with her phone, but Tom grabs it from her. "Give it back!"

"I think this counts as evidence," he crows.

Nathan frowns. He obviously dislikes Tom as much as I do, but I don't know if Tom's right. Does her phone count as evidence? Nathan holds out his hand. "Please give me the phone. We'll hold it in our safe room, and we won't go through anything until we can get the authorities here." Reluctantly, Tom does as he's told.

"Thank god we got these back," Mrs. Sutopo says, bending over and stroking the pile of jewelry as if it's a baby.

Jacqueline shakes her head and whispers to Maureen, "How could you?"

I didn't think Maureen could look any worse, but when Jacqueline says that, Maureen's face crumples.

"I didn't mean to—I just—"

Nathan places a hand on Maureen's shoulder. "I think it's best if you don't say anything else for now. Let's go to my office." His tone is reassuring but firm, and I realize then that he's trying to help her. My chest tightens painfully. I want to reach out and touch him, thank him for showing some compassion.

"Your office?" Tom says, with a sneer. "You can't be serious. This isn't your problem anymore, it's a criminal offense. I'm calling the cops."

"No!"

Everyone stops and looks around in obvious confusion. Maureen and Jacqueline both shouted it at the same time.

"Babe," Tom says, taking Jacqueline's hand, "you don't understand—"

"I do," she says quietly. "And I don't want to press charges."

Maureen sucks in a breathy gasp. "Thank you—"

"Okay, that's just crazy talk." Tom lets go of Jacqueline's hand and does this totally humorless laugh. "I mean, I know she's your friend or whatever, but she *stole* from us."

"And our friendship is over because of it. But we've found the gifts now, and I just want to move past it, put it behind us."

Tom snorts, an ugly sound. "Okay, babe, I don't think you're thinking straight right now. Maybe you're all confused 'cause it's the wedding day, but this is a serious crime."

"We found the gifts! What more do you want?" Jacqueline snaps.

"Well, you know what? I hate to say this, but the gifts were mostly from my relatives, so I think I get to decide what happens to the thief who tried to steal them."

"What?" The word comes out poisonous. I'm pretty sure no one in the room is breathing, and honestly, wow. Tom Cruise Sutopo, going even lower than the very low bar I set for him.

He must have felt the tide turning against him, because he sputters, hesitates before he decides to push on. "I just mean—ugh, Pa, help me out here. Talk some sense into her!"

Mr. Sutopo takes a few steps forward and places a hand on his son's arm. "Come on, son. I think it's best to let it go."

"Yes," Mrs. Sutopo says, "like we always tell you, whenever possible, choose to be generous. So be generous now." She turns to Nathan and says, "Thank you, the matter is done. We won't be pressing charges."

Nathan nods, ignoring the wail of complaint from Tom.

"Thank you, Jackie," Maureen sobs. "I'm so sorry—"

"I want you to leave," Jacqueline says, still in that very calm voice. "I don't want to see you ever again. Is that okay?" she asks Nathan. "Is there a yacht available?"

"I'll make arrangements." Nathan nods at one of the guards, who escorts Maureen, still weeping, out of the room. "I'm sorry for all the trouble. Is there anything else I can do for you?"

Jacqueline shakes her head, and we all leave the room, deep in our own troubled thoughts.

25

Outside, Jacqueline's mom checks her watch and says, "Oh my god, it's almost time for the ceremony."

"But what about the family portraits?" Mr. Sutopo says.

"No time. We can do them after the ceremony, maybe?" Mrs. Sutopo gives me a questioning glance, and I nod.

"Yeah, definitely, we can squeeze them in then," I say in the most reassuring tone of voice I can manage.

"I just got a storm warning headed our way," Mr. Sutopo says, looking at his phone. "I hope it doesn't hit us during the ceremony. That'll be a bit of bad luck, eh?"

"It'll be fine," Nathan says, quickly. "We've got the ball-room set up in case it starts to rain."

"Good. Okay, we need to go and touch up your makeup for the ceremony," Jacqueline's mom says. "Meddelin, can you call your auntie and ask her to meet us at the bridal suite?"

"Sure." I take out my phone and dial Second Aunt's number while everybody else rushes off to prep for the ceremony. Why's she taking so long to pick up?

Noise floods through the receiver. "Hallo? Meddy?" Second Aunt's practically shouting.

"Second Aunt? Where are you?"

"Aduh, Meddy. Got a bit problem."

Oh no. My chest tightens, and my free hand clenches into a fist. No, whatever it is, please don't let it be too, too bad. I've just handled one crisis, can't I have a break? It's a struggle to keep my voice level. "What is it?"

"Ummm. Well, you see. Well. Hard to explain whose fault, you know? Because nobody telling anybody what anybody do, so then everybody doing everything."

"Second Aunt, you're killing me. Please just tell me what's happened."

"Well, hmmm. Hard to explain."

Could I be any more frustrated? Pretty sure I'm so freaking anxious and annoyed right now I could choke a horse. Though I wouldn't. But I could. "Second Aunt!"

"Well, no matter, nothing can do. What you call me for?"

I shake my head a little, trying to clear it of the angry fog. Deep breaths. Inhale. Exhale. Focus on the wedding, on poor Jacqueline. And anyway, I can always ask Ma what the hell's going on. Ma can never keep a secret from me. "The bride needs you to touch up her makeup before the ceremony."

"Ah, okay! I go there now."

As soon as she hangs up, I scroll through my contacts to dial Ma's number, but someone clears his throat, interrupting me.

"Nathan!" Oh no, how long has he been there? What has he heard? What have I said?

"Sorry, I didn't mean to startle you."

"Ha, no, you didn't." He did. "Can you I help?"

"What?" He frowns.

I wince. This is what happens when I try to speak while frantically rifling through my conversation with Second Aunt for anything incriminating. "Sorry, I meant, did you need something?" Did that come out too brusque?

"Um. I wanted to apologize for——" Nathan gestures around him with a sigh. "You know. Everything that just happened. I tried to dissuade them from searching your room. I know that was a real intrusion."

Everything inside me melts. "Thank you for saying that. I know you did everything you could. But it's okay, I didn't mind, and it all got sorted out in the end, so." I love you. I'm still in love with you. *FOCUS*. Sweet as he's being, I can't let myself get too distracted right now. I need to call Ma and find out what's going on. "Anyway——"

"Where's your boyfriend right now?"

"My what now?"

Nathan takes a deep breath, obviously trying not to show that he's feeling a bit hurt by whatever he's about to say. "Your boyfriend? The guy who was in your room before."

Everything that just melted inside me moments ago freezes into sharp points. Shit. Step. Carefully. "Oh, um, he went for a walk around the resort," I say, weakly. Oh god, he must think I'm the biggest asshole ever, having kissed him twice and then telling him I have a boyfriend. Argh!

"Really. That's . . . interesting." His handsome face is unreadable. "Only I took a look at the yacht passenger list, and he's not listed as a passenger when you came to the island."

"That's—yeah. Uh huh." Think! Quickly! "That's because he's actually one of the staff members?" I blurt out. My mind struggles to keep up with my mouth, going over the words. That's actually not a bad idea. "Yeah, he's actually not my boyfriend, he's sort of a one-night stand. Or a one-morning stand, if you will." I give what sounds like the world's fakest laugh.

"So one of my staff members left his post to have a—a thing with you, and then took a nap in your room? I've gotta tell you, as his employer, I'm not very pleased to hear that."

Can this possibly get any worse? "I don't want to get anyone in trouble," I warble. "I just—he wasn't asleep for very long, we'd just—you know."

Nathan sighs, his broad shoulders sagging a tad. "I know. I'm probably just letting my jealousy get in the way. Honestly, it's fine. You're both consenting adults. It's been a bit of a day, that's all."

"I'm so sorry." And oh, how I mean every word of that. I can't even describe just how sorry I am about every-thing.

A small smile flickers across his face, turning it into the Nathan I know and love. If I could just reach out and kiss him. "No, don't apologize. It's okay. The crisis is over. I should go. Make sure everything's running smoothly for the cere-mony."

"Right, yeah. I'll see you around."

"See you, Meddy."

Just the sound of my name coming out in that low, rich tone is enough to send a shiver down my spine. I watch him leave, and then I shake my head to clear it once more. I've been doing a lot of that today. It's hard for my mind to keep up with all the crazy that's going on today. I take out my phone once more and call Ma.

"Hallo, Meddy?" In the background, people are hooting and laughing loudly.

"Ma, what's going on?"

"Got small problem. Very small." Something crashes and breaks from her end. It sounds large.

"What's happening?"

"Aduh, is your Fourth Aunt, lah, she never tell anyone, she just come here, she give them that drink, you know, abstinence?"

"Abstinence?" For a blissful second, I'm confused. Then the penny drops, and horror floods in. "Absinthe? She gave who absinthe?"

"All of—ah!"

"Ma?"

"Do not listen to your mom."

"Is this—Fourth Aunt? Is that you?"

"Yes, of course, who else would it be?"

"Please tell me what's going on. Who did you give absinthe to?"

"Okay, that's not exactly true. I mean, yes, I did bring some absinthe, but your mother brought her usual Chinese medicine crap," she hisses, her voice coming out triumphant. I can practically see her and Ma glaring each other to death. Something else crashes behind her and she yells, "Hey! Stop it! Animals."

244

"Her Chinese medicine crap," I echo. "I don't understand—"

"Well, it's not actually a bad thing, I guess. Look, don't worry too much, it's for the best."

An alarm goes off, and it's not just the ones going nuts in my head. I look at my phone. Shit. It's the alert for me to be at the pool for the ceremony.

"I've got to go. Please—" Please what? "I've got to go." I hang up and rush off to Jacqueline's room.

As always, it's in chaos, though now the burly guards have been replaced once again with the bridesmaids. Jacqueline's makeup has been retouched and she looks flawless, no traces of the ugly incident with Maureen on her face except for the tiny tremor that flickers across her chin once in a while. When she sees me, she smiles. "Girls, can I have a minute with Meddy, please?"

Second Aunt, who's fluttering around Jacqueline, adding little invisible finishing touches to her hairdo, glances at me and gives me a look. I have no idea what the look is supposed to convey. I'm dying to pull her aside and shake her until she tells me what's going on, but instead, I watch her leave the bedroom with the bridesmaids.

Once they're all gone, Jacqueline sighs. "Meddy, I'm so, so sorry."

"What—why?"

"The whole thing about the tea ceremony gifts and searching your room! I feel awful about it."

"Ah, right. Yeah, no, don't worry about that, please. I'm just sorry that you had to go through all that stressful stuff."

She clasps my hands. "I just—Maureen was so sure that you'd taken it. I still can't believe she did that." A choked sob escapes, and she looks up at the ceiling and blinks furiously to stop her tears from falling. I grab a piece of paper from the table and fan at her face. "She's my best friend, has been for over ten years. I still can't—" Her eyes glisten, the tears threatening to drop and ruin all of Second Aunt's hard work.

"It's okay," I say, hurriedly. "Let's not think about that right now. You'll have all the time in the world after the wedding to go over everything."

"I couldn't even tell any of my friends because they're all my bridesmaids and Tom said if any of them knew, we'd lose face, because it shows that I was stupid enough to get duped by my own maid of honor, so I've just been sitting here, dying to talk to someone about it, someone who understands—"

"I get it. But you're not stupid." Seriously, Tom? What the actual fuck? "You really aren't. Nobody saw it coming."

She sniffles. "Thank you."

"You look so radiant. Your pictures are going to turn out beautifully."

"Really?" She brightens a little.

"Yeah. Easily the most beautiful bride I've photographed. And definitely my favorite client. Well, top five anyway."

She laughs. "Top five? Not even top three?"

I wrinkle my nose. "Maybe top ten." We grin at each other, then I help her up, brushing lint off the front of her poufy dress. "You're a vision." I check my phone for the time. "I've gotta take position at the venue. I'll see you there, Jacqueline.

You'll be amazing." I give her hands another squeeze before leaving.

In the living room of the bridal suite, I look around for Second Aunt, but she's nowhere to be found. Damn it. I rush down the hallway, into the open air, and revel in the fresh ocean breeze. The wedding ceremony has been arranged to take place on the water. Literally on the water; the resort is built in the shape of a semicircle, with the huge, sprawling building gently curving around a giant infinity pool. A stage has been built right on top of the pool, so it looks like it's floating. Rows upon rows of flowers adorn the sides of the aisle, and bowls of flowers with lanterns in the middle float serenely on the pool's surface. The whole setup is breathtaking.

There are two thousand seats set up around the infinity pool, and they're all full. Ironically, two thousand is on the smaller side for a Chinese-Indonesian wedding. In Jakarta, the average middle-class wedding would have over three thousand attendees. The guests look happy, which is a relief; I suppose none of them knows of the mishaps that have happened behind the scenes. For all they know, this amazing wedding is going off without a hitch. I look around for Ma and my aunts, but they're nowhere to be seen. Seb waves to me from a distance, and I give him a thumbs-up. He'll be covering the whole ceremony from afar with his 18-200mm. Taking a deep breath, I attach my 35mm lens to my first camera and the 24-70mm lens to my second camera and get to work, capturing pictures of the entire scene as well as close-ups of as many details as I can get without being too obtrusive.

Then the music begins and the MC's voice booms out over the speakers.

"Ladies and gentlemen, please stand to greet the parents of the groom!"

Tiffany chairs scrape back as the guests get to their feet.

"Mr. and Mrs. Sutopo, everyone!" the MC says, as Tom's parents walk down the aisle, smiling and waving to their family and friends. I nimbly step to one side of the aisle, making sure not to fall into the swimming pool, and take pictures of them.

"Behind them are the groomsmen. Let's give them a round of—um."

I'm adjusting my shutter speed when the MC's faltering voice catches my attention, and I look up to see the first groomsman turn the corner and walk down the aisle. Or rather, lurch down the aisle. He's visibly stumbling, his shirt half untucked. My insides cramp up sickeningly. The second groomsman isn't faring any better, and neither is the third.

"A round of applause for the groomsmen, everyone!" the MC's voice comes again, a tone of uneasiness in it.

Lukewarm clapping starts up, and then murmurs start as the fourth and fifth groomsmen stumble down the aisle drunkenly, laughing, their arms around each other. The MC keeps up a cheerful chatter, trying to drown out the murmur, and then the sixth, seventh, and eighth groomsmen come out, and it's even worse because one of them is so drunk that he's unable to stay on his feet; the other two guys are practically carrying him, the points of his shoes trailing across the carpet of fake petals. The rest of the groomsmen file in rowdily, hooting and swaying at the now silent crowd.

I have no idea what to do aside from continue taking pictures of them. I suppose, for once, this isn't my problem to fix, which is a nice thought to—

Oh.

My.

God.

As the groomsmen take their place at the altar, I'm now close enough to see that the eighth groomsman, the one that I thought was too drunk to walk, the one who was being carried by the others . . .

The eighth groomsman is Ah Guan.

PART 3

GIRL GETS BOY

(Or tries to, anyway. It's tricky because there's a corpse and everything.)

26

I won't scream. I won't. This is fine. It's absolutely not a problem. Yep. I can handle this. Who can't handle a little problem like a fucking corpse propped up on the altar like some macabre puppet in front of two thousand people?

I am totally fine. Toh-tah-lee.

I think I'm going to throw up. Or faint. Or spontaneously combust. What the hell is going on? Why did they bring him out?

I study the two groomsmen propping Ah Guan up. Since I'm only a few feet away from them, I can see that behind their sunglasses, they're drunk AF. All twelve of the groomsmen are. They're all swaying on their feet and giggling and pointing in random directions, and none of them seems to know what the hell's going on. Can absinthe have such a dramatic effect on people? Just how much did Fourth Aunt give them?

Sweat trickles down the back of my neck. I need to do something. These guys aren't going to stay on their feet for long, and once they go down, there's no telling what'll happen with Ah Guan's body. I look around and try to catch the wedding planner's eye without calling too much attention to myself, but it's useless; she's behind the crowd, overseeing her various staff members, probably coordinating the bridal party's entrance in time with the music.

"And now, here he is," the MC booms, getting back into his rhythm after the interruption of the groomsmen, "the man of the hour, the handsome groom, Tom Cruuuuise Sutopo!"

Snapping out of my panic, I raise my camera and capture the moment as Tom swaggers down the aisle with a smug smile. Each time I press the trigger to take a photo, I want to laugh hysterically. Why am I still bothering to do my job? There is a literal corpse on the altar! Things can't possibly get any worse than they are right now. Still, somehow, through my panic, I keep taking photo after photo, even adjusting the shutter speed in between pictures. Here's Tom looking smug; here's another of Tom looking even smugger; here's yet another one of Tom, looking nice in his suit but also smug. And the whole time, Ah Guan's body is only a few feet away from me. It's as though I can feel the coldness of his aura creeping up my back. I have to keep stopping myself from turning around and looking at him.

As Tom nears the altar, his smile wavers. Ah. He's spotted his groomsmen. He tries his best to keep the smirk on his face, but his eyes flash as he takes in their rumpled tuxedos, their sunglasses, and their unsteadiness. He takes his spot next to them.

"What the fuck, guys?" he says, his lips still stretched in a fake smile. "Seriously, what the fuck?"

The groomsman next to Tom turns to stare at him, mouth agape. It takes a few moments before his brain apparently catches up and he says, "Whur?"

"Unfuckingbelievable," Tom mutters. "You guys are in so much trouble."

I swallow. Tom's only separated from Ah Guan's body by seven groomsmen. He's so close to him. When he leans forward to look down the scraggly line of groomsmen, my heart squeezes like a fist and I very nearly pass out. But all Tom does is sneer and shake his head at them before straightening back up.

The music winds down to a pause and the MC says, "And now, ladies and gentlemen, let's welcome the bridal party!" Pachelbel's Canon in D Major starts playing, and the first bridesmaid comes out.

With all eyes on her, I'm the only one who spots the first groomsman's head bobbing down slowly before jerking back up. Oh no. He looks like he's about to fall asleep.

I inch closer to Tom. When I'm within whispering distance, I say, "Tom, I think we need to dismiss your groomsmen."

He glances at me like I'm an irritating fly, and scoffs. "Right, and be groomsmen-less on my ceremony like some fucking loser? Not happening."

"Look at them. They can barely stay on their feet." I nod toward the groomsmen, at least three of whom are swaying more dramatically. Shit, one of them's holding Ah Guan up. If he falls . . . "If they fall over, it'll make such a huge scene," I hiss, my voice rising with panic. "It'll ruin everything!" Like my life, for example.

A flicker of uncertainty crosses Tom's face, but then he lifts his chin, his jaw working into a stubborn clench, and says, "If they fall over, I'm gonna sue the shit out of them."

"Sue them?" How does his twisted little mind even work? Sue his own friends? I mean, sure, from his point of view, his friends have let him down majorly, but still, that's not a good reason to let this go on and ruin his own wedding. Talk about cutting off your own nose to spite your face. Also, with a twist of guilt in my guts, it hits me that it's not even really the groomsmen's fault. Fourth Aunt was the one who got them drunk out of their minds. I need to fix this, but how? I take out my phone and dial the WP's number.

"A round of applause for our gorgeous bridesmaids," the MC announces, his voice dripping with obvious relief that none of the bridesmaids, so far, seem drunk.

"Hello? Meddelin?" the wedding planner says. "What is it? Aren't you on duty—"

"We need to get these groomsmen off the stage."

She sighs. "Yeah, they seem really drunk, the shit-heads. I don't know how we can do that without stopping everything, though."

The fourth bridesmaid's already walking down the aisle. I'm running out of time.

"Ask the MC to announce it, make it seem like it was the plan all along to have just the bride and groom on stage. Have him be like, 'And now the bridal party will leave so the groom and the bride can have the stage to themselves.'"

"Huh. That could work. Yeah. Good idea. I'll let him know. God, those fuckers, they look like they're about to fall over." She hangs up and I release my breath. Please, please let it work. Let the groomsmen hold it together long enough to get off the stage. Of course, once they're off the stage, I have no idea what's going to happen with Ah Guan, but one step at a time.

When the last bridesmaid has taken her position at the altar, there's an expectant hush. In Chinese-Indonesian weddings, by the time the ceremony starts, the groom and close family members would have seen the bride, but the rest of the wedding guests have not. The MC shouts, "And now! The moment you've all been waiting for! Here comes our beautiful bride, Jacqueline Wijaya!"

Everyone oohs and aahs as Jacqueline, flanked by her parents, rounds the corner and walks gracefully down the aisle. She looks like a fairy queen. Her dress billows gently in the wind, making her look ethereal, and behind the sheer lace veil, her face is radiant. But as I zoom in and take pictures of her, I see that her smile is forced, her chin trembling slightly. Tante Yohana says something to her, and she gives a small nod.

In the distance, I can see the wedding planner running to the MC and whispering something to him. He frowns and shakes his head. My heart sinks. He's refusing to make the announcement for the bridal party to leave the stage. The wedding planner says something else, gesturing wildly, and the MC looks over at the stage, wincing when his gaze lands on the groomsmen. Jacqueline arrives at the stage, embraces both her parents, and then turns to face Tom, who smirks at her.

"And here we are, the bride and groom, oh what a lovely couple," the MC says. "Before the ceremony begins, will all the bridesmaids and groomsmen please leave the altar so that the bride and groom can have some privacy?"

A murmur ripples through the crowd, and Jacqueline and Tom turn around in confusion.

"What the hell's going on?" Tom says.

I walk over to them as discreetly as I can and say, "I think it's for the best. The groomsmen look ill. You don't want them to cause a scene during the ceremony."

Jacqueline's eyes widen as she notices the groomsmen in their disheveled state for the first time. "Oh my god. Yeah, you're right. Yeah, tell them to go."

"No!" Tom snaps. "They're MY groomsmen, I get to decide what to do with them, and I say they stay."

"They're not *things*, Tom," Jacqueline hisses. "Look at them, they're a mess. They need to go lie down." She leans over and raises her voice. "Yes, thank you all so much for being here. Um, the ceremony's going to run pretty long, so you guys can take a seat." She gestures at her bridesmaids to leave as well.

The bridesmaids start walking back toward the aisle, but the groomsmen continue swaying in their spots until Jacqueline nods to one of the bridesmaids. She walks across the stage and takes the first groomsman by the hand, apparently intending to lead him down the aisle.

"No! Don't any of you dare move," Tom barks, loud enough for the guests in the front to hear. They shift and look at one another, and the murmur gets louder.

"You're not being reasonable," Jacqueline says. "Go on," she says to the bridesmaid, "take them out of here."

The bridesmaid does as she's told, looping her hand through the groomsman's arm and gripping it tight with her other hand, staggering a little when the groomsman sways and rests some of his weight on her.

"Stop," Tom says, but it's too late. All the bridesmaids, who obviously despise him, have rallied around and are helping the groomsmen off the stage. "No, wait—WAIT!"

It all happens in slow motion. I see Tom reaching out desperately, angrily, grabbing anything he can reach. I see it unfold so slowly, as though he's moving underwater, or in a dream. Or a nightmare, rather. Because right then, the nearest man to Tom is groomsman number seven. One of the guys holding up Ah Guan. My mouth drops open, and a "Nooo" comes out, low and slow and much too late.

Tom grabs the groomsman, jerking him backward, and in his inebriated state, groomsman number seven tumbles over like a bowling pin. Groomsman number six, who's propping up Ah Guan's other arm, stumbles too, his feet staggering across the stage until he reaches the edge and falls with a dramatic splash into the infinity pool. Without any support, Ah Guan falls down onto the stage floor like a log.

I'm going to be sick. This is so bad—this is—it can't be happening.

People are screaming. More groomsmen have fallen into the water and—oh god—they're too drunk to swim.

"Save them!" someone screams. There are more shouts,

but I can't make any of them out. The world is a blur of noise and movement.

Several of the guests take off their jackets and plunge into the water. Nathan is running from the back of the ceremony, where he must've been standing, overseeing the proceedings. His security guards run ahead of him and jump into the water.

Reality comes rushing back and I realize that in the chaos, no one's noticed the body. Ah Guan still lies on the stage, undisturbed while people clamber everywhere. This is my chance. I've got to get him out of here. I grab his arm and I don't hesitate, not one bit. I put all of my strength into it, and the adrenaline coursing through my veins propels me up, up, up, and before I know it, I'm standing, Ah Guan's arm flung across my shoulders. I grip his waist tight, not even grimacing a little at the fact that I'm holding a dead man, not giving my brain that space to freak out, and take a step forward. And another. I can do this. I can walk him out of here.

"Oh god, he's completely passed out," Jacqueline says, rushing forward.

No. No, no.

"It's okay!" I cry.

"Let me help—"

She's reaching for his other arm. Her fingers brush his hand. His cold, stiff, dead hand. The expression on her face freezes. "Wait—"

"No!" Instinct overtakes me and I shove her aside—I

can't let her find out, not beautiful, pristine Jacqueline, not like this, not—

She stumbles back, eyes wide, and before I know it, she topples over the aisle and splashes straight into the water.

27

For the first time in my life, I don't hesitate. There isn't even a split second of "What do I do now?" The moment Jacqueline crashes into the pool, I drop all of my precious camera gear and go in after her.

We're in the deep end—the pool is about seven feet deep here, and all that tulle, the frothy layers of lace, they look light and airy, but on land alone the whole thing weighs over fifteen pounds. Underwater, her dress might as well be metal armor. I catch her arms and pull up, but it's like trying to move an anvil. I don't even have time to think "Oh my god, she might drown." I yank up, my legs going *kick, kick, kick* frantically. Somehow, we both break the surface of the water. Jacqueline draws in a desperate, wheezing gasp before my strength gives out and we both go back down. My lungs are screaming, my chest is on fire, and my muscles are water. I kick again, but my legs are so feeble.

Bubbles froth around us all of a sudden. Feet and legs spear down. Bodies dive in. Hands reach out and catch us, wrapping around our arms with viselike grips, and before I know it, I'm breaking the surface for the second time. Air rushes in, clear and sharp and painful. I try to gulp it in. Cough, maybe throw up a little, try to breathe again.

"Easy, easy, it's okay," a low voice says.

My eyes keep rolling back in my head and I feel like I might pass out at any moment, but still, somehow, I recognize the voice and the arm wrapped around my chest, keeping me buoyant.

"Nathan—" I say. Or try to say, rather. It comes out as a choked gurgle.

Jacqueline. Save Jacqueline!

"She's okay, she's okay. The lifeguards got her."

Sure enough, a few feet to my right, there are two lifeguards helping Jacqueline. They've thrown a float around her and are heading to the side of the pool. My relief is short-lived. I glance up at the stage, where about half of the bridal party is still struggling to rush off, and as though the entire universe has been waiting for me to look, it's at this moment that one of the bridesmaids, in her hurry to run off the stage, trips over Ah Guan's prone body.

She falls heavily; even from where I'm wading in the water, I can hear the thud.

"Nearly there," Nathan says reassuringly, but I barely register it.

The bridesmaid scrambles up, her face a mask of horror. As she stands, she accidentally kicks Ah Guan. He doesn't move, merely lies there like a sack of potatoes. Her mouth drops open. Her shriek pierces through my entirety, stabbing through all of the chaos and panic of the crowd.

"He's dead!"

They don't hear her at first. Not most of the crowd, anyway. They're all too focused on the spectacle that is Jacqueline. Phones have been whipped out, all of them aimed at the frothy white mass being tugged to the side of the pool by muscled lifeguards.

But then another bridesmaid comes to help the first one up.

"He's dead!" the first one screams again.

"What?"

"That guy! He's dead!"

The second bridesmaid looks at Ah Guan. Sticks out a hand, her face disbelieving. "Yo, dude." She pokes him. And then she rears back, her face a mask of horror. She doesn't shout, but when her mouth moves, I can see clearly what she says. "Shit. He's dead."

The hotel's security team are doing their best to keep the peace, but it's next to impossible to keep the peace when two thousand privileged guests have just discovered a dead body. There are screams, dramatic gasps, even more dramatic swoons, and a lot of demands to "speak to the person in charge." The person in charge is Nathan, and he's currently giving orders to have the altar cordoned off and the guests to be escorted back to their rooms while he calls the sheriff's office.

Someone's wrapped a towel around me, which I quickly soak through, drenched as I am in my clothes. The previously warm sea breeze has turned cold. The storm is coming, and the wind bites through my wet towel and clothes like a knife. I shiver. I should go inside, but I can't bring myself to leave, not when the dead body of the man I killed is right in the middle of everything and there are thousands of people around me pointing and shouting.

Nathan's striding everywhere, giving orders into his walkie-talkie. He's also drenched, but he doesn't seem to notice. He stations two guards to block anyone with morbid curiosity, which as it turns out is everyone here, from getting down the aisle. Even though the guests seem horrified, they also seem fascinated, hopelessly drawn to the dead body.

"Meddy!"

I very nearly cry when I turn to see Ma and my aunties rushing through the crowd. Even as I watch, Big Aunt elbows a tall man out of the way to make room for Ma and the other aunties. Love swells through my heart. My bossy, loud, overwhelming family is here. Everything is—well, it's unlikely that anything would be okay, but at least I won't be going through it alone.

Ma finally squeezes out of the crowd, and I rush to greet her with a hug. She's never been a hugger, but I don't care, not right now. I just want to smell her scent. For one fleeting, precious moment, I catch the smell of home—freshly laundered clothes and a hint of fish sauce—and I breathe it all in, taking strength from it.

"Meddy, you okay? How? What happen?" my aunties cluck around us. "Aduh, why is the body there?"

"I don't know, I—" I am surrounded by people. "Let's get out of here first." Together, we cut a path through the crowd, my aunts elbowing chests and stomping on feet whenever they need to (and sometimes even when they don't need to), until we're well away from the crowd and round the side of the main resort building. There's no one here. I guess everyone who's in the vicinity has followed the noise and energy of the crowd to satisfy their curiosity. Still, we all look around for a few moments to make sure we're completely alone.

"Okay, so." I take a deep breath. "I have no idea how Ah Guan ended up on the altar. Do any of you know what happened?"

Am I surprised when my family members look down guiltily for a moment's breath before they all point at each other and say, "It's her fault"? I mean, I guess I am, but also not really.

"Okay." Another deep breath. "Let's see." Big Aunt is glaring at Second Aunt, who's pointing an accusatory finger at Big Aunt. Ma and Fourth Aunt are both pointing at each other. Right. So, nothing new, then. "Why do you think it's each other's fault?" I hold my hands up. "Wait, one person at a time. Big Aunt, you go first."

"Why her first?" Second Aunt demands.

I shrug. "I don't know, 'cause she's the eldest? Isn't that how the rules go? Anyway, we don't have all day, so . . . Big Aunt? What happened from your point of view?"

Big Aunt shoots Second Aunt one last magnificent glare before dragging her gaze to mine. Her face softens, and she begins telling her story in rapid Mandarin.

"I went back to the kitchen to look for a waiter's uniform for Ah Guan. There are so many waiters and other sorts of

266

servers around, I thought it would be the perfect disguise. It's a good idea, right?"

It takes a moment before I realize she's actually expecting an answer, and I hurriedly nod. "Yes, very good idea."

"So I made sure to be extra careful. I went to the locker room and checked that no one was inside, and then I looked inside the lockers one by one and aha! I found one! A waiter's uniform. I even got his shoes. I remembered, you see, that Ah Guan didn't have shoes on. I'm all about the details, you know, because of my work," she adds with obvious pride.

It takes a moment for me to work out all the Mandarin words, and when I do, I say, "Yes, you are very detailed, Big Aunt. So you found a waiter's uniform . . . but why is Ah Guan not wearing it?"

"Exactly! Why he not wearing it? You ask her!" Big Aunt says triumphantly, switching to English and pointing a finger straight at Second Aunt's face. God, she's good. Now that she's done telling her part, she's switched to English to goad Second Aunt into relaying her story in English too.

"You take so long!" Second Aunt says, rising to the bait. "And I know you will make mistake, forget this and that. Already you make such big mess of everything. Why I should stay there and wait for you to make more mistake, I ask myself? Why? No. This time, I will take charge. I have to go to groom's suite because groom and groomsmen want hair done, so okay, I go. Inside, I see, waduh, got so many of them. So many! And all their groomsmen clothes just lying around, and these silly boys all drinking and not pay any attention, so I think, aha! This is perfect disguise. Got so many groomsmen here, who will notice one extra one? So when they not looking, I take a set and I rush back to room."

"If it makes you feel any better, your mother and I helped to put the groomsman's clothes on him," Fourth Aunt pipes up.

How's that even remotely supposed to make me feel any better?

Ma must have read the look on my face, because she says, "We are always listening to Big Aunt—" She turns to Big Aunt and adds, "Da Jie, you always give very good advice, but this time we think maybe give Er Jie a chance, since she come back with the groomsman uniform so fast."

I slap my forehead. "It's not about who to listen to, it's about assessing who has the best plan!"

Big Aunt nods smugly.

"Well, at the time, it seemed like dressing him up as a groomsman was the best plan," Fourth Aunt says.

"I just—I mean—no offense to you, Second Aunt, but it's a terrible idea! What about the poor groomsman you guys stole the suit from? Where is he?"

"Probably snoring, dead drunk, in a closet someplace," Fourth Aunt says with a wave of her hand.

"But—"

"Stop interrupting," Fourth Aunt says. "Anyway, so we dressed him up as a groomsman and decided that while everyone's busy getting ready for the ceremony, we'd try to get rid of him then."

"So we each take one arm and then we carry him out the

room," Ma says. "We think maybe we can carry him to the back garden, leave him there on the bench, then will take long time before people find him. Nobody go to back garden, right?"

"This is not a well thought-out plan," I moan.

"It is very well thought out! How will anyone know we have something to do with groom man dead body?" Ma cries.

I open and close my mouth, but no words come out.

"But halfway to back garden, you all come to hallway on your way to look for tea ceremony present," Second Aunt says. "We panic! Waduh, what if they see us with body? So we quickly hide behind room service cart."

Oh god. This is getting worse by the second.

"It was an awesome room service cart. It had all these bottles of champagne in it," Fourth Aunt says. "Which gave me an idea. I ran back to my room and got a bottle of absinthe—"

"Why do you have a bottle of absinthe?" I can't keep the shock out of my voice.

"Yes, why do you have bottle of absinthe?" Ma says, the world's most judgmental smile dancing on her lips.

"I'm an entertainer!" Fourth Aunt snaps. "None of you understands the amount of energy we need to have to even get ourselves out on stage, and then afterward, we need something to help us come down. You should be grateful my drug of choice is just a shot of absinthe. Most other entertainers go with coke."

"Coke got so much sugar." Big Aunt sniffs. "Better drink Coke Zero, otherwise later you get diabetes."

"She means cocaine—never mind. So then what happened?"

"I got the absinthe and we carried the body to the groomsmen suite. I just burst in there and went, 'You boys ready to party?' while waving the bottle around. The groomsmen were like, WOW, beautiful girl AND alcohol?"

"I think they only notice the alcohol," Ma mutters.

"They were whistling!"

"At the alcohol!"

"Okay, okay," I whisper-shout over them. "Then what happened?"

"Well, I used my womanly wiles to lead them to the far side of the living room, and while we opened the bottle and poured shots for everyone, your mother and Second Aunt carried the body inside and put him in one of the bedrooms. Everything went smoothly, and THEN your mother had one of her crazy ideas—"

"Not crazy," Ma huffs. "I just want to make sure they not so—you know—not so alert. Because if they so alert, if they find out too early that there is dead body in the bedroom, then that will be very bad."

"Ma, just tell me, what did you do?"

"I just—I see many bottles of champagne in their kitchen, so I open one or two and I put some—you know."

I take a deep breath. Be strong, self. "I don't know. What did you put in the bottles?"

"Just Chinese medicine, very good for health."

"It's weed," Fourth Aunt says, triumphantly.

"WHAT?" Good grief, I don't even know where to begin.

There's the fact that my mother has drugged a dozen grooms-men. Or maybe the fact that my mother carries around a stash of marijuana with her. What in the actual F?

"No, no, it is traditional Chinese medicine," Ma huffs. Spare me from yet another round of sibling rivalry.

"Traditional Chinese medicine doesn't include mari-juana!" I almost scream, but at the last minute remember to lower my voice.

"No, original recipe call for a type of fungus—it is called dong chong xia cao," Ma admits. "But wah, dong chong xia cao so expensive! So I look everywhere for substitute, and then someone on Internet tell me there is this very good herb, called Tetris Hydro Canned Oil. Very good for pain."

"She means tetrahydrocannabinol," Fourth Aunt says. Fleetingly, I wonder if she's memorized what THC stands for just for this moment.

"THC? Ma, that's the active ingredient in marijuana!" Oh my god.

"No, this one is different. This herb is very good for blood flow. You know how winter really affect my bones, very bad, so painful, these are helping me. It has a bit of side effect, make me feel a bit woozy."

"They get you high," Fourth Aunt says.

"No high, just a bit woozy."

I close my eyes. "So between the two of you, those poor groomsmen got drunk AND high? You could've killed them!"

"Aduh, touch wood, don't say such bad luck thing," Second Aunt says, knocking on a nearby tree.

"Don't say such bad luck thing?" I cry, torn between

laughing and crying. "I mean, it's a bit late for that, don't you think?"

"Tch," Ma tuts, "don't be rude, Meddy. I raise you better than that."

This is unreal. Another deep gulp of air. "Right, so you guys drugged the groomsmen, and then . . ."

"And then we leave, that is all," Ma says. "When we leave they all still happy happy, all laughing."

"But how did Ah Guan end up on the altar?"

My aunts and mom shrug, but I don't need them to answer. I can piece it together by now. I see it so clearly in my mind's eye. One of the groomsmen would've gotten a call from a panicky WP, asking where the hell are they, the ceremony's starting soon. They would've scrambled to get dressed. The room would've been spinning, they would've been stumbling everywhere, and then one of them maybe went in the bedroom to get something and saw Ah Guan in bed. I watch it unfold like a movie in my mind. He totters to Ah Guan and nudges him. Figures that maybe Ah Guan had passed out, and in his absinthe-marijuana-addled mind, he thinks the best course of action is to drag Ah Guan to the ceremony. He calls the others inside to help, and one other groomsman appears. Together, they lug Ah Guan out of bed, laughing over what a lightweight he is. The floor tips under their feet and they nearly fall, but it's all part of the fun. They no longer even know which side is up.

And that's how a corpse ended up on the altar.

28

The minute Ma and my aunties finish filling me in on what's happened behind the scenes, they erupt into argument with a flurry of Mandarin, Indonesian, and English.

Big Aunt: "Tuh kan? You see, this is what happens when you don't listen to me!"

Second Aunt: "Ha! You're just jealous because for once, I take control of the situation, we're not just following you around like zombies."

Ma: "Why did you give them so much absinthe? They're not drunkards, like you!"

Fourth Aunt: "Excuse me, it's not my fault if the grooms-men can't hold their alcohol. And also, I wasn't the one who drugged them."

This is so typical of them. Big Aunt and Second Aunt with their rivalry, Ma and Fourth Aunt with their jealousy. I can't take another second of it, so while they argue with one another, I stalk off.

As though to reflect our mood, the wind's picked up and is howling like a grieving widow. It snatches at my ponytail, whipping it into my face. Up to this point, the adrenaline has rendered me oblivious to my surroundings, but now, I realize that I'm freezing in my wet clothes. My teeth are actually chattering, and each breath I take makes my jaw clack. I hug the towel around me tight and walk toward the infinity pool. I'm dreading the sight of what was going on while I took stock with my family, but I have to. I have to know.

I'm half-expecting the scene to be crawling with cops, to hear the wail of sirens and see the red and blue lights flashing. But when I get there, the place is almost devoid of people. The hotel's security team is ushering the last remaining guests away from the site, telling everyone in stern voices to go back to their rooms and stay put. Jacqueline and Tom—thank god—are nowhere to be seen. I check my phone and see half a dozen messages from Seb, telling me he's been ordered to go back to his room. My heart skips a beat when I spot Nathan on the stage, his tall profile silhouetted against the stormy sky. He's staring down at the body, and from my vantage point, it's impossible to see the expression on his face. His back is straight, but his head is bowed as though he's deep in thought.

"Miss, please, you need to return to your room," a guard says.

Nathan turns and sees me. "No, she's fine, she's with me," he calls out, hurrying toward us.

Just as I'm about to walk to him, voices are raised, and I turn around to see the sheriff I'd seen earlier that morning shouldering past a couple of the hotel's security guards.

"Coming through," he says pompously. "Sheriff coming

through." When he gets near me, he places a meaty hand on my shoulder, even though the path is wide enough for the two of us, and pushes me aside like I'm a shopping cart in his way. "Step aside, ma'am, sheriff coming through," he says in that self-important voice that makes me want to punch him. Instead, I watch wordlessly as he swaggers down the aisle toward Nathan.

I step closer, not close enough that they'd tell me to go away, but just close enough to hear what they're saying. It's not hard to hear the sheriff; even over the howl of the wind, he's practically bellowing every word.

"Knew something bad was gonna happen," he says by way of greeting. "You fancy folk think you can just turn up on my island and build your giant resorts—ha! I've been waiting for this to happen, boy."

Nathan places his hands in his pockets, maybe to stop himself from punching the sheriff too.

"And now one of my little birdies tells me you got a dead body—oh, hello, what do we got here? A dead body."

To my shock, the sheriff actually sticks one of his feet out and nudges Ah Guan's arm with the tip of his shoe. That does not strike me as correct crime scene protocol, but then again, who am I to judge what's correct protocol? All I have to go on are episodes of *CSI* and *Law and Order*. For all I know, maybe all sheriffs use the tips of their shoes to—okay, who am I kidding? This guy is a nut.

"Sheriff McConnell," Nathan says, "so glad to have you here again."

The sheriff snorts, and it's amazing how much he reminds

me of a seal. "Hah, yeah, I bet you're glad. What a mess. But no worries, you've all got someone who knows what he's doing here," he calls out to the small audience. He looks around and frowns. "Where's everyone?"

"We thought it best to have as few people here as possible, so we sent all the guests back to their rooms."

"Oh ho! Don't want any witnesses, is that it?" The sheriff scratches his jaw with conscious effort, as if it's something he's seen some TV detective do and decided he'd do it too.

A crease forms between Nathan's eyebrows. "Well, no, everyone's witnessed the body—"

"Why's he wearing that silly outfit, then? Is he one of these New Age performers? Baton twirling or whatever?"

"Baton twirling?" Nathan looks so confused I want to hug him and apologize for everything. "Er, no, he was a groomsman."

"A groomsman, eh?" The sheriff walks around the body and, again, nudges it with the tip of his shoe. This time, though, he pushes harder, until Ah Guan flops over onto his back. I get a glimpse of his slack face before I look away, bile lurching up into my throat. With a superhuman effort, I swallow it back down. "I need to talk to the other groomsmen."

"Sure, they should all be back in their rooms; would you like to follow me—"

"No, bring them here."

"They're—uh, I don't know how mobile they are."

The sheriff narrows his eyes. "Bring. Them. Here. Don't make me charge you with obstruction of justice, boy."

My hands tighten into fists. Could this man possibly be any more odious? Nathan activates his walkie-talkie and asks someone to escort the groomsmen back to the altar. When he's done, he looks at the boiling gray clouds and says, "Should we take the body indoors? It looks like it's about to start pouring."

The sheriff gives what he probably thinks is a really sly side-eye glance. "I see. So you want to move the victim from the crime scene, eh?"

"Er . . . no? Do whatever you think is best," Nathan says. He takes out his phone and types something. A moment later, my phone buzzes.

Nathan [4:25PM]: I really hate this guy. He's such a hack.

Meddy [4:26PM]: Seriously. How did he become a sheriff??

Nathan [4:26PM]: Nooo idea. My guess is he killed off the competition. Or maybe there was none to begin with. It's a small island.

Meddy [4:27PM]: True. I hope this gets resolved quickly.

Nathan glances in my direction and sends me a small smile that melts all of my muscles. Muscles that almost immediately tighten up at the sight of two security guards escorting a couple of groomsmen down the aisle. I step aside to let them pass. The groomsmen are still clearly out of it, their eyes wild, their heads lolling.

"These are the most sober ones, sir," one of the guards says to Nathan apologetically.

"That's fine. I'm sorry for making you guys come out here again," Nathan says to the groomsmen.

In reply, one of them smiles dopily and says something like, "Shokay," and the other one just stares blearily at Nathan. I cringe. Ma and Fourth Aunt have really done a number on these poor guys.

Sheriff McConnell wastes no time. He strides toward the groomsmen and points at Ah Guan's body. "Who was this man?"

They both look to where he's pointing, and seem startled all over again at the sight of the corpse. I don't blame them. Even after a whole day of moving it around, seeing an actual dead body is still shocking to me.

"I don't know, man," the first groomsman says. The second groomsman continues staring at the corpse, mouth agape. I swear he's about to start drooling.

"He must've been one of your good friends? He's a fellow groomsman?"

The first groomsman laughs. "Nooo. Don't tell anyone, okay?" He leans forward as if he's about to reveal some secret, but his voice is still as loud as ever. "The groom ain't got no friends. So he hired us to be his groomsmen. Most of us never met each other until last night." He laughs again. "It's the funniest shit."

Now it's time for my mouth to drop open. This explains

so much. No wonder Tom's been so weird around his groomsmen. No wonder he's been ordering them around as if they're his employees. Because they are! He's employed them for the day. *And* it explains why the groomsmen quite happily carried Ah Guan down the aisle; aside from the fact that they were drugged and drunk out of their senses, they just plain didn't recognize one another.

The sheriff shakes his head. "So none of you knew this guy?" He nudges Ah Guan's shoulder again with his shoe. What is up with him and the need to keep prodding Ah Guan with his foot?

Both groomsmen shake their heads.

"Would the others know him?"

The first groomsman shrugs. "I mean, who knows? Maybe? Tom had to hire people from three different agencies because he needed so many bodies. Oops, bad word choice, lol." He says "lol" as if it's an actual word.

Someone nudges my elbow, and I turn to see Ma and my aunties behind me.

"What are you doing just standing there?" Ma whispers. "Come, we go back in, otherwise later you will catch cold."

I can't help snorting out loud. Here we are, with the sheriff and the dead body, and Ma's worried about me catching a cold? "You guys done fighting?" I say, unable to keep the bitterness out of my voice.

At least they have the decency to look somewhat abashed. "For now," Fourth Aunt says. She eyes the sheriff and groomsmen and switches to Indonesian. "What've they figured out so far?"

"Not much. But I want to stay here, see what else they come up with."

"I'm going in." Fourth Aunt pinches my cheek and then turns around and walks back toward the rooms, followed by my other aunties. Only Ma stays with me.

A few feet away, Sheriff McConnell is fast losing patience. "Get me the other groomsmen," he barks at the two security guards. They glance at Nathan, who nods. As they leave, Sheriff McConnell paces around the altar, his weight making the whole stage shudder. Thunder rolls, and I can't help but jump.

"We really should go inside, it looks like nasty weather," Nathan says. "We could question the rest of the groomsmen in their rooms."

"Oh, I bet you'd like that, wouldn't you?"

Nathan looks confused. "Um, yeah, I guess? Won't the rain—I don't know—do something to the body? Make it harder to gauge when it died or something?"

"Hey, I'm the professional here," the sheriff barks. "All you mainlanders think you're so sophisticated with all your fancy equipment and technology and all this newfangled DNA shit."

"What?"

"Well, I've got news for you: I'm going to solve this without all that fancy-schmancy techy shit. I'm going to solve it with good old detective work." Sheriff McConnell taps the side of his head with another one of his trademark cunning looks.

"Um. Okay. I still think we should go inside—"

He's interrupted by the arrival of two more groomsmen. They're in worse shape than the previous two—these ones keep giggling and pointing at random things in the air.

"Ma, are you sure you haven't like, permanently addled their minds?" I whisper.

"Aduh, of course not, lah. Traditional Chinese medicine is very good for your health. Very good!" Still, I can't help noticing how worried Ma actually looks.

Sheriff McConnell asks them if they recognize Ah Guan, and they both giggle and shake their heads. "Hey, man, time to wake up. You're lying on the altar," one of them says.

"Which agency are you from?" Sheriff McConnell asks them.

"Best Days Agency," one says.

"Party Peeps," the other one slurs.

"And presumably you would know who's from which agency?"

The two groomsmen stare at him blankly. "I what now?" one of them says.

Sheriff McConnell pinches the bridge of his nose. "What I'm asking is: This man, he's definitely not from either of your agencies?"

One of the groomsmen shakes his head confidently, while the other says, "Iono."

I'm expecting Sheriff McConnell to be frustrated by this, but instead, he rubs his hands with satisfaction and nods. "You two can go. I know who did it."

I can't help squeezing Ma's hand. She squeezes back and

pats it reassuringly. "Oh, Tuhan," she mutters. "It's okay. It's okay."

It's not okay. I'm about to be arrested. I watch, rooted to the spot, every part of me leaden, as Sheriff McConnell walks off the altar and onto the aisle. Coming straight toward me.

Except he stops in front of Nathan and says, in a thunderous voice that matches the weather, "Nathan Chan, you are under arrest for the murder of this man." He pulls out a pair of handcuffs with relish and, smiling proudly, latches them around Nathan's wrists.

29

Sheriff McConnell barely spares Ma and me a glance as he brushes past, his meaty hands on Nathan's shoulders. Nathan is wide-eyed, but as he passes me, he whispers, "It'll be okay."

And I'm—

I'm—

Furious. How pathetic does Nathan think I am, that he'd need to comfort me while HE'S literally in handcuffs? What is it about me that makes people around me want to take care of every problem? Do I exude incompetence? Helplessness? I've had just about enough of it. I swing around. I want to yell at Nathan, to tell him to stop protecting me, stop treating me like I'm this breakable thing, because I'm not. I want to lash out at someone, at anyone, and unfortunately, the closest person to me right then is Ma. Ma and my aunties.

They're just standing there, gaping as the security guards all file away, following Nathan.

"It's going to be okay," Big Aunt says in Indonesian, her voice full of uncertainty, and I take it. I take this chance to lash out.

"It won't be okay!" I cry. "It won't be. Stop saying it will, because it won't! I didn't want any of this to happen. I just wanted to—I just—" I just what? What would I have done without my family? I would've been stuck at home with a dead body in my car and no way of explaining it. But maybe that would have been better than this. Anything would've been better than having Nathan get arrested for something I did.

"Meddy, you are upset, I know, but we are just taking care of you," Ma says.

I shirk away from her outstretched hand, and the hurt that slashes across her face enrages me even more. "I don't need you to take care of me. I'm not a baby anymore, Ma. God, all of this is such a burden!"

They startle at the B-word. It's their worst nightmare, to be a burden to their children.

"Meddy, how can you say that?" Big Aunt says in English, her chest rising. "We are family, we work together, we always there for each other."

"Yeah, and that's exactly the problem. We're always there. I don't know what life is like without any of you in it. I had a glimpse of it when I went to college, and then after that I moved back home and it's back to being in the fold. I don't know who I am without you all breathing down my neck. I don't even know if I want to be a wedding photographer, but I can't do my own thing, I can't just abandon the family business, because you always talk about sacrifice and how much you've all sacrificed for me, and so this is it, the cycle of sacrifice that'll go on and on and on."

They look like I've slapped them. "You don't want to be wedding photographer?" Ma whispers.

"I hate weddings!" I cry.

They stagger back a step, their faces lit up with horror.

"I do, I hate them—"

"That's not true. I've seen the way you look at wedding dresses," Fourth Aunt says. "It's like you've got horny eyes on; it's quite honestly disturbing."

I sigh. "You're right, there are things I love about weddings. I love the brides; I love seeing them looking all beautiful and happy and wearing a big white dress. But everything else, everything else I hate. I hate that brides and grooms are driven nuts by this unrealistic expectation that the day has to be perfect. I hate that it's turned into an industry that makes people spend way more than they should, and I hate that we're part of that!"

They're all quiet for a while. "So you saying that we are holding you back?" Ma says, after a while.

I don't answer. I can't. Whatever I say, it won't be enough. It won't be accurate. It's not a no, and it's not a yes. And, in the end, I have only myself to blame. My cousins grew up in the same environment and managed to leave, to spread their wings. I'm the only one who remains in the same old nest, and surely that proves that the blame lies on me.

After an eternity, I shake my head. "I don't blame you." See, that's not totally accurate either. I blame everyone, including myself.

Ma utters a sob, and immediately all of my aunties,

including Fourth Aunt, catch her by the arms. They coo soothing words in Indonesian at her.

"It's okay, she's just a child, she doesn't know what she's saying."

"My Hendra used to say things like that too, it's okay."

"These kids, they'll only understand what we've given up after they have children of their own."

This is what always happens when one of my generation dares to talk back to our parents. They band together and reduce us to kids having a tantrum, dismissing our words so we can't pierce their armor. Part of me wants to kick crazily at the ground and scream until they listen, but of course that'll only confirm their belief that I'm nothing more than a silly child.

I close my eyes and take a deep breath before speaking. "I'm sorry, Ma, I don't mean to hurt you. Just—please. Don't try to help me here. Go back to your rooms and I'll handle this. I love you all, but it's time for me to grow up and clean up my own mess."

Ma's eyes meet mine, and despite the hurt creasing her face, I see understanding dawn in her eyes. But it's underneath a blanket of sorrow and anger. She doesn't say a word, merely shakes her head in disappointment and lets my aunties escort her away. Big Aunt glares at me, Second Aunt is busy cooing over Ma, and even Fourth Aunt doesn't have anything mean to say to Ma, which is how I know for sure that Ma's heart is broken.

Still, I harden myself against going after them. Because I've always gone after them, and then I end up apologizing and assuring them that I'll be a less shitty daughter, and that's how I find myself at twenty-six still living at home and spending my weekends shooting huge weddings and pretending I love the whole production.

No. I have more pressing things to attend to. Like Nathan. The thought of him fires me up even more. I stride toward the main building, climbing the impressive stone steps up to the lobby. There, I corner a receptionist and ask where Nathan's been taken.

"I'm not at liberty to say, ma'am," he says smoothly, but I catch a glimmer of hesitation in him. Unbidden, an image of Big Aunt comes to mind. Big Aunt, who carries herself with her back ramrod straight and her chin always up. Big Aunt, who always manages to get people to listen to her. What would she say? I lift my chin and glare at him imperiously. "I've been in touch with LAPD and they've said that the sheriff has no jurisdiction to arrest anyone. I am not going to stand aside and let that idiot make a mockery of the justice system, and neither are you. You're not going to obstruct me. Now lead me to where he's keeping Nathan." Obviously I don't give a tiny rat's fart about the justice system, but it seemed like a good term to throw in.

After a moment's hesitation, the receptionist says, "He took him upstairs. To Mr. Chan's office. Said the storm's getting too bad for him to drive in."

"Good. Take me there. Now," I add, when the receptionist opens his mouth.

"Right away, ma'am." He hurries out from behind his desk and nods at me to follow him. As soon as his back is turned, I sag a little. I can't believe it worked. I channeled my inner Big Aunt, and now I'm being led to Nathan. Phew, I should try that more often. This feeling is honestly pretty addictive.

He leads me through a side door to an employee elevator. We get inside, and he uses his key card to get to the top floor. I try to keep looking imperious, which is a lot harder to do in the dead silence of the elevator. I have to stop myself from sighing with obvious relief when the doors finally whoosh open.

The top floor is taken up by numerous offices. I've never been to this part of any hotel before, but I guess it makes sense that large resorts would have offices to oversee the running of things. The receptionist leads me past half a dozen offices until he gets to the end. There's a security guard standing outside. When he sees us approaching, he shifts his stance so that he looks like he's standing to attention.

"Hey, Dave," the receptionist says. "This is—uh—"

"I'm Meddy, Nat—Mr. Chan's lawyer."

The guard's eyes widen. "Thank god you're here," he says in a low voice. "I don't even—why was I asked to guard his office? I don't believe for a second that Mr. Chan did it."

I nod at him, take a deep breath, and stride through the door.

Sheriff McConnell's seated behind Nathan's desk, with Nathan perched on a chair opposite him.

"What's this?" Sheriff McConnell says, eyeing me from top to bottom with a languorous leer that makes me want to take a long, hot shower.

"This is Mr. Chan's attorney," the guard says.

Sheriff McConnell's eyebrows raise. He looks me over again, but this time, the look is several degrees less lecherous and shows more disbelief, as in how the hell can someone who looks like me be an attorney? I'm about to be affronted when I realize that, welp, I'm still in my all-black photographer's outfit and I'm as wet as a drowned rat. My hair is dripping water onto my towel. Ugh, Ma and my aunties were right. I need their help. I have always needed their help. They haven't been holding me back. I've reached my potential. This is it, this is where I peak—as a wedding photographer for the family business, always protected from the world by my family.

But there's a glimmer in Nathan's face. Something I've seen before, so many years ago, when he asked me to go east with him. Just a flicker, but it's there, still. Fierce, naked hope.

My cheeks burn. Even after all this time, even after everything, he still has hope for us. And I—

I feel it. Fluttering from deep inside my chest, as though waking up from a deep slumber. Hope. I've squashed it down for the last four years, shoved all thoughts of being independent to the side, told myself I'm being stupid, or selfish, or unrealistic. Unrealistic—that's always been my mantra, passed down from Ma and my aunties. "Don't be unrealistic," they'd say. They had to be pragmatic all their lives; there was no room for dreams or idealism. Just look at Fourth Aunt, Ma would say. She chased her dreams all the way from Indonesia to Los Angeles, and look where it got her. This is what happens when you're unrealistic, when you let the dream take over.

But everything that's happened the past few days has been unreal. If ever there was a time to use the word, it's now. Ma pretending to be me online, that's pretty fucking unreal. Me accidentally killing my date. I mean, how much more unreal can it get? And all the domino pieces falling over one by one—the body getting shipped here, the body ending up on the altar—none of it has been anywhere near realistic. Why am I still trying to play by realistic rules?

My back straightens, my neck lengthens, and I stare down at Sheriff McConnell and see him for what he truly is: a fish out of water, completely at a loss as to what to do. Nothing like this has ever happened on this island, and he's torn between the sudden rush of power and a whole ocean of fear. I pounce on that fear.

"My name is Meddelin Chan, and I'm an attorney. What have you charged my client with?" My voice comes out like an iron fist, thudding onto the desk.

There's a beat of silence, and then Sheriff McConnell scrambles forward, placing his elbows on the desk before second-guessing himself and sitting back and folding his hands on his lap. "Ahem, yes, his attorney, eh? You got here fast." He pauses. "Hang on, I'm pretty sure I've seen you around . . ."

"Yeah, I've been here awhile, taking care of some papers."

Nathan gives a small shake of the head, but I don't need him to guide me. I won't have this joke of a cop derail me. I lean forward, place my hands on the desk, and say the words ever so slowly.

"What. Have. You. Charged. My client. With?" Never

mind thudding, my heart is kicking. I swear it's grown legs and is sprinting, crashing over and over into my rib cage. Any moment now, it's going to kick its way right out of my chest, *Alien*-style. But somehow, my face remains straight, my gaze unwavering, locked on Sheriff McConnell.

He shifts his weight again, and unfolds and refolds his hands. "Right, yes. Well. There's been a murder."

"What have you charged my client with?"

His gaze flits away like a spooked butterfly before coming back to rest on my face. "Well, that is to say, er—"

"If you haven't charged him with anything, then you can't keep him locked up. I'm taking him out of here."

"Well, then I charge him with murder!"

Shit, shit, shit. Somehow, I stare him down, even though everything inside me is screaming Noooo, you've done it now, you've gone and made everything worse! "For the murder of whom?"

The sheriff gives a little shake of his head, reminding me of a horse. "Of the body. Down there, at the altar."

"So you haven't identified the body?"

"Well, no, of course not, that'll come later—"

"What was the cause of death?"

"I don't—"

"Time of death?"

"Well, I mean to say—"

"Found a weapon on my client, did you?"

"Not yet—"

"So you don't have a cause or time of death, but you've arrested my client. On what grounds?" Seriously, who am I right now? It's as though Big Aunt has taken over my consciousness and is just bulldozing over everything, and holy smokes, it's actually working. Sheriff McConnell is sweating as if he's just run a marathon in the dead of summer. I actually feel kind of sorry for him. "Sheriff, I think we both know you're in over your head. Have you even ordered the body to be brought in out of the rain?"

He stares at me balefully. "Protocol states that . . ." His voice trails off. It's obvious he has no idea what protocol states when there's a mysterious body and a rainstorm. On the one hand, he should leave crime scenes as undisturbed as he can. On the other hand, the rainstorm might destroy a lot of evidence.

It's good that he doesn't know what the protocol is, because I sure as hell have no freaking clue. Hopefully protocol is whatever Sheriff McConnell hasn't done. "Protocol states that you should preserve as much of the crime scene as possible, which in this case means asking the hotel employees to erect some sort of covering, maybe? To try and keep as much of the rainwater away from the crime scene?" I say it as if it's obvious, as if I haven't just pulled it out of my ass, and the look on Nathan's face almost makes me burst out in hysterical laughter. Nathan is looking at me like—I don't even know how to describe it—like he's seeing the most amazing sunrise ever, his handsome face lighting up with awe.

"Well, I was just about to do that when you barged in," Sheriff McConnell mutters.

I look pointedly at the glass of whiskey in front of him.

"Really? It looks to me like you're making yourself comfortable in my client's office."

He looks down at the glass and flushes, his face turning beet-shade. "This was his."

"Mhmm. Well, it's obvious to me that you have failed to follow any sort of protocol, so I don't think you can legally charge my client with anything without further evidence." What are these words coming out of my mouth? I'm pretty sure that any legit cop would've called my bluff a long time ago, but Sheriff McConnell is caught completely off-guard. His eyes are perfect circles, his mouth moving, but no words are coming out. "So ple—so, uncuff my client. Now," I add, when I feel the need to say "please," and to my disbelief, Sheriff McConnell actually stands up. I tense, half expecting him to—I don't know—pounce on me and catch me by the scruff of my neck and arrest me.

He walks over to the other side of the table, his steps echoing in the large office. He approaches Nathan, who I can tell is trying his best not to laugh. He takes out a keychain, grabs Nathan's hands, and—

Oh my god. I did it.

Sheriff McConnell lowers Nathan's hands. They're still cuffed.

Shit. I haven't done it. He's on to me. Is he? What's going on?

Sheriff McConnell puffs out his barrel chest. "I don't care what fancy law firm you're from, but this here's my territory. And I smell something bad. I don't know what it is your client here's done, but I know he's done something, and I'm going to find out what it is."

"You can't just keep him here because you think he's done something. That's not how the law works. You need to actually have found evidence and then charge him," I snap. At least, that's what it seems like on *CSI*.

"If you've got a problem with how I handle things, you can take it up with the mainland police." He looks around the room dramatically, hands cupped behind his ears. "Oh, huh, I don't hear the wail of sirens, do you? That's because those pansy fancy-pants cops don't dare to come here in the storm, so it looks like I'm in charge. And I say he stays here."

"When they arrive, you are going to lose your license." Or whatever the hell it is that cops have.

Sheriff McConnell shrugs, his meaty face squishing into a sly smile. "Yeah, they've been saying that for years, and yet here I am."

The ground is crumbling underneath my feet. I grasp for anything I can think of. "I need to speak with my client. Alone. He still has that right."

"He does indeed. Five minutes." With that, Sheriff McConnell saunters out, hands in pockets. He's practically whistling with joy.

As soon as the door clicks shut behind him, I sink onto the sofa and put my head in my hands. I was so close. I thought I had it.

"You did great, Meddy."

I remain with my face buried in my hands. I can't stand to look at the disappointment that must be on Nathan's face.

"Meddy." Nathan kneels in front of me, gently pulling my hands away from my face. "Hey," he says, softly. "There you are." There is so much in his expression. All of it, our history, every fight, every kiss, every laugh, written plain as day across his flawless face.

"I'm so sorry." The words come out broken by sobs. "I made a mess."

"No, you helped. He wouldn't have let us speak in private if you hadn't done all that—I mean, that was amazing, all those things you said to him." He laughs. "You were on fire."

"You don't understand," I moan. "I—I did it." It's time. The truth, all of it. I'm so tired of keeping things from him. I could lie to the entire world, but not to him. Not Nathan. "That dead body. I killed him."

There it is, the truth, falling out of my mouth like a snake, twisting in the air between us. I don't take my eyes from Nathan's face because I want to memorize the way he's been looking at me. He's never going to look at me the same way again, not with this horrible thing I've just dropped in his lap. I brace myself for the horror that'll no doubt take over his face as soon as my words sink in.

But it doesn't come. Nathan just sighs. And then he says two words that leave me speechless.

"I know."

30

"What?" I cry. "Wait. What?"

"Shh." Nathan puts a finger to his lips, glancing at the door.

I struggle to lower my voice. "Sorry. But what the fuck, Nathan?"

He sighs. "I know. I figured it out."

"When? Wha—how? What?"

"Meddy, you and your family have been acting shady as shit the whole day. And you guys were lugging around that ridiculous cooler everywhere—I didn't know what to make of it. I thought maybe something had gone wrong with the wedding cake and you guys were trying to hide it or something? But then I went to the kitchen to check, and the wedding cake was fine, so then I thought maybe it was something else with the food. Then when the body appeared on the altar . . . it doesn't exactly take a rocket scientist to put two and two together."

I gape at him. My lips form words. Nothing comes out. My mouth just flaps idiotically, nonsensically. Still no words.

"Can you tell me why you did it, at least?"

Somehow, I manage to get my voice working again. "Um, it was in self-defense, and I didn't mean to—it happened so fast."

Anger ripples across his face. "Self-defense? Did he hurt you?"

I shake my head quickly. "He was about to, but I, uh. It's a long story."

Nathan releases his breath. "Well, I'm glad he didn't hurt you." He squeezes my hands. "It's okay, I'm not going to tell anyone."

"But—why?" I burst out. "Why wouldn't you? You've been charged with murder. You should be telling everyone it wasn't you, it was me."

"I'd be surprised if the sheriff can make it stick. There's no evidence that I had anything to do with the body."

"You don't know what he might do, how he'd paint it. He strikes me as the type of guy who colors outside the lines. I don't know that he'd care if he got the wrong person, as long as he got someone." Nathan winces, and I realize I'm gripping his hands so tight that my fingernails have dug little crescents into his palm. "I'm sorry." I release his hands, but he catches them again and brings them to his lips.

"I've failed you once, Meddy," he says, his eyes never leaving mine. "I didn't fight for you, and I've regretted it ever since. I don't want to lose you again."

My cheeks flush. Hell, my entire body flushes. I lean forward and catch his mouth with mine, our lips molding to fit perfectly, two pieces of the same puzzle. Our breaths mingle, and I swear I can feel his heartbeat right next to mine. This is why I haven't had a serious relationship since college. No one else can compare to this; no one can hold my heart in his hands the way Nathan does.

"I can't let you go down for this," I whisper. He runs a thumb across my lower lip, tracing a searing line to my chin, and a delicious shiver runs through me.

"I won't. Really."

Summoning the last of my strength, I pull away. "But—" My thoughts are a mess. My breath is coming out in shallow gasps. I struggle to think straight. "It'll be such bad publicity. If there's even a shred of suspicion on you, the resort—"

A shadow crosses his face, and I know, then, that I've hit the truth of the matter. Sheriff McConnell is likely not going to make the murder charge stick, not with so little evidence. But the accusation will be enough to scare the investors. And then what will happen? In my mind's eye, I see a roomful of people in sharp suits sitting around a large conference table. Someone asks for a vote to remove Nathan Chan as the CEO of Ayana Lucia. And one by one, they all raise their hands. They can't have someone so notorious be the face of their company. And that'll be that. Nathan's dreams would be over. This gorgeous resort he's planned, designed, and built—he'll lose it. They'll probably give him a tidy severance package, but he'll never again be able to find investors for another venture, not with this rumor hanging over his shoulder, casting its long shadow.

"Oh, Nathan." I can't stand looking at the sadness he's trying so hard to hide from me. I know what it looks like when he's trying to hide something so I won't worry.

"It'll be fine," he says, his voice gruff.

But it won't.

As though reading my mind, Nathan pulls me right up against him so I feel the intoxicating heat of his body. "Please let me do this for you," he says in a low voice that makes my legs wobble.

"But—"

"If you come forward and admit you did it, I'll do the same. I'll insist that I did it, and then I'll definitely, 100 percent lose all of this." He's absolutely serious. He'd really choose to lose everything to stop me from turning myself in.

"Nathan." His name comes out in a choked sob, and I kiss him again. I never want to feel his lips leaving mine.

A chair outside creaks loudly and we break apart, right before Sheriff McConnell opens the door. He narrows his eyes at us. What a sight we must make—both of us out of breath, my hair all rumpled, our cheeks flushed, sitting away from each other in the most awkward position. We must look like guilty, horny teenagers. Sheriff McConnell frowns. Surely he must realize I'm no lawyer—

"God, I hate lawyers," he rumbles.

Huh. Maybe he hasn't put two and two together. "Yeah, you and everyone else," I say, standing up and brushing myself off as calmly as I can. "I'm just about done here. Thank you, Sheriff. I'll be . . ." I glance back at Nathan, who raises his eyebrows. "I'll be back after consulting with my firm."

"Take your time," Sheriff McConnell says, lowering himself onto Nathan's plush leather chair with obvious relish.

He leans back, puts his feet up on the mahogany table, and rests his hands on his stomach.

I try to send silent messages to Nathan as I walk out. *I'll be back. I won't leave you here like this. I'll set you free. I'll clear your name.* I don't know if he got any of that.

As soon as I'm in the privacy of the elevator, I sag against the wall and bury my face in my hands. What a mess. What am I to do? I should just gather all the evidence I have against me that'll clear Nathan and present it to the sheriff. I'll turn myself in. I—

But that'll implicate Ma and my aunties. In the eyes of the law, my family is very, very guilty. And to add to the towering pile of calamities, Ah Guan wasn't dead when we stuffed him in the cooler. He died suffocating inside it. Which means I wasn't the only one who killed him. My entire family did.

Maybe I can spin it so that I'm the only guilty one. Maybe I can make it out so that I tricked my whole family, stole into Big Aunt's kitchen, and stowed the body in her cooler without anyone's knowledge. Yeah, that could work. Excitement and dread stir inside me. I might be able to make this work. I'd go to prison for a very long time. But it's no less than what I deserve. At the very least, this will, for the first time in my life, be a decision I'm making all on my own. Not a decision I'm making because I'm caving to Ma's wishes or to familial duty or anything. I guess I can at least feel good about that.

At the lobby, they've shut the giant wooden windows to protect the place from the storm. It completely transforms the place, turning it from a tropical paradise into a shuttered castle with fierce winds and rain raging against it. The mood is somber. I don't know how much the staff know about Nathan's arrest, but it's obvious that they're all aware that something is wrong. Though they smile politely at me as I walk by, their expressions are strained and tight with fear. I walk quickly down the hallway that leads to the rooms. First, I'll go back to my room and change out of these wet clothes. Then I'll ask Ma to come with me to Big Aunt's, where I'll tell everybody my plan to shoulder all of the blame. I take a big breath. It isn't going to be easy convincing them. Ma will for sure 100 percent cry. Big Aunt will get mad and insist that I listen to my elders and let them handle the problem. Second Aunt will probably launch into some weird Tai Chi pose, and Fourth Aunt will flap her feathery nails and tell me to stop being so melodramatic. But I'm resolute. No one can stop me from doing the right thing.

At my room, I take out Nathan's master key card and wave it against the door lock. It unlocks with a snick, and I push the door open, saying, "Ma, can I have some tea—"

The rest of what I'm about to say dies in my mouth. I stand there, frozen, as the door swings shut behind me with a final click. All of my plans, all of the courage I've built up in the past few minutes, everything leaks out of me, leaving me empty.

Because sitting on the bed are Ma and all of my aunts, their hands tied together, and standing behind them with a gun pointed at their heads is Maureen.

"Ah, Meddy," she says, and swings her arms up so the gun is now pointing straight in my face. "Now we can properly begin."

I guess someone can stop me from doing the right thing after all.

31

You see guns being pointed at people all the time on TV. It's become so commonplace that I don't blink whenever it happens on the screen. But in real life, oh man, in real life it's very, very different. With the barrel of the gun staring down at me like a—well, there's no comparison, it's a fucking gun aimed straight at my face, how much more terrifying can it get? My legs turn to water, and as I take my first step, my knees wobble and I stumble forward.

The room explodes in a burst of "Don't shoot!" "Aiya, no!" "No shoot!"

"Shh. Jesus, stop freaking out, please," Maureen says to my aunties and mom.

"Sorry!" I cry, as I straighten up. "I just—I'm so scared. I can barely walk." Come to think of it, I can barely breathe.

Maureen rolls her eyes. "I'm not going to shoot. Just go sit in that chair over there. God. You guys. Calm down." She looks at her gun, as though remembering it's there. "Right. Okay, look, I'll point this elsewhere for now." She lowers her arms so the gun's pointed at my legs. I guess that's a liiittle tiny bit better.

I practically crawl to the chair and sink into it gratefully. My entire body is basically a puddle. Now we know, when it comes to fight or flight, I am neither. I am: freeze like a hamster and then melt into a useless shivery puddle.

"Sayang, you are okay or not?" Ma calls out.

I manage a small nod and watch helplessly as Maureen stands and walks toward me. When she's a few steps away, she says, "Don't even think of jumping me." It's a laughable thought; my limbs are lead. Somehow, I manage to shake my head. Now she's right in front of me, and my heartbeat is no longer a beat. It's going too fast. It's basically a buzz. Maureen swings the gun back, and my eyes squeeze shut instinctively. My family members draw a sharp intake of breath, and Ma cries, "Please no!" Oh god, here it comes.

But nothing comes.

I crack open one eye. Maureen sighs. "Damn it, I've been daydreaming of this moment for hours. I was going to pistol-whip the shit out of you."

I cringe. Again, it's something you see on TV, but now that I'm actually living it, the idea of being hit by a gun is sickening.

"But I don't have it in me to do that." Maureen sighs again.

A sigh of relief is just halfway out of my mouth when Maureen suddenly darts close and puts her face right up in front of mine, like a striking snake. Ma and the aunties cry out again. I jump back and smack the back of my head against the vanity mirror.

"Aiya! Don't scare her!" one of the aunties snaps.

"Oh, shit! I'm sorry, I didn't think you'd jump like that," Maureen says. "Are you okay?"

Dizzy, I sit back down. I think I nod.

"I won't do that again. That was kind of an asshole move on my part. I just wanted to scare you a bit; I didn't think you'd react like that. Geez, girl."

"You are so naughty ah!" Ma scolds. "You don't scare her like that again!"

To my surprise, Maureen looks contrite. "Sorry, Auntie. I won't do that again." She straightens up and brushes her hair back. "Okay, let's get one thing straight: I need you to do something for me."

I manage to croak out a single: "What?"

"The tea ceremony gifts, dummy. What else did you think?"

I must have looked confused, because Maureen rolls her eyes again and says, "Get them. For me."

"Oh, right. How?"

Maureen throws her hands up. "I don't know, figure it out! Trick them, tell them you want to take photos of the gifts. Hold the bride at gunpoint—no, not the bride. Hold the groom at gunpoint."

"I don't have a gun."

"Here." She fishes in her back pocket and throws something at me. A gun. The thought *Holy shit, it's a gun being thrown at me* barely has time to flash through my mind before it hits me smack in the chest.

I don't even register the pain. I'm scrambling to— something—I don't know, I'm half-convinced the thing's going to go off and kill somebody, when it thuds to the floor. I squeak. My family cries out again. Maureen shakes her head at me. "Dude, your reflexes, seriously."

I pounce on the gun and grapple with it until I'm pointing it at Maureen.

Maureen frowns. "Okay, I'm not a TV villain, so I'm not gonna draw this out. That gun's not loaded."

I swallow. Look down at the gun. I've never touched one before. I don't even know how to check to see if it's loaded.

"You press the thingy," Maureen says. "That button, yeah."

The . . . ammo thingy slides out, and sure enough, it's empty. I push it back into place and put the gun down on the dresser. "I don't—I can't point a gun at someone. Not even an unloaded one." Even as I speak, I realize I'm absentmindedly wiping my hands on my pants.

"I mean . . . you get used to it," Maureen cajoles. She waves her own gun and points it at me again. "See?" I wince and move my head so it's not directly in the line of fire. Maureen lowers her gun again. "Okay, yes, it feels pretty shitty, but needs must, you know?"

"I don't know!" I cry. "You don't need to do this. Why are you doing any of it?"

"Because it all sucks!" she cries. "I don't want to do any of it. It's all gone wrong. The gifts weren't even supposed to—they were supposed to be returned to Jackie once it all died down. I just wanted to—I don't know, I wanted to—" Her voice wobbles, and she pauses to blink away her tears. "Anyway, it doesn't matter now, because it's all gone wrong and it's all because of *you*."

"Why me?" But even as I say it, it all comes rushing back. Of course. It IS because of me. Because I killed her partner in crime.

"Because you killed Ah Guan. He was supposed to help me with all of this, hide the gifts and then put them back and everything, and you killed him and—god, Meddelin. I may be a thief, but you and your fam are killers," she says in this super-judgy tone of voice.

"What makes you think we killed him?" I say in my most innocent voice.

"I heard you guys talking about it round the side of the hotel as I was coming back. Sorry, Aunties, but you're all very loud, and I speak Indo very well. And Chinese. You guys know how it is."

"Wah, she speaks Indonesian and Chinese very well," Ma says wistfully. "Your parents must be so proud." She gives me a pointed look.

I ignore Ma. "Weren't you being escorted off the island?"

Maureen shrugs. "I have a black belt in karate." At my look of horror, she sighs and says, "I didn't do anything, gosh! I just knocked the guy out a little and took his gun. That's still not as bad as you guys killing Ah Guan."

"We didn't—I didn't mean to! He was going to attack me. I panicked, and then when I woke up, I thought he was dead. Please, let my family go. They were just trying to help me; we didn't know he was still alive when we put him in the cooler," I cry.

Maureen digs a phone out of her pocket and taps on the screen. "Ha, got your confession on tape. Okay, here's what's going to happen: I've set this voice recording to be blasted on all of my social media in an hour's time. If you don't get me the tea ceremony gifts, everyone will know what you and your fam did. If you get me arrested or whatever, the recording will be blasted on social media. Get me the tea ceremony gifts and I'll delete the recording and we can go our separate ways."

"Wah, this girl very smart," Second Aunt muses, nodding grudgingly.

"Iya, pinter ya," Big Aunt says. "Meddy, should learn to be more like her. Very smart. Must do good business."

Now it's my turn to throw up my hands. "Seriously? She's literally blackmailing us at gunpoint!"

Big Aunt tuts. "Aduh, of course we no mean you should point gun at people. But just saying, this Maureen very—what's the word—so business-mind—"

"Evil? Crazy?" I cry.

"Hey," Maureen snaps.

I gesture wildly at her. "You're pointing a gun at me and asking me to rob your best friend. How much more evil can you get?"

"She see opportunity, she take it," Second Aunt says. "You should be more like that." Big Aunt nods, and the two of them look at each other for a moment, as though surprised to find that they're agreeing with each other for once.

"But don't point gun at people, very rude," Ma says.

"Oh, well, I'm glad we have this distinction, at least." FFS. My family, I tell you. They just know how to push all of my buttons. I'm never good enough for them, not even compared to a gun-toting homicidal robber.

Then I realize that the rage they've stirred up inside me has given me newfound strength. I'm so fired up. I need to find a way to prove them wrong, to show them that I'm not this useless ball of tears they seem to think I am.

"If you guys like her so much, then maybe she should be your stinkin' photographer." Even as I say it, I know how petty and childish it sounds.

"Aiya, Meddy, don't be like that," Ma says. "We only give you advice for your own good. Must learn to be smart like Maureen. You see, Maureen want to take tea ceremony gift, so she got to think of every possibility."

Maureen simpers. "It did take me a while to figure it all out."

"You be good, you figure out how to take tea ceremony gift and save all of us, okay," Ma says.

"Yep, we're all counting on you," Fourth Aunt says.

I shake my head in disbelief. "I can't even with you guys right now." I grab the unloaded gun from the dresser and stuff it into my back pocket.

"Okay, that's way too obvious. It's bulging out of your pocket," Fourth Aunt calls out.

"They're a lot bulkier than they look, aren't they?" Maureen says, sympathetically.

"I don't need help from you," I spit out as Maureen reaches out.

"Okay, sheesh."

"Meddy, don't be so rude," Ma says. "Maureen just trying to help."

It takes all of my will not to scream at all of them. I grab my camera bag and take out two of my lenses, placing them with utmost care on the dresser. "Don't touch these."

"Yes, no touch, they are very expensive. You break, you pay," Ma says.

"I won't," Maureen says, holding up her hands.

I stuff the gun into the bag and glare at them. "Right. So all I have to do is hold people at gunpoint before robbing them."

"You can, I believe in you," Ma says.

"Jia you!" Second Aunt gives me the traditional Chinese cheer.

"They're so supportive. I wish my family were more supportive," Maureen sighs.

"You can have mine," I snap, and leave the room before I say something I'll no doubt regret.

32

Compared to how it was earlier in the day, the bridal suite is practically deserted. Jacqueline's parents are in the living room, talking quietly. They glance up at me with lined faces when I come in. The sight of their exhaustion might as well be a knife in my chest. I wish I could hug them and beg for their forgiveness.

"Hi, Tante, Om. Is Jacqueline here?" I say, hating every word, hating the fact that I'm intruding at such a sensitive time. I half-wish they'd throw me out right now. Instead, Tante Yohana nods and smiles.

"Ah, Meddy. Maybe she'll talk to you. She's in the bedroom."

Swallowing, I head there. I swear my chest must be visibly moving, my heart's kicking so wildly. I reach the impressive double doors and knock lightly. When there's no answer, I grit my teeth and push it open just a crack. "Um, Jacqueline? It's me, Meddy. Can I come in?"

There's a sob. I can't tell if that's a yes or a no, so I push open the door and walk inside, closing it behind me. Jacqueline is buried under about sixteen layers of frothy tulle, and I have to peel away layer after layer for what feels like an entire minute until I unearth her.

"Go 'way," she sobs, batting away my hand feebly.

"Hey," I say, softly.

She glances up and utters another sob. "Oh, it's you. Is it just you? I don't wanna talk to anyone right now, especially not people who I thought were close to me!" The last few words come out in a dramatic half-shout, and she buries her face in the pillows once more and wails into them.

"It's just me." Not knowing what else to do, I perch carefully on the side of the bed. I glance to the corner where the safe is and quickly look away. How awful of a person am I, to be thinking of stealing from this miserable person who's been betrayed by practically everyone on her wedding day? I guess I'm pretty freaking awful, because my gaze keeps creeping back to the safe, and I have to consciously drag it back to Jacqueline. Or maybe I should try to get into it now, while she's not looking? But I don't know the safe combination.

"You know what the worst part of today is?" Jacqueline cries, suddenly sitting up.

"Um." I sift through my mind. There are so many contenders. The corpse showing up at the altar? The tea ceremony gifts going missing? Her fiancé hiring random actors to act as his groomsmen?

"Whenever something good or bad happens, the first person I turn to is Maureen. And now I can't, because even she turned out to be a dirty traitor!" She devolves into sobs again. "What is it about me? Am I so horrible that people close to me can't help but lie to me? My own fiancé can't even trust me enough to tell me that he doesn't have enough friends to have as groomsmen. How messed up is that?" she cries, staring at me with her wet face.

What's the right thing to say here? I mean, it is SO messed up, but then again, I don't think that's what she wants to hear. "Um. It's not great, but it's also not the worst thing a guy could do." Except Tom has done worse, aside from being named Tom Cruise. He also happens to be a world-class douche. I shouldn't be defending him. "Okay, yeah, it's pretty shitty. Look, you want to know the truth? Tom's kind of a shit."

Jacqueline's mouth drops open, and those huge eyes stare at me. Oh my god. I can't believe that just slipped out of me.

"Sorry, I didn't mean that. Ignore me, I'm not really thinking straight, I hit my head back there, when—uh. Yeah." Oh my god, I almost said, "I hit my head back there, when Maureen scared the crap out of me with her gun." Keep it together, self.

To my surprise, something like a laugh squeaks out of Jacqueline's mouth before she covers it. "I can't believe you just said that."

"I'm sorry, really, I am—"

"No, don't be sorry. After today, I think you're right," she says in a whisper, and then she does a horrified sort of laugh. "I can't believe I just said that about the guy I'm about to marry."

"Are you? Still marrying him, I mean." I know what I hope her answer is. I haven't known these people very long at all, but talk about beauty and the beast. It's not even that Tom's particularly unattractive; he's just so *ugh* in every possible way.

"Yeah, of course—" she falters and looks horrified. "I—I don't know. Our families are so good together. Our parents get along so well, they've got investments with each other, and they're so keen for us to be married—"

I know all too well what she's talking about. Within the rich Chinese-Indonesian communities, parents scheme and plan so that their sons and daughters will be able to marry the wealthiest sons and daughters. Given the Sutopos' vast conglomerate of corporations and real estate, Tom is a catch, regardless of his odious personality.

Her last words come out in a whisper: "But he really is a shit, isn't he?" She half-sobs, half-laughs. "God, I wish Maureen were here. She's always hated him, you know? Well, she's always hated whatever guy I dated, but with Tom, god, she was always ranting about how gross he is, and I just never saw it. Honestly? I think I'm more upset about Maureen than any of it. Does that make me a bad person? I haven't even really thought of that poor dead guy—I mean, Jesus, there was a dead guy at our ceremony! How much more of a bad omen can you get? I can't believe one of the actors Tom hired turned up dead."

I blink at her. It takes a while to sink in. Of course. She doesn't know that Ah Guan wasn't one of the groomsmen. She doesn't know anyone in the groom's bridal party. Nobody does.

"I wish I could talk to Maureen!" Jacqueline wails again, burying her face in her hands. "I miss that asshole so much."

Great. Of course, the one person she misses just happens to be the woman currently holding my family hostage at gunpoint. My family who's probably fawning over her and telling her what a great daughter she'd make instead of me.

Ugh, freaking Maureen. Okay. What would Maureen do if she were here? Aside from grabbing the tea ceremony gifts and running away with them, that is. The thought of it makes me frown. Despite everything that's happened, I can't reconcile the image of Maureen stealing gifts that were meant for Jacqueline. My mind keeps reeling away from the wrongness of it and resting instead on all those times I caught glimpses of real friendship between the two women. The way Maureen anticipated Jacqueline's needs and brought her water before she even asked for it. The way Maureen supported Jacqueline's arms as she stepped into her huge dress. The way the two of them finish each other's sentences. There's so much love there. A lot more than whatever's between Jacqueline and Tom, that's for sure.

And that's when it clicks. Everything falls into place. The theft of the tea ceremony gifts, but the intention to return them. How distraught Maureen was when they found the gifts in her room. She was sorrowful, grieving, not because of the loss of the gifts but because of the loss of her friendship with Jacqueline.

Because Maureen's in love with Jacqueline.

My hands start flapping like Ma's and Big Aunt's and—come to think of it—the rest of my family's do when they get excited. There's a squealing sound emanating from somewhere. Takes a while to realize it's coming from me. Oh my god, oh my god—

"Why do you keep saying 'Oh my god'?" Jacqueline interrupts her crying to snap at me. "And why are you flapping like a chicken at a slaughterhouse?"

"Oh, sorry. I didn't realize I was saying 'Oh my god.'" I clear my throat. Gotta buy myself a bit of time, try to figure out how I should tell her—should I tell her? It's not exactly my secret to tell, and would it help matters? I don't know—my head's spinning with so many different pieces of information, like the fact that Maureen is still back in my hotel room with my family as her hostages. Am I putting their lives in danger by telling Jacqueline the truth? What do I do? I'm not equipped to handle this, I can't—

I can. All my life, I've told myself I'm incapable of handling whatever. Whether it's moving east with Nathan or moving out of Ma's house or breaking away from the family business and starting out on my own. Again and again, I tell myself I'm not ready. I still lack whatever skills are needed to strike out. But there's nobody to count on now. Nathan's been captured by a Podunk sheriff drunk on power, and the rest of my family's being held at gunpoint. It all comes down to me. I'm the one who started it all. I should be the one who finishes it.

Deep breath. I force my hands to stop flapping. Inhale. I take Jacqueline's hands. Look her in the eye.

"Jacqueline, do you trust me?"

She takes in a shuddery breath and then nods.

"Good. Then there's something I need you to do."

33

I knock on the door to my room and open it a crack before calling out, "It's me, Meddy. Don't shoot, I'm coming in."

A few cheery shouts of "Oh, you back!" and "Ayo, masuk, masuk!" greet me. My family's way too chipper for people who're being held at gunpoint, I must say. When I enter, they're all sitting around sipping tea, even Maureen.

"Seriously?"

"What?" Ma says, looking all surprised, like I haven't just caught her drinking tea with the literal enemy.

"Nothing. Of course you'd be drinking tea with your kidnapper, because why not?"

"I'm not a kidnapper," Maureen says, looking affronted.

"Yah, why you being so rude, Meddy? I raise you better than this," Ma says.

I raise my eyes to the ceiling. "Whatever. Here you go. I got it." I toss the duffel bag onto the floor, grimacing when it hits the floor with a loud tinkle. Shit, I hope I haven't just broken some priceless Cartier watch or whatever.

"Hati-hati!" Big Aunt cries.

"Sorry, I wasn't thinking—" It's hard trying to make a statement.

"Oooh, exciting," Maureen says, getting up from the chair. She starts to bend over, stops, then points her gun at me and says, "Open it."

I do as she tells me and step back as she uses her toes to prod at the bag. Jewelry and watches glitter from inside it.

"Wow," Maureen says after a pause. "I didn't think you'd pull it off."

"I tell you, my daughter is very smart," Ma says, nodding and smiling proudly at me.

I feel a flush of pride before I realize how fucked up it is to feel proud about this. Still, it's nice to be complimented.

"How did you do it?" Maureen says, staring at me. "How did you even get inside the safe? The bridal room must be full of people. How'd you get past them?"

"Well, let's see. I told them I was there to talk to Jacqueline, and then I talked to Jacqueline alone and told her you wanted the gifts, and she let me have them."

They all stare at me like I've just grown another head.

Maureen lets out a bark. "Oh, right, yeah, she just let you have them."

"Yeah, she did. She said she doesn't want them anyway, now that they're tainted with all the bad stuff that's happened, and she said you might as well have them."

"You're lying. Stop lying!" Maureen grasps the gun with both hands and aims it straight at my head.

There's a squawk from my family. "Aduh, don't point gun at people," Big Aunt says.

"Please, Maureen, put the gun down, be good girl," Ma pleads.

"Quiet, I'm trying to think!" Maureen glares at me. "How did you really get it?"

"I told them I wanted to talk to Jacqueline. She was in the bedroom all alone. I went in, held her at gunpoint, and told her to empty the safe or I'd shoot."

Maureen's chin trembles. "Was she okay?"

"No, she wasn't okay. What did you think was going to happen?"

"I don't know! I didn't think you'd actually go through with it!"

"Well, I did, and here's your stupid stash, now you can take it—there must be at least two million dollars' worth of stuff in there—and GO."

Maureen's eyes dart to the bag. Back to me. Down to the bag. "Did—um—did she ask about me at all?"

"Why do you care? You literally just had me rob her."

"Only because I didn't—I wanted—"

"What?" I snap, taking a step toward her. "You wanted what?"

"I was going to—I thought maybe this way, Jackie would come here and talk to me. Without calling the cops or anything. If she saw that I have the gifts, but I gave them back, maybe she'd—I don't know—"

"Why would she want to talk to you again after you stole from her? Twice!"

"I wasn't going to steal from her. That wasn't the plan!"

"What was the plan? How did you even get to know Ah Guan in the first place?"

"I—we were friends. He was the one who got me to suggest your mom as a florist to Jackie. Said she'd get a good deal. He knew I was upset about the wedding, so he came up with this whole plan to get it canceled. He said we could take the tea ceremony gifts, hide them for a while until the wedding's called off, and then we'd return them."

Knowing what I know of Ah Guan, he probably had no plans to return them, but I trust Maureen's telling the truth. I take another step toward her. "Why did Ah Guan think you'd be upset about the wedding?"

"Because—"

"Why, Maureen?"

"Because I love Jackie!"

There's a collective gasp from my family.

"I love her, okay?" Maureen cries, tears running down her face. "I've loved her since we first met, when we were in college. I told myself not to be so selfish, that she's not into girls. I would've supported her through all of her relationships—I did support her through most of them, but Tom is such a—"

"A shit!"

We all turn to look at the doorway, where Jacqueline's burst in, chest heaving. Once again, there's a collective gasp from my family.

"Wah, her makeup still okay," Big Aunt says approvingly. Second Aunt glances at her older sister in surprise. We all do, actually. For as long as I can remember, it's the first time Big Aunt's said something nice to Second Aunt. "Er—yes, mascara no run. Is because I apply eyelash glue on top of it, you know," Second Aunt says, smiling with obvious pride.

"Sshh," I hiss.

Jacqueline storms inside. Even though she's no longer in her huge white dress, there's just something about her that commands your attention. Maybe it's how ethereally beautiful she is. Or maybe it's the way she's looking at Maureen, half-glaring, half-something else. She's incandescent. It might be rage or sorrow or—

"Jackie—"

"I love you too!"

Love. It's love that's blazing so brightly from her, love that's caught all of our attention, love that now propels her inside this room.

I was right. The two women love each other. It was a gamble, but I was willing to risk it all for this. I step aside to let Jacqueline pass, and at last she's standing face-to-face with her best friend.

Slowly, Jacqueline raises her hand and places it on the gun. Maureen doesn't put up a fight as Jacqueline takes it from her and releases the ammo thingy. I really should brush up on my gun lingo.

"Empty," Jacqueline says, a smile touching her mouth. "I knew you couldn't hurt anyone. Not really."

"I—Jackie—how long—"

"Meddy got me to wait outside while she took the bag

in. I heard everything." Jacqueline places a gentle hand on Maureen's cheek. "Why didn't you tell me before?"

"I didn't think—I—you're straight, I didn't want to—"

"I only dated guys because I didn't want you to even suspect that I might be into you," Jackie cries. "I didn't want you to get scared. I thought *you* were straight."

She and Maureen laugh, then they fall into each other's arms. Jacqueline's chin tips up, Maureen lowers her head, and finally, their mouths meet in a heart-stopping kiss that makes my eyes well up. I look away to give them some semblance of privacy and see that Ma and my aunties are just sitting there, openly staring and smiling, not even pretending to look away or anything.

"Tsk," I tut at them, and they look sliiightly abashed. I stand there awkwardly, staring at the ceiling while my family steals glances at them. After what seems like an eternity, the two finally break apart, breathless and grinning.

"Look, her lipstick still stay on," Second Aunt says.

"Yes, your makeup number one. Excuse me, sorry to bother, but can untie us or not?" Big Aunt says. "My hands very painful."

"Oh! Yeah, of course. I'm so sorry," Maureen cries, and we all hurry to the beds to help untie the wrist bindings.

I kneel down in front of Ma and start working at the knots around her wrists. Now that I'm crouched so close to her, I can see every line on her face, every familiar crease and fold, all of the laugh lines and the worry lines, the pathways of her life so clearly written across her features. "You okay?" I say softly. There's so much I want to say to her, but at the same time, it feels like in this moment, she knows everything, every secret I've kept buried in my heart.

"Yes," she says, smiling at me. Her eyes are bright with unshed tears. "I so proud of you, Meddy."

And in that moment, I've never felt prouder of myself and my family.

34

"So let me get this straight," Sheriff McConnell says. "The dead guy's dead because . . . wait, why?"

It takes everything inside me not to leap out of my chair and throttle the guy. Luckily, I'm surrounded by my family, plus Jacqueline and Maureen. Jacqueline squeezes my shoulder and gives me one of her encouraging smiles. I can do this. I can spin a story to fool this man and let us all off the hook. "It's really all quite simple, Sheriff. You see, Ah Guan—that's the deceased—he wanted to steal the tea ceremony gifts—"

"That's them gifts you people get before the wedding ceremony?"

I wince at the words "you people," but keep going.

"Yes, in Chinese tradition, we usually have a tea ceremony, where the bride and groom's relatives give them money or jewelry and so on. After the tea ceremony, Maureen and I took the gifts back to the bridal suite."

"Hang on, aren't you the lawyer?" Sheriff McConnell says. Good grief, did he just notice that? I suppose I have changed into dry clothes, but still. As though reading my mind, he shakes his head and mutters, "You all look very similar to me."

"Yes, because we are all family," Ma says, beaming proudly.

"What, you're all related?"

"No, she meant a few of us are," I say quickly. "And I'm sort of . . . a lawyer-ish type of person." In that I watched every season of *The Good Fight*. "Anyway, so Maureen and I took the gifts back to the bridal suite and rejoined the procession, and that was when Ah Guan took the gifts. He must have been there all along, disguised as one of the groomsmen. I don't think he expected the bride and groom to discover that the gifts were missing so early; usually, they don't look at the gifts until the next day, but—I don't know, maybe Tom wanted to look at what kind of Patek Philippe he got. When Ah Guan heard that they were conducting a search, he must've panicked and stashed the gifts in Maureen's room. She's the likeliest suspect because she was the last one with the gifts."

Sheriff McConnell nods slowly, frowning at us the whole time.

"And then he needed a place to hide, and where else to hide but within plain sight?" I say, moving my hands animatedly. "He was disguised as a groomsman anyway, and the other groomsmen were drunk and weren't really aware of what was going on, plus they don't even know one another."

"Yes, wah, they are so drunk. One of them—I don't know who, but one of them"—Ma says meaningfully—"bring, you know, that alcohol, the very bad one. I think it is called 'abstinence.'"

"Well, I heard that one of them brought weed," Fourth Aunt says.

"Good grief," Sheriff McConnell mutters.

"Yeah," I cut in. "So he went into the groom's suite, and when the search party went through the suite, he panicked and hid in a cooler. See, one of the baker's coolers went missing earlier in the day, and I think Ah Guan was planning on using that to stash the stolen jewelry. We found the cooler in the groomsmen's suite. It got locked by mistake, and he suffocated in it and died."

Sheriff McConnell's eyes are so wide right now they look like they're about to pop out. But, as much as I brave myself for the inevitable cry of, "This is horseshit!" it doesn't come. Instead, what he says is, "And then what happened?"

"Then the groomsmen must've found him at some point, and by then they were all drugged out of their minds, they were tripping hard, so hard they didn't even realize he was dead. They must've thought it was a joke. They hauled him out and carried him cheerfully down to the altar. You can question them; we did, and they remember bits and pieces. Some of them remember finding Ah Guan and carrying him to the altar. They thought he was just passed out."

"I don't—wha . . ." Sheriff McConnell leans back, looking dazed. I can't blame him. It's a hell of a story we've all cooked up. But it's the best we could come up with. I hold my breath as he rubs his forehead. "How did you all figure out all these details? You weren't there, were you?"

"No, we pieced it together based on information we gathered from witnesses," I say, my voice a lot more confident than how I actually feel. "You could talk to the groomsmen if you want. They're right outside the office."

He nods silently, still looking dazed.

Jacqueline hurries to the door and opens it. As promised, the groomsmen are all waiting outside, and they look terrible. Their clothes are bedraggled, their hair is all messed up, and a handful of them have what look like vomit stains down their fronts. Sheriff McConnell wrinkles his nose and grimaces. Can't blame him; they smell so bad I can practically see the stink fumes radiating from them. It's a stench of sweat, vomit, and other bodily fluids I don't care to think of. They stumble inside and blink owlishly at us.

"So," Sheriff McConnell says, getting up from Nathan's chair. "You boys are the groomsmen."

They squint against the bright lights in the office and shrug. A couple of them mutter, "Worst job ever."

"Which of you boys are sober enough to tell me what the heck happened?"

A couple of hands are raised, hesitantly. Sheriff McConnell picks one. "You go first. State your name and occupation."

A short, friendly-looking guy steps forward. His hair is sticking out in every direction and his shirt is torn, but his eyes are the least bloodshot out of all the men. "Um, my name's Henry, and I'm an actor."

"And you know the groom . . . how?"

"I don't. Not really. I've only met him once before today. We were all hired to play his groomsmen."

"Millennials," Sheriff McConnell grumbles.

"Um, Tom hired most of us separately. I don't know about these other guys, I think a couple of them are from agencies, but most of us are independent actors."

Jacqueline shakes her head sadly, and Maureen hugs her close and kisses her cheek. Despite everything, the sight of them makes my heart melt, just a little.

"He paid us for like, a whole wedding experience, so that included a bachelor's night, which took place last night. We partied hard; I guess none of us wanted to let him down. God, I remember drinking and seeing the sky lighten and I was like, 'Shit, is it morning already?' It was wild, man. And the morning was just a blur, like—I don't know, people kept coming in and telling us to get ready or whatever, so we peeled ourselves off the floor and tried to get dressed, but it was a mess. The suite was a dump by the time we got through last night, everyone's clothes were all mixed up and shit, I think one of the guys lost his tux, another lost his pants, and people kept coming in and out of the room. It was horrible. Oh, and a lot of us were puking from the party." Henry sags into the chair and grabs his head. "My head's killing me. Is that all you wanted to know?"

"No!" Sheriff McConnell snaps. "No, you idiot, I want to know about the body."

"Oh, right, yeah of course. Yeah . . . man, I have no idea how that happened."

Sheriff McConnell looks as if he's about ready to explode. When he does talk, his voice comes out slow and deliberate, like he's talking to a particularly slow child. "Well, let's start with when you first realized there was a dead body."

"At the altar, when Joshua—er, was it Joshua or was it Kegan—I really have no idea who was holding the body up. When they dropped him. Then I realized there was a dead body. No, wait, it was after that. 'Cause I was laughing, I thought the guy was just really drunk, but then someone screamed that he was dead, so then I knew," Henry says, nodding with pride as if he's solved the whole mystery.

I don't dare meet anyone's eye. I might burst out laughing, or crying. It's surreal to see our plan actually get carried out.

"Before that," Sheriff McConnell urges, "do you know who found the body? It must've been in the groom's suite, right? And one of you must've found him; otherwise, how did he end up at the altar?"

"Um, I guess? I don't know who found him. I told you, it was a mess. I don't even know—oh man, I don't even know how I ended up at the altar. It was like I blinked and then there I was. It was crazy. I was seriously tripping."

"Who drugged you?" Sheriff McConnell roars.

"I mean, I don't know. I'd like to know, that was some good stuff—er, I mean, yeah, that was really uncool, drugging us like that," he finishes lamely. "You could wait until the rest of these guys sober up and question them. But I doubt any of them would know. We were all tripping haaard."

Sheriff McConnell leans back in his seat with a groan and barks, "Just get out. All of you, out!"

"Aren't you going to release Nathan?"

He glares at me, and there's so much hate and anger behind his eyes that I almost take a step back. Almost, but not quite, because behind me, Ma places a reassuring hand on my back and I stand tall.

"I'm not leaving until you release him. You see, I think we've established that it was all an unfortunate accident that has nothing to do with Nathan, and you don't have a case against him, or anyone. So close it. We've solved everything for you. You can tell mainland police you figured everything out on your own; we'll back you on that. They'll be so impressed by your work. Can you imagine the articles that'll be written about you? You solved a death and a theft involving two million dollars' worth of gifts!"

"Wah, you are the best police," Ma says.

"Very best, number one!" Big Aunt says, holding her thumbs up.

"Oh yes, I tell all my WhatsApp friends, wah, lucky got such great police," Second Aunt says.

"What a strapping hero," Fourth Aunt simpers.

He's torn, anyone can see that, between the implausibility of the situation and wanting to believe what we're saying. He wants to believe it so badly. He knows he's in way over his head, that he's bungled this up beyond all measure. Better to claim that he's solved everything before the big boys from the mainland march in and take over.

Then, Maureen, accountant extraordinaire, steps in and says the words that tip the sheriff over to our side once and for all: "I'll help you with the paperwork."

EPILOGUE

I take a deep breath and push open the swing doors to Top Dim Sum. Noise spills out, a cacophony of Mandarin, Cantonese, Hokkien, and other Chinese dialects I can't identify. At the reception desk, the host is already overrun by throngs of loud aunties and uncles asking about their tables.

"Oof," I breathe out. I don't know if I'll ever get used to the noise of Sunday dim sum. A strong hand finds mine and gives it a reassuring squeeze.

"I'm hungry," Nathan says, grinning down at me. "I can't wait."

"Ha!" I give him a weak laugh. I'm still half-convinced that one of these days he'll realize what a crazy mess my family is and decide he's better off without me. But no—I catch myself. No, he's lucky to have me. I'm lucky to have him. We're meant for each other. I smile up at him, and this time, my smile's less nervous. "Come on, they've got a table already."

We weave our way through the heaving crowd, into the main dining room.

"Meddyyyy!" someone yells over the noise, and I look

over to see Ma and Fourth Aunt waving their arms like they're one of those dancing balloon thingies outside of car dealerships. "Over heeeere!" they shout again, even though I've already waved in acknowledgment and we're very clearly walking toward them. My family, I swear.

"Wah, finally you arrive," Ma says, standing up and giving Nathan a hug. She squeezes my cheek like I'm all of two years old. We greet the rest of my aunties, and they all smile and start piling food on our plates.

"Ayo, makan!"

"Makan, makan!"

For a few minutes, we're quiet as we tuck into delicious, steaming plates of siu mai and har gow.

"You look healthy, Meddy," Big Aunt says in Mandarin.

"Yep, you really do," Nathan says. Unlike mine, his Mandarin is flawless. Yet another reason why Ma and my aunts adore him.

"Really? I think you look a bit tired, dear," Ma says, before Fourth Aunt obviously kicks her under the table.

"Remember, you're supposed to be supportive?" Fourth Aunt whispers in a volume loud enough to be heard over the din of the restaurant.

Ma nods and faces me again. "Ah yes, I was wrong. You don't look tired. You look radiant, very well fed, so different to when I last saw you." Still, when she smiles, it's obvious that she's trying her best to hide her sorrow.

I reach out for her hand. "Ma," I say, gently, "I see you literally every day. You know exactly how I look." Which is true. The woman pops up at my apartment first thing every morning with a stash of home-cooked food, and most nights I have dinner at her place. It's not so bad; my apartment's on Broadway, one block away from the Asian supermarket she goes to, so she makes every excuse she can to drop by. And as much as I hate to admit it, I love seeing my mom every day. It's made moving out a lot less hard on both of us.

"Aiya, your mom just misses you," Second Aunt scolds without any bite.

"I know, I miss you too," I say, squeezing Ma's hand.

"I don't like this whole modern thing where young women live on their own," Big Aunt says.

"Yes, it's very dangerous," Second Aunt agrees. They're so much more annoying now that they're agreeing with each other.

"Yes, Nathan, this is all your fault. Meddy moved out of my house because of you," Ma says.

"Whoa, why me?" Nathan cries, raising his hands and looking incredibly adorable.

"Maybe so you can be having all the sex," Ma grumbles in English.

"Ma!" I give Nathan an apologetic grimace, but he just shakes his head with silent laughter. I mean, she's not wrong, but STILL.

"It's okay, I am very modern," Ma says, switching back to Mandarin.

"Since when?" Fourth Aunt mutters.

"I'm so modern I don't even care if you get married or not, as long as you give me my grandbabies."

"Ma," I groan. But Nathan looks far from being scared off. He's laughing easily, his eyes twinkling as he watches me interacting with my family. "Are you done embarrassing me? Because I actually have something to show you," I say.

Ma waves at me to go on, and I rummage in my bag and take out a glossy magazine, which I put in the middle of the lazy Susan. There's a moment when Big Aunt and Ma look around for their reading glasses. Then they all lean forward and squint at the magazine.

"*Martha Stewart Wedd*—oh my god," Fourth Aunt says. "No! Really? We're in there?"

I grin at them. "Yep, really. It's on page 20. A three-page spread with pictures of everything—the cake, your flowers, the amazing makeup."

"The resort," Nathan adds. "All captured beautifully by Meddy." He grins at me, and my heart splits wide open. It always does at that smile.

My mom and aunts squeal and chatter happily as they flip to the pages showcasing Jacqueline and Maureen's wedding. "Wah, the cake is so, so pretty," Second Aunt says.

Big Aunt smiles at her and says, "And the brides look very beautiful."

Ma beams through her tears. "Look, our business name is there." And sure enough, underneath the big title is a list of vendors, clearly listing the name of the family company. And, below that: Photographed by MC Photography.

I'm no longer part of my family's business. We're affiliated, and I'm always referring clients to them and vice versa, and sometimes, as was the case with Jacqueline and Maureen's wedding, we work together. But other than that, I'm mostly done with big weddings. Breaking away was hard at first for all of us, but they soon got used to Seb, which is unsurprising because he's amazing, and I soon found my niche: photographing the in-betweens. I do just about everything, from engagements to newborns to families who just want to capture the joy in their lives, and I love it. My website is filled with kissing couples and laughing babies. I guess it doesn't hurt that I often suggest Nathan's gorgeous resort as the location of their shoot. The cross-pollination has been good for all of us.

"And *Martha Stewart Weddings* is only the first to publicize our story," Nathan says. "We've lined up a whole lot of other online wedding publications too. Prepare to be booked out for the next two years."

Big Aunt, who handles all the bookings, has been sworn to silence. But at this she yelps, "It's true! We're already book out this year!"

The other women stare at her. "What? Just the other night you were talking about being worried because we have no customers," Ma says.

"Aiya, obviously I was just making it up. You see, Meddy? I'm good at keeping secrets, right? Meddy was very sure that I wouldn't be able to keep it a secret." She grins proudly while the others shake their heads and then says, "Aaand, guess who booked us last night." She doesn't give anyone time to guess before squealing, "The Sutopos!"

"What?" we all squawk.

"Sutopo as in . . . Tom Cruise Sutopo?" I say. "Why in

the world would they want to hire you guys again after what happened last time?"

"Tsk, they know it's not our fault," Big Aunt says, flapping her hand at me.

"I mean, it sort of definitely was our fault," I mutter.

"Okay, they don't know that. When they saw us in *Martha Stewart Weddings*, they said to us: 'You are the best in this area. We must top Jacqueline and Maureen's wedding so that we can save face! We'll pay you double; make sure the wedding is better in every way.'"

"Wow. Here's to Tom, I guess. I hope he's found someone more . . . suitable for him." Someone who's less likely to take his bullshit.

Ma sighs loudly. She waits until all the attention is on her before saying in English, "All these people get marry." She looks pointedly at me and Nathan.

"Ma, come on," I groan. "You said you wouldn't—"

Nathan gives my hand another squeeze and says, "It's fine. I know, Auntie, I'm sorry we're taking our time. There have been a lot of things we had to take care of, but you're right."

"I am?" Ma says.

The table falls silent. "Nathan," I whisper, "I think they're getting the wrong idea."

In answer, he nods at a nearby waiter, who grins and walks toward us with a small bamboo steamer. *What*? As though in slow motion, I turn to look at Nathan. He smiles at me. I look at the waiter.

"Oh god," I whisper.

336

The bamboo steamer is placed before me, and the waiter opens it with a flourish, revealing a navy blue velvet box inside.

"Nathan. Really?" I can't say anything else. My throat has closed up with tears. Dimly, I sense my family members flapping like headless chickens, and the commotion catches the eye of the other diners, who turn and watch us with unconcealed interest.

Nathan takes the box out of the steamer and gets down on one knee. Without taking his gaze from mine, he smiles and says, "Meddelin Chan, will you marry me?"

"YES!"

I look around in surprise. The yes had come from my mother. The aunties yank her back. I turn back to Nathan. The man I've loved for all of my adult life. The one who got away. The one who, against all odds, found me again. The man of all my dreams.

I've hidden him from my family for so long. It's only fitting that I make this declaration in front of them, here and now, in this heavily quiet dim sum restaurant.

"Yes."

The roar envelops all of us, a heady rush of congratulations all around, and I know then, as I have never known before, that Nathan and I are home.

AUTHOR'S NOTE

Thank you so much for reading *Dial A For Aunties*. This book is a love letter to my family—a ridiculously large bunch with a long history of immigration. All four of my grandparents came from China to Indonesia between 1920 and 1930, and when they arrived in Indonesia, they changed their Chinese names to Indonesian ones to avoid xenophobia. Chen became Sutanto. Ho became Wijaya. As they fully integrated themselves into Indonesian culture, so too did their offspring. My parents grew up speaking Bahasa Indonesia as a first language and Mandarin as a second language.

With my generation, my parents sent us to Singapore to avoid the nineties riots—clashes in Indonesia against the Chinese population. Fortunately, now Indonesia is a wonderfully diverse country in terms of race and religion, and we are afforded the kind of freedom our parents didn't have. While in Singapore, my cousins and I quickly adopted English as our first language. Some of us (cough, cough, me) forgot how to speak Indonesian almost entirely. Whenever my parents visited, we struggled to communicate with each other.

The result of all this moving around is a mish-mash of

languages. My family is technically trilingual, but each of the three languages we speak is broken in some way. I'm most comfortable in English, then Mandarin because I spent ten years studying it in Singapore, and then Indonesian. My parents are fluent in Indonesian and Mandarin, and speak halting, broken English. When we speak to each other, the sentences are jagged and cracked, and we often struggle to convey what we're trying to say. This is the price my parents have had to pay to ensure that my brother and I were safe and sound.

Some of the aunties in *Dial A For Aunties* speak the sort of broken English that my parents' generation does. Their grasp of the English language is not a reflection of their intelligence, but a reflection of the sacrifice they have made for us. They are, in essence, trilingual, and I am so proud of this heritage. I'm aware while writing this that I'm straddling a very fine line between authenticity and stereotype, and it's my hope that this book defies the latter. It is by no means representative of the Asian community as a whole; no single book can possibly represent such a large community of individuals.

I hope *Dial A For Aunties* gives you a little peek into the fierce love with which my family raised us and protects us to this day.

—Jesse

ACKNOWLEDGMENTS

Dial A For Aunties is hands down the most joyous publishing experience I have had. From the writing to the submissions to the publishing process—all of it has been so wonderful and smooth that if I were to see this publishing timeline on a TV show, I would've snorted and said it's unrealistic.

Many, many people are responsible for making this journey as magical as it has been. My agent, Katelyn Detweiler, was the best ever champion for the book. Her excitement upon reading it was a delight to see, and she handled the submissions process so masterfully, despite all the panicking and flailing from my end. Thanks to Katelyn, *Dial A For Aunties* found the best possible home at Berkley.

Cindy Hwang was my dream editor, and working with her has turned out to be even better than I had dared to hope for. Thank you for helping to mold the book into its current form, and for working so patiently with me on the most challenging edits of all. It was such a joy to open up the document and see that Cindy had corrected my Chinese spelling; truly a moment when I knew without a doubt that I was in the best hands.

To the rest of the Berkley team—Angela Kim, who is always ready with a response even past midnight; Jin Yu for her endless creativity; and Erin Galloway and Dache Rogers, who are pure magic when it comes to publicity. Thank you, too, to the team at Jill Grinberg Literary Management—Sophia Seidner, Denise Page, and of course Sam Farkas, for bringing the aunties to all over the world.

I am so excited that *Dial A For Aunties* will be a Netflix movie. This wouldn't have been possible without the efforts of Mary Pender and Olivia Fanaro of United Talent Agency. They pitched the project flawlessly and found the perfect producers, Nahnatchka Khan, Chloe Yellin, John Davis, and Jordan Davis. I'm so glad that the project is being handled by Lisa Nishimura of Netflix, who will no doubt turn it into a wonderful, rollicking film.

On the personal side, I am wildly grateful to Nicole Lesperance for urging me to write this batty story, Bethany Hensel for talking me through all of my indecisions and helping me envision the right ending, Lani Frank for being such a sharp, brilliant critique partner, and Elaine Aliment for her expertise on writing romance. And of course to the rest of my writing family: Toria Hegedus for being empathetic even when I'm at my most unbearable, SL Huang who is quite possibly the smartest person I know, Tilly Latimer for all the reality checks, Rob Livermore for the laughs, Maddox Hahn for all the entertainment, Mel Melcer for the wisdom, Emma Maree for the faith in humanity, Grace Shim for the hours of heart-to-heart when I needed them, Sajni Patel for all the virtual donuts, Marti Leimbach for sharing all of her publishing expertise, Alechia Dow for always checking in on me, Kate Dylan for being such a hilarious fish, and all the folks of Absolute Write, without whom I would have quit writing a long time ago.

To my husband, Mike, who supported me for years while I struggled to write. Without his confidence in me, I would've definitely given up after my first book. In fact, I probably wouldn't have even finished my first book. To my little girls, Emmeline and Rosalie, who will one day read this when they're grown (I hope. Or I shall guilt them into reading it!) and hopefully gain more understanding of our heritage from it. Or at least some laughs.

And most importantly, to my Mama and Papa and the rest of the Sutanto and Wijaya families. Growing up, I never experienced true fear because I always knew that my parents and the entire strength of the Sutanto and Wijaya clans would catch me if I fell. Thank you for bringing me up with that assurance. Thank you for giving up everything so that you could give me everything. This book is about families, for my family.

Terima kasih, Mama dan Papa tersayang.

Meddy and her amazing aunties will return in

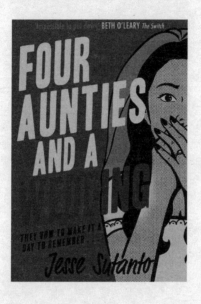

After Meddy Chan and her aunties got away with *literal* murder, she's hoping for a quieter life. She's happily coupled up with love of her life Nathan, and excited to plan her dream wedding. She just needs to keep her family from interfering *too much*.

Meddy has dreamt of her wedding day but with the Chans involved, this is going to be a wedding day you'll never forget . . .

Keep reading for the first chapters . . .

1

I try not to breathe as the last corset hook is yanked into place. "Ow, that's digging into my rib cage."

Yenyen huffs a breath through his teeth and gives one last vicious tug, which forces a squeak out of me. "In the past, brides would break their ribs to fit into their wedding dresses," he says, and it strikes me that he's not saying it in a horrified tone, but rather a wistful one, which is somewhat worrying. "How do you feel?"

I risk breathing again, and to my surprise, despite the torturous time I had getting stuffed into the dress, once I'm in, it's actually—dare I say it—comfortable. What sort of black magic is this? I could've sworn I would hardly be able to take even the tiniest sip of air. I blink at him in surprise. "I can breathe in it."

I can't quite see his eyes behind the round, purple-tinted sunglasses, but I'm pretty sure I hear them roll.

"Aduuuh, of course you can breathe in it, silly. Yenyen's creations aren't just beautiful, they're also build for maximum comfort."

I can't help but smile at him. Yenyen has a tendency to

refer to himself in third person, which should sound mildly deranged but actually comes off somewhat endearing. His real name is Yenzhen, but nobody is allowed to call him that. Within the Chinese tradition, it's common to have phonetically repeated names as a pet name, and as Yenyen says, he's everybody's best friend, so we must call him Yenyen.

"Now, are you ready to see it?" he says.

Am I? My heart rate rises. My cheeks grow warm. This will be the forty-millionth dress I've tried on. I swear I've tried on every wedding dress L.A. has to offer, and each time, there's been something that Ma or my aunts didn't like. Over the last few months, as we exhausted every bridal boutique in greater Los Angeles, their comments have seared themselves onto my brain.

"Sequin not shiny enough."

"The lace look itchy, is making me itchy, is making you itchy?"

"Body too slutty." (Second Aunt meant bodice. I think.)

And so on and so forth, until Nathan announced that he'd arranged for Indonesia's premiere wedding dress designer to come to L.A. with custom-made dresses. Including—and this is the pièce de résistance—dresses for the mother and aunts of the bride.

I swallow and nod at Yenyen. "I'm ready."

"Okay, keep your eyes closed, though!" He gathers the skirt behind me as I turn slowly to face the floor-length mirror. After a minute of rustling and fussing, he says, "Open your eyes."

I do as he says.

My mouth drops open. "Yenyen—" My breath catches in my throat. There are no words to describe this dress. I know, in that moment, that this is it. This is The One. The bodice is swathed in the softest, most delicate lace that looks like it was sewn by fairies using spider silk. The skirt is a gorgeous frothy affair that somehow remains light enough for me to move around in. The entire thing hugs my body in all the right places and accentuates my curves in a way that is at once sexy and conservative. I feel as though I'm wearing a cloud. Tears rush to my eyes. "It's perfect," I whisper.

Yenyen waves me off, but it's obvious he's fighting off a huge smile. "Shall we show your family?"

Here we go. Deep breath. I don't know what I'll do if they say they don't like it. I steel myself, tightening my hands into fists. I'll fight for this dress. I've acquiesced to their never-ending laundry list of complaints, despite many of the dresses I've tried on being perfectly fine. This one isn't just perfectly fine, though. It's actually perfect. And I won't let them ruin it for me. I won't. I—

"Ta-da!" Yenyen cries as he yanks open the bedroom door with a flourish.

I grit my teeth, awaiting the cascade of complaints, but there are none. In fact, there is nobody around. The sofa and chairs arranged in a semicircle in Ma's living room are empty.

"Aduh," Yenyen cries, throwing up his hands. "Yenyen can't work like this. You know how important a good entrance is? This isn't just a dress; it's an experience!"

"I'm so sorry. I don't know where they went. Maybe to

the bathroom?" I'm about to call out for them when footsteps thunder down the hallway.

"Meddy? That you? Sudahan ya?" Ma calls out.

"Yes, she is done!" Yenyen snaps. "Please take your seats so your daughter can show you her beautiful wedding gown."

"Eh, tunggu! Meddy, you close your eyes!"

"What?" Yenyen's face is turning red. His whole moment is being ruined, poor guy.

"Just go with it." I pat him on the shoulder.

"Unbelievable!" he snaps, but takes control of himself and arranges my skirt and train so it cascades flawlessly across the hardwood floor.

"Ready or not, ah?" Second Aunt shouts.

"Yes." I close my eyes, half-dreading what I'm about to see. Ma and the rest of my aunts come out of Ma's bedroom giggling like schoolgirls. But before they get to the living room, Yenyen mutters, "This feels wrong," and rushes over to the hallway to see them.

His gasp can be heard all the way over in Santa Monica. "Those are *not* the dresses Yenyen brought you!"

"No, it's the dresses *Jonjon* brought them," someone else says regally.

Okay, not even the strongest-willed person can keep their eyes closed through this. I crack one eye open just as a tall, thin man wrapped in a tight-fitting snakeskin suit emerges from the kitchen.

Yenyen gasps again. "Jonjon. How dare you?"

"What's going on?" I say.

"Hello, nice to meet you. I'm Jonjon, you might have

4

heard of me? Voted most avant-garde fashion designer in Indonesia? I was featured in *Tatler* and *Vogue*?" He extends a hand dripping with various chunky rings. Unsure what to do, I shake it limply. "Your family asked me to design their gowns for your wedding."

"But Yenyen designed their gowns!" Yenyen cries.

Jonjon snorts. "Those lumpy brown sacks? I don't think so. These ladies deserve better. Ready to see them?"

"Wait, wait!" Yenyen grabs a wool blanket off the couch and throws it around me. "Okay, when the time is right, throw off the blanket with a flourish, ya?"

"Um. Okay." I hug the blanket tight around me and nod at Jonjon, half-dreading what I'm about to see.

"Behold!" Jonjon waves grandly, taps on his phone, and tinny pop music plays as one by one, my family struts down the hallway.

I turn around. And stare in shock-horror at the spectacle before me.

Big Aunt, Second Aunt, Ma, and Fourth Aunt are all decked out in the most blinged-out, most aggressively purple dresses I have ever laid eyes on. Ever. How do I describe the particular shade of purple? It's as if flamingo pink and electric blue had a baby and then that baby snorted a line of coke and proceeded to punch you in the face. It is a LOT of purple. And it's a LOT of different kinds of material. I'm talking taffeta, and embroidery, and sequins, oh god, so many sequins. With every move my mother and aunts make, crystals and jewels flash and threaten to blind me. And that's not even the worst part.

"What are those things on your heads?" My voice comes out hushed with horror, but Fourth Aunt must have misheard it as awe, because she simpers and flutters her fake lashes at me.

"Aren't these just gorgeous?" She pats the—the thing—on her head gently. "It's called a fascinator. They are a must-have for English weddings. We're going to fit in so well."

"With that THING on your head? I mean, what—I—but—" I sputter.

"Aiya, you hate it!" Ma wails. She turns to her sisters. "I tell you, I say, Komodo dragon is not good choice, we should have gone with flamingo!"

My mouth opens and closes, but no words come out. What does one say when faced with four women wearing ten-inch-tall Komodo dragons on their heads? Well, not actual live ones, at least. I think. "They're not real, are they?" I don't know that I'd be able to forgive my family if they were.

At this, Jonjon smiles smugly. "They look real, don't they? I understand why you'd think they are; the craftsmanship is flawless, isn't it?"

Again, no words come. The dragons are in various positions, each one weirder than the last, but also somehow compatible with each woman's personality. Big Aunt's dragon is standing on its two hind legs, the front ones akimbo, like an Asian auntie who disapproves of your life choices. Second Aunt's dragon is—of course—stretched into some bizarre Tai Chi pose. Ma's is sitting down, primly sipping tea. Yes, there is an actual tiny teacup in its paws. And Fourth Aunt's is doing karaoke.

I turn to Yenyen. Maybe he can play bad cop for me and shoot this whole ridiculous getup down in flames. Like me, he's also staring open-mouthed at their fascinators. He extends an arm and touches Fourth Aunt's dragon as gingerly as though expecting it to come to life and take a chunk out of his hand.

"Amazing," he says.

I sidle over to him and whisper, "Don't you mean 'ridiculous'?"

His gaze flicks over to me and I see belatedly that the expression he's wearing isn't so much shock as it is wonderment. "Look at the craftsmanship. The scales, those eyes!"

"You mean how they follow you around the room?" I can't help but shudder.

"It's called the Mona Lisa effect," Yenyen says.

My mother and aunts preen.

"You do realize he's calling the dragons Mona Lisa, not you," I point out. Which is probably a petty thing to say, but really, now. There is no way in hell I can let this happen. I can't have them meeting Nathan's parents wearing Komodo-freaking-dragons on their heads.

"Okay, yang bener ya. Serious time," Big Aunt says, straightening her back and smoothing down the front of her ruffled skirt. "What you think, Meddy?"

I tear my eyes from the tops of their heads to her face, and that's when I realize it: Big Aunt is nervous. It's the first time I've seen that vulnerable look on her face. Well, I guess

7

I have seen it one other time before, when she had to move the body of a man I'd just killed. The naked worry and hope in her face make my chest squeeze painfully. My eyes move from Big Aunt to the others and find all of them wide-eyed with anticipation. Ma is wringing her hands, and Second Aunt looks like she's one mean comment away from plunging into a Tai Chi pose. Fourth Aunt is studying her nails, but now and again, she steals glances my way, and I know then that she's just as nervous as the others.

Well, crap.

"Um." My voice falters. I clear my throat and try again. "Well. Um. More importantly, what do *you* think, Big Aunt? Do you feel good in it?"

She starts to nod, but Jonjon shrieks, "Be careful!" and she jerks her head upright. Her Komodo dragon wobbles precariously for a few tense seconds as we stare with bated breath. Then it rights itself.

Sensing an opportunity, I pounce. "Well, uh—as incredible as they look, if you can't move freely in them, then I don't know if they're a good idea. I want you to feel completely comfortable at my wedding, Big Aunt."

"True . . ." she says.

Hope flutters in my chest.

"Oh, not a problem. On the day of, you just tell your hair and makeup artist to sew the fascinators to your wig," Yenyen says. "That's how most celebrities get them to stay on, you know."

"Thanks, Yenyen, very helpful," I hiss through gritted teeth. He's supposed to be on my side.

8

"So you like?" Big Aunt says, her eyes searching mine.

"I . . ." Six pairs of eyes bear down on me like six searing-hot laser beams. I know when I'm defeated. "If you like them, then I like them too."

Ma and the aunties' faces melt into huge grins, and for just this one moment, I'm glad I went along with it. Then common sense returns and I kick myself inwardly. What have I just done? What did I agree to? What is Nathan's prim English family going to think? The thought of introducing my batty family members to his well-dressed, eloquent mother is almost enough to make me break out in hives. Of course, as always, as soon as I think this, the guilt comes in full attack mode. I shouldn't be ashamed of my own family, not even with Komodo dragons on their heads. They've gone through so much for me, like cover up an actual murder. The least I can do is pretend to like their hideous outfits.

But I don't get a chance to say anything as Yenyen crows, "Okay, Yenyen's turn!" and whips the blanket off me. My family gasps at the sight of my dress.

"Wah, bagus, bagus," Second Aunt says.

"Mm, I love it," Fourth Aunt agrees. "Sexy, not trampy."

I turn to Ma. "What do you think?"

Ma is blinking away tears. "Oh, Meddy." Her voice catches and she grasps my hands.

A lump forms in my throat and I nod through my tears at Ma.

"Yes, so very pretty, so beautiful bride," Big Aunt says, patting my cheek fondly. I smile back at her. The Komodo dragon atop her head grins down at me. "You going to make big splash in Oxford."

Well, some of us will, at least. The mention of Oxford fills my stomach with butterflies. Ever since I cracked open *Harry Potter and the Sorcerer's Stone* at age ten, I was hooked. And when I visited Nathan's family all those years ago, he'd taken me on a tour of Oxford University. It had cemented my love for the gorgeous city. It was a no-brainer when he'd suggested having the wedding at one of the oldest and biggest colleges at the university: Christ Church College. With its expansive gardens and magnificent cathedral, Christ Church makes the perfect wedding venue. I'd thought Ma and the aunties would be against it, but when I told them, they'd literally whooped with joy, especially when we offered to pay for their airfare. And, as horrible as it sounds, there's an additional benefit to having a wedding in England—I won't have to invite the rest of my humongous family.

Not that I don't love them; it's just that there are so many of them—all of my cousins and their families, for one, and then my mother's cousins and their families. Chinese-Indonesian weddings tend to have thousands of guests for a reason; everyone is related to everyone else, and if you fail to invite your cousin's cousin's spouse's cousin, there would be such Slighted Feelings. Generations of family feuds have stemmed from this uncle not inviting that cousin's brother-in-law's father-in-law to his daughter's wedding. With a destination wedding, we can just tell the rest of the family that we don't want to impose, and that they shouldn't feel obligated to spend thousands of dollars to travel all the way to

England just to watch me get married. In the end, the only people from my side of the family who are attending are Ma, the aunties, and a handful of cousins, which is such a huge relief. None of my aunties' sons are coming. I had a video call with them and we all agreed that the aunties would be so emotional and overbearing that it would probably be best for everyone's sanity not to have them there. The relieved expression on my cousin Gucci's face was so palpable that I couldn't help laughing and taking a screenshot, just in case I needed to blackmail him in the future. They promised that we'd celebrate ourselves when we next had a family gathering. We've somehow ended up with over two hundred guests anyway, thanks to Nathan's numerous business contacts, which appeases Ma and the aunties' need for big weddings.

Ma waves her hand in my face. "Eh, Meddy, hello, you paying attention or not, ah?"

I snap back to reality and jerk back at the sight of her Komodo dragon. Those dragons, I swear. "What is it, Ma?"

"We have surprise for you," she says with obvious glee.

Uh-oh. The last time my mother sprang a surprise on me, I ended up killing it. Or him, rather. "Um. What is it?" My voice comes out thick with worry.

"Wedding vendor! We find perfect one for you."

"What? But—" Too many things crowd through my head. The first and foremost being a childish wail of *But this is my wedding. I want to be the one who decides who to hire!* But before I can shoot her down, I realize something: Ma couldn't possibly have found a wedding vendor. The only ones she knows are, well, us. "Ma, I told you, I want you all to be there as guests, not vendors."

"Of course not us," Big Aunt says, waving me off like I'm a gnat. "Mana mungkin? How we can cater to your wedding when we wearing this outfit?"

Huh. Maybe I should ask them to cater to my wedding after all. Anything to get rid of those dragons.

"I told you Meddy would want to find her own wedding vendors like a normal bride," Fourth Aunt says, glancing up from admiring herself in the mirror. "Right, Meddy?"

The glare Ma shoots her could have melted plastic. Dammit, why did it have to be Fourth Aunt who said that? I can't possibly agree with her. To Ma, that would be a betrayal, and I'd never live it down.

Then another realization sinks in: how could they have found any vendors in England? They don't know their way around the Internet. Well, my mother did catfish a guy for months.

"So, what you think, Meddy?" Ma says, her eyes shining with hope. Big Aunt and Second Aunt stare at me. Even Fourth Aunt looks at me in the mirror.

"I can't agree without knowing who—or what they do. I mean, Nathan and I have been looking for vendors too—"

"Aduh, of course I not expect you to agree to hire them now," Ma says, flapping her hand at me. "What you think, I so unreasoning I expect you to just agree without even knowing who?"

Well, yes, actually. But I don't say it out loud.

"Of course I don't. I very reasoningable. You meet them first, pasti you will love, I am sure."

"Meet them? But they're in England, surely?"

"Ah, no. They in here. But they do destination wedding. And they family business, just like us. And best of all, they family!"

I blink. "They're family?"

Big Aunt nods. "Mereka itu, your grandmother cousin niece cousin sister-in-law. Very close family."

I try to go over the familial connection, but give up after grandmother's cousin's niece. "Do they have a website, at least?"

Second Aunt waves her index finger at me. "No need website. We meet them for dim sum, they can show you all their photos."

"Uh." I suppose I might as well agree to get them off my back. "Okay. But I want Nathan to come along, and if we don't like them, please don't—"

"Aiya, of course we not push you into hiring them if you not like," Ma cries. "What you think we are? Dictator?"

"No, you're Chinese mothers, which is as good as dictators," I mutter, squeezing Ma's arm with affection.

"Oh ho ho, you so funny. My daughter so funny. Wait until you become mother also. Then you understand. Okay, you go undress. We all go undress. Then we go."

"What, now?"

"Of course now! If not now, then when?"

Of course. I should've known. Still, I can't help but smile as I watch my family scurrying out of the living room,

Komodo dragons teetering crazily as they move. I turn around to look into the mirror and sigh happily at the reflection of me in my amazing dress. Even Jonjon is grudgingly admiring Yenyen's handiwork. How did I manage to end up with the dreamiest gown that was ever made? This wedding is going to be wonderful.

2

Less than an hour later, I wait outside our favorite dim sum place for Nathan while my mother and aunts go inside to meet this mysterious vendor they've decided we're related to. I can't help the grin that stretches across my face when I spot him walking across the parking lot. I mean, dayum. He is fine. And he's mine, all mine!

Okay, settle down, creeper. I suppose part of me does feel like a creep whenever I see Nathan from afar. I can't help but undress him with my eyes, which I know sounds really gross. But seriously, how can I not? Look at him, all strong jaw and broad shoulders and muscled arms and those pecs and—

"You've got your horny face again," he says.

"I'm just hungry."

"For me?"

"Okay, ew. But yes." I inhale the scent of him as he bends down and gives me a chaste peck on the cheek; the dim sum bunch is mostly made up of Chinese uncles and aunties who openly stare disapprovingly at every young couple, and Nathan knows I'm not comfortable with PDA in front of this particular crowd. Horny eyes, acceptable. Actual kissing, hells no. "So, before we go inside, there's something I need to tell you."

"Uh-oh." His eyebrows knit together with concern and he lowers his voice while taking my arm. "Is it about . . . the thing?"

My stomach knots. I hate that I've put this weight on his shoulders. It's been almost a year since Ma set me up on a blind date with Ah Guan that ended with me and my aunties accidentally killing him. Emphasis on "accidentally." As if that wasn't bad enough, Ah Guan's body was then mistakenly shipped to a wedding at Nathan's hotel, where through a series of mishaps caused by my aunties, it ended up appearing at the altar as one of the groomsmen. Only a magical combination of quick thinking, false bravado, and sheer dumb luck allowed us all to get away with it. To this day, I can't quite believe how fortunate we were that someone like Sheriff McConnell was in charge of the case. His incompetence was vital in ensuring that nobody ended up charged with anything.

Even though Ah Guan's case is closed—declared an unfortunate accident—Nathan still worries that it'll come back to haunt us, and I hate that he worries. Nathan had figured out the truth behind Ah Guan's death in record time and decided to help us cover it up. Though he's never held the incredible sacrifice he's made over my head, I never let myself forget it. I hate that he has to carry this burden because of something I did. "No," I say quickly, and Nathan's shoulders relax. "My mom and aunts found some wedding vendors that are apparently related to us and they're really keen on us meeting them."

"Oh. Is that all? You looked so worried I thought it was going to be something really bad."

"Well, I mean, it kind of is," I sigh. "I've been dreaming about our wedding for so long, and I've been looking forward to searching for the right vendors with you. I wasn't really expecting my family to swoop in and find them for us. Well, I don't know why I wasn't expecting it from them."

"Aw, hey, c'mere." Nathan wraps his arms around me and pulls me closer, to the immense interest of all the random uncles and aunties around us. "It'll be okay. Your mom and aunts are just really excited about the wedding."

"I know." I sigh and rest my head against his chest. An idea begins to form, and I pat his pecs. "Wow, these are getting really big; you've been working out hard. What a manly man you are."

Nathan grins at me. "I know you're just buttering me up, but I am here for this. Please keep telling me what a manly man I am."

"Well, I was thinking, we'll meet with these vendors . . ."

"Uh-huh?"

I trail a finger down his chest. "And if we don't like them, you put your foot down like the big manly man that you are and tell my family we'll be hiring someone else."

Nathan laughs. "Me? Say no to your Big Aunt? Hell to the no."

I punch him on the arm and he laughs. "We'll do it together," he says, kissing the top of my head.

"Okay," I sigh. "Well, get ready to meet them."

"What, now?"

"Yep, come on, manly man."

"Nathan, over here, Nathan! Nathan!" Ma shouts, standing up and waving madly as we weave through the dim sum crowd. Nathan waves back at her, but she continues waving and shouting his name.

"How come she's never that excited to see me?" I grumble.

"Because I am, in her words, 'the perfect specimen of a man.'"

I roll my eyes. I mean, I agree with Ma, obviously, but Nathan doesn't need to know that. Over the past year, my family has doted on him as if he's their long-awaited prodigal son, and instead of being scared off as I feared he might be, Nathan has quite happily accepted all the attention.

As we near them, I see that there isn't one, nor two, nor three new faces at the table, but—

"Five vendors?" I hiss.

Nathan squeezes my hand. "It'll be okay. We'll eat with them and look at their portfolio and then politely but firmly tell them no."

I take a deep breath. I can do this. I'm an adult, dammit. I can stand up to my family, especially for my wedding. And despite all of his jokes, I know Nathan would back me up if I wanted him to.

Everyone smiles and waves when we get to the table, and Nathan and I go around greeting them—Big Aunt first, then

Second Aunt, and so forth. Even though I arrived here with Big Aunt and the others, I still need to make a show of greeting them again. After I greet my family, I'm left with the vendors. They're not quite what I expected. There's an elderly woman who looks about Big Aunt's age, three men who could be anywhere from thirty to fifty-five, and a young woman who looks about my age.

The young woman stands up and comes around to shake my hand and Nathan's with a big, friendly smile. "Meddy, it's so nice to finally meet you. I've heard so much about you, and I'm just so excited about your wedding."

Her smile is infectious, and I find myself beaming back at her before catching myself. I don't want to appear like I approve. I squeeze my mouth into a thin line. But then the woman hands me her business card, and I know then that she and I are destined to be friends. Because her card says this:

Staphanie Weiting Tanuwijaya
Photographer

Stop weiting around, we're here for all your weidding needs!

I chomp down on my bottom lip to keep from laughing.

"That's not a typo, by the way. It really is spelled with an *a*," Staphanie says.

I meet her eye. "I relate very hard to this."

"I knew you would, Meddelin," she says somberly. "When your mom texted me your name, I was like, 'Okay, I need to

19

meet her. She'll understand what it's like to grow up with an unfortunately spelled name.'"

"I do!" I laugh. "I really, really do. Oh god, you poor thing. I'm guessing you get lots of staph infection jokes?"

"Mhmm. And coupled with my Chinese name, Weiting? Forget about it. 'I'm wei-ting for my staph infection to clear up.' I hear that one at least five times a day."

I'm still laughing as we sit down next to each other.

Big Aunt clears her throat and Staphanie and I go quiet. When all the attention is turned to her, Big Aunt gestures at me. "This Meddy, the bride, and that one Nathan, the groom."

The elderly woman nods and smiles in a very grandmotherly way at us. "Wah, cakep sekali ya? Will give you so cute babies," she says to Ma. Ma simpers, and the elderly woman continues, "You must have babies right away, okay, not be like these modern people nowadays, waiting and waiting, later your womb will dry up."

"Ama!" Staphanie scolds. She turns to us. "I'm so sorry. This is my grandmother, she's just, uh, she's—"

The sight of Staphanie's mortification about her family warms my heart. Finally, someone who truly understands what it's like growing up with my family. "It's okay, I understand," I tell her.

"Oh, you so right," Ma says to Staphanie's grandmother. "Yes, I don't know why all these young people they want to waiting, waiting, until they too old to make the baby!"

Nathan places a comforting hand on my back. I can tell

he's struggling to bite back his laughter. I'm glad he finds Ma funny, at least.

"Please, eat," Staphanie says, placing a har gow on my plate. I quickly reciprocate by spearing a char siu bao and putting it on her plate. Around the table, our families are doing the same, rapidly picking up dumplings and placing them on each other's plates—a battle to show which family is more well-mannered. Nathan is used to this by now and jumps in with gusto, giving Big Aunt the biggest siu mai and Staphanie's grandmother the fattest cheung fun. Cries of "Aduh, don't mind me, you eat, you eat," and "Wah, you such good boy," fill the air and soon, everyone's plate is full and the battle ends in a draw. Now we can finally start eating.

Staphanie takes a small bite of her bao. "So, to give you an overview of our company . . ." She gestures at her family. "Like yours, ours is a family-run business. My ama is the wedding organizer—"

"Oh, wow." I don't even have to fake the amazement in my voice. "That's really amazing, Tante." I say, using the formal Indonesian term for Auntie. "Wedding organizing is so complicated, especially when it comes to Chinese-Indonesian weddings."

Staphanie's grandmother nods with barely restrained pride. "You can call me Ama."

Calling someone else "Grandmother" feels like a betrayal of my late ama, but there's just something about Staphanie's grandma that is so grandmotherly. I totally want to call her Ama, even though we've just met.

"Okay, Ama." Nathan gives her his boyish smile. She

beams back at him, and I know then that we have found our wedding organizer.

"Ama is known for having the sharpest eye in the industry," Staphanie says. "She doesn't ever miss anything."

"Ooh, that very important," Big Aunt says, nodding her approval. "Yes, sharp eye very important for wedding, because this and that, need to keep track, ya?"

Ama nods and smiles politely.

"Ama used to hunt when she was younger. She has the keenest eye in the industry and doesn't miss a single detail, so don't you worry, you've got the best wedding organizer in the biz," Staphanie says.

I don't bother hiding my amazement. "That's so cool."

Ama does that pursed-lip thing people do when they're trying not to grin too hard, which looks adorable.

"And this is Big Uncle," Staphanie says, gesturing at the man sitting next to Ama. "He does the flowers and decor."

"Hi, Om," I say. Om is Indonesian for "Sir" or "Mister."

He waves me off and says, "No, no, you call me Uncle James."

"Spelled J-E-M-S," Staphanie whispers, and I have to bite back my giggle. "Anyway, Big Uncle's well-known for his lily bouquets—"

"That what I well-known for!" Ma pipes up. "Until my lily guy—uh." She falters as she probably realizes what she's just about to say. *Until my lily guy was killed by my daughter.*

"Until she moved on to peonies," I quickly say, my heart thumping wildly.

"Oh, iya, peonies, yes." Ma smiles weakly.

"Maybe we can see photos of the flower arrangements?" Nathan asks. I shoot him a grateful look.

"Yeah, of course." Staphanie takes out a tablet and opens up the gallery before sliding it over to Nathan and me. "Here you go."

The bouquets and flower displays are beautiful, well-balanced, and artfully arranged to showcase the vibrant blooms. "Very pretty, Om—I mean, Uncle Jems," I say. "Do you have any photos of bouquets with hydrangeas? I have a soft spot for them."

A frown crosses Uncle Jems's face for a second, and I squirm inwardly, wondering if I'm being too demanding. No, right? I mean, it's normal to ask for your favorite flower in your wedding bouquet.

"Yes, of course," Staphanie cuts in, taking the tablet back and scrolling through the photo album. "Um, maybe not in here, but I'll look up our old photos at home and send them to you."

"Okay, thanks."

"Anyway, Second Uncle is hair and makeup," Staphanie says, pointing at the man next to Uncle Jems.

"Uncle Henry," he says, waving at me.

"There's a rogue *d* in the middle of his name," Staphanie whispers. I didn't think I could love her more, but I do. Where has this girl been all my life? She opens up a different photo album and slides the tablet back to me and Nathan.

As expected, Uncle Hendry's handiwork is beautiful and—dare I say it—rivals that of Second Aunt. As though she could hear my traitorous thoughts, Second Aunt actually gets up from her seat and walks over to us, so she's literally breathing down our necks as we look at the pictures.

"Wah, bagus sekali," she says, "you do that curled plait thing very well, that one very tricky, ah?"

Uncle Hendry nods. "Yes, very tricky, but I take lesson and practice on Staphanie hair."

"Mm, yes, I always practice on Meddy hair also," Second Aunt says, still peering down her nose at the photo album. "Oh, this photo!" She plucks the tablet out of my hands and stares at it closely. "This one your photo?"

There is a second of silence as Uncle Hendry stares at her. "Yes?" he answers cautiously.

"Wah! This one I see everywhere on Pinterest! So very popular. Wah, turns out you are the artist behind it!" The admiration on her face is palpable. She's gazing at Uncle Hendry as if he's just saved a child from a burning building. I exchange a glance with Nathan, who's openly grinning and wiggling his eyebrows at me. I can tell he's thinking the same thing—is Second Aunt in insta-love?

Uncle Hendry breaks the eye contact. "Aduh, is nothing, is very easy technique."

"I been trying to figure, you know, how to do the hair like that? And I cannot get it correct, waduh, drive me crazy. I try on Meddy hair so many time, still not look nice. You have to teach me how to do like that!"

Poor Uncle Hendry looks like he's just about ready to jump out of the nearest window. He's no match for Second Aunt. Or any of my aunts, really.

"Ahem," Big Aunt says. She doesn't even bother pretending to cough. "Please ignore my Er Mei, she lupa her manners, asking people to share trade secret. Hendry, you ignore her, okay?"

Second Aunt's lips thin into a tight line, and for a mortifying second, I'm half-afraid she's about to get into it right then and there with Big Aunt. Or lunge into some Tai Chi position. But then she exhales and smiles at Uncle Hendry. "So sorry, my Da Jie is right, I get carry away. You don't have to reveal your trade secret to me." With that, she returns to her seat and slurps her tea very deliberately.

The tension is too much for me to withstand, so I blurt out, "Second Aunt, I'm sure Second Uncle would love to hear all about the Komodo dragon fascinator and how it'll fit in with your hairdos."

"Oh yes, we have traditional British hats for wedding," Second Aunt says.

"Traditional British hats with Komodo dragons?" Nathan whispers.

"Don't ask," I mutter.

"Sounds exciting," Staphanie says. "Second Uncle would love to take a look at them, wouldn't you, Second Uncle?"

Second Uncle nods quickly. "Yes, of course. Maybe I can come your place and see this dragon sometime?"

Second Aunt's smile lights up her entire face. She's practically glowing like a light bulb. "Okay, boleh," she says, and grins down at her teacup, clearly blushing.

Staphanie and I exchange knowing glances before she says, "And last but not least, Third Uncle is our MC."

"Ooh, nice." Again, I don't have to fake the admiration in my voice. The master of ceremonies is one of the most stressful jobs at Chinese-Indonesian weddings. They're basically the wedding organizer's mouthpiece, the one who herds the thousands of wedding guests along and gathers them into appropriate groups for photos, the one who provides entertainment whenever there's a lull, and the one who hosts the reception. MCs need to be loud and personable and shameless and charming and energetic, and I don't know how anyone does it.

"You can just call me Francis. I'm too young to be an uncle," he says.

"No!" Big Aunt booms, loud enough to make us all jump. "No such thing as calling your elder by first name."

I look helplessly at Staphanie's Third Uncle and say, "How about Ko Francis?" Koko means "older brother" in Indonesian.

"That'll do. You two need to tell me how you met and everything. I bet you have a juicy love story that I can compile into the best speech ever."

Ha. It's too bad our love story doesn't involve saving baby otters, but rather getting away with literal murder.

The longer lunch goes on, the more I realize that I really, really like Staphanie and her family. How can I not? They're clearly just as bonkers as mine. As expected, her photos are wonderful—slightly overexposed like mine are. She captures the brightness of her weddings with soft, pastel colors.

"Which camera do you use?" I can't stop admiring her

gallery. The colors scream of film photography, something I've always wanted to try but never had the guts to.

"Same as yours, the 5D Mark III."

"Really? Wow. I could never get my pictures to have these pastel shades. I would've guessed the 1D."

There's a beat of silence, then Staphanie laughs. "You're so kind. No, these are not taken by the 1D."

"Well, I'm impressed. You'll have to teach me how to get the backgrounds so smooth on the 5D."

"Mhmm, for sure!" She grabs a pork rib and places it on my plate.

If I don't reciprocate—or rather, retaliate—Ma would tell me off later for being rude. "Stop doing that. You're making me look bad." I put down the tablet and take a har gow for her.

Staphanie grins. "How else can I show everyone that my Ama has raised me well? Also, I really just wanted more food, and if I take food for myself Ama will tell me I've brought shame to the family."

I laugh, relating to every sentence she just said. "Okay, you tell me which dishes you want and I'll tell you which ones I want."

"Deal."

As our two families chat with each other, Staphanie and I pile all sorts of dumplings on each other's plates. By the time lunch is over, I know that against all the odds, Ma and my aunts have actually done something right and picked the perfect vendors for my wedding.

ONE PLACE. MANY STORIES

Bold, innovative and
empowering publishing.

FOLLOW US ON:

@HQStories